Superstition

David Ambrose began his distinguished career screen-writing for Orson Welles. He read law at Oxford and has worked internationally in theatre, television and film. David Ambrose's two highly acclaimed novels, *The Man Who Turned Into Himself* and *Mother of God*, and a collection of short stories, *Hollywood Lies*, inspired by his life in Hollywood, are available in paperback from Pan Books.

'HITCHCOCK MEETS HAWKING'

Also by David Ambrose

**the man who turned into himself
mother of god
hollywood lies**

DAVID AMBROSE

Superstition

PAN BOOKS

First published 1997 by Macmillan

This edition published 1998 by Pan Books
an imprint of Macmillan Publishers Ltd
25 Eccleston Place, London SW1W 9NF
and Basingstoke

Associated companies throughout the world

ISBN 0 330 36744 7

1 3 5 7 9 8 6 4 2

A CIP catalogue record for this book is available from
the British Library.

Phototypeset by Intype London Ltd
Printed and bound in Great Britain by
Mackays of Chatham plc, Chatham, Kent

To Lulu, Mick and Daisy

In whose house this book was conceived and by
coincidence completed eighteen months later

Whatever coincidence means

Acknowledgements

This novel is based on an experiment which actually took place in Toronto in the early seventies, and which has been widely written about in the literature of parapsychology. The best account is that written by two of the participants, Iris M. Owen and Margaret Sparrow. Their book, *Conjuring Up Philip – An Adventure in Psychokinesis*, unfortunately out of print and hard to obtain, is a classic in its field.

I am indebted to Brenda J. Dunne and Michael Ibison of the Princeton Engineering Anomalies Research (PEAR) program for taking the time to show me some of the extraordinary work they are doing in the field of consciousness-related physical phenomena. *Margins of Reality* (Harcourt Brace) by Robert G. Jahn, the director of PEAR, and Brenda J. Dunne is essential reading.

John Beloff's *Parapsychology – A Concise History* (Athlone) provides an admirably clear and restrained overview of the subject, and led me to the challenging and closely argued articles and papers of, among others, Helmut Schmidt and Brian Millar.

Other writers whose work has been particularly stimulating include Kit Pedlar, Stan Gooch, Michael Harrison, Alan Gauld and A.D. Cornell.

My thanks to Joanne McMahon of the Eileen J. Garrett Library at the Parapsychology Foundation Inc., New York, for her help when I was researching this book. Also a special thanks to Michaeleen C. Maher, the New York-based investigator of paranormal phenomena, for talking to me at length about her work and impressing on me the rigorously high standards with which it is carried out.

'There is a superstition in avoiding superstition'

Francis Bacon, 1561–1626

'Superstition: An ambiguous word, it probably cannot
be used except subjectively'

Encyclopaedia Britannica

Prologue

PROLOGUE

He gazed across the street at a house indistinguishable, except in detail, from the ones on either side. It had a door of a green so dark that it was almost black, with its number – 139 – picked out in plain brass characters. To one side and above it were symmetrically proportioned windows, their light lending a haze of warmth to the chill November dusk. Framed within them he could see an interior of clean lines and ordered spaces; from where he stood he had an angular glimpse of paintings, furniture and works of art arranged in what looked like a pleasing mixture of the antique and the new.

It was a prospect that he would normally have found inviting, but all he felt now was a profound apprehension, verging on dread, of what and who he was about to meet in there.

Sam had spoken to Ralph Cazaubon on the phone only once – less than an hour ago. He knew nothing of him apart from what Joanna had told him, which did not include the fact that they were married. 'My wife' was how Cazaubon had referred to her. It made no sense that Joanna and this man should be married, and it filled him with an aching sense of something far more disquieting than jealousy, and to which he could not yet give a name.

He noticed a couple of passers-by dart curious glances in his direction, and realized that he had lost track of how long he had been standing there. A few minutes at most. He waited as a cab picked up a fare in front of him and pulled away, then stepped off the kerb.

The house seemed to grow, filling his field of vision as he approached. He had the fleeting impression that it was reaching out to him, enfolding him, preparing to absorb him. He felt a moment of irrational panic, but forced himself on without breaking his stride.

As a scientist Sam was committed to a rational response to all things. Reason and logic, he believed, were the only tools at man's disposal in any attempt he might make to penetrate the mystery of his being; though how far they could take him on that quest was becoming, at least to Sam, increasingly open to doubt. These past months had seen the widening of a gulf between things that had happened and any ability he may once have had to make sense of them. It was a gulf into which the shadow land of superstition had begun to insinuate itself, spreading into every corner of his mind like the grey mist of the Manhattan twilight that settled all around him into every crack and crevice of the city. Superstition, he now knew from painful personal experience, was the one thing against which reason offered no defence.

He climbed the stone steps and reached out to push the bell, deliberately suppressing any hesitation that he felt. He heard it ring somewhere distantly, then waited, forcing from his mind any preconception of the man whose footsteps he half imagined he could hear coming towards him.

A moment later the door was opened by someone tallish with a well-groomed mass of thick, dark hair. The man's eyes were dark, with an inquiring, steady gaze. He wore a comfortable tailored jacket in a good tweed, grey trousers, a knitted tie. His shoes were polished wingtips in a rich burgundy and looked handmade. Sam would have put him in his late thirties.

'Mr Cazaubon? I'm Sam Towne . . .'

They didn't shake hands. Cazaubon looked as though he might under normal circumstances have had a pleasant smile, but at the moment he was as wary of Sam Towne as Sam was of him. When he stepped back from the door in a wordless invitation to his visitor to enter, there was an assurance in his movement that was more than just physical; it spoke of breeding, a sense of who he was – and probably, Sam thought, of old money.

'As I told you on the phone, my wife isn't here yet,' he said, leading the way into the drawing room.

It worried Sam that she wasn't there. He wanted to ask where in God's name she could have been since the events of that morning – events of which, he felt reasonably certain, this man in front of him knew nothing. But he held his tongue. He must tread warily, proceed with caution. As much as he needed to know that Joanna was safe, he had to avoid antagonizing Cazaubon. He needed to talk to him, find out who he was, and many other things about him; he had to ask more questions than any stranger had a right to ask.

Sam knew he must have sounded odd on the phone. Yet he could see that the other man was at least initially reassured by his appearance. There was nothing very threatening about Sam Towne. Of medium height and build, about the same age as Cazaubon, he looked like what he was – an underpaid academic with little in the way of worldly ambition or material achievement. He glimpsed his reflection in the big Venetian mirror over the carved stone fireplace, and realized how shabby he looked in these surroundings, with his raincoat hanging open over a well-worn corduroy jacket, denim shirt and jeans.

'I'm sorry,' Cazaubon said, as though correcting an omission of protocol on his part, 'can I take your coat?'

Sam slipped it off and handed it over. 'I don't intend taking up any more of your time than I have to,' he said, as though by way of reassurance.

Cazaubon nodded and went out into the hall, where he hung the coat on an antique iron stand. 'Can I offer you a drink?' he said as he returned, good manners not entirely concealing the suspicion he still felt.

'No – thank you very much.'

'Then why don't you sit down, and tell me what this is about?' Cazaubon indicated an Italian sofa in oatmeal fabric, then sat in an armchair across from it, and waited.

Towne leaned forward, caught himself twisting his hands, and laced his fingers to keep them still. 'This is all going to sound very strange. I gather from what you said on the phone that your wife has never spoken of me or the work that I've been doing . . .'

'To the best of my knowledge she hasn't, Mr Towne – sorry, *Dr* Towne I believe you said.'

'I'm a research psychologist at Manhattan University,' Sam began. 'I run a project investigating various kinds of anomalous phenomena.' He felt his fingers start to twist again, pulled them apart and made an open gesture as he ran through the usual brief litany with which he began any explanation of his work. 'Basically, we've been looking into the interaction of human consciousness with measurable physical devices and systems. It covers fields

6

such as telepathy, precognition, psychokinesis, remote viewing . . .'

Cazaubon's eyes narrowed slightly. 'You mean you're some kind of psychic investigator?' he asked.

'Broadly speaking, yes, though I dislike the word "psychic". It's vague and implies a prejudgement of the phenomena we're observing. We're psychologists, engineers, statisticians and physicists. There are seven of us, though we work with other departments in the university as well as outside groups and individuals.'

'What does all this have to do with my wife? To the best of my knowledge she has no experience of such things, nor any interest in them.'

Sam had to be careful here. He still didn't know who or what he was dealing with. The man across from him looked normal enough, civilized, thoughtful. But he couldn't be sure of anything any more.

'Someone with your wife's name, or I should say using her maiden name, Joanna Cross, has been involved in a programme I have been running for some time.'

Cazaubon looked at him with a disbelief that bordered on hostility. 'That's impossible. I would have known about any such thing. You must have made a mistake.'

'Perhaps. If so, I'm here to clear it up.'

Cazaubon got to his feet with a restlessness that, it seemed to Sam, he was trying to conceal. He walked over to the fireplace, looked down into the empty grate, then turned once more to his visitor.

'You mean that some woman has been going around using my wife's identity? Is that what you're saying?'

'I don't want to alarm you. I'm sure there is some explanation . . .'

'Forgive me, I think this is very alarming indeed,'

Cazaubon said, his tone hardening. 'And quite possibly a matter for the police.'

'No, it's not something for the police,' Sam responded with more weariness than urgency, as though such a course would merely be a waste of time. 'As a matter of fact the police are already involved – in a way.'

'How?' Cazaubon shot back, his voice tightening with concern.

'Two men have died today.'

Seeing the flash of alarm in the other man's eyes, he added quickly, 'Your wife – or this woman calling herself your wife – was not directly involved. She wasn't even present when it happened.'

'Then why are you here?'

Towne hesitated. How could he begin to explain without sounding like a lunatic? His fears for her, like his deep misgivings about this man across from him, were not the kind that could be summed up quickly or expressed in any easily intelligible way. 'I'm sorry,' he said eventually, 'it's very hard to explain without your wife actually being here.'

Cazaubon frowned. 'Look, Dr Towne, my wife is an intelligent woman and a free agent, but I'm not sure I can have you upsetting her with a wild story about some total stranger pretending to be her – especially at the moment.'

He stopped, as though deciding not to elaborate on those last words, but his tone implied that she might be in some particularly delicate state: unwell perhaps; burdened by some problem; or maybe simply pregnant. Whatever the reason, Cazaubon made it clear that he was prepared to defend her against any intrusion or unnecessary worry.

'I understand how all this must sound,' Sam continued lamely.

8

'Do you? I don't even know who you are, apart from what you tell me.'

'You can call up the university.'

Cazaubon was silent for a moment. Sam felt that he would make the call, if not immediately, then later. He hoped he would.

'Look,' he said, attempting the conciliatory tone of a reasonable man, 'perhaps we can clear this thing up without troubling your wife. Do you happen to have a photograph of her that I could see?'

'Of course I do. Though I'm not sure what that would prove – except maybe to show you that this woman you're talking about is obviously not my wife.'

'At least it would be a first step.'

Cazaubon started across the room towards an ornate Chinese cabinet, but stopped as he pulled open a drawer. They had both heard a sound in the hall.

As she entered, Sam felt himself pulled to his feet more by sheer nervous tension than politeness. Cazaubon had already crossed the room to kiss her lovingly on the cheek, clearly happy and relieved to see her.

'Darling,' he was saying, 'this is Dr Sam Towne of Manhattan University. He's been telling me a rather odd story . . .'

He stopped because Sam had gasped audibly. Both Cazaubon and the woman who had just entered turned their gaze toward the man who stood with his mouth slightly open and his pale blue eyes staring, unblinking, at her. His face was white and he looked on the verge of passing out.

Sam Towne had not been ready for this.

Something impossible had happened.

One Year Earlier

1

Eleanor (Ellie) Ray was not quite sixty, though most people meeting her would have guessed her to be at least ten years older. It was an impression she cultivated; the grandmotherly touch was worth hard cash in Ellie's business.

It was difficult, looking at her now, plain and dumpy, barely five feet tall, to imagine Ellie as she once had been – the high-kicking, fish-net-stockinged, feathered and sequined glamour half of 'Wanda and Ray', a comedy and magic act that had somehow eked out a living for twenty long, hard years on the road. She had been 'Wanda', and 'Ray' had been Murray Ray, her husband. She was a dancer when they met, but too short for the chorus line, and not talented enough to be a single act. She worked up a couple of novelty numbers with another girl who was over six feet and they played a few dates in the Catskills, but their bookings quickly dwindled from a handful to none, and Ellie was thinking about getting out of the business altogether when she met Murray.

He was only a year or two older than her, but already established and a pro, though not a star. He probably never would be. He was a funny-looking little guy, not much taller than she was, but kind of sweet. They'd found themselves on the same bill a few times that season, and he'd started showing her magic tricks backstage as a way, he hoped, of getting her into bed. She knew perfectly well what he was up to, and had already made up her mind to cooperate. It was easy come, easy go in those days. Sex was as good a way as any of passing the time after the show or between jobs.

But the magic was something new, and the fascination she found in it took her by surprise. She started practising some of the tricks he'd shown her. Murray told her she had talent. All it takes, he'd said, was application – and that she had. To Ellie it was a last chance to avoid waiting tables, which was probably all she'd get offered outside the business.

They married three months after they met, but it was another year before she joined him on the stage. It took time to work up a new act, and Murray had been right about application. It was the little tricks, the throwaway stuff, that were really gruelling to master. The big illusions were surprisingly simple and largely mechanical. But that wasn't their style; for one thing they didn't have the money to buy and transport the equipment that was needed. So they did it the hard way, with timing, patter, careful misdirection and muscular dexterity. By the time she trod the boards with Murray, Ellie's small, short-fingered hands concealed a strength that few men could equal. She could flip cards, hide chiffon scarves and switch marked dollar bills – all with a smile on her face that never flinched, even when the pain shot up to her elbows and sometimes all the way to her shoulders. It'll get better, she told herself. Practice makes perfect. When I'm really good, it won't hurt so much.

Ellie sat back and looked down at her hands, wrinkled

now and speckled with liver spots. She turned them over, curling them like claws. The strength was still there when she needed it. There was no screw-top jar or bottle that didn't yield to her iron grip. She smiled as she remembered that weight lifter who'd got fresh with her one time in Atlantic City, until she'd grabbed him by the balls to let him know she wasn't happy. He'd never been the same man again.

She came out of her daydream and looked up. The murmur of voices was growing. Glancing through the rectangle of glass in front of her that from the other side was just a mirrored fragment in one of the twin starbursts flanking the stage, she could see the auditorium was already almost full. She looked down at her watch, an ostentatiously cheap one with a plastic strap that she always wore for work; the Cartier that Murray had given her on her last birthday was kept carefully in a drawer at home. Time enough to show that off in a few months when they were out of here, enjoying the bonanza they'd been building towards these last few years.

Negotiations for the sale of the place were discreetly in hand, and looked certain to net them enough to live out their days in comfort. Ellie had never been to Europe, and dreamed of seeing Paris, Rome and London. Annual winter cruises in the Caribbean beckoned. And of course – this was the jewel in the crown for Ellie, the fulfilment of a life's ambition – there would be a town house in central Manhattan. The girl from New Jersey would end her days as an upper east side matron, living in the kind of house to which her mother had taken that long subway ride to scrub and clean every day of Ellie's childhood. It was a triumph that would lay some ghosts for Ellie – the only kind of ghosts that she believed in.

A thin smile played on Ellie's lips at the thought, but died almost at once. It would have been so nice, she couldn't help thinking, to have had it all thirty years ago.

But still, better now, far better now than never.

Joanna Cross found a seat towards the back and to one side. It was a vantage point from which she could see everything without being conspicuous herself. It was already enough that she was younger than most of the people drawn to this place and others like it. Even the staff were largely middle-aged or more, apart from some of the behind-the-scenes and maintenance people, who didn't on the whole have much contact with guests.

There was, however, one trance medium who couldn't have been more than thirty, but he was the exception. And he was talented. His seances involved a luminous tin trumpet that floated in the dark and through which spirit voices spoke. Occasionally billowing clouds of ecto-plasm spewed forth from his body, taking on the forms of dead departed loved ones of the sitters, while glittering points of light skipped and shimmered over people's heads. That it was all just some gigantic conjuring trick was obvious to Joanna. The only thing that amazed her was other people's inability to see what they didn't want to see, and their willingness to believe what they wanted to believe. Or needed to.

That was what got to her. On one level it was just silly but relatively harmless. On another it was the merciless exploitation of people who had suffered loss and tragedy and who needed help. Instead they had been tagged as suckers and taken on a cynical ride that, more often than not, would leave them penniless. That was why Joanna

16

was going to put Ellie and Murray Ray where they belonged: in jail if she could, but at the very least she meant to expose and ruin them as a warning to others of their kind.

And there was no shortage of others like them. Since she had started researching these articles for the magazine, Joanna had been amazed at the size of the psychic industry. From the corner clairvoyant and palm-reader to organized compounds like this, it was a business that turned over millions, maybe billions of dollars every year – most of it in cash, with the rest largely sheltered by well-meaning but misguided legislation which allowed any fraudster to pose as the founder of some church and claim charitable status. That was, no doubt, why the auditorium in which Joanna now sat was referred to on the plan of the Camp Starburst compound as 'The Cathedral'.

Her gaze drifted from one to the other of the glittering glass and mirror structures on the walls at each side of the stage. They were, in all their vulgar ghastliness, an obvious reflection of the 'starburst' theme. And behind one of them, Joanna knew, was the place from where Ellie Ray was able to look out, as she was probably doing now, and control the proceedings.

Joanna looked down at her watch. It would be starting soon. With any luck, for sure if she had her way, it would be the last seance that would ever be held in this place.

The pattern of swimming fish and drifting sea anemones disappeared from Ellie's computer screen as she hit a key. She called up the file that she'd assembled earlier in the day when she got the list of who'd be coming. They were mostly first or second-timers who'd heard about the place from friends. Handled right, most of them would be good for several visits, and some of them represented potentially rich pickings. These latter would be singled out for longer individual seances with key mediums in the next day or two.

Ellie scrolled the information up the screen. Everything was there, all the data she needed, ordered, concise and detailed – and duplicated in the box files that she kept for back-up. Of course, she would have to put the right names to the hundred and fifty-odd faces out there, most of them belonging to people she had only spoken to for ten or fifteen minutes at the most. But she had a mnemonic for that, a trick she'd learned from a memory act years ago.

A sound behind her made her turn. Murray came in, wiping his nose with a huge, white handkerchief. He'd had a chill and she'd been quite concerned about him this past week, but he'd worked through it and never missed a seance. He seemed to be picking up now, though he was still unhealthily red in the face. She absolutely had to get him on a diet soon. He was carrying far too much weight for a man of his age. All his suits had been let out to the limit, and half of them he couldn't get into at all any more.

'Ready to rock'n'roll,' he said, stuffing the handkerchief back in his pocket. He picked up the slim battery pack by the computer and sat down with his back to Ellie. It was their usual routine. He fixed his earpiece securely in place, then sat still as she fed the threadlike filament that ran from it down the inside of his shirt collar and out through the little opening cut just below the shoulder blade. She pulled the end of it around and under his arm and plugged it into the battery pack, which he slipped into the special pocket in the lining of his jacket. She tapped the microphone in front of her, and he nodded. The connection was live.

Ellie waited a moment, checked once more through the rectangle of glass that everyone was ready, then cued Mark, their stage manager, to get the show under way.

Mark's stage-trained voice resonated impressively over the big speakers in the auditorium. 'Ladies and gentlemen, the seance is about to commence. Mrs Ellie Ray is here to welcome you with a few words of introduction.'

The curtain rose on a stage that was empty except for a massive, straight-backed chair placed dead centre – a throne in red velvet and mahogany. A rainbow of pale pastels moved constantly though all but imperceptibly across the ornate drapery behind. Ellie strode out from the wings, all smiles and holding up her hands to both acknowledge and arrest the ripple of applause that greeted her appearance.

'Now then, my dears,' she began, 'we're all friends here, so just relax and let yourselves enter that quiet frame of mind that will help you touch your loved ones on the other side. The vibrations are very good in here. Very good. I can feel the spirits are drawn here and to all of us gathered here today. Always remember, the spirits *want* to make contact. They're just waiting for you to open your hearts and your minds, as I know you are doing at this minute, and they will come to you. My husband Murray. You all know Murray . . .'

Murray waddled out, beaming over the assembled faces, took the hand that his wife held out to him, and gave a little bow, but not too much of one: the last thing he and Ellie wanted people to think was that they might once have been in show business.

'Murray will be with you on your journey to the spirit world today,' Ellie continued, 'and for those of you with us for the very first time, let me explain what's going to happen . . .'

As she spoke, Murray seated himself on the throne and Ellie produced a black silk scarf which she made a big show of tying securely over his eyes.

'If you want to make contact with anybody on the other side, all you have to do is raise your hand and one of our two volunteers – that's Merle and Minnie, there they are, on either side of you, giving you a little wave – will bring you a microphone. Now the microphone is only so the rest of us can hear you. If you don't want to speak your question out loud, the spirits will understand. They'll know what's in your heart, and they will respond through the medium, through Murray here. All you have to do if Merle or Minnie points you out is direct your thoughts to the spirit world, and your loved ones will respond through the medium. Alternatively, if you prefer, you can hand over some personal object, a watch or a key-ring or a piece of jewellery or whatever, either your own or belonging to a loved one who's passed on. The vibrations will pass through the medium to the spirit world, and to whoever it is that you wish to make contact with.'

Finally satisfying herself that the blindfold was secure, Ellie stepped back a few paces.

'Now I'm going to leave you, but before I do I'm going to ask you all to remain very quiet for a short time while the medium enters the spirit world. After that you'll hear an announcement asking those of you with a question to raise your hands. Now very quiet, please, ladies and gentlemen . . . very, very quiet . . .'

The lights dimmed as Ellie slipped into the wings and Murray assumed the pre-trance position – head down, chest heaving with slow, deep breaths. Gradually a white spot opened up on him from directly overhead, glowing like a ray of heavenly light. After about a minute Murray slowly raised his head as though listening to something above and slightly to one side. Then he nodded as though in acknowledgement of some unseen presence.

Mark's voice came softly once again from the speakers over the expectant, waiting heads. 'Ladies and gentlemen, the medium is ready. Please hold up your hands to indicate you have a question.'

From her vantage point at the computer, Ellie watched as Merle appeared uncertain which of the sea of waving hands to give the microphone to first. In an acting job of the first magnitude, she seemed to make a random choice – but it was no mistake when she handed the mike, as instructed earlier by Ellie, to a plump woman in her sixties whose husband had recently died leaving her a high, seven-figure fortune in securities and gilt-edged stock.

Very smooth, thought Joanna, admiring the performance despite her contempt for it. Murray had answered several unspoken as well as spoken questions, each time drawing murmurs of amazement from his audience. Now he was giving a demonstration of psychometry, turning over in his stubby fingers a brooch that a woman near the front had sent up. He mentioned names and places, cleverly playing out and embellishing the information that Ellie was whispering in his ear. It was impressive, but only if you didn't know how it was done. And Joanna knew.

Nobody showing up cold at the gate of Camp Starburst would ever be admitted then and there – not even if they waved a wad of hard cash under Ellie's acquisitive nose. If the wad was big enough they might be given tea in the Rays' private quarters, and maybe even taken on a limited tour of the compound. In the course of all this they would invariably say enough about themselves to give the Rays a starting point. From then on it was routine.

The first step was to check them out on the psychic network that extended across the country and beyond. There was a surprisingly large army of believers who went from seer to medium to mystic, one after the other, often travelling long distances for a consultation. Had anyone told them that the information they were being fed about themselves had been faxed or e-mailed from the last hustler who had duped them, they wouldn't have believed it. Because they wouldn't want to. They preferred to hang on to the myths of spiritism.

If the network didn't come up with the goods, Ellie simply called up a detective agency to which she paid a regular retainer and had them dig up what they could. One thing was certain: by the time Ellie or Murray or any of their colleagues sat down for a seance with a sucker, everything that was about to happen had been planned and rehearsed to the last detail. There were no surprises in the spirit world.

But there was going to be a big one very soon. Joanna slipped a hand discreetly beneath the dark wig she was wearing and pressed the earpiece more firmly into place. The receiver in her purse was picking up every word that

Ellie fed to Murray, and a recorder was getting it all on tape. Some of it was pretty juicy stuff; Ellie didn't bother to disguise her contempt for the suckers out there who bought what she and Murray were selling.

It was going to make good reading.

Ellie squinted through the glass to identify the woman near the back who had just handed something to Merle. It was that young woman, Rachel Clark, who was staying in Clouds Wing for the weekend. Ellie brought her file up on the computer screen. There wasn't much – just the fact that she had consulted seven mediums in the last few months, all in and around Philadelphia where she lived. She had wanted the same thing from all of them: to get in touch with her father whom she had nursed through a long illness until his death the previous year. There was obviously some unresolved stuff there, though what it was remained vague.

'Dirty old sod probably been schtupping her since she was ten,' she muttered into the mike. 'It's that girl with the dark hair that you noticed the other day – good tits under that baggy cardigan. Trust you to notice! Mother died when she was fifteen, never been married, engaged once, name of Johnny – nothing known about what happened to him. The old man manufactured kitchen equipment – sounds like there was money in it from the schools she went to.'

Ellie read off the remaining details as she peered through the glass to see what Rachel Clark had given to Merle. Murray was answering the previous question as Merle mounted the steps at the side of the stage. Careful timing meant that she had to pause long enough right

23

next to Ellie's little window to offer a clear view of what she held, along with subtle finger signals to denote gold or gold plate, real jewellery or fake – anything that might usefully be passed on to the blindfolded Murray.

'Man's gold watch, father's I guess,' Ellie was saying as Murray wound up his previous reading, simultaneously taking in Ellie's information over the sound of his own voice. 'The old man's name was James Anthony Clark. Mother was Susan Anne with an "e", née Ziegler. The kid's half-Jewish, that's a nine on the fucked-up meter for starters . . .'

Joanna had to fight to hide the grin of glee that wanted to spread across her face. They'd bought into every last detail of the phoney identity and background she'd set up on those boring trips to Philadelphia these past few months. The proof was coming out of Murray's mouth as he regurgitated every empty lie she'd set to trap them.

And it was all on tape!

At just twenty years of age, Jeremy Holland was a general dogsbody around Camp Starburst. He got the job because his mother was a cousin of one of the resident mediums at the camp, and was learning the trade himself. Today, however, he was manning the switchboard, and a situation had arisen which he was unsure how to handle. Ellie looked up with an air of surprise as he approached apologetically.

'I've got the police on the phone,' he said.

Ellie's heart skipped a beat. She knew that some of what they did was marginally illegal, but took comfort in the thought that it would be almost certainly unprovable in court. But any contact with the law made her uncomfortable.

'What do they want?'

'They won't say. They want to talk to one of the guests. A Mrs Anderson. Eileen Anderson.'

'She's in there,' Ellie said, nodding towards the auditorium. 'She can't talk now. Tell them they'll have to leave a number or call back.'

'I've told them. They insist.' Jeremy's voice shook slightly. Like all staff on the compound, he feared Ellie's wrath; above all feared being the cause of it. 'They said they want to talk to somebody in charge – now.'

'Fuck!' Ellie muttered, thinking. 'Listen, can you work this end for five minutes?'

'I'll do my best,' he said, brightening at the opportunity and the confidence she was showing in him.

'He's just starting on this guy – him in row "J" next to Minnie. The stuff's on screen. All you've got to do is read it out – not too fast.'

'No problem.'

Ellie whispered a few words to Murray to explain the switch, then made way for Jeremy at the mike and bustled out. She had the call switched through to her office.

'This is Ellie Ray. How can I help you?'

'Sergeant Dan Miller, New Hampshire State Police. As I told the young man I was speaking to, I have to speak to Mrs Anderson in person.'

'I'm afraid Mrs Anderson is in a . . . in a religious service right now. But I'm a very good friend of hers. If there's any way I can be of help to you or to her, I'd be very happy.'

She heard him hesitate, then decide.

25

'Well,' he began, obviously not relishing the task he had to perform, 'I'm afraid I have some tragic news. I'm calling from the county morgue. Mrs Anderson's husband was fatally injured in a traffic accident two hours ago . . .'

At first Joanna tried to tell herself it was a joke. Or she had misheard. Every instinct strove to deny that what she thought was happening could really be happening. Like the victim of some sudden catastrophe, she was paralysed by disbelief.

It had started when Ellie took back the microphone from the young man who'd been struggling to keep the show going for the last five minutes. 'Listen,' she'd said to Murray with a new urgency in her voice, 'I've just had the police on the phone. Something's come up. It's that Anderson woman . . . I'm getting her bio up . . . first name Eileen, comes from Springfield . . . has some problem with a twin sister who died when they were kids . . . Now listen to me, Murray, her husband just got killed on the interstate . . . Now this is what we're going to do . . .'

Joanna slipped a hand under her wig as though her earpiece might be somehow malfunctioning. She refused to believe what she was hearing. They could not possibly be about to do this awful thing. Not even these people could be as heartless as that.

Ellie's voice buzzed on in her ear.

'It's *got* to bring Joyce Pardoe back into play. Once this gets into the newsletters, she's sure to improve on that last offer. We could even get an auction going between her and the Thomases . . .'

Joanna was only vaguely aware that her mouth was hanging open as she listened to this woman cold-bloodedly planning to boost the sale of her real estate by exploiting a tragic bereavement. Even then she couldn't believe that Murray would go for this. She watched him sitting imperturbably, finishing off a rambling answer to a question from some man near the front, betraying nothing of the callousness and greed being poured into his ear. Surely he would just ignore his wife's words and carry on. He wouldn't go for this. He couldn't.

'The husband's name is Jeffrey Dean . . . Jeffrey Dean Anderson . . . Salesman – that's all I've got, nothing about what he sells. Two kids, teenagers, Shirley and Richard . . .'

Murray signalled for the next question. Merle had an object for him, a brooch or clip or something of the sort. She started across the stage and Murray held out his hands for it as he always did.

Then he froze without warning. His whole body remained rigid for some seconds, then he inhaled a shuddering breath and slumped back in his chair as though unconscious.

People were on their feet in alarm, thinking he was ill. Merle hurried towards him, but quickly realized that all was well as he pulled himself forward and stood up. He raised his arms theatrically, and the audience watched, puzzled, as he placed his fingers on his temples in an attitude of intense and painful concentration. His breathing remained heavy for some moments more. Then, still blindfolded, he spoke.

'Jeffrey . . . Jeffrey Dean Anderson,' he intoned, 'is speaking to me now as I stand before you . . . Eileen, he has a message for Eileen . . . he says she's here . . . he has a message for you, Eileen, and the children . . . Shirley, Richard . . . He wants you to know that he loves you, all

27

of you, and he doesn't want you to be sad . . . he has simply . . . crossed over . . .'

People ran to help the thin, drawn-looking woman who had collapsed in the aisle.

Outside, Joanna ran through the slim, tall silver birches until she had to stop, doubled over, retching from disgust and nausea.

Afterwards she walked briskly to the ludicrously named Clouds Wing, one of the two hotel blocks on the compound – wooden-built, plain and over-priced. There she paused only to pick up the few possessions she'd brought with her, and to check again that she had the whole episode securely on tape.

Then she picked up her car keys and hurried to the parking lot.

2

Sam Towne was watching an upturned plastic pudding basin crawl crab-like back and forth across the smooth surface of the laboratory floor.

The technical name for the device was a tychoscope, derived from the Greek 'tukhe', meaning chance, and 'skopion', meaning to examine. The prototype had been invented by a Frenchman, Pierre Janin, in the late seventies. It rested on two wheels, set parallel to each other, and a fixed pivot leg, enabling it to move in a straight line either forward or backward, or rotate clockwise or anti-clockwise.

All these movements were radio-controlled by a Random Event Generator (REG) in the next room. An REG was essentially no more than an electronic coin-tossing machine, its circuitry governed by some unpredictable physical process such as radioactive decay. A computer, programmed to sample this process at pre-set intervals, generated arbitrary series of numbers or movements accordingly.

The tychoscope's next move, in consequence, was always anybody's guess. Statistically, there was a known probability that it would make any one of the possible moves open to it, just as a coin, every time it is tossed, has a 50/50 chance of coming down heads or tails. Over ten, a hundred, or a thousand tosses it will come down approximately half the time heads and half tails. That is the law of probability.

Yet what Sam and his assistant, Pete Daniels, were witnessing was a consistent and dramatic violation of that law. The little pudding-basin robot was literally huddling in one corner of the floor. Each time the REG switched it to a new tack that looked like taking it away, the next few switches would inexorably bring it back to the same area.

Sam and Pete exchanged a look, neither concealing his excitement from the other. Both knew that this was a historic moment: a repeatable demonstration, under laboratory conditions, of something utterly inexplicable.

'Okay, let's move the cage,' Sam said.

There was an anxious twittering from the fifteen seven-day-old chicks as their world swung up into the air and came to rest two yards from where it had been. It took only a few moments for them to re-orientate themselves and begin calling for the featureless moving object that they had been conditioned to regard as 'mom', and which was now further away from them than they found comfortable.

Pete came back from the next room with a print-out from the computer. He handed it to Sam in silence. The numbers spoke for themselves.

'That's almost three times,' Sam said, doing a quick bit of mental arithmetic. 'The goddamn thing spent three times longer hanging around the cage when the chicks were in it than when it was empty.'

'In-fucking-credible.'

'But true.'

They both turned as the chirping of the little birds

grew more agitated. The tychoscope was making a turn of almost three hundred and sixty degrees. Sam caught Pete's eye, each of them knowing the thought that had shot through the other's head, followed by a jolt of self-reproach at such a cock-eyed notion. It was absurd to think, as they both instinctively though briefly had, in terms of the tychoscope actively searching for its brood. It was a mindless machine without even the pretensions to ratiocinative thought of the simplest computer program. Any kind of program was an ordered process, and the whole point of the process by which the little robot's movements were controlled was that it lacked all order.

The only possible force causing the machine to move as it had been moving for the past twenty minutes was the will of the tiny caged chicks to keep it near to them. Like most baby birds, they had adopted as their mother the first moving object they had come in contact with on hatching from the egg. After their birth they had spent one hour every day for six days in the presence of the robot as it meandered on its random path. Today was the first time they had been caged and therefore unable to follow the machine in their accustomed way.

So, instead, they were making it come to them.

An hour later Pete brought in another cage of chicks to replace the first. The only difference was that these chicks had never seen the tychoscope before and therefore had no attachment to it. To establish this Sam did a twenty-minute control run during which the robot, as the computer print-out confirmed, followed its normal random path while the chicks in their cage paid it no attention.

'Okay, Pete, pull the blinds, will you?' Sam said as soon as he had satisfied himself about the result. The lab became pitch dark, and the twittering of the chicks grew agitated.

'See what I mean?' Sam said. 'They hate the dark during waking hours. It throws them into a panic.'

The noise that the chicks were making certainly bore him out. They subsided somewhat as a small flame leapt from Pete's lighter, which he touched to a candle. He attached the candle to a clip on top of the tychoscope, which had remained stationary on the far side of the floor since the end of the previous run.

When the candle was in place – the only source of illumination in the room – Sam pressed the switch on his remote. The tychoscope began to move.

The chicks clamoured for the light to come to them . . .

'I'll never eat one of those things again,' Pete murmured as they analysed the data after several runs. 'The little buggers are magicians.'

Sam smiled. 'Then you'd better become a vegetarian,' he said, 'because anything more awake than a carrot could pull off what you just saw. And some people have theories about carrots.'

'You want to run a test with a basket of vegetables?'

'Nah – people would think we were nuts.'

'They already do.'

'Yeah, well,' Sam shrugged, 'maybe we are.'

Pete shot a covert glance in his boss's direction. Sometimes he didn't understand Sam. By rights he should have been ecstatic at the results they were getting, but a sudden despondency seemed to have settled on him, as though everything they were doing was a waste of time.

'What's up?' he asked. 'You found a flaw in the procedure, or what?'

'There's no flaw.' Sam's voice was flat.

'So why the long face?'

There was a flash of annoyance in Sam's look that warned the younger man to back off and not push the question further. But Pete wasn't in this job because he liked being told what to do or what to think. He respected Sam, liked him and admired what he was doing; because of that he wanted to be taken into his confidence.

'Don't look at me like that,' he said, aware of a slightly whining note of protest in his voice that he disliked. 'If there's something on your mind, I'd like to know.'

Sam sighed. It was a form of apology. 'It's nothing to do with the experiment.'

'Then what's the problem?'

'The problem is figuring out what, if anything, it all adds up to.'

3

Joanna had appeared on television only once before. It had been an afternoon talk show following a series of articles she had written about junk diet treatments and the doctors who pushed them. She'd found the experience surprisingly painless. The trick, she realized, was not to perform; it was more effective to underplay than overplay, because the cameras captured everything. Keep your sentences short and the thoughts behind them clear.

Today's show was for the same slot, taped in the morning for transmission that afternoon. Joanna's article about the sleazy tricks at Camp Starburst had provoked the furore she'd hoped it would. Now she found herself sitting alongside a male 'channeller', a female astrologer and the author of a book about the ghosts of famous people who, supposedly, still walked the earth. The fifth guest was a psychologist called Sam Towne who was, apparently, doing 'scientific research' into the paranormal at the University of Manhattan.

Joanna found the whole subject distasteful and the programme pointless, but her editor had insisted that anything which hyped the magazine's profile, and incidentally hers, could only help circulation.

'Are you saying,' one woman from the audience asked,

'that it's all a lie, all religion and everything, and there's nothing after death?'

'I'm saying,' Joanna replied, 'that nobody knows what happens when we die, and anybody who claims to know for sure is a liar – and probably a crook as well.'

'But what about religious belief?' the host of the show asked, moving among the audience with his microphone. 'Are you saying that all religion belongs in the same category of fraud as what you've been writing about?'

'No, of course I'm not. Religion is a different thing.'

'D'you mind if I ask if you have any religious beliefs yourself?'

'I was brought up in a protestant family, I've never been a big church-goer, but if you're asking whether I believe in God . . . I'd be hard pressed to say positively no.'

'Can I say something here?' The interruption came from Sam Towne, the psychologist. The host asked him to go on.

'Miss Cross was writing about people who claimed knowledge of the afterlife,' Towne said, 'specific and detailed knowledge about people who had, as they like to put it, "passed over". Now we shouldn't confuse religious belief with that kind of knowledge, or indeed any kind of knowledge in the generally accepted sense. I *know* that I'm sitting in a television studio; so do you. There's no way we can disagree about that. But I may *believe* something about how I come to be here, how the studio comes to be here, how the world in which it exists comes to be here – and you may believe something else. Both our belief systems may be consistent with the facts as we know them, but inconsistent with each other. The phoney psychics that Miss Cross was writing about had nothing to do with either religious belief or knowledge. They were running a straightforward confidence trick to make easy money.'

Predictably, the other three guests began protesting their agreement: the Camp Starburst affair had been a scandal but an isolated incident, and should not be used as a brush to tar the whole psychic world.

As Joanna listened, the low opinion she had formed of them during the past hour did not improve. She had to admit a sneaking regard for Sam Towne, however. When she'd heard there was going to be a spook-hunter on the show, she'd imagined some dour eccentric who spent his weekends in haunted houses trying to video the ghost. He turned out to be in his mid- to late-thirties, with an easy manner and a sense of humour. It was obvious that he was intelligent, his mind darting quickly but always clearly between topics; she could see from the monitor screens that he came over well on television.

The presenter gave Joanna the final word when he came to wind up the show. She confined herself to remarking that the psychic world may be one thing, but the multi-million dollar industry it gave rise to was something of which people should be very suspicious indeed. The host signed off with a few words about the next day's show (incest – again), and a production assistant approached to unhook the guests' microphones.

Joanna declined an offer of coffee in the hospitality room. She wouldn't have minded talking longer to Sam Towne, but the other three depressed her, coming as they obviously did from the same mould of parasitic hypocrites as Ellie and Murray Ray.

As she stepped into the elevator and began the high-speed descent to the Sixth Avenue lobby, a wave of depression swept over her. What had been obvious from the questions asked was how much the public *wanted* to believe. She found something sad in their need to reach out for something beyond their daily lives. She understood the impulse, of course, even shared it to some extent. But it meant that people like the Rays would always flourish. She had stepped on a couple of ants, but the ant hill was as busy as ever.

The huddled figure on the low wall by the stunted evergreens had attracted barely a glance in the forty minutes she had been sitting there. Like a cat waiting for a mouse to emerge from its hole, Ellie Ray had not taken her eyes from the revolving door. The psychic mafia had done her this one last favour, even though outwardly they were obliged to disown her and join in the universal chorus of condemnation. She still had friends, and word had been passed along that Joanna Cross was in the building to record a TV show with some members of the profession.

So far every attempt that Ellie had made to confront the young woman had been frustrated. She wasn't listed in the phone book, and security at the building where she worked had threatened to call the police if she showed up there again. Ellie hadn't been too worried. She'd known that she'd get to her sooner or later, and today was perfect. Today of all days. She felt a power in her that she had rarely felt before.

Although she had only ever seen Joanna Cross in the unflattering disguise that she had worn at Camp Starburst, Ellie had no trouble recognizing the smartly dressed, dark-haired young woman in the grey raglan-sleeved coat who stepped briskly out onto the building's slightly raised forecourt.

Joanna didn't notice the form that moved in the corner of her vision. Only when she reached the last of the four broad steps down to the sidewalk did she find her way blocked. The sight of Ellie Ray's face gazing up at her with stony hatred gave her a jolt. She knew that the woman had tried to get into the magazine offices, and had resigned herself to the fact that sooner or later an unpleasant confrontation was inevitable. Having it here and now, out in the open, was probably as good a way as any of getting it over with.

'I've been looking for you.'

Ellie sounded as though her jaw and throat were rigid with tension, strangling her words and at the same time giving them an abrasive edge.

'I know,' Joanna replied. 'I have nothing to say to you, so please get out of my way.'

'Bitch!'

Joanna moved to step around the diminutive figure, but felt a hand grip her arm like a steel claw.

'Murray's dead.'

Ellie spat the words out before Joanna could even try to pull free. She froze for an instant. The death of anyone you've known, no matter how slightly or under what circumstances, always has a certain impact. But the news of this death hit her hard, because she could see in Ellie's face what was coming next.

'You killed him, and you're going to pay for it.'

'I'm sorry to hear about your husband,' Joanna said, keeping her voice level, measuring her words, 'but I can't accept that I had anything to do with—'

38

'We lost everything because of you.' Ellie spoke as though Joanna hadn't even opened her mouth, dismissing her protest. 'Six more months and we'd have been out of that place with a small fortune in the bank. Now it's unsellable, except for its real estate value – which is nil. You fucked us over good, young lady, and you're going to pay.'

'Let me go!' Joanna tried to shake the little woman off, but the grip on her arm tightened so sharply that she gasped in pain.

'When I'm ready. I'm stronger than you – and don't you forget it.'

'If you don't stop this at once, I shall call the police and have you arrested.'

The older woman's eyes bore up into hers with a feverish concentration. They were dark-ringed, as though she hadn't slept in several days.

'He started three nights ago, chest pains. I called an ambulance but he died before they reached the hospital. His last words were, "Fix her, Ellie. Fix that bitch." And I promised him I would.'

Suddenly Joanna didn't want to struggle any more, or even protest. It wasn't that she was afraid, just that she was transfixed by an awful, morbid fascination. She felt oddly passive in the face of it, the way you were supposed to feel in an accident when time slows down and stretches towards infinity. She knew she had to let the moment play out to its natural conclusion, accepting the torrent of abuse in the knowledge that it would then be over. Somehow she knew she wouldn't see this woman again.

There was the twitch of a bitter smile at the corner of Ellie's mouth, almost as though she had read Joanna's thoughts.

39

'Don't worry, you won't see me again. This moment is all I need. You're going to remember it. And before you die, you're going to wish you'd never been born.'

She paused, enjoying the feel of having her victim hooked. 'You think I'm a fake, do you? A phoney. You'll find out.'

Her face took on the rapturous look of a fanatic entering the hallowed presence of the supreme power.

'It's done,' she whispered. 'You're on your own now.'

Joanna shivered. It was a silly, empty threat uttered by an angry and bitter old woman. But the moment had been charged with such emotion that a cocoon of silence seemed to have descended on the two of them, isolating them in a strange and loathsome intimacy. The people pushing past them on the sidewalk could have been a million miles away or on another planet.

Then, abruptly, it was over. The circulation-blocking pressure on Joanna's arm was lifted, and the woman who had filled her field of vision for the past few moments was just a short and unimposing figure scurrying off amid the shoppers and office workers on their way to lunch.

A shudder ran through Joanna, stronger than before, as though her body was shaking off the memory of the old woman's repugnant touch. She took a deep breath, and felt her heart beating fast. A delayed reaction of anger welled up in her.

And fear. There was no denying the fear.

She started walking north towards the park, telling herself that the exercise would calm her. But two blocks on she felt no better. The anger she now felt was less with the dreadful little woman who had buttonholed her and more with herself for being so easily shaken.

'Miss Cross?'

She jumped. The voice had come from just behind her as she waited to cross the street. She turned and saw Sam Towne.

His smile immediately faded as he saw the look on her face.

'I'm sorry,' he said, 'I didn't mean to startle you.'

'No, you . . .' she stammered, 'it's all right, I . . . I . . .'

'Is something wrong?' he asked, concerned now.

She didn't mean to tell him anything. It was too absurd, and she felt she would only make herself look foolish by talking about it. She would just say, Yes, of course she was all right, perfectly all right. They would have a polite, brief conversation, and then part.

But instead she heard herself saying, 'Something really horrible just happened . . .'

4

They sat down and he looked across the table at her. His face still wore an expression of concern.

'Feeling better?'

'Thanks – I'm fine.'

'What would you like? Water, wine, coffee?'

'A little water to begin with.'

Sam signalled the waiter. He had suggested they go somewhere, maybe have lunch if she had time. He told her that Mario's was one of his favourite haunts, then apologized for the unintended pun. She laughed, and it released some of the tension in her.

'Seriously, don't feel bad about getting spooked,' he said. 'Those people are professionals. They know exactly what buttons to push to trigger all your superstitions.'

'But I'm not normally a superstitious person.'

'Everybody's superstitious, even those who say they aren't. We're rational beings, so we have no choice.'

One of her eyebrows twitched slightly, the way it always did when she reacted to something with scepticism.

'Wait a minute – are you saying that superstition is a rational thing?'

'Absolutely.'

She looked at him slightly sideways and with the faintest narrowing of her eyes. 'Could you just run that by me again?'

He shifted his weight a little and leaned forward. 'Opposites define each other – black/white, vice/virtue, order/disorder, and so on – including rationality and irrationality. One can't exist without the other. And somewhere in the middle there's a grey area where you can't be sure which is which – a no-man's-land where anything can happen.'

'This sounds like the opening to *The Twilight Zone*.'

He laughed. 'You should know – from what you say you've just been there.'

True, she thought. For a while she had been genuinely afraid. But it was over now, the memory fading with each moment that passed. She ordered a salad and the special fettuccine that Sam said she should trust him about. She even had a glass of Chianti, although she normally never drank at lunch. Today, she thought, she had an excuse.

'The thing that really shook me up,' she said, putting her glass down after a first welcome sip, 'was when she told me that her husband had died. Without that, I don't think she would have got to me.'

'There's no way you can blame yourself for that man's death,' Sam told her firmly. 'It's obvious that he must have had a heart condition already. Anything could have triggered it.'

'I know,' she said, 'but that's the rational me talking. And as you've just pointed out, there's an irrational me, too.'

'Acknowledging its existence doesn't mean we have to give it the upper hand,' he said.

As he spoke, he gave her a smile that was somehow

so understanding and sympathetic that it took her by surprise.

'I'll try,' was all she could think of in response. They were silent for a few moments as their lunch was served. She made noises about the excellent fettuccine and how right he'd been to recommend it, then she asked him to tell her something about his work. He gave a shrug as though wondering where to begin.

'What would you like to know?'

She thought a moment, then said, 'There's one question I'd like to ask you as a scientist. It sounds kind of rude, but it isn't meant that way.'

'Go ahead.'

'Why do so many scientists that I've talked to think that any kind of investigation into the paranormal is a waste of time?'

'Well,' he said, not remotely discomposed by the question, 'there are two answers to that. One is that scientists, when they poke their noses outside their own narrow, specialist field, are as prejudiced and dumb as anybody else – only worse, because they *think* they're so smart.'

He forked some more pasta into his mouth and dabbed his lips with a linen napkin.

'And the other?' she prompted.

He smiled again, this time with a hint of resignation. 'The other answer,' he said, 'is that maybe they're right.'

'Presumably, that's a view you don't share.'

Again he gave a small shrug, as though not sure how to answer. 'All I know is I've seen some pretty strange things. I'm not sure what they add up to or what conceptual framework they fit into, but I can't ignore them any more than I can explain them.'

'Give me an example.'

'I'm not talking ghosts and banshees and messages from beyond. I'm talking about anomalies. Things that just don't fit into anything we understand.'

'Such as?'

He described to her the experiment in which the chickens were persuaded to adopt a machine as their mother. She laughed at first, then grew serious as she understood its significance.

'We've had cats in boxes with a heat source controlled by the same kind of random event generator. The cats, of course, liked the warmth – and we found the heat source would be on significantly longer when there was a cat in the box than when there wasn't.'

'If that's true, it's amazing.'

'Oh, it's true.'

'Can people do it too?'

'Come to the lab some time and try some of our tests. I promise we won't lock you in a box or anything.'

'I'll talk to my editor. Maybe we should do something – kind of a "mind over matter" piece.'

She shivered suddenly and convulsively.

'What is it?' he asked, concerned.

'I don't know,' she said, genuinely puzzled. 'When I said mind over matter I suddenly had a picture of that horrible old woman and the way she looked at me.'

She thought for a second that he was going to reach out and take her hand where it lay on the table, but he seemed to check the impulse. 'Remember what I told you,' he said, his eyes focused searchingly on hers. 'Those people are clever. They plant a fear and hope you'll worry yourself sick over it. Don't let them scam you that way.'

'I won't,' she said. 'I'm fine, really. Thanks.'

Over coffee she told him that she'd be seeing her editor

that afternoon and would suggest writing something on 'scientific' parapsychology. 'I'll call you if he bites,' she said.

Sam scribbled down his work number on a crumpled receipt culled from one of his pockets.

'Call me anyway,' he said, handing it to her.

5

Taylor Freestone took himself and the job of editing
Around Town very seriously indeed. Joanna watched as
he crossed his elegantly tailored legs, placed his fingertips
together and leaned back thoughtfully in his suede-
upholstered editorial chair.

'Might it not seem a little odd,' he asked, looking at
her from beneath a delicately furrowed brow, 'to have
just done an exposé of the whole business, then to be
saying maybe there's something in it after all?'

'Two totally different things,' she shot back, knowing
full well that he was going to agree, but only after they
had completed this little ritual dance of petition and
assent in deference to his authority. 'Sam Towne's work
is genuine research, and some of it's pretty mind-bending.
All we did with Camp Starburst was expose a scam, but
we didn't say there was nothing to the paranormal.'

He thought a moment, alternately pursing and
stretching his lips as though tasting a questionable wine.
She hadn't told him about her encounter with Ellie Ray,
though she had mentioned that Murray had died. The
news made little impression on Taylor, who had a curious
way of not connecting with the human reality behind any
of the stories that he published. His life was bounded by
the fashionable cocktail circuit of the upper east side,

although the magazine he edited with such conspicuous success took its stories from wherever in the world they might occur. Taylor's skill, Joanna knew, was in sensing what the sort of people who bought his magazine had been talking about at their fashionable health clubs, or may have seen on public television recently, and now wanted to go into slightly more deeply. It was a skill she admired and which she knew was far from being as simple as it sounded. Nonetheless, the man's fey posturings irritated her unreasonably, and she had to force herself to remain still and silent until his deliberations were over.

'Do a little groundwork,' he said eventually. 'Sketch something up for me next week. We'll see where we go from there.'

The apparatus was attached to the wall of a small room in the lab. It resembled a huge pin-ball machine – which in a sense, Sam said, it was.

'There are nine thousand of these polystyrene balls,' he said, pointing to a compartment at the top, 'which are dropped one by one in the centre of this first row of pegs. Watch . . .'

He turned the machine on. Balls started dropping and bouncing down through about twenty rows of plastic pins, ending up in a row of collection bins at the bottom.

'The pins are set like theatre seats, where you're always looking between two heads in front of you instead of sitting directly behind somebody. You can see that, as the balls drop, each hits one pin in every row, bounces one way or the other and hits another pin in the next. The further they drop, the more they tend to cascade out to one side or the other. But most of them, as you would expect, tend to stay more or less in the middle, with only a few bouncing all the way out to one side or the other. So you wind up with the balls distributed through these collection bins at the bottom in the form of a Gaussian curve . . .'

'Er . . .?'

'Bell shaped – tapering equally on both sides towards a central summit. That's the normal pattern of random distribution. The point of the experiment is to try to influence the balls to fall more towards the right or more towards the left, so that you wind up with the summit of the pile off-centre, more towards one side or the other.'

'And you do this just by thinking?'

'Sure. You sit here,' he indicated a sofa about eight feet from the display, 'watching the balls drop through the system, and willing them to go in one direction or the other.'

'And it works?'

He smiled at the incredulity in her voice.

'Over several runs, the deviations from pure chance are millions to one against. So to that extent, we have to say it works.'

'But how?'

'We don't know – yet. Come on, I'll show you some more.'

They continued their tour of the lab, which was housed in a collection of semi-basement rooms abandoned by the engineering faculty when they moved to better premises. Joanna was shown a kind of clockface with lights in place of numbers. The lights flashed on and off in a random pattern, and the point of the experiment was to try to 'will' them into moving consistently clock-wise or anti-clockwise.

There were computers which produced random numbers which 'subjects' were supposed to 'will' upwards or downwards. There was a randomly con-trolled water fountain where the subject would attempt to vary the height of the jet; a pendulum where the swing responded to conscious though non-physical inter-vention; and other ingenious devices on the same theme, including a television monitor on which two images inter-acted while a viewer concentrated on one of them until it dominated the whole screen to the exclusion of the other.

'Of course,' Sam told her, 'you don't get results in just one session. That's why volunteers have to work over a period of weeks or months. It's the aggregate of small but persistent deviations from the norm that becomes significant – increasingly so the longer you continue.'

He introduced her to four of the full-time members of his team who were present that morning. The youngest, his assistant, Pete Daniels; the oldest Peggy O'Donovan, an experimental psychologist, who was the lab manager. She had thick grey hair pulled back from her face in a bun and wore a kaftan of rich colours over an ample figure. Joanna was captivated by her smile and the aura of calmness that she exuded – something which must, Joanna felt, be invaluable in any crisis. The other two were Bryan Meade, an electrical engineer who designed and maintained the experimental equipment; and Jeff Dorrell, a theoretical physicist who designed and implemented the department's data processing.

Missing were the final two members of Sam's team, psychologist Tania Phillips and physicist Brad Bucklehurst, who were out in the field running remote perception studies with a group of volunteers.

'One volunteer, the "agent", is stationed in some randomly selected location at a given time,' Sam explained. 'Another volunteer, the "subject", is located somewhere far from that location and with no knowledge of it. The point is for the subject to guess what the agent is seeing.'

'And you're going to tell me they can, aren't you?'

Sam grinned. 'Sometimes with amazing accuracy. And believe me, we've done this thousands of times. The weirdest part is that sometimes we have the subject guess what the agent is seeing even before the agent goes to the location – sometimes days before. And we still get results.'

Joanna felt a surge of irritation with the sheer improbability of what she was hearing. 'But how . . .?'

He held up his hands before she could even get the question out. 'I don't know. All I can tell you is it works. Though what "it" is . . .' He gestured as though it was anybody's guess. 'We call it "psi".'

6

Over the next few days Joanna spent as much time at the lab as she felt she could without getting under everybody's feet and becoming a nuisance. They were a good-natured group and gave her all the help they could. Sam didn't hide the fact that funding was a problem for the kind of work they were doing. That was obvious to Joanna from the shabbiness of the premises in which they were housed. A little favourable publicity, Sam mentioned casually one day, would be a great help in going after fresh grants.

She tipped her head on one side and regarded him with amusement. 'What makes you so sure it's going to be favourable?' she asked.

He was genuinely nonplussed for a second. It simply hadn't occurred to him that anyone could be other than impressed by his work. 'I'm sorry,' he said hastily, 'you're perfectly right. I shouldn't have made that assumption.'

Joanna felt suddenly sorry for teasing him. He was, she had decided, a very sweet man with no guile and an almost boyish enthusiasm for what he was doing. That slight naïvety combined with obvious intelligence and a rare breadth of learning made him undeniably attractive – something she was coming to realize with every hour spent in his company.

'It's okay,' she said, 'I'm kidding. I'm fascinated by everything you've shown me. All we have to worry about is whether my editor will print it.'

A look of concern crossed his face. 'You mean it isn't certain?'

She shook her head. 'I need to find some hook for the story – something that'll make people sit up and say, "I have to read this".'

'But the implications of it all are fantastic. Machines controlled by thought process. A direct interface between mind and computer. Some practical and usable degree of human telepathy . . .'

'I know – but it's all abstract and in the future. I need to show my editor something more than interesting theories and promising statistics. And I don't have it.'

They walked up the steps and across the concrete campus, heading for the street. Somewhere, incongruously, a piano was playing a Chopin waltz. Joanna assumed it was a recording or the radio, until the music faltered and the player repeated the phrase. Then they passed through a narrow passage and were hit by the noise of the city.

By the time they had settled at their now regular table at Mario's – paid for, Joanna insisted, by the magazine – the frown on Sam's face had lifted and she could see that he was bubbling with some new idea.

'There's something I've wanted to try for years,' he said after they'd ordered. 'It's been done before, more than once, so I know it works. If this isn't a "must read" story, I don't know what is.'

'Tell me.'

'A group experiment, with you as one of the group. We're going to create a ghost.'

He watched her face for a response as he spoke. She returned his gaze, wondering how seriously to take him.

'Just so I know what I'm getting into,' she said with a note of caution in her voice, 'would we be planning to create this ghost by, well, killing somebody? Or did you have another method in mind?'

'Nobody is going to be murdered,' he assured her with a laugh. 'This will be a ghost of somebody who has never existed. We're going to make him up – or her.'

She looked at him for a while before speaking, taking time to absorb the idea. 'All right,' she said eventually, 'tell me how we create a ghost.'

'First of all we have to define what we mean by a ghost. What does the word "ghost" convey to you?'

'Well, I suppose something from beyond the grave that drifts around moaning and goes bump in the night.'

'Returning to avenge murder, bring a warning, or just because it can't stop hanging around its favourite spots?'

'Something like that.'

His hand flicked dismissively. 'I don't believe in that kind of ghost.'

'I never suspected that you did. What kind *do* you believe in?'

'Have you ever heard of *tulpas* . . .?'

'No.'

'It's a Tibetan word – means a "thought form". You imagine something in the right way, and it becomes real.'

She felt her sceptic's eyebrow twitch again. 'Now this I would have to see to believe.'

'That's the whole idea – you *will* see it.'

'Go on.'

'Think of any haunting you ever hear about. It's always the same story. Things start with unexplained noises, footsteps, doors opening and closing, cold spots, even odd smells – a general sense of some kind of "presence". You may get an outbreak of poltergeist phenomena, and sooner or later people start seeing things – a vague form, some kind of drifting cloud, or even somebody perfectly real-looking crossing a room or peering in a window. All the usual spooky stuff.'

'None of which,' Joanna interrupted with a note of caution, 'has ever happened to me personally.'

He shrugged. 'Nor me. But the evidence that it does happen is overwhelming. By far the hardest thing to swallow is the kind of explanation usually offered. Ghosts, when you think about it, are a pretty corny idea. If you dig back far enough into the history of any house, you'll find that something unpleasant once happened to somebody in it. Even if it's a new house, you'll probably find there used to be another house on the same site. You'll always find an explanation for a haunting if you look hard enough – the same way you'll see faces in a fire or passing clouds if you watch long enough.'

'So what are you saying?'

'I'm saying why are ghosts so repetitive and unoriginal? They're always doing the same thing and dressed the same way, no matter how often they're seen and how many people see them. They're more like a snapshot or a memory than an actual event. And a memory is something that's stored in the brain. And that's where I think ghosts come from: from the brains of the people who see them.'

'Hallucinations?'

'Of a kind.'

'How many kinds are there?'

'Well, there's the kind that only one person sees, and

there's the kind that a bunch of people see together telepathically.'

'Assuming that telepathy is a fact.'

He accepted her point with a wry glance. 'There are medical reasons to suspect that it is.'

'Such as?'

'There's a standard clinical procedure for measuring the brain's physical response to some stimulus such as a light shone in the eye or a tuning fork held to the ear. It's a matter of recorded fact that a thought projected at another person is capable of producing that same physical response.'

She looked at him a while, her face unable to hide the misgivings she felt. 'I guess I have to take it on trust that you're not bullshitting me. After all, I can always check.'

He laughed. 'Go ahead, check. Telepathy's more commonplace than most people realize, but I'm not going to get into a fight over it, because you'll believe what you want to believe. We all do. All I'm saying is that telepathy is the most likely reason why ghosts are sometimes seen, heard or sensed by several people at once. And the experiment I'm suggesting will provide evidence of that.'

'You say this experiment has already been done?'

'More than once. And it's time someone created another ghost and looked into the implications a little further.'

They did so for the rest of lunch, by which time Joanna knew that she had what she was looking for. It took less than twenty minutes to type up her notes for Taylor Freestone and take them into his office that afternoon. He held the few pages limply in his hand as though the effort tired him, then dropped them as he finished reading.

'Go for it,' he said languidly.

Joanna walked out with a sense of triumph. 'Go for it' was as close as Taylor Freestone ever came to foaming at the mouth with enthusiasm.

7

Looking back, she saw that her elation at Taylor Freestone's reaction was more than just professional. It had
provided her with an opportunity to go on seeing Sam
without the formalities of dating and everything that
involved. She was surprised when she realized how much
she wanted to go on seeing him. Thinking about it, she
had to admit that he was certainly one of the more
interesting men she'd met, and he wore well the longer
she spent with him. She came to see very quickly that he
wasn't just an act, a piece of cleverly polished performance art, sustainable for an evening or two until the
routine became stale and repetition set in. What made
Sam interesting was his interest in everything. When he
spoke it was a process of discovery – as much for him as
for his listener. He never taught or lectured. Even when
speaking of things with which he was familiar, he would
put them together in new ways and find patterns that he
hadn't noticed before. He was, on the whole, exhilarating
company. And he made her laugh often.

There's a weakness somewhere, she found herself
thinking one day when she got home. There always is,
there has to be. In the end it'll show, something obvious
that I should have seen all along.

Then she stopped herself, ashamed of the distrustful

nature that such a thought revealed. That wasn't, she knew, the way she really was.

Nearing thirty, Joanna had behind her a love life that she liked to call 'mature' – which she defined as having more good memories than bad, her only regrets being not things she'd done but some of the things she hadn't. She wasn't yet consciously thinking of any kind of permanent relationship. She'd tried that once – a live-in affair that had lasted three years, until he'd met somebody else. They had parted without bitterness. She had realized very quickly that she had liked Richard more than she had loved him, and had secretly rejoiced to have her freedom back.

That had been eighteen months ago. Since then she had been alone, except for a brief but romantic liaison with an Italian architect who turned out to be rather more married than he'd led her to believe. For the past six months she'd missed him more than she'd cared to admit, so her interest in Sam brought her, at the very least, the assurance that she was over Jean-Pierre.

Yet she knew no more about Sam now than she had after their first lunch together. She had no idea whether he'd ever been married or whether he was still married, though there was no evidence of any family life either in his conversation or in the odds and ends, postcards and snapshots, scattered about his untidy office. She had broached the question obliquely once by asking him whether he had any children, but had received only a simple 'No' in reply. On one occasion he'd let slip that he'd been at Princeton, but she knew nothing about his family or even where he'd been born.

The idea crossed her mind that she could always formally interview him and find out everything she wanted to know. After all, if she was writing a story about his work she would have to write something about the man. But she dismissed the possibility at once, annoyed to find herself in such a state of mind that she would even consider such devious strategies.

She hadn't been prepared for this at all.

The phone rang just after seven and brought her groggily out of a deep sleep. It was her mother, full of apologies for calling so early but making the excuse that she'd tried three times in the last two days and always got her machine. She hadn't left a message because there wasn't anything special. She just wanted to talk.

Joanna could tell that something was wrong. Or at least that there was something on her mother's mind. She asked her what it was.

There was a hesitation at the other end of the line, followed by an uncharacteristic awkwardness in her mother's voice as she said, 'Darling, I know it's silly, but I've had the most terrible dream about you three nights running. Are you all right?'

Joanna assured her that she was perfectly all right, and asked her to describe her dream.

'There's really not much to it, and it makes no kind of sense that I can figure out. All I know is that it's night, and it's raining very heavily outside, and I'm here alone waiting for your father to get back from work. Then something happens – I don't know what – but suddenly you're outside banging on the door trying to get in, but I won't let you. For some reason I'm terrified and have to keep you out. You're screaming and I'm hiding somewhere, terrified, and I can hear this pounding rain the whole time and . . . it's awful.'

Her mother's voice broke slightly, but she pulled herself together and said, 'I'm sorry. I told you it was ridiculous. But I've had it three times now, and it's got me really worried.'

Again Joanna promised her that there was nothing to worry about, but the fact that her mother was so upset bothered her. Despite the fact that Joanna was an only child, Elizabeth Cross had never been an anxious or over-protective mother. This kind of thing was totally unlike her.

'It doesn't make any sense to me either, mom. But there has to be some reason for the dreams we have. Have you told dad about it?'

'Each time I have it I wake him up, moaning and crying out. He doesn't know what to make of it either.'

They were both silent a moment. Joanna could feel that her mother was feeling better just for having spoken to her. 'You know what, mom?' she said, trying to lighten the mood a little. 'It sounds to me like you're hiding something from me, something you don't want me to see and feel bad about. Have you done something outrageous to your hair, or what?'

Her mother managed a brief laugh, slightly forced. 'I've looked at it every which way, and I can't figure it out. Why would I ever feel about my own daughter that I can't have this person in the house. What could you have done?'

'Jesus, mom, I hate to think. But whatever it is, I haven't done it.'

Another pause. Then Elizabeth Cross said, 'Maybe I feel somehow that you're hiding something from me, and

I'm, you know, resisting whatever cover-up you're giving me.'

'I'm not giving you any cover-up.'

'You're not working on some story like that last one, are you?'

Joanna's mother, for some reason, had been deeply uneasy about Joanna's involvement with the phoney psychics at Camp Starburst. She hadn't known until after the event that her daughter had been in there alone, under cover. 'Those kind of people are evil and dangerous,' she'd said. 'I'm shocked that the magazine let you do that. Call me superstitious if you like, but I think that kind of thing is best left alone.'

'I'm working on a story about a psychologist at the University of Manhattan,' Joanna said, uneasily conscious of not telling quite the whole truth, but knowing it was wiser for the moment to withhold further details.

They talked a while longer as Joanna got out of bed and went through the kitchen to put on a pot of coffee. Gradually their conversation took on its usual half-joking, half-serious tone as Elizabeth's fears receded. 'Any movement in your love life?' she asked after a while. 'Not that I'd want to seem like I was prying, of course.'

'Oh, mom, nobody would *ever* accuse you of prying.'

It was a running gag between them, one which allowed either to 'cut to the chase' whenever they saw fit.

'But since the subject's come up . . .'

Joanna laughed. Her mother was sounding quite her normal self now.

'Since the subject's come up, mom, all I'm going to say is that the answer to your question is somewhere between no and I'm not sure yet. I'll keep you posted.'

8

Sam gathered the members of his department together twice a week to review current projects and consider new ones. They couldn't all fit into his office, so they sat informally around a central reception area where visitors and volunteers normally waited to be called into one of the adjoining rooms. This particular morning the topic under discussion was the new group experiment proposed by Sam. Joanna, with everyone's permission, was taping the meeting and making notes. She had also been told to feel free to make comments or ask questions.

'Essentially it's a reconstruction of the Victorian seance,' Sam was saying, 'with the difference that they thought they were conjuring up the dead, whereas we know it's PK – psychokinesis,' he added for Joanna's benefit. 'The observable effect of mind on matter.'

'What I don't understand is why you have to invent a ghost to achieve this – aside, that is, from giving Joanna a good story, of which I'm all in favour.' The speaker was Tania Phillips, one of the members of the department Joanna had not met before. She had short dark hair, a wide mouth with an aggressive jaw but gentle eyes. 'We're already getting measurable PK effects with all our work with individual test subjects and REGs, so why use different methods for a group?'

'Because whenever this experiment's been tried, no amount of heavy concentration or earnest meditation has ever produced results. The best approach is a relaxed, sociable group treating it as a kind of parlour game. The imaginary ghost, so the theory goes, serves as a focal point for "psi" forces that we all supposedly have in ourselves, but which we don't know how to make conscious use of.'

'But why does it have to be an *imaginary* ghost, instead of – I don't know – Julius Caesar or Napoleon?' The question came from Bryan Meade, the engineer in the group.

'We probably could whistle something up and call it Julius Caesar or Napoleon,' Sam said, 'though we'd soon discover that he knew no more about the Roman empire or French history than any of us around the table did.'

'Sam's right. Inventing a ghost who never existed makes the point more clearly.' The comment came from Jeff Dorrell, the theoretical physicist. 'I read just recently some stuff on that Toronto group twenty years ago. I agree – it's time somebody tried something like it again.'

'They created a ghost called Philip,' Sam said, looking around the group, his enthusiasm mounting as he spoke, 'who was supposed to have lived in the English Civil War, then committed suicide after an unhappy love affair. He never materialized physically, but after a while he started talking to them through table rapping. And they got some spectacular poltergeist activity – all of which exists on tape and film.'

Peggy O'Donovan had been listening to the discussion from a corner, balanced on an impossibly ancient bean bag and hugging her knees beneath her usual flowing kaftan. 'Okay, let me just ask one thing. I presume everybody here has read *Magic and Mystery in Tibet* by Alexandra David-Neel?'

Everybody had, with the exception of Joanna, who had never heard of it. 'I think I know what you're going to say,' Sam said, 'but go ahead, tell Joanna.'

Peggy's almond eyes turned in Joanna's direction; there was an almost hypnotic quality in their depth and stillness. 'Alexandra David-Neel was a French woman who travelled through Tibet around the turn of the century. She describes at one point how she heard of holy men who were able to create these thought-forms – *tulpas*.'

Joanna glanced at Sam as she recognized the word from their earlier conversation.

'Eventually, through study and practice,' Peggy continued, 'she managed to produce a *tulpa* of her own – a monk, who took up residence in her house. When she travelled, he would follow. Other people saw him and assumed that he was real. To begin with he was friendly and funny and nice to have around. Then she sensed that he was changing into something that made her feel increasingly uneasy, something malevolent. So, having materialized him in the first place, she decided to dematerialize him. Except he wouldn't go. She had six very difficult months getting rid of him.'

Jeff didn't hide the amused scepticism that the story had provoked in him. 'My favourite part of that book is where she tells about the hat that walked.' He looked over at Joanna. 'Apparently a hat was blown from some traveller's head and landed in a distant valley. Some villagers found it but didn't touch it. They'd never seen anything like it and thought it was some sort of animal. After several days of skirting around it, afraid to get too close, their fears imbued the hat with a life of its own –

and it started to move around by itself.' He chuckled, like a man who thought he'd made his point neatly. 'I don't know how literally we're supposed to take Ms David-Neel, but I smell a little literary licence here and there.'

'The point is,' Sam summed up, 'that she doesn't deny that her little monk disappeared in the end, nor did he do any mischief when he was around – aside from making her feel uncomfortable for a while. With the Toronto group, their "Philip" vanished the moment even one member of the group got bored with him.'

'Incidentally, what size and kind of a group do you have in mind, Sam? Regulars, volunteers, or what?' The question came from a tall, fair-haired man – Brad Bucklehurst, another physicist and the only other member of the department, apart from Tania, whom Joanna had not met until this morning.

Sam said that by all accounts the optimum number for such a group was six or eight. Because spontaneity was such an important element, it might be an idea to have mainly new volunteers. Joanna, of course, would be among them as well as Sam himself. Above all, he wanted to avoid anyone who had or even claimed psychic or mediumistic gifts: the aim of the experiment was to demonstrate the power of the normal human brain, not the exceptional one.

Peggy said she'd start drawing up a list of possibles and put out feelers through the usual newsletters, personal ads and websites. Of the department members only Pete Daniels pressed to be allowed to join, and Sam agreed. The others, though interested, were too busy with their own projects to devote several hours a week to a new one.

When the meeting broke up, Joanna headed for her office, which was a pleasant, twelve-block walk on a dry, cool day. Sam accompanied her, on his way to a meeting with the administrator of some research foundation out of which he was trying to squeeze an extra few thousand dollars a year – part of the endless battle for funding in a field that didn't enjoy the kind of support given to cures for cancer or even attempts to build a better mousetrap. They walked in silence for a while, and he glanced sideways at her several times before asking if there was something on her mind.

'I was just thinking about what Peggy said,' she told him.

'What about it?'

'You're quite sure there isn't any risk?'

'Of what?'

'I don't know. Starting something that we can't stop.'

'We just took a bigger risk crossing the road, and didn't even think about it.'

'So there is *some* risk.'

'I don't believe so. But you don't have to go through with it if you don't want to. You can write about it without being part of the group.'

'No,' she said quickly, 'I want to be part of it.'

They walked on in silence another half block. 'By the way,' he said as they paused at a 'Don't Walk' light, 'I've been meaning to ask you, is all that business of Murray Ray and the old woman still bothering you?'

Joanna was surprised that he'd remembered Murray's name. It had been some weeks since their first meeting, which was the only time they'd spoken of him. She also realized that he'd made a connection that she hadn't made herself between that unnerving incident and the

67

sense of slight misgiving that Peggy's comment had provoked in her.

She replied honestly. 'Whenever I think about it, I tell myself I'm not responsible for his death. I know I'm not. But yes, I do still think about it.'

'And I suppose you think about that "curse" the old woman put on you?'

Joanna hesitated. She didn't know whether the problem was admitting to him or to herself that she did. 'Sometimes,' she said. Then, more brightly: 'Then I tell myself it ought to be working by now, but I don't feel anything.'

He laughed. 'You're fine.'

A surge of pedestrians came towards them across another intersection. They were briefly pushed apart, then he reached out to hold her at his side, slipping his arm beneath hers and wrapping his fingers around her wrist.

She found that she enjoyed being touched by him.

9

In the end she decided that not to do a proper in-depth interview with him would be a betrayal of her obligations as a writer, putting personal considerations before professional ones. There was a twisted roundness to that logic, when she arrived at it, which pleased her.

He agreed at once when she brought the matter up, suggesting, rather to her surprise, that they go over to his place where they could talk undisturbed. Perhaps one afternoon this week, he said, for tea? She said fine, accepting at once the obvious point, which only occurred to her then, that she couldn't hope to write interestingly about the man without seeing where he lived. She could send a photographer along later, if she felt it was a good idea.

Promptly at four p.m. on the appointed Thursday, she stepped out of a cab at the address he had given. Sam lived in a megalithic building way up on Riverside Drive, on the fifth floor with a fine view of the river. The apartment was rambling, shabby and (most important) rent controlled. He had inherited it from one of his friends from college days. The place had a long academic tradition; half the furniture and a large number of the books that lined every wall still belonged to previous tenants who, despite the best intentions, had never returned to collect them. It didn't matter; everything was used, enjoyed, and nothing thrown out until it absolutely and irreparably fell apart.

Over Earl Grey tea and some exotic petits fours from a Belgian deli on the west side that he said he would be glad to introduce her to, they began to talk. Joanna's compact tape recorder spooled silently on the table between them, and she changed cassettes several times before they were finished. By then she knew that Sam's father was a doctor with a practice on Cape Cod. He had been promising his wife that he would retire next year for the past five years, but still showed little sign of doing so. It sounded like a happy childhood, sailing and horseback riding, scrambling over rocks and up trees with his two older brothers, one of whom was now a professor of history at Harvard, and the other a heart surgeon in Chicago. Sam himself had a master's in physics and a doctorate in psychology from Princeton.

'A high-achieving family. I'm impressed,' she commented.

'That was dad. He never made us work, just made things interesting. If any of us asked a question about anything, no matter what, dad either had a book in his library, or he'd pick one up next day and leave it lying around. It was just a talent for opening up kids' minds.'

'And your mother . . .?'

'Mom's an enthusiast – paints, plays oboe in the local orchestra, and writes novels.'

'Have I read her?'

'I doubt it. She only ever got one published over twenty years ago, but that doesn't stop her. She also runs a travel group – went to China last year.'

'They sound quite terrifying.'

He laughed. 'Just your average American family.'

'Not where I come from.'

Joanna's parents were by no means unsophisticated, but paled by comparison with the gifted eccentrics Sam had described. Her father had learned to fly with the navy, gone on to be a civil aviation pilot, then become an airline executive. Mom had always just been mom, and still was: no mindless cookie-cutter, but no world-travelling bohemian artist-writer either. And Joanna, as an only child in a non-bookish household, had got all her early intellectual stimulation, such as it was, from television. But she'd worked hard, gone to Wellesley and majored in journalism. The nice thing about the job, she always thought, was that learning was part of it; she could make up for lost time while getting paid for it.

'By the way,' she said eventually, and with what she hoped was not an exaggerated casualness, 'have you ever been married?'

'No,' he replied equally casually, as though his answer needed no elaboration.

'D'you mind if I ask if there's any particular reason for that, in your view?' she inquired, with the smile of someone trying to draw her subject out on something about which he was being unduly modest.

He shrugged non-committally. 'Luck, I guess.'

'Would that be good luck or bad luck in your book?'

'I suppose the word I should have used was "chance". More neutral. Came close a couple of times, but it never happened.' Another shrug. 'We tend to be late marriers in my family.'

She decided after a moment's reflection against pursuing the topic further; it was not, after all, a matter of great journalistic importance.

'So tell me,' she said, adopting a change of tone and shifting her weight slightly in the deep and well-worn leather armchair, 'how did you get started on the work you're doing now?'

He thought a moment. 'I'm not sure I can answer that. It just happened a step at a time, with a kind of inevitability, the way things do.'

'But it's an interesting series of steps. You started as a physicist, became a psychologist, then a parapsychologist. Did something happen, or what?'

He shook his head, as though searching for an answer and apologizing for not finding one. 'I've always just followed through on whatever interested me most. So far this is where it's brought me.'

'But you told me once that you've never had any paranormal experience, seen a ghost, dreamed the future – anything like that. So it's purely intellectual curiosity?'

Again he paused a moment before answering. 'I suppose something did happen once, a long time ago, that might have had something to do with it.'

A distant look came onto his face as though he was focusing on some faraway time and place. 'All I remember is that I was walking down a road on the Cape. It was a beautiful day in early June, but nothing otherwise exceptional about it. I was alone, and without any warning, right out of nowhere, I was hit by a thought that took my breath away. It was like an explosion in the head. I don't think I even broke my stride. Nobody looking at me would have realized that anything had changed. But I suddenly had an overwhelming sense of something extraordinary happening.'

He paused, then started to speak again, and stopped, chewing thoughtfully on the corner of his lower lip as though striving to find the right words. 'This "extra-ordinary thing" was simply the fact of being there – alive, conscious, part of this body that I could see if I looked down, with feet at the end going one after the other along the road. I was somehow inside and outside of this body at the same time. And in a way that I'd never realized before I was also part of the landscape around me – a landscape that was suddenly strange and new but at the same time totally unchanged. It was a feeling that was frightening and exciting in about equal parts. It couldn't have lasted more than a couple of minutes, but while it did time meant nothing. In a way it hasn't meant much ever since.'

He looked at her with an apologetic smile, as though hoping that he'd answered her question because he didn't know what else to say. 'Just your plain, ordinary sensation of oneness with the universe, I guess. The only strange thing about it is that we call it strange, when civilizations we label primitive take it for granted.'

She pondered her next question for a few seconds, then asked, 'When did this happen?'

'Oh, a long time ago.'

'How long?'

'Longer than I care to remember.'

'How old were you?'

'Seven.'

10

By the time they'd finished talking it was dusk. He offered her a glass of wine and produced a remarkably smooth, dry white from his fridge. When she remarked on it, he said it was a Condrieu from the northern point of the Rhône Valley in France – a gift from a friend who imported fine wines for restaurants all up the east coast.

'By the way,' he said, glancing at his watch, 'I really should have asked before, but if you happen to be free, can I offer you dinner?'

'That's very kind of you,' she said, dismissing as abruptly as it crossed her mind her mother's rule that a woman is never free for at least three days, five for a first date. 'I'd like that.'

Then he surprised her again. 'I've got a new recipe a friend of mine just e-mailed me from California. If you don't mind being a guinea pig I'd like to try it.'

'Sounds good,' was all she could think of in reply. As he refilled her glass, she vaguely wondered whether this was some standard technique of his, a carefully planned prelude to seduction. Once again she dismissed the thought as unworthy; the poor man was obviously broke and, unlike her, didn't have an expense account for eating out in restaurants. 'Can I help?'

'Only if I get into a hopeless mess, but I think I'll be okay. Bring your glass and come and talk to me.'

The kitchen was cavernous and unmodernized, though plainly still much used. There were racks of herbs and spices, hanging pans, skillets and casseroles of gleaming steel and copper, and sets of knives with blades kept razor-sharp and well-worn wooden handles. Sam had put some music on in the main room, and it was piped through into two large speakers with a brilliant sound quality. A concerto by Poulenc danced and pirouetted in the air as she watched him go to work. They talked of everything and nothing while he poached a fillet of cod in sake, then prepared soy sauce, sesame oil, scallions, ginger and coriander separately. Served with Basmati rice and accompanied by another bottle of Condrieu, it was delicious.

They ate by candle light at one corner of a long oak table in the adjoining dining room, panelled where its walls were not obscured by shelves of books. For dessert he had prepared fresh-sliced mangoes with a rich lemon sorbet. He offered to make coffee, but she declined. He came around the table to pour what remained of the wine into her glass, and stayed to kiss her long and tenderly.

'All right,' she said about an hour later as they lay in bed in each other's arms, still elated by the suddenness and vigour of their lovemaking, 'off the record, what's the real story on how you've stayed single all these years?'

'Hey, I'm not *that* old,' he protested in a tone of mild reproach.

'I didn't say you were. But I get the feeling that you like women, which means that if you haven't stuck with one you must have had an awful lot of them.'

75

'Are you one of those women who thinks there's automatically something wrong with a man who isn't married by the time he's thirty?'

'I'm not "one of those women who" anything.'

'No, you're not, are you?' He ran his hand over the lightly muscled smoothness of her back and pulled her gently towards him once again.

Later they perched cross-legged on the window seat of Sam's living room, eating fruit yoghurt and popcorn washed down with champagne. 'That proves it,' she exclaimed triumphantly when he produced the bottle.

He looked at her questioningly. 'Proves what?'

'You planned this whole thing – even down to a bottle of champagne in the fridge to celebrate.'

'It was left over from a party,' he protested, spreading his arms in a gesture of innocence. 'I'd forgotten it was there.'

'Can you really cook? Or do you always do that same dish to impress your girlfriends?'

'Come back tomorrow and try me.'

She leaned over and kissed him. 'I might.'

They talked some more about themselves, their backgrounds, their lives up to the present, then wandered back to the subject of the experiment and the things that remained to be arranged, principally the composition of the group. He broke off in the middle of something he was saying and looked out over the dark waters of the Hudson. She was already becoming familiar with these moments of distraction in him, as though his mind abruptly travelled to some place of its own, cut off from the world until it had dealt with whatever preoccupied it at that moment. It was an oddly attractive quality because it was so wholly without self-consciousness. It implied an unexpected vulnerability, a certain loneliness.

'You know something,' he said after a while, 'if I could get Roger Fullerton into this group, it would not only be the coup of a lifetime but an absolute blast.'

'Who's Roger Fullerton?'

'My old physics professor at Princeton. He's actually very famous, twice nominated for the Nobel, though they haven't given it to him yet. Having him in the group would really get some attention from the kind of people who dismiss any and all paranormal research as something between group hysteria and outright fraud.'

'Would he do it?'

'I don't know.' Sam laughed softly, turning his attention from the river back to her. 'He's always been one of the people who dismiss this kind of work as something between group hysteria and outright fraud.'

'You told me this thing could only work if everybody involved had an open-minded, uncritical approach. Now you're saying let's have a sceptic.'

'The thing about scepticism is it cuts both ways. *Real* sceptics *have* open minds. Roger worked with Einstein and Niels Bohr. He was on the tail end of that whole generation who discovered that reality disappeared the closer they looked at it. You'd think telepathy and psychokinesis would be food and drink to guys like that.'

'So why aren't they?'

Sam shrugged and reached out to pour the last of the champagne into her glass.

'Ask him yourself. Are you free Saturday afternoon?'
'I could be.'
'Come out to Princeton. I think you'll like Roger. And I know he'll like you.'

11

It started to rain as Sam parked his car. Huddling beneath the old umbrella that he had found in the back, they hurried down tree-lined walks between the neo-Georgian carved-stone buildings of the campus. On the second floor of one of them Sam knocked at a door, and a crisp voice called out, 'Enter.'

'Spry' was the word that came to Joanna's mind to describe Roger Fullerton. He wore an immaculate three-piece suit in excellent tweed and sported a white moustache with a waxed twirl at the ends. The twinkle in his eye as they were introduced left her in no doubt why Sam had suggested that her influence with the old man might well exceed his own.

They settled into leather armchairs and someone brought in tea. The room was where Fullerton had taught and held discussion groups for over forty years. It bore the imprint of a long, distinguished life. Framed photographs of people she knew but couldn't quite place, some of them also featuring a young and good-looking Fullerton, hung casually at rakish angles on the panelled walls. Books and papers were scattered everywhere in what seemed like carefully ordered chaos. A computer sat on a table by a window with a stained glass pattern.

'So,' Fullerton said, shifting his gaze back to her face

from her legs, where it had lingered for a moment with an appreciation so open and innocent as to be wholly inoffensive, 'I gather the purpose of this visit is to persuade me to get involved in one of Sam's lunatic "experiments", as he likes to call them.'

There was a faintly English inflection in his speech that made Joanna think of Ray Milland or Cary Grant in some of the old movies she'd seen on late-night television. She glanced in Sam's direction, but he had his nose in his teacup and seemed oblivious of Roger's brusquely dismissive tone.

'I think he's more or less abandoned that ambition,' she said guardedly. 'On the way over he said he'd probably have to settle for just another argument, but at least it keeps him in shape.'

Roger chuckled. 'Well, I'll try not to let him down.'

Since their first conversation about Fullerton, Sam had filled her in on the background of his relationship with the older man. They had met when Sam used to go to his lectures and always asked questions at the end. The friendship they struck up had survived even when Sam abandoned physics for psychology – a non-subject, in Fullerton's view, lacking clear parameters. But that disapproval was nothing compared to the outrage he had expressed when Sam became interested in parapsychology.

Within minutes of setting tea things aside and getting through the basic requirement of social niceties, the two men had picked up their ongoing quarrel like a game of chess played on and off whenever the opportunity arose. No piece had been moved since last time, and both knew exactly where they were.

'You're simply ignoring half of the thinking that's gone

in the last hundred years,' Sam was saying. 'At the end of the nineteenth century there was an explosion of interest in psychic phenomena . . .'

'Foolish old women and nervous bachelors,' Roger interrupted scornfully, 'holding hands in darkened rooms, waiting for a sign from mother on the other side. Good God, you're not calling that science, are you?'

'Some of the best minds of their day were involved, here and in Europe – doctors, physicists, philosophers, people whose work in their own fields still stands today—'

'And it's that work for which they're remembered – not for dabbling in senseless mumbo-jumbo that led nowhere.'

'On the contrary, they saw that something very interesting was happening, and they had the intellectual curiosity – and honesty – to try to find out what it was. You taught me that the essence of the scientific method is the willingness to place one's own ideas in jeopardy.'

'Which they did, quite rightly – and came up with nothing! As long as there is not a single repeatable experiment to prove the reality of ESP—'

'There are many repeatable experiments that prove beyond doubt the effect of consciousness – both human and animal – on random events. The statistics are there to be seen.'

'Statistical proof is a contradiction in terms.'

'The laws of physics are statistical.'

'Quantum events may be unpredictable, but they average out to give us laws which are consistent – enough so that we use them in everything from digital watches to space shuttles. Your so-called experiments add up to no more than a scattering of anomalies from which no

81

coherent pattern emerges, and for which there appears to be no practical use. All you have is some vague unknown force called "psi" which is supposed to account for whatever minor deviations from chance you've observed.'

' "Psi", my dear, bigoted Roger, is no less definable than what you call the "observer effect" in physics. Now are you going to tell me that *that* doesn't exist?'

'You can't extrapolate from the micro world to the macro.'

'You can't draw a line between them, either. They're not two different things, just opposite ends of a spectrum.'

'At my end of which are the basic limiting principles of science, and at yours anything goes. So-called "psi" abilities' – he spoke the word with deliberate scorn – 'are supposed to operate as though space and time were meaningless. Forget the inverse square law, relativity and thermodynamics – "psi", which we can neither measure, predict nor otherwise define, rules the universe. You're running a religious cult, not practising science.'

'If you're so keen on basic limiting principles like cause and effect, why don't you come and look at what I'm doing before you make up your mind about it?'

'Because I know without looking that I can't disprove any of your claims, and that's why they don't interest me as a physicist and never will. The essence of any scientific theory is that it remains open to being proved false in the light of fresh evidence. The essence of any crackpot idea is that it cannot be proved either true or false in any circumstances.'

'What if you sat in a room and watched a table move about and even levitate of its own accord – all in broad daylight?'

'I would applaud an excellent conjuring trick.'

'It's been done more than once. I'm going to repeat – note that word repeat – the experiment, and it is not a conjuring trick.'

'Then I would echo the view of David Hume on miracles – that it is more rational to suspect knavery and folly than to discount, at a stroke, everything that past experience has taught me about the way things actually work.'

Joanna had been sitting like a spectator in the stands as the two men batted their argument back and forth across the room. She wanted to get the exchange on tape for use in writing her magazine piece, but hesitated to do so openly without the professor's agreement. So she had furtively slipped her hand into her bag and pressed the start button, hoping that the machine would pick up at least some of the exchange. She felt a moment of guilty unease as Fullerton suddenly looked her way.

'What do you think of all this, Miss Cross? As a journalist?'

'As a journalist, professor, I'm not supposed to have a view. I just try to write about both sides of the argument.'

It sounded a little mealy-mouthed, and was in fact untrue. But this was not an argument that she particularly wanted to find herself in the middle of.

'But you must have some personal feelings,' Fullerton persisted. 'Everybody does, one way or another.'

'Well, I suppose I think, you know, maybe there are "more things in heaven and earth" . . .'

She broke off the quotation without bothering to finish it.

'But I can't give any good reason. Except my father, who's a very down-to-earth man, claims to have seen a flying saucer one time when he was a pilot in the navy.'

'Wait a minute,' Sam interrupted, 'I don't mean to be rude, but just for the record, UFOs, ley lines and crop circles have nothing whatever to do with parapsychology.'

Joanna gave him a look which, in the sweetest possible way, warned him not to patronize her. 'Jung thought that UFOs were *tulpas*,' she said. 'I researched the subject after you mentioned it the other day – thought-forms either created in the past but still manifest, or being created now by the collective unconscious.'

Sam held up a hand. 'I stand corrected. You're right.'

Roger beamed his approval. 'It's nice to know,' he said, 'that somebody can make him acknowledge the error of his ways.'

'I wish I could say the same about you, Roger,' Sam retorted, 'but I can see you're determined not to join us in an experiment that might shake some of your rigid preconceptions.'

'Not join you?' the old man said, eyebrows shooting up in mock astonishment. 'If you imagine that I'm going to pass up the chance of holding hands around a table with this young lady for the next few weeks, not to mention watching you make a buffoon of yourself, then you're even crazier than I thought you were.'

It had stopped raining by the time they walked back to the car. Every step of the way Sam was grinning from ear to ear.

12

Joanna's parents came in from Westchester county one weekend out of three. They stayed at the same small hotel behind the Plaza that they'd used for twenty years, and where they were gold star clients and got a preferential rate. Their usual routine was to take in a show, maybe catch a movie or an exhibition, and see their daughter.

Elizabeth Cross was an attractive woman with a good figure and a flair for simple, stylish clothes. She looked a good deal younger than her fifty-six years, as did her husband Bob, who would be sixty in the spring. Although of only medium height and balding now, he still had the trim physique and confident agility of a much younger man. Joanna was always proud to be seen with her parents. Normally the three of them would dine in some favourite restaurant. Tonight was no exception, aside from the fact that they were going to be four: Joanna had invited Sam to join them.

To get the introductions over in as relaxed an atmosphere as possible, she had everybody over for a glass of champagne at her tiny apartment in Beekman Place. Sam, as Joanna had expected, was charming and amusing and completely at ease. She could tell that her father liked him at once, though her mother was less than comfortable with his choice of profession.

'Is it anything like that film *Ghostbusters* that's always on television?' she asked.

Sam smiled. It was a question he was familiar with. 'Nothing so dramatic,' he said. 'I only wish it were. But we're just scientists investigating hard-to-categorize phenomena.'

'Something like *The X-Files*?' her father suggested.

'A little, I guess, in some ways. Except we're nothing to do with the government.'

'But this thing about creating a ghost,' Joanna's mother persisted. 'It sounds positively morbid.'

During the cab ride to the restaurant, which was in the sixties between Lexington and Third, Sam explained in as much detail as he could what the experiment was designed to achieve. Joanna could see that her mother wasn't much reassured, but her father was fascinated.

'So let me see if I've got this right,' he said, after they'd been seated at their table and placed their orders. 'Telepathy is communication mind to mind, while clairvoyance is seeing some place or event, as opposed to the contents of another mind.'

'Correct,' Sam said, 'although there's obviously some overlap. Seeing at a distance often involves seeing what somebody else is seeing.'

'Precognition,' Joanna's father went on, ticking the subjects off on his fingers, 'speaks for itself, though why these people who can do it don't just get rich at the race track I don't understand.'

'Well, sometimes people do predict a winner,' Sam demurred. 'It just isn't reliable enough to beat the odds consistently.'

'And finally there's psychokinesis, which means mind over matter – moving solid objects by thought alone.'

'And maybe creating solid objects,' Joanna added. 'Or at least solid-looking.'

'Well, I think it all sounds very strange, and I'd rather have nothing to do with it,' Joanna's mother said. 'Call me superstitious if you like, but I think there are some things in this life that we should just leave alone.'

'Elizabeth, if we all took that attitude, we'd still be living in caves,' Joanna's father said. 'Today's technology is yesterday's magic. People were burned at the stake for ideas that led to teflon and television. Hey, Sam, did Joanna ever tell you that I saw a flying saucer one time?'

'Oh, Bob!' Elizabeth said reproachfully, as though he'd made some social faux pas in polite company.

'Yes, as a matter of fact she did, Mr Cross.'

Elizabeth got on with her dinner as her husband told the story that she'd heard too many times. She had always felt that some unspoken stigma attached to any claim to have seen UFOs, ghosts, or anything else sufficiently out of the ordinary. It was something that set you apart from other people, and she dearly wished that her husband would not talk so freely of his experience.

'I was flying an F-14 off the *Nimitz* in the west Atlantic. I came out of some high cloud around twenty thousand feet – and there it was. It was about three miles east, just hovering there, a silver disc-shape, no windows, no lights as far as I could see. But solid. I reported in. They said they'd nothing on their screens. I turned to investigate, and as I approached it just kind of shot off like it was on a wire or something. It didn't accelerate the way any regular craft would. It just went straight from zero to bat-out-of-hell. Disappeared in two, three seconds – just like it hadn't been there. But to my dying day, I'll know what I saw.'

They talked around the subject for a while, but Joanna was conscious of Sam subtly steering the conversation towards other topics in deference to her mother's unease.

Later, when Elizabeth left the table to go to the women's room, Joanna went with her. She watched her mother as she re-applied her make-up in the mirror. There was something clipped and too brisk in her movements, as though she wanted to communicate that she was unhappy but didn't want to say it.

'You okay, mom?' Joanna ventured cautiously.

'Yes, of course, darling. Why?'

'I just thought you were a little quiet.' The comment drew no response, so she continued. 'Are you still having that dream that you told me about on the phone?'

'Dream? Oh, that – no, I haven't had it since we talked.'

'That's good.' Joanna checked her hair in the mirror, turned, flicked an end. 'I didn't much care for that idea of being locked out in the rain all night.'

Another silence as her mother snapped her compact shut and took out a lipstick. 'If you're waiting to hear what I think of Sam,' she said after a moment, 'I think he's very nice.'

'Nothing was further from my mind,' Joanna said airily. Then added, 'But . . .?'

'I didn't say "but" . . .'

Joanna waited as her mother applied a touch of colour to her mouth and pressed her lips together. 'But, since you mention it, it does seem a rather strange choice of profession.'

'He's a psychologist. What's strange about that?'

'You know perfectly well what I mean. A psychologist is a doctor. That's not what he does.'

'A psychologist is not necessarily a doctor. It's someone who studies some aspect of human psychology.'

'Exactly – *human*.'

'Mom, he's not weird. In fact he's one of the sanest and most intelligent men I've ever met.'

'I'm sure he is. It's just that I find this whole thing you're getting into very – I don't know – uncomfortable.'

'What whole thing?'

'This whole world of weirdness. I wish you'd go back to writing those travel pieces you used to do. Or more of those reports on the environment.'

'I'm a journalist,' Joanna objected stiffly. 'I have to cover whatever the magazine wants.'

'Well, as soon as you've covered this particular subject and moved on, the happier I'll be. I still feel a shiver down my spine every time I think about those horrible people you wrote about at that Camp whatever it was called. It's better not to get involved.'

'That was a scam that had to be exposed.'

'So what's the difference between that and what Sam's doing?'

'There's no comparison. This is scientifically-based research.'

'Then I'm probably wrong and we won't talk about it . . .'

Elizabeth Cross gave her reflection one last check, and started for the door. Joanna followed her out, catching her up in the corridor.

'Mother, that is your most irritating habit.'

Elizabeth gave her a look of innocent surprise. 'What is?'

'You know perfectly well – saying something provocative just as you walk out the door and before anyone can call you on it.'

They had reached the stairs. Elizabeth Cross paused with one foot on the first step and turned to her daughter.

'I wasn't aware that I had said anything provocative.'

Joanna felt her lips twitch, and was immediately aware of her mother's amused reaction. That twitch had been a habit of Joanna's since she was a child, and she cursed herself for never having mastered it. It meant that she had put herself in the wrong – said too much or something she didn't mean – but would die before admitting it.

'All I meant,' her mother said in a conciliatory tone, 'was it's an unusual job, and it must take an unusual person to do it. That doesn't mean he isn't very nice, I already said he was. Now come along, or the poor man will be wondering what we're saying about him.'

Joanna followed her mother through the leather-upholstered door at the top of the stairs and across the restaurant to their table. She felt a curious unease. Something in her mother's words, more particularly in the unspoken misgivings behind them that she couldn't quite identify, had brought back the image of Ellie Ray's face, twisted with black rage and pushed into hers that morning on Sixth Avenue.

But the feeling passed as they sat down. For the rest of the evening they talked of shows to see and events to catch in the coming season.

All the same, when the two couples bade their good-nights outside the restaurant before going their separate ways, Joanna sensed her mother's continued reserve. It both irritated and troubled her. She knew about her mother's instincts, and for most of her life had trusted

90

them – often, as things turned out, with good reason. But this was different. This time her mother was simply mistaken. That was all there was to it.

She slipped her arm through Sam's and enjoyed the feeling of their closeness. He dipped his face to hers and kissed her lightly on the mouth as they walked into the wintry, glistening Manhattan night.

13

The first meeting of the group was on a Tuesday evening, just after seven. They were in a basement room beneath Sam's main lab. Until now it had been used for storage – mainly junk which he'd been glad to throw out finally. High on one wall two small windows opened to ventilate the place, but a metal grille on the outside meant that they let in almost no light. Whenever the room was in use, even in bright daylight, the overhead strip lighting had to be kept on. It reflected with a clinical coldness off the white-painted brick walls from which the odour of fresh paint had not yet quite evaporated.

In the centre of the room was a square wooden table around which were eight straight-backed chairs. An old leather sofa was pushed against one wall; next to it was a card table on which stood a coffee machine and paper cups, and next to that was a small fridge containing cold drinks. Video cameras on tripods stood in adjacent corners, and four small microphones hung from the ceiling with cables leading to a bulky transformer and a power outlet on the wall.

Joanna sat on the left of a married couple in their early forties who had been introduced to her as Drew and Barry Hearst. Barry was a heavy-set man with a dark beard trimmed short and a taste for open-necked

Hawaiian shirts even in the middle of winter. He was a plumber, Joanna knew, running a successful business out of Queens and employing nearly thirty people. His wife, Drew, sat next to him, slim and fragile-looking, but with a stillness that suggested a wiry strength and considerable determination.

Next to Drew was Maggie McBride, a soft-spoken, motherly woman in her sixties whose voice still carried a lilting trace of the Scottish Highlands where she had been born.

On Maggie's right was an austere-looking man in his fifties who wore an expensive and well-cut business suit and introduced himself as Ward Riley. All that Joanna knew about him so far (the idea was that they should get to know each other better in the course of their twice-weekly sessions) was that he was a lawyer turned investment banker who had made a great deal of money and retired ten years ago. According to Sam he was a man full of fascinating contradictions: a successful businessman drawn to eastern mysticism and paranormal research; a lifelong bachelor and an intensely private man who funded, anonymously, a string of scholarships for young artists and musicians he would never meet, as well as sponsoring a small poetry magazine and occasionally contributing generously to Sam's research.

The rest of the group comprised Sam; his assistant, Pete Daniels; Roger Fullerton; and Joanna herself. Sam inevitably acted as chairman of the proceedings, while making an effort to keep everything as informal as possible.

'As you know,' he said in the course of his general introduction, 'Joanna Cross is here to write about this whole thing for *Around Town* magazine. By mutual agreement she isn't going to use any of your actual names or otherwise identify you in print – unless, of course,' he added with a smile, 'you want her to, in which case I'm sure she'll oblige. Obviously I too will be writing something for one of the professional journals, but the same rules apply – no names without your permission.'

After that he went around the table, inviting everyone in turn to say a few words about themselves. Maggie McBride was coaxed, reluctantly, into going first, but it quickly became obvious that her natural shyness covered a canny intelligence and a strong sense of who she was.

Maggie had been born in Elgin, Scotland, from whence she had emigrated with her parents to Vancouver, Canada, at the age of twelve. There she had met and married fellow Scot Joseph McBride. They had worked as cook and chauffeur to a wealthy businessman, eventually moving with him to New York. Maggie's interest in things psychic had been kindled by her employer's wife, who was a devout spiritualist. Maggie originally 'played along,' as she put it, 'as part of the job, but never really believed there was much to it.' She and Joe had two children, of whom they were deeply proud: a son, an industrial chemist, married with one child; and a daughter, unmarried, who was an investment analyst on Wall Street. When Joe died of cancer five years ago, Maggie had stayed on as housekeeper to her now elderly employers. A couple of years ago she had come across an appeal for volunteers in a copy of the Parapsychology Association newsletter and had applied out of curiosity. She had worked with Sam on some of the experiments that Joanna had seen demonstrated. Her results had been good within normal limits. She had never had any kind of psychic experience, and suspected that most such claims were phony, though she kept an open mind.

Barry Hearst spoke for himself and Drew, but deferred to her unquestioningly whenever she corrected him on some point of emphasis or detail, which was not often. They came from the same part of Queens and had known each other since childhood. Both came from working class families. As a teenager Drew had contemplated becoming a nun, while Barry had been constantly in trouble with the law. They were vague about how they had come to get married (Joanna suspected an accidental pregnancy), but the union had been beneficial to both. Barry had channelled his rebelliousness and was now, at the age of forty-one, the owner of a flourishing plumbing supplies business. His claims to be uneducated were flatly contradicted by Drew, who said that he had his nose in a book every spare minute and was widely read in history and philosophy. He also had, she added with barely disguised pride, a large collection of classical recordings and often whistled Mozart at work. Barry admitted, under pressure, that he supposed he was 'something of a success story – at least in the neighbourhood'.

Tragedy had almost shattered their lives ten years ago when their only child, a daughter, had been killed in a road accident at the age of eleven. Barry had been almost destroyed by his grief and claimed that only Drew's strength had pulled him through. Nonetheless, he remained an agnostic in contrast to her devout Catholicism. It did not seem to be a source of friction between them. They were there, Barry said in conclusion, because he had read something about Sam's work in a magazine and had written in for more information.

Roger Fullerton described himself modestly as a

physics teacher who already knew that the universe was irrational, but wasn't yet sure how deep the problem went and hoped all this might help him find out.

Pete Daniels, who was awestruck even to be sitting at the same table as Roger Fullerton, said that he was twenty-four, born in Kentucky, and had studied physics at Caltech. He claimed that a chronically low boredom threshold had kept him from going into industry or doing anything either profitable or practical with his skills, which was how he'd wound up working with Sam. (Sam had already told Joanna that Pete had the soul of a pure researcher and was worth his weight in gold, despite being paid in peanuts.) He was funny in a naïve-smart kind of way, and Joanna sensed that the whole group felt an immediate affection for him.

Finally Ward Riley managed to say even less about himself than Joanna had learned from the thumbnail sketch that Sam had given her. 'A retired businessman with a lifelong interest in all forms of paranormal phenomena,' was all they got out of him. Curiously, however, nobody seemed to want or need more; there was about him a quality – oddly indefinable, Joanna thought – that disposed people to accept him at face value and demand no more than he chose to volunteer.

That left only her. Since they already knew who she was and why she was there, she invited them to put any questions they might have to her. Barry Hearst asked whether, in view of her revelations about Camp Starburst, she had any belief whatever in the supernatural. She said that she supposed she had as much belief as any of them present; certainly, the material she had read describing previous experiments of the kind they were embarking on was pretty convincing, but she wouldn't really know for sure what she thought until she saw with her own eyes the table they were sitting around move or, better still, float in the air.

Roger smiled and said that such an occurrence would pretty much take care of his misgivings too. After that the session broke up into a series of casual chats over coffee. Sam moved happily among his little group, obviously satisfied that the atmosphere he had hoped to create was evolving successfully. When he felt that they had accomplished as much as could be expected on this first occasion, he unobtrusively brought the proceedings to a close. They were to meet again in three days.

'At which time,' he said, 'we'll start to invent our ghost. And then, to paraphrase Bette Davis, fasten your seat belts – because with any luck, we'll be in for a bumpy ride.'

14

'What is it?' Joanna peered at the pale blue liquid in the metal container. It was warm, viscous and odourless.

'Paraffin wax. Watch.'

Sam pulled back his sleeve and dipped his hand in it up to the wrist. When he withdrew it, it was evenly coated with what looked like a tight-fitting, partially transparent glove. 'It dries almost immediately and comes off easily,' he said, pulling a strip from the back of his hand. 'And look, you can see every mark of the skin, even tiny hairs, perfectly imprinted.'

'This is very interesting. I assume there's a point.'

They were in a back room of the lab that housed some photographic developing equipment, a gas stove and a few shelves of chemicals. He finished cleaning the stuff off his hand as he explained. 'Sometime in the twenties there was a Polish banker called Franek Kluski, who discovered at the age of forty-five that he was a prodigiously gifted physical medium. According to people who were there, he held seances in which he produced mysterious creatures out of nowhere – human forms, semi-human, animal, semi-animal. The only problem was that at the end of the seance they disappeared, so there was never any tangible proof that they'd been there, even though people had seen them and touched them. So one of the researchers investigating him came up with this idea of asking these spirits if they wouldn't mind dipping their hands into a bowl of paraffin wax, so that when they dematerialized they could leave the wax casts behind. Very obligingly, the spirits agreed – and at the end of every seance after that there'd be these empty wax casts lying on the floor. All the researchers had to do was fill them with plaster to get a perfect cast of . . . whatever it was that had been in the room.'

Joanna stared at him. 'You have to be making this up.'

He made an open, non-committal gesture with his now wax-free hand. 'There's a set of plaster casts in Paris at the Institut Metapsychique. They call them "phantom hands", and they were reportedly created in the way I've just described.'

'I've got to see Roger's face when he hears this.'

Sam laughed. 'I'd rather see it when something dumps a wax cast in his lap and tells him to explain that away.'

'You know,' she said thoughtfully, 'you were so right to want Roger in the group. As you said, if he buys into this, it's going to be very hard for the sceptics to dismiss it.'

'Believe me, it won't stop them trying.'

'All the same, if he'll let me use his name, I'd like to do a special interview with him – once before we start, and again later if something happens.'

'Steady on there – your interview technique is what got us on first name terms.'

'What's the matter? Jealous of an old professor?'

'Of *that* old professor, yes. He's been married four times, and I wouldn't put it past him to try a couple more before he's through.'

'*Four* times?'

'He's a scientist – repeatability is the essence of any good experiment.'

'I think you just cured me of a dangerous crush.'

'Glad to hear it.' He pulled her to him and kissed her.

'D'you think they know?' she asked in a soft voice.

'Does who know what?'

'The others in the group. About us.'

He shrugged. 'They've probably made an educated guess. Anyway, it's no secret – is it?'

'No.' She ran her hand through the thick hair on the back of his head and pulled his lips to hers once again. 'Absolutely not.'

Inventing the ghost proved to be a slow process fraught with unanticipated pitfalls. Under Sam's guidance they applied such logic to it as they could. The first question was should it be a male or female ghost? Roger suggested that tossing a coin might be the fairest and fastest solution. Everyone agreed, so Roger spun a quarter. The ghost was male.

The next question was what period should their ghost have lived in? Everyone waited for everyone else to make a suggestion, then Sam said why didn't they all give their opinions one at a time, starting on his left with Maggie. Somewhat diffidently, claiming she knew little history and would defer to those who did, she suggested mid-eighteenth-century Scotland, the time of Bonnie Prince Charlie and the Jacobite uprising. There was a brief silence while everybody wondered whether to comment on that idea rightaway, or hear other people's views. Sam proposed that they carry on around the table with their own suggestions, then go around again for comments.

Riley suggested the Hermetic period in ancient Egypt. Drew picked Renaissance Florence. Barry picked the American Civil War. Joanna picked the French empire under Napoleon. Roger said that anywhere in Europe at any time in the seventeenth or eighteenth centuries – the 'Age of Reason' – would be fine with him. Pete Daniels said he would have picked Renaissance Italy, but since that had already gone he thought he'd 'run classical Greece up the flagpole and see if anyone saluted'. Sam said he thought that was quite enough to be going on with and he would be happy with whatever the group chose. He invited Maggie to start the round of comments.

'It seems to me,' she began hesitantly, as though apologizing for stating the obvious, 'that it would be a help if we invented someone whose language we all spoke. And I have to admit that French, Italian, Ancient Egyptian and Greek are a bit, well, double Dutch to me.'

'It's a good point,' Roger said at once. 'There's no point in complicating things unnecessarily. I suggest, if we all agree, that we choose an English-speaking ghost.'

Everyone agreed, after which the discussion grew freer. Sam invited those who had chosen 'foreign' ghosts to make new choices in their native tongue. Drew opted for Victorian England; Roger said the ghost could, of course, be an English-speaking traveller anywhere in the world; Riley suggested the Russian revolution, where it was a matter of historical fact that there had been several English-speaking observers; using the same excuse, Joanna stuck with the French empire.

Going around the table again, Maggie endorsed France – 'the auld alliance', in any period – as a second choice.

101

Drew said she hadn't read enough history to be able to imagine any particular period in much detail, but it might be interesting to pick a time when something was happening other than war and bloodshed. She liked Roger's idea of the Age of Enlightenment, when cultures were flourishing and new ideas exploding everywhere.

Barry said that the elements of war and cultural evolution had always overlapped throughout history, and the American Revolution was a perfect example. He was sticking with that.

Joanna suggested that, as three revolutions had been proposed so far, perhaps it might be an idea to settle for one of them. Riley conceded that the Age of Enlightenment was perhaps a more attractive choice than the Soviet experiment, by which time reason had grown over-confident of its ability to solve everything, thereby provoking disaster. During the French and American Revolutions things were still more finely balanced.

Roger agreed. It was, he said, a time when people believed in the scientific process but didn't take its products for granted as they did today. After all, the late twentieth century had televisions and refrigerators and rockets to the moon as proof that science worked. Two hundred years ago, its achievements weren't so obvious. They were ideas more than achievements: an approach, not an answer.

Sam said that if it came to a choice between the American or French Revolutions, then Maggie's point about language should probably hold the balance.

'English was spoken in Paris,' Drew said, loyally, though perhaps unconsciously, siding with her husband. 'Jefferson was in Paris then. And Benjamin Franklin. And what about Lafayette?'

Roger admitted to being no military historian, an ignorance which Joanna doubted because she had seen him notice the brief look of unease on Maggie's face as she realized that she knew next to nothing about Lafayette. Roger, she surmised, was merely being gallant – and wondered vaguely whether there was any truth in Sam's joke about him looking for a fifth wife.

Barry volunteered a brief sketch of Lafayette's life. Born into an immensely rich aristocratic French family in 1757, he had been a courtier of Louis XVI, but in 1777 had gone of his own accord to America to fight against the British in the American Revolution. He was appointed a major general, struck up a lasting friendship with George Washington, and distinguished himself at the Battle of Brandywine in Pennsylvania. In 1779 he returned to France and persuaded the government to send a six-thousand-man expeditionary force to help the colonists. He was central to the Americans' decisive victory over the British at Yorktown in 1781. A hero now in both countries, he returned to France and there became leader of the liberal aristocrats, championing religious toleration and campaigning for the abolition of the slave trade. In 1789 he was one of the first leaders of the French Revolution, but found his essentially reformist instincts outstripped by the revolutionary zeal of Robespierre and others. After failing to save the monarchy, he fled to Austria in 1792. He returned to France under Napoleon in 1799, and lived for more than thirty years as a gentleman farmer and member of the Chamber of Deputies. His popularity in America had never dimmed, and when he paid a visit in 1824–5 he was received with wild adulation and given every conceivable honour.

'It's a good story,' Sam said, 'but we can't use him because he's a real person.'

'But we could easily invent an American who went back to France with him,' Barry countered. 'Some hero-worshipping kid from New England who gets idealistically involved in the Revolution and winds up on the guillotine.'

Murmurs of approval greeted the idea all around the table, the general feeling being summed up by Maggie McBride.

'I think that's a very good idea, I really do. An American in Paris. Very nice.'

15

His mother's eyes were red from having cried all night. He wanted to put his arms around her and promise her that everything would be all right, that they would see each other again one day. But that was not how things were done in their family. He could no more tell her that he loved her and would weep for missing her than she could tell him how bitter was the sense of her impending loss. Her only son was going to France with the great General Lafayette, and in some part of herself she knew with certainty that she would never see him again. Yet when he'd asked her why her eyes were red, she'd brushed him aside with an impatient answer. The dust was troubling her. She had a sensibility to the grass and flowers in the summer, and to the fine white powder that hung like a mist in the air of the grain mill. 'Eat up, now,' was all she said. 'You have a day's ride before you and you cannot journey on an empty stomach.'

She busied herself with unnecessary tasks, frowning sternly through the noise and clatter that she made with pots and pans and crockery while her son ate his final breakfast in her kitchen. Through the window she could see her husband John saddling up the horses with Edward, the young groom. He started towards the house, moving with his habitual solemn gait, and she knew the moment was upon them. She took a deep breath and prepared herself for parting.

They embraced stiffly, mother and son, unused to such contact. He gripped the Bible she had pressed into his hand and promised he would treasure it. She watched from the yard as he rode with his father down the track and towards the trees. He turned back once and raised his hand. She raised hers, too far away for him to see it tremble. As they disappeared beneath the dense green foliage, she turned quickly and walked back into her kitchen.

Adam Wyatt felt a weight fall gradually from his shoulders as he rode beside his silent father down the Hudson River towards New York. The lack of contact between them that had been at first oppressive ceased to trouble him, and his thoughts turned towards the great adventure that was opening up before him. It was pure chance that had brought him to the notice of the great Frenchman, an unthinking deed that passed for bravery in the crucible of war. A horse had broken loose and would have betrayed the position of Lafayette's troops as they dug in to lay final siege, under General Washington's command, to the British at Yorktown. It mattered little whether Adam's bold action in preventing the animal's escape had made one jot of difference to the outcome of the engagement; General Lafayette himself had witnessed the incident and had the young man brought to him for commendation. He had taken a liking to the young American and had him transferred to his command. Adam's intelligent and questioning nature – about everything from political theory to science and philosophy – had further commended him to the sophisticated and good-hearted Frenchman. He had even arranged for the boy to have lessons in the French language when he showed interest in it. Now here he was, not two years on and just turned twenty years of age, heading for France as one of the general's personal staff. He would see and learn things he had so far never dreamed of; and of course he would be seen as something of an ambassador for his new and vigorous young country with its commitment to equality and freedom, ideals which were fast gaining currency in Europe.

He shook his father's solemnly proferred hand on the outskirts of New York, then John Wyatt turned to head for home. His only reason for making the journey had been to take back the horse that Adam had ridden, and he had no wish to linger amid the festive crowds still celebrating George Washington's triumphant return to the city. Adam had wandered happily for several hours, drinking in the sights and sounds of celebration, then presented himself at the appointed quayside for embarkation on the great ship that would set forth at first tide on the five-week voyage to Bordeaux in France.

The sickness of the first few days (it was the first time he had been to sea) soon passed, and he found himself invigorated by the salty cleanness of the wind that gusted them briskly on their way. He didn't see a great deal of the general on the trip – or 'Marquis' as he was instructed to call him henceforth; the war was over and military titles could be set aside. He was given daily lessons in French, and instructed on protocol in readiness for his arrival. The Marquis de Lafayette, for all his commitment to libertarian politics and the dignity of man, remained an aristocrat who moved in the highest court and diplomatic circles, and those who moved with him were expected to behave appropriately. During those five weeks at sea

Adam learned how to speak, move and even think more like a nobleman than the farmer he had always been. The food on board was simple, but he grew accustomed to having it served to him by deferential crew members, who also filled his glass with wines of an astounding subtlety and richness of taste the like of which he had never known. The Adam Wyatt who finally set foot on French soil in the port of Bordeaux was no longer the same Adam Wyatt who had embarked in New York.

The next months saw the transformation complete. Lafayette was as much the hero of the hour in France as he had been in America. At every level of society the French people revelled in the defeat of their old adversary, Britain, and were proud beyond words of the role played in it by Lafayette and the troops he had persuaded the government to send. Lafayette was lionized not only in France but in all the liberal courts and salons of Europe; and, wherever he went, Adam Wyatt went with him. At Versailles he was presented to Louis XVI and his beautiful young queen, Marie-Antoinette. In Paris he was introduced to Thomas Jefferson, there to negotiate trade agreements with America. He spoke at length with the elderly and still brilliant Benjamin Franklin, present as a roving ambassador. They were heady times for a young man of his origins. Sometimes it seemed to him that those years of puritan simplicity were all a dream from which he had now woken. At other times he feared that his new life was the dream, and that he would awake to a scolding from his mother for some minor infraction, then have to go out on a cold morning to bring in the herd for milking.

But he didn't wake up, and after a couple of years of his new life he stopped fearing that he was going to. He wrote home dutifully, though infrequently, and received short, awkwardly written letters from his mother, usually with a brief postscript added by his father. The news they contained struck him as increasingly banal and uninteresting, evoking a world that seemed remote and unattractive, a far cry from the life of one of the principal secretaries to the Marquis de Lafayette, to which exalted rank young Adam Wyatt had now been appointed. Although his patron had made a return visit to America in 1784, Adam had not accompanied him; he was, he wrote to his parents, too busy with his master's affairs to think of leaving France. Later, of course, it would be possible, though he could not be sure exactly when.

What he did not mention was that he was in love not only with Paris but with Angelique. She was the daughter of a noble family who were friends of the marquis. They shared his reforming zeal and his conviction that the future must belong to all men and not just the privileged few. At the same time, like the marquis, it never occurred to them that the monarchy was any obstacle to such reform. The king was king of all men, a symbol of the country's unity. That there was unity in the country, sufficient at any rate to carry through such democratic reforms as might be necessary, was something taken for granted by everyone in the rarefied atmosphere in which Adam moved. The young queen, Marie-Antoinette, might be criticized for her extravagance and occasional folly, but these were minor matters. The king, though indecisive and a poor leader, was nonetheless accorded the respect due to his position and enjoyed the loyal support of even the most liberal of the nobility and the great majority of the country.

Angelique had become a favourite at court and was a regular companion of the queen. Adam himself began increasingly to be received there. The fact of his being an American hero with a quick wit and a now near perfect command of the language made him a fashionable and fascinating figure. When he and Angelique married in the summer of 1787, their wedding was one of the season's more glittering affairs. His wife's dowry was sufficient for the purchase of a fine house in the Faubourg Saint-Honoré in Paris and an estate in the Loire. Adam Wyatt was now a man of substance, treated as an equal by those he had originally come to serve. If America had pointed out the direction in which the future lay, Europe and especially France, he believed, was the place where it would be most swiftly and successfully achieved.

He continued to believe this throughout the summer of 1788 even as evidence mounted that the country was on the verge of bankruptcy. The single greatest contribution to this state of affairs was the cost to France of its involvement in the American War of Independence. Adam noted with interest that nobody pointed the finger of accusation either at him or his country; the only subject of debate was how to make up the deficit. In the autumn it was agreed that the Estates General should be called in the spring of 1789. This was a kind of national parliament made up of clergy, nobles and elected representatives of the people. It had not met since 1614 and was the only body with the constitutional authority to decide how new taxes could be levied to deal with the crisis.

No one, least of all the liberal and enlightened minority to which Lafayette and now Adam Wyatt belonged, anticipated how this event would serve as a focus for discontents that went back far in time and ran deep throughout the country. An arctic winter had triggered food riots and fuelled the deep resentment that the vast majority of the poor felt towards the privileged few. When those privileged few, in the form of the clergy and the nobility, tried to assert their will over the newly-elected representatives of the people in the Estates General, the dam broke.

The court, Angelique among them, continued to amuse themselves as usual, unconscious that anything was seriously amiss. The enlightened nobility, such as Lafayette, welcomed and participated in the changes that were now becoming inevitable. None of them, however, imagined that these changes would amount to anything more than a controlled redistribution of power: a constitutional instead of an absolute monarchy; a fairer distribution of wealth; a lifting of the grinding poverty to which ninety per cent of the population, labourers and peasants, had for too long been subjected. Nobody anticipated outright, bloody revolution.

Perhaps because he was a foreigner and for all his newfound wealth and privilege still an outsider looking in, Adam sensed that what was happening here was very different from the so-called revolution in America. The enemy there had been the old colonial power in Europe; here in France the enemy was visible through the windows of the royal palaces and fine houses such as Adam's own. He walked the teeming streets, sometimes accompanied by two armed servants for protection, sometimes alone but dressed in rags to avoid becoming the target of attack or robbery. He saw the king and queen and ministers of government burned in effigy; saw shops and warehouses broken into by the starving poor, their owners beaten and murdered for protecting what they thought of as their own; watched as mobs tore down the hated ring of customs barriers around the city and overran the frightened soldiers sent to quell their rioting. He was present when the Bastille, the hated feudal prison and symbol of oppression, was stormed and the heads of its governor and guards mounted on pikes and paraded through the streets to cheering crowds. Adam sensed that there was worse, much worse, to come, and felt a kind of fear that he had not known before.

After the fall of the Bastille Lafayette was made, by popular acclaim, commander of the National Guard, a new volunteer army that would henceforth be the ultimate authority behind each step of the revolution – for such all now acknowledged it to be. Yet there was still no suggestion from the men who emerged as its leaders – Robespierre, Danton, Mirabeu, Desmoulins – that the monarchy should be forfeit. On the contrary, hated though it was by the people, it was seen by thinkers and reformers as essential to society's stability, its safety guaranteed by Lafayette and the same National Guard that was born out of revolution.

Adam was with Angelique at the court at Versailles on the 5th of October, 1789. There had been a grand banquet celebrating the arrival of the Flanders Regiment for a routine change of garrison. Fine food and wines had led to expressions of sentimental support for the king and queen in the face of continuing criticism from the revolutionary National Assembly. Adam looked on with misgivings as the revolutionary red and blue cockades which the soldiers had been ordered to wear were torn off and trampled under foot. He knew too well that these excesses would be reported and could only aggravate the situation. Sure enough, an angry mob descended on the palace, slaughtering guards and breaking into the royal apartments. The king and queen and all their court had feared for their lives. Adam had hidden with Angelique in a cupboard of one of the royal bedchambers. Only the intervention of Lafayette and his National Guard had saved them. But Lafayette's authority was slipping; the mob threatened to turn on him and hang him unless he and his troops forced the royal family to return with them to Paris and live henceforth in the more modest Tuileries Palace, where they would in effect be prisoners.

It was the turning point in Adam's life in France. He loved his wife and was caught between the now doomed world they had so happily inhabited for too short a time and the rising tide of blood that the revolution had become. Events proceeded with an almost hypnotic inexorability. Adam knew that he and Angelique would be forced sooner or later to flee, but they were held for the moment by bonds of loyalty, he to Lafayette, she to the queen. Faction after faction seized revolutionary power, each one sweeping forward on fresh tides of blood. The guillotine worked day and night, the stench of death was everywhere. By the end of 1792 Lafayette had been arrested in Austria and thrown into prison as a 'dangerous revolutionary'. Shortly afterwards the king was executed in Paris. Suddenly it was too late to run. Adam and Angelique went into hiding, living in daily fear for their lives. He held her in his arms and tried to stifle her heartbroken sobs as they watched the queen dragged to the scaffold, only thirty-seven but looking like an old and broken woman, her hair prematurely white. The crowd around them danced and cheered with a vicious joy . . . and someone, seeing a young couple not sharing the revolutionary fervour of the moment, pointed them out to the local militia.

They ran, but it was hopeless. The crowd had them in its power, and Adam feared they would be torn limb from limb. It was in that moment of raw panic that he did the thing that would haunt him to his grave and beyond: when he saw his wife seized and, in her despair, screaming her love for the dead queen and her contempt for the wretches who had killed her, he protested that he did not know this woman.

The lie did not work. Worse, Angelique had witnessed his betrayal. She became strangely quiet, gazing at him as though across a void of time and space, no longer caring what would happen to her.

He saw her carried off, to what fate he never knew, and called out after her to beg forgiveness and swear his undying love. But it was too late. Too late for everything.

That night he gazed out through the bars of a prison cell, oblivious of the stinking mass of humanity around him. Tomorrow they would all be dead. Until then was time enough to mourn for his life, regret the country he had left, the new life he had too easily been seduced by, the errors he had made by loving first too well, and finally not well enough.

Come morning, he embraced his fate with a bitter equanimity that passed, in others' eyes, for bravery. He gave a grim laugh, remembering it was something which passed for bravery that had brought him to this present circumstance. With that thought he mounted the steps to the scaffold on which the queen had died the day before, and on which for all he knew his wife had died already; then knelt as though in prayer, hands tied behind his back, and closed his eyes to meet his death.

16

The members of the group read their copies of the document with nods and murmurs of approval. All had contributed something to 'Adam's story', though it was impossible to say now who had come up with which specific element or detail. They'd all spent every free moment they had reading up on the period. Not only was the French Revolution exceptionally well documented, it was also widely popularized. Lavishly illustrated general histories were complemented by academic tomes on particular events and personalities. They spent two sessions discussing what they'd read and passing around any pictures that had caught their attention – portraits, drawings, sketches and cartoons of the time.

Drew, who had a flair for charcoal sketching, drew a head-and-shoulders portrait of Adam as she imagined him. She gave him a strong face with high cheekbones, a fine, slightly Roman nose, dark eyes that had a steady, questioning gaze. He was beardless but had thick, dark hair that he wore relatively short and which fell boyishly across his forehead. His mouth was full and had a hint of humour to it. The picture appealed to everyone else in the group, and from then on hung on the wall as a permanent reminder of the man they were trying to create. Eventually Joanna, as the only writer among them, had been given the job of 'typing up' the story and putting all the elements and details they had discussed into some coherent form.

'Barry's checked it out,' Sam said, 'and I've had a colleague of mine in the history department do the same. Nobody can find a trace of any Adam Wyatt, or anybody remotely like him, having returned to France with Lafayette.'

'So what do we do now?' Roger asked after a brief silence. 'Sit here until he comes knocking at the door?'

'I don't think ghosts knock at doors, Roger,' Sam replied. 'It rather defeats the point of being a ghost, I'd have thought.'

Barry rapped the table with his knuckles and made a funny voice. 'Let me out, let me out!'

Maggie smiled. 'You know, I'm still not sure we should have called him Wyatt. Every time I hear the name I think of Wyatt Earp. It makes it a bit hard to take him seriously.'

'According to Sam, if we take him too seriously he's not going to work,' Ward Riley said, leaning back, arms folded. 'If I've understood the principle of this thing correctly, we could have sent Mickey Mouse to France and got the same results.'

'Or lack of results,' Roger added with a twitch of his moustache, then quickly held up his hand to forestall what he felt was a general protest. 'All right, I know . . . give it time. Meanwhile, what precisely do we do?'

'We sit and talk about Adam,' Sam said, 'and any other subject that might take our fancy. The important thing is we get used to being in each other's company. When that happens, maybe Adam will choose to join us.'

*

Joanna's arrangement with her editor, Taylor Freestone, was that she would be regarded for the moment as on full-time assignment to the 'ghost story'. She knew, however, that this exclusivity would last three weeks at most. If results had not begun to appear by then, she would be regarded as available for other jobs in between her twice-weekly sessions with the group.

She copied Taylor on Adam Wyatt's fictitious life story and gave him digests of her notes on the theory and process of what they were attempting. After two weeks, these memos began to look more like delaying tactics than dispatches from the front. She could feel scepticism beginning to replace enthusiasm in Taylor Freestone's attitude. 'It'll take as long as it takes,' was all she could tell him.

'I suspect we haven't filled out Adam's story enough for us all to believe in him,' Sam said at the beginning of their next session. 'Until we imagine his day-to-day life better than we do he's still no more real than a character in a book.'

Barry said that he thought they all sensed his day-to-day life pretty well. It was true, they'd added a lot of detail. They knew where he lived in Paris, they'd described the house, and they'd imagined at length his small château and estate in the country. They'd even wondered why, in an age before routine contraception, he and Angelique didn't have children. Their answer was that it simply hadn't happened. Although there were any number of medical conditions that might have been responsible, they hadn't settled upon one, making the excuse that neither Adam nor Angelique had been particularly troubled by the matter and had assumed that, given time, she would inevitably get pregnant. By common consent it was agreed that they were physically attracted to each other and had a good sex life.

'We've talked about what they eat, the sort of places they go, the people they see,' Roger said. 'What else is there? Inner monologue? Dreams? Personal growth?'

'I don't think they'd invented personal growth then,' Ward Riley said with a half-smile. 'That only happened when psychoanalysis connected with California.'

Joanna noted with interest that Ward Riley was showing the least sign of impatience of anyone in the group. There was a calmness in him that became more apparent the longer one was in his company. She supposed it was a consequence of his preoccupation with eastern philosophy. She wondered if he meditated or practised yoga or followed any other special discipline, and made a mental note to ask him.

' "By his friends shall ye know him." '

Everybody looked at Pete, who had spoken.

'I think it's a quote, but I'm not sure where from.'

Joanna said she thought the quote was 'deeds' not 'friends', but she wasn't sure either, and certainly couldn't say where it came from. But they all got the point.

'The question is,' Drew said, 'do we *invent* his friends, or use real people? If we invent too many characters we risk losing focus on Adam.'

'Drew's right,' Barry said, 'about losing focus, I mean. What we need to do is place him among real people who aren't so famous that they feel like storybook figures.'

The trouble was they'd all been reading up on the revolution, so that all the main players in it were fixed in their minds and difficult to manoeuvre into some new scenario of their own without striking a fatally false note. Joanna smiled to herself, remembering the Hollywood screenwriter she'd had a brief fling with a few years ago. He'd told her about 'the curse of the Hollywood biopic' where characters in top hats and tailcoats greet each other in the street with lines like, 'Morning, Ibsen,' 'Morning, Grieg.'

'There are perhaps one or two characters from history who aren't quite so well known as to be almost clichés.' Riley leaned forward slightly as he spoke, crossing his legs, hands cupping his elbows. 'Also they're colourful enough to – what shall I say? – spice up the story a little, stimulate the imagination.'

Everyone looked at him expectantly. 'Go on,' Sam said, as though he had a shrewd idea what was about to come up.

'I was thinking about Cagliostro and Saint-Germain,' Riley said.

Pete laughed. 'Sounds like a conjuring act in Vegas.'

'Well, you're not far from the truth,' Riley told him. 'They were magicians in a sense, though not a double act. They were adventurers, charlatans, and quite possibly geniuses. Both claimed to have occult powers and to belong to secret societies going back to the dawn of time. Interestingly, there is evidence that they were responsible for a number of remarkable cures, not to mention good old stand-by miracles like turning base metal into gold.'

'Alchemists!' Roger said with a snort of disdain.

'Yes, alchemists. But there was more to it than telling fortunes and deluding the gullible.'

'They believed in astrology.'

'And numerology. And so did Jung, who said that the ten years he spent studying alchemy were some of the most important of his life.'

'All psychoanalysts are mad. I wouldn't send my dog to one.'

'I'm with Ward on this,' Barry said. 'You can't just dismiss all of that stuff out of hand. I'm sorry, Roger, I know you're a smart guy and all, but that's just narrow-minded and arrogant. There's too much evidence. You may not like it, but it's there.'

'I stand corrected,' Roger said amiably, holding up his hands in surrender. 'By all means, write them in if you want to.'

'The only problem,' Barry continued, turning to Ward, 'is that from what I've read Cagliostro left Paris just before the revolution, and Saint-Germain had died.'

'Cagliostro was at the height of his fame when Adam arrived in Paris. They could well have met in fashionable salons. Then in 1785 he got mixed up in a financial scan-dal involving some woman friend of Marie-Antoinette and a devious cardinal. He was thrown into the Bastille for a spell – along with the Marquis de Sade, incidentally – then banished from France. He died in Italy in 1795.'

Maggie had given a little shiver of distaste at the mention of the Marquis de Sade. 'I don't think we want to get involved in all that, do we?'

'I'm not suggesting we do,' Ward said. 'But the fact is these people were around. And whatever else you may think of them, they were remarkable men. Adam could easily have met Cagliostro or De Sade in the circles he moved in in Paris. Saint-Germain died in 1786, but the legend was that he'd lived many times before and has been reborn since. Witnesses claim to have seen him in Paris in 1789 trying to warn the king of revolution. Since then he's been seen in the Himalayas as a monk, and even in Chicago, of all places, in 1930.'

120

There was a murmur of amusement around the table at this last reference. 'Shit, let's have him over to supper,' Pete said. 'Oh, excuse my French, Maggie.'

'That's all right,' Maggie said. 'But I'm not sure that I like all this talk at all. Our Adam was a nice, clean-living young man and we're getting him involved with some very strange people. I don't know why, but it makes me uneasy.'

'We're not getting him involved with anyone unless we all agree,' Sam said.

'I think it's too late for that,' Drew said quietly, oddly thoughtful. 'We've talked about them, so they're in our minds now, just as much as Adam is.' Her tone of voice suggested that she shared Maggie's misgivings.

'I wouldn't worry about it,' Sam said. 'When you think how many bogeymen we already have in our heads who haven't done us any harm so far . . .'

'I wasn't thinking about us,' Drew interrupted him, not contradicting him but clarifying what she meant. 'I was worried about Adam.'

There was a silence in the room. Then Drew spoke the thought that they were all thinking. 'Did you hear that? I talked about him as though he was real.'

17

Taylor Freestone sniffed in the haughty way that he thought befitted a member of the east coast establishment, of which he considered himself a prominent member. Joanna's latest memo had not impressed him. Its bottom line was that the group had still made no progress in conjuring up its ghost, and the three-week deadline had been passed. He mentioned a couple of stories that he said he'd like her to start thinking about. One was about the private lives of UN delegates in New York; another involved new whispers of scandal in the endless Kennedy saga. Naturally, if the ghost story became live, as he put it with no intended irony, he would put her back on it full time. He still knew that if this thing worked out it was a cover story.

Boredom was the main problem facing the group, especially someone like Roger Fullerton, who simply wasn't used to it. The idea of meeting regularly with the same people, however agreeable, for unstructured sessions of talk, speculation and occasional jokes was beginning to wear thin. Sam confided to Joanna that they were going to lose him if something didn't happen soon.

'We're going to have to try something new,' he said to her one night in her apartment, late.

'I thought we just did.'

He laughed and shifted on the bed so that his body covered hers in a gentle, sensual embrace. She could feel him hard and urgent, ready to enter her again, and gave a little moan of pleasure. 'What exactly did you have in mind?' she whispered.

'Tell you later,' he mumbled, teasing the lobe of her ear with his teeth, his excitement mounting as her breathing grew faster.

'A ouija board!'

The protest came from Barry, who seemed to regard the suggestion as almost an insult.

'Jesus, Sam! I thought this was supposed to be a *scientific* experiment, not a board game.'

'A ouija board, or an equivalent, was used in China and Greece from at least the sixth century BC. The Romans used it in the third century AD, and the Mongols in the thirteenth. Europe discovered it in the 1850s. Native Americans had their own version of it, which they used to find missing objects and persons and talk with the dead. It didn't become a "game" until some smart American slapped a patent on it about a hundred years ago and started marketing it commercially.'

'Okay, okay. But I still think it's a weird idea.'

'How does everybody else feel about it?' Sam looked around the table. 'Remember, we don't do anything unless we all agree, or unless we all agree to a majority vote.'

Ward Riley observed that ouija boards were widely used in Victorian seances. It obviously served to externalize physically something in their collective consciousness. 'I think we should try it,' he said.

Maggie said she had heard it described as a 'dangerous toy', but had tried it once as a young girl without ill effects – or, for that matter, any positive results either.

Drew had no objection. Pete said maybe it would help them break through whatever was blocking them right now.

Roger didn't have an opinion either way and was happy to go along with the majority.

Joanna had tried it at school, like Maggie without results, but had no objection to trying it again. Barry said what the hell, let's do it.

The device that Sam brought down from his office was something that he hadn't used since his earliest experiments with the paranormal. The large, hand-painted board bore all the letters of the alphabet, numbers through 0 to 9, and the words 'Yes' and 'No' standing opposite each other. The pointer was heart-shaped and stood on three small felt-tipped legs. It was large enough for all eight of them to place a fingertip on it – so lightly, Sam told them, as to be barely touching.

Although they got into the procedure without fanfare or ceremony, there was undeniably a new sense of drama in the air. The physical coordination required of them – all leaning forward at the same angle, arms extended, forefingers resting on the pointer head like leads emerging from a battery – gave a focus to what had so far been an abstract intellectual exercise. They were keyed up, alert, ready for something to happen.

'Is anybody there?' Sam asked in a normal conversational tone.

There was a silence. They waited. Nothing happened.

Sam asked the question again. 'Is there somebody who wishes to talk to us?'

Again nothing happened. Joanna found herself involuntarily holding her breath. She quickly glanced at the others and saw that most of them were doing the same. Her finger was resting so lightly on the felt top of the pointer that she could barely feel the contact, but suddenly she became acutely conscious of it, like an irritation or an itch that you have to do something about before it drives you crazy. But she couldn't, because she knew that her finger must stay where it was as long as the others kept theirs there, all waiting intently for something to happen.

Then it did. She gave a little gasp. There were murmurs of surprise, curiosity, suppressed excitement from the others. The thing had distinctly moved about an inch. However much she rationalized it in the terms that Sam had explained to her, she felt her heart beating faster.

'Is somebody there?' Sam asked again, his voice steady. 'Please indicate yes or no.'

A brief pause. Then, in a single, straight movement, the pointer slid to 'Yes'.

'Somebody's pushing,' growled Barry.

'Nobody's pushing,' Sam said. 'Keep your fingers in place. Will whoever is there please spell out your name for us?'

Gradually, almost hesitantly, the pointer moved back to the centre of the board, described a circle as though getting its bearings, then headed for the letter 'A'. It barely paused before looping out again, everyone leaning and swaying to follow it, moving in unison like some kind of precision dancing team. It went to 'D' and back to 'A', then across to 'M', after which it came to rest once again in the centre of the board.

'He's not going to spell out his second name,' Joanna heard herself saying. As though in response, the pointer started to move again and all of them with it: 'W – Y – A – T – T'.

'I tell you, somebody's pushing it!' Barry's voice was high with incredulity.

'If that's what you think, try it,' Sam told him. 'Ask it a question to which only you know the answer, then try and push it to spell it out.'

Maggie had removed her finger, but Sam said quickly, 'No, Maggie. Everybody keep your finger there. Don't resist Barry, just try to follow him. Okay, ask it a question.'

Barry frowned a moment, then asked, 'What's my cousin Matthew's middle name?'

The pointer didn't even get to the first letter. It was obvious that Barry was pushing, and equally obvious that the others were not resisting; yet he couldn't even get it to move in a straight line. He conceded with a grudging, 'Okay, I guess I'm wrong.'

'Let's carry on,' Sam said. 'Does anybody have a question they want to ask Adam?'

Roger said he did. 'I'd like to know whether Adam thinks he's real, or knows that he's just a projection of our thoughts?'

The pointer didn't move. 'Which is it, Adam?' Sam said. 'Are you real or not?'

Once again the movement began. 'I – A – M – A – D – A – M – W – Y – A – T – T'.

' "I am Adam Wyatt",' Roger repeated. 'Well, that's nicely inconclusive.'

'If we're not pushing it, which we're not, is there any

126

reason why this thing couldn't move by itself?' Joanna asked.

'Psychokinesis? Let's try,' Sam replied.

They all removed their fingers.

'All right, Adam,' Sam said, 'can you move the pointer by yourself without our touching it?'

It seemed an age as they sat motionless, watching, though in fact it was barely a minute.

'Maybe it's a little soon for that,' Sam said finally. 'Back to the old method.'

They all replaced their fingers on the pointer's felt top.

'Anybody else got a question?' Sam asked.

Pete said, 'Why don't we ask him *why* he can't move this thing by himself?'

With a swiftness that startled them, the pointer started moving around the board until it had spelled out 'I CANNOT'.

'Why not?' Barry repeated.

This time there was no response. The thing remained as dead as it had been when they weren't touching it.

'According to the theory, if I understand it correctly,' Ward Riley said after a while, 'what we're learning now is that we don't believe in Adam enough to give him a life of his own. Isn't that so, Sam?'

'According to the theory, that's right,' Sam said.

'Why don't we ask him if he can do anything to prove that he's real?' Drew said.

With a suddenness that made them all recoil in shock, a sound came from the table that was unlike anything they had heard before. It was a sharp rap, but more like a detonation than a knock, something that came from within the fibres of the wood itself rather than from the collision of two hard surfaces.

Joanna had felt the vibration run up her arm. She could see that the others had too.

'I think that's him,' Sam said. There was a note of quiet triumph in his voice.

Joanna's heart was beating fast.

18

On reflection, Joanna decided to say nothing to her editor about what she had initially regarded as a breakthrough. A single rap, even though captured on tape, as was the reaction of the group on video, was far from conclusive proof that anything out of the ordinary had taken place. So she diligently started to research her story on the UN delegates in New York, while remaining privately convinced that she would soon be back on the Adam story full time.

She had seen her parents only once since their evening with Sam. On their last visit to the city he had been in Chicago taking part in some weekend-long symposium, and since then Bob and Elizabeth Cross had been in Europe. They were spending three months between London, Paris and Rome. Her father had managed to swing it with the company as part work, part vacation: a kind of dry run for retirement, he called it. They had travelled increasingly in recent years. Her father's job with the airline provided them with almost unlimited free travel and offered major discounts at some of the world's best hotels. As her mother said, it was the best part of growing old – being no longer too poor or too busy to travel, and still young enough to enjoy it. Of course grandchildren would be nice, but she didn't want Joanna to feel any pressure on the subject.

A couple of nights after the first rap, and before the excitement had quite worn off, Joanna stopped by the lab around six to pick up Sam. They had planned to catch an off-off Broadway theatre group, then have dinner at a new Thai restaurant they'd heard about. When she got there, he and Pete had something to show her that they were very excited about. A friend of Pete's in the engineering department had analysed the table rap that they'd got on tape. It had proved to be as radically different from any ordinary kind of knock as it had sounded. She pored over graphs and print-outs that meant little to her aside from the obvious differences that Pete pointed to.

'In an ordinary rap,' he said, 'if I hit the same table with my knuckles or a hammer or any hard object, the sound starts with maximum amplitude and dies away. This rap, on the other hand, builds up gradually and ends with maximum amplitude. It's exactly the opposite of normal.'

'They found the same thing in Ontario with the "Philip" experiment,' Sam added triumphantly. 'We're on our way.'

The theatre show was interesting enough to keep them in their seats until the end, and the restaurant was worth waiting for. It was way up on the west side, so they decided to spend the night at Sam's place. On the cab ride back he fell silent and she sensed a change in his mood. He was unaware of her watching him as he gazed out into the passing night. It was one of those moments of distraction she had learned to accept in him. It couldn't have lasted more than a minute, but when he turned to her it was with the look of somebody waking from sleep

130

to find a loved one watching over them. He took her hand.

'Well . . .?' she said softly.

He shrugged. 'Just the usual question. What does it all add up to? And if it doesn't add up to anything, why is it there?'

'I thought science didn't ask why. Just how.'

'I know. But as Roger likes to point out, his end of it has built the microchip and the teflon frying pan, while we're no closer to understanding the paranormal than William James was in 1910. He wrote something that I've never had to memorize, because ever since I read it I've not been able to get it out of my head.'

He paused a moment, his gaze going out again to the Manhattan night. ' "I confess",' he began quoting softly, ' "that at times I have been tempted to believe that the Creator has eternally intended this department of nature to remain baffling, to prompt our curiosities and hopes and suspicions all in equal measure, so that although ghosts and clairvoyances, and raps and messages from spirits, are always seeming to exist and can never be fully explained away, they also can never be susceptible to full corroboration." '

'Good quote. I'll use it in the article.'

'You can add,' he said, with some of the usual vigour returning to his voice, 'that it didn't stop him trying.'

She increased the pressure of her hand on his. 'Can I tell you something?' she said.

'Sure.'

She leaned over and kissed him. 'I love you.'

He looked deeply into her eyes. 'Funny,' he said, 'I've been thinking the same thing.'

'Telepathy?'

'No, I don't think so.' He kissed her again. 'Just coincidence.'

The tub of warm paraffin wax excited much interest at the start of the group's next session. Sam repeated the story he'd told Joanna about the phantom hands in Paris.

'Now that's funny,' Maggie said pensively when he'd finished. 'That's Paris three times.'

'How d'you mean, Maggie?' Sam asked.

'These plaster casts you're talking about are in Paris. We put Adam in Paris. And Joanna was just telling me that her parents are on holiday in Paris.'

Sam thought about it, raised his eyebrows, then he laughed. 'You're right. I wonder what it means.'

'The point of synchronicity,' Roger said, taking his usual place around the table, 'is that it has no point.'

'Except in so far,' Ward Riley demurred, 'as it points to what Jung called "a unifying principle behind meaningful coincidences".'

'The logic of that argument is flawed,' Roger responded, happy to have found someone he could dispute with almost as vigorously as he did with Sam. 'It rests on the assumption that coincidences are meaningful, for which there is no evidence. To say that a meaningful coincidence has meaning is to say nothing.'

'Steady, Roger,' Sam said, not wanting to be left out of this, 'Wolfgang Pauli was on Jung's side. They even wrote a book on the subject.'

'I knew Pauli,' Roger said with a sniff of disapproval. 'A genius, but given to flights of fancy, and he drank too much.' He pulled his chair up to the table in a way that suggested the subject was now closed.

When he'd got them all around the table, Sam announced the test results on the rap recording that Joanna had heard two days ago. Even Roger, she could see, was genuinely interested.

'The last session,' Sam continued, 'marked a significant breakthrough, and I'm sure we're going to build on it. I suggest we try to get a conversation going with Adam, first of all putting questions to him and having him answer one rap for yes, two for no.' He glanced around the group, and received nods of general assent.

'All right,' he said, 'let's give it a try.'

He placed his hands lightly on the table in front of him. The others did the same.

19

Perhaps the strangest part of it, Joanna reflected later, was how quickly they all accepted the situation, talking with the imaginary Adam as though it were the most normal thing in the world. Admittedly, the need to phrase everything as a question to which a straight yes or no answer could be given was limiting, but after a while they streamlined the process. They would talk among themselves, sometimes rummaging through the stack of books on the period that they kept in the room, then place their hands on the table and toss a question to Adam which allowed him to confirm or deny something they'd been discussing. Did he know so-and-so? Had he seen this or done that or been there?

'What was the name of those shady guys Ward mentioned?' Pete asked after a while.

'Cagliostro and Saint-Germain,' Ward replied. 'And of course the Marquis de Sade?'

'Did you meet any of those guys, Adam?' Pete asked.

A single rap confirmed that he had. Joanna noticed Ward's eyebrows arch slightly with interest. 'All of them?' he asked.

Another single rap.

'This boy got around,' Pete remarked under his breath,

and jumped slightly when a rap came from the table directly where his hands rested on it.

'Did you ever see any evidence,' Ward asked, cutting through the murmur of amusement that had run around the table, 'that any of them possessed unusual powers?'

This time there was a pause, then a slightly less firm single rap.

'You mean you did see something?'

Another slightly tentative single rap.

'Can you tell us what it was?'

This time two raps for no.

Sam caught Ward's eye, and took over the questioning. 'I don't believe you saw anything at all, Adam. You're just making this up to please Ward, aren't you?'

There was a silence lasting for some time, broken by Maggie.

'Perhaps he doesn't want to talk about it,' she said, clearly not relishing this line of questioning herself. 'Is that so, Adam?'

There was an immediate and loud single rap from the table.

'Very well, Adam,' Sam said, 'if that's what you want, we'll change the subject.'

Ward shrugged his acquiescence.

'I want to ask about the political situation,' Barry said. 'Adam, was there any point during those five years prior to 1789 when you realized that a violent revolution was inevitable?'

There was only a slight pause before the table gave two raps for no.

'Looking back,' Barry continued, 'can you see with hindsight that it was – inevitable, I mean?'

A clear, firm rap for yes.

'Looking back from where exactly?' The question came from Roger and was addressed to Barry.

'Yeah, that's a good point,' Barry said. 'Where exactly is he looking back from?'

'From here,' Sam said. 'He knows everything we know because he's part of us. Isn't that right, Adam?'

Two very firm raps came from the table. Everyone looked at Sam.

'It seems that he has a mind of his own,' Roger remarked with faint amusement. 'Or thinks he has.'

Sam grinned, keeping his hands on the table, as did the rest of them. 'All right, Adam,' he said, 'if you're not here with us, we're going to have to find out where you are.'

He was about to phrase a question when there was a sound they hadn't heard before. It came from the table, but instead of a rap it was a strange scratching noise, as though something inside the wood was trying to get out.

They looked at each other in bewilderment, wondering what it meant. Then suddenly Maggie said, 'He's trying to write!'

The explanation was so obvious that no one bothered to comment on it. Sam leaned back and reached behind him for the ouija board, and they all lifted their hands from the table to make room for it, then placed their fingertips on the pointer.

Sam repeated his question. 'If you're not here with us, where are you?'

Again there was a silence – long enough for them all to wonder whether they were going to get an answer at all. Then the pointer began to move, slowly at first, but gaining speed. It spelled out 'I DO NOT KNOW'. And stopped.

'That's kind of a tough one to follow,' Joanna said. 'What do we ask for a supplementary?'

There was a ripple of amused agreement from the others.

'Why don't we just ask him if there's anything he wants to tell us?' Pete suggested. 'Is there, Adam? Anything at all?'

Again there was silence. One by one they all put further questions, each time without response.

'D'you think he's gone?' Drew asked.

'Perhaps the problem is that we asked a question that we ourselves have no answer to,' Ward Riley said thoughtfully. 'Knowing that Adam is a composite personality created by all of us is one thing. Knowing exactly where he exists between us all is quite another.'

'Maybe we should go back to asking straight yes or no questions,' Maggie said. 'If he needs to spell something out, he'll make that scratching noise again.'

Once again Maggie's pragmatic common sense was accepted without comment. They went around the table, asking a question each. And once again they were met with silence.

'He's gone,' Drew repeated. This time it was a statement of fact.

They all sat back, taking their hands from the table as though acknowledging the truth of what she'd said.

'I guess that's a wrap for today – no pun intended,' Sam said. Then glanced at his watch. 'Though we've still some time if anybody wants to try anything.'

No one seemed in any hurry to get away. But neither did they have any ideas. Barry wandered over to get some coffee. Maggie followed him. Pete got up and stretched luxuriously. Roger turned in his chair and began talking to Joanna.

'You know what they did in Toronto with the "Philip" experiment?' Pete said, taking the coffee pot from Maggie and pouring himself a cup. 'Sometimes they used to sing to him and tell jokes. Hey, Adam, how about that? Would you like us to sing to you?'

The rap that came from the table took them all by surprise, not just because of its strength, but because nobody was anywhere near it. They all stopped what they were doing and turned to look first at the table, then at one another, as though seeking confirmation of what had just happened.

'He's back now,' Joanna said, 'and with a vengeance.' She turned to look at Pete. 'Okay, Pete, it's your idea. You'd better decide what you're going to sing.'

'Hey, I can't even hold a tune,' he protested. 'You're all gonna have to give me some help here.' Nobody spoke. 'Oh, come on, now,' he appealed to them, 'we're all in this together!'

Once again they all exchanged looks, this time in a general attitude of, well, what the hell, why not?

'So what do we want to sing?' Sam asked. 'Show tunes? A Gregorian chant or two? Elvis? The Beatles? "Greensleeves"?'

Since they had no sheet music, it had to be something they all knew the words of by heart, which significantly limited their choice. They finally settled on 'Ten Green Bottles', reducing it to eight since there were only eight of them around the table.

Ward said he thought he could recall how it went, but he still had to be reminded of the tune by a quick solo from Barry.

Pete started, and they all joined in the chorus at the end of his verse. Then Maggie took over, surprising them with a powerful and attractive soprano. Sam sang with great energy, but slightly off-key. Next came Ward, revealing a singing voice considerably richer and more resonant than his speaking voice. It was during the chorus following Ward's solo that the table started to beat time.

Once again it was obvious to everyone there that no one was touching the table with hand or foot. At first they faltered, but the table thumped on with such emphatic rhythm that they picked up the tempo and sang more loudly. When they'd finished their eight verses, the steady drum beat they'd been hearing became a series of pitter-patterings that seemed to roll around the table top, creating a sound that was uncannily like applause.

They were all so taken by this unexpected and somehow touching development that they broke into delighted laughter, like children.

'He likes us! Guess you want another one – right, Adam?' Pete said, and there were no protests when the table, still untouched by any of them, delivered a reverberating rap in the affirmative. It took them only moments to determine that they could all manage at least a few lines of 'John Brown's Body', but the tune was so strong that it didn't seem to matter if they sang nonsense lyrics when they forgot the real ones. Certainly it didn't bother Adam, who thumped along as enthusiastically as before, and delivered an even louder round of applause at the end.

'Okay, what now?' Pete asked, looking around the group.

The table gave several more thumps of encouragement, obviously not wanting the fun to stop yet.

'Pete, for heaven's sake,' Drew protested, laughing, 'if you keep on asking, he's going to keep on saying yes.'

'Only if we want him to! As long as he wants more, it means we're enjoying ourselves. Anybody got an idea for a song?'

'Anything you like,' Sam said, 'as long as it's not "My Way".'

They managed a robust verse or two of 'America the Beautiful', then Barry suggested the 'Marseillaise', the words of which were in one of the books they had in the room. However, their combined French accents being nothing to boast about, they dispensed with the words altogether and merely bellowed the tune at the tops of their voices. They wound up with a ragged and hoarse 'Hello, Dolly!' Then, with much laughter and clearing of throats and some coughing, and accompanied by Adam's vigorous applause, they got up to pour themselves coffee or to get cold drinks from the fridge.

'My goodness, will you look at the time!' The exclamation from Maggie caused them all to glance at their watches. To their surprise, they had overrun their usual two hours by almost forty minutes. 'I have to meet my daughter. I'll be late if I don't hurry.'

She bustled around, picking up her purse and coat. As she did so, a curious rumble started in the centre of the room, causing everyone to turn.

The table was moving of its own accord, vibrating and bumping across the concrete floor, picking up speed as it went. It travelled in a dead straight line, finally slamming with the force of a hammer blow across the door through which Maggie was intending to depart, blocking it completely.

Nobody spoke. It was as though they couldn't believe

the literal truth of what they'd just seen and were waiting for someone to confirm it for them.

Finally it was Sam who said quietly, 'He doesn't want her to go. Is that right, Adam?'

A firm thump, deep and resonant, came from the table, which stayed where it was.

Maggie made a little gasping sound, and the hand that went to her mouth was trembling.

'It's all right,' Sam said, watching her. 'He likes you, that's all. Which isn't surprising, because we all do.' He started forward. 'Give me a hand, will you, Barry?' he asked casually.

There was no resistance as, one at each side, they picked the table up and carried it back to the centre of the room and put it down where it had been. It stayed there, as though whatever force had been in it had been neutralized by their touch.

'Sorry if we've made you late, Maggie,' Sam said. 'Our apologies to your daughter – and we'll see you next week.'

'Yes. Goodnight.' The words were barely a whisper as she hurried across the room, through the door and disappeared up the stairs.

Those who remained were strangely subdued, not wanting to talk about the incident and using the lateness of the hour to leave quickly. In the end only Joanna and Sam remained, along with Pete, who was busy with the cameras and recording equipment at one side.

'Got it!' he exclaimed triumphantly, after playing back a fragment on a small monitor screen. 'It's fantastic, Sam. We've got the whole damn thing in perfect living colour!'

20

Two things got Joanna off the hook with her editor. The first was a video of the table slamming about the room of its own accord. The second was Roger Fullerton's offer to let his name be used in her article.

'One of the world's leading physicists endorsing a spook hunt? That's historic! I won't ask how you did it, but congratulations.'

He winked. She wished he hadn't. Taylor Freestone did not have the gift of casual intimacy, though he liked to believe it was one of his many social graces.

'Forget the UN. I'll put somebody else on the Kennedys. You're back on this full time.'

She walked to the restaurant where she was meeting Sam and Roger for lunch. Roger's offer to let his name be used had surprised her as much as it had delighted Sam. 'I still think it's all a waste of time and probably a complete dead end,' he'd said, typically enough. 'But there's obviously something going on, and I don't mind standing up and saying so.'

The rest of the group, aside from Pete and Sam himself, still chose to remain anonymous. Barry didn't think it would do much for his plumbing sales to be thought of as something out of the ordinary. Joanna told him he reminded her of her mother. He laughed and said he would try to take it as a compliment.

Drew went along with Barry. Maggie shrank from the idea of any invasion of her privacy. Ward Riley, too, preferred not to be named.

Sam and Roger stood up as she approached. It was the same restaurant and the same table at which she and Sam had first lunched together after the incident with Ellie Ray outside the television studio. She marvelled for a second at how far in the past all that seemed now. They could see that she was pleased about something, and she told them about her editor's decision. Roger, whose treat lunch was, ordered a bottle of champagne.

'Here's to you both,' he said, raising his glass. 'I'm willing to admit, Sam, that you've proved your point. My only question now is, what exactly *is* your point?'

Joanna pressed the start button on her tape recorder, which she had set down on one corner of the table. The real purpose of this lunch, apart from general sociability and an enjoyment of one another's company, was to provide further background for what she was writing.

'My question,' Sam said, 'is whether what we have seen is a violation of local causality or not.'

Attuned as he was by now to the slightest interrogatory twitch of Joanna's eyebrow, he leaned forward and picked up a metal pepperpot, moving it a few inches on the white tablecloth. 'That is local causality. If, however, I'd moved my hand through the air, and somebody else's pepperpot on another table, or even in a different restaurant, had moved ... that would be non-local causality.'

'Or at least,' Roger demurred, 'it would appear to be.'

'Local causality is a central plank of our concept of

143

reality,' Sam continued. 'On a common sense level it's obvious that nothing moves unless you push it.'

'But we've seen that it does,' Joanna said.

Roger held up a cautioning finger. 'Ah, but have we? If there were some invisible force that emanated from our minds and pushed things around in the way that that table was pushed around the other day, then local causality would be restored. Unfortunately there is absolutely no evidence that such a force exists.'

'But we saw that it exists,' Joanna protested. 'Surely it could be electromagnetism or "mindwaves", or some function of the nervous system. Or something – "psi",' she added as a last desperate suggestion, and saw Roger's mouth turn down with disapproval. 'I know,' she said, 'you're allergic to that word.'

'Unexplained phenomena do not suddenly become explicable just by sticking a meaningless label on them.'

'At least we've got you to accept that unexplained phenomena exist,' Sam remarked with a chuckle, proferring his glass as the waiter returned to top up their champagne and distribute menus.

'I've never doubted that such things exist,' Roger responded imperturbably. 'Lightning was unexplained until man discovered electricity.' He opened his menu with a deft flick of his fingers, like a conjuror producing something out of thin air. Conversation was suspended for some minutes while they ordered.

'I want to go back to what you were saying about nonlocality,' Joanna said. 'The general impression that people like me have, non-scientific laymen, is that quantum physics has been coming up with stuff since the turn of the century that makes nonsense of all our common sense ideas of cause and effect.'

'That's true only up to a point,' Roger said. 'I've always thought there should be some remedy at law against the kind of psycho-babbling New Age halfwits who invoke quantum physics as justification for any and all of their grab-bag of muddled theories...'

He stopped as Sam began mischievously winding an invisible handle in the air.

'All right, all right, I know you've heard me before on the subject. All I'm saying is we should look at other explanations before jumping on a bandwagon which is already so full of crooks and phonies that there's very little room left on it anyway.'

'You know as well as I do, Roger,' Sam continued, 'that Bell's Theorem leaves the door wide open to non-local causality.'

Roger sniffed disdainfully. 'I know that a facile interpretation of Bell might do. But as to what he actually said...'

Joanna was about to ask for an explanation, but instead let them fight it out uninterrupted, in the knowledge that she could play back her tape later and pose any questions she needed to. Sam was arguing that certain experiments had proved that communication faster than the speed of light was a reality; Roger insisted that such a view was simply a misinterpretation of what had actually happened.

'The price you have to pay for a naïve and simplistic interpretation of Bell,' he said, summing up and giving his adjectives the bite of an actor playing in a Coward revival, 'is that the universe is woven together in a fabric that makes absolutely no sense in terms of anything we have so far discovered or even conceived. Once you've accepted that, you've opened the floodgates to every kind of nonsense from astrology to numerology and all the rest of it. Sheer intellectual anarchy.'

They paused for a moment as the waiter brought their starters. Sam forked up a mouthful of delicate, lobster-filled ravioli. 'You know, Roger, any minute now you're going to start denying that that table actually moved the other day.'

'Sam, that's unfair,' Joanna protested. 'Roger has volunteered to go public with this and put his credibility on the line.'

'Thank you, Joanna,' Roger said, beaming her his most winning smile.

'You're right. I'm sorry, Roger,' Sam conceded. 'And I'm not saying that just because you're buying lunch – honest.'

Roger ignored the cheerfully backhanded apology. 'I'm merely saying that our assumptions as to how this effect works must be as circumspect as our observation that it does.'

'The only assumption I'm working on,' Sam said, 'is that the effect is a mental one and the source is ourselves. I take it we're agreed on that.'

'Demons or the dead would make a lot more sense than some of the ideas you've been hawking.'

'Roger, Joanna's getting this on tape. Now tell her you're not serious.'

Roger twirled a forkful of spaghetti and seafood, then held it suspended in the air as he delivered his final word on the subject. 'On the contrary, I would give precedence to the impossible over the merely unintelligible every time.'

*

146

It was just after midnight when Joanna let herself into her apartment. She'd spent the evening with Sam but taken a cab home because she wanted to make an early start on her story. She switched on the light, slipped out of her coat, and started to flip through the mail that she'd picked up from her box in the hallway. It was mostly the usual bills and circulars. There was an invitation to a wedding, which she'd been expecting for some time; a letter from a girlfriend working for a bank in Sydney, which she decided she would read in the morning; and a postcard from her parents in Paris.

She read the message, a hastily scribbled list of where they'd been and what they'd done, written by her mother and with a kiss from her father squeezed in at the bottom. Then she turned it over to look at the picture.

It was a reproduction of what must have been a large painting in oil. She thought for a moment that she'd seen it before. It reminded her of some of the illustrations in the books she'd been researching on the French Revolution and looked as though it came from the same period. It had an artificially staged quality, the kind of formal portrait that captured some significant event in which its subject played a central role. She thought she recognized the languid figure in the uniform and cockaded hat, and sure enough, when she turned the card over and read the details printed in one corner, she saw that it was Lafayette taking his oath to the constitution in Paris, in 1790.

She turned the card again to study the picture in more detail. She knew now that she hadn't seen it before, but at the same time something in it tugged at her memory. She looked at Lafayette and at the carefully posed figures surrounding him. Some of them were classically idealized with an almost saintly purity glowing from their faces;

others were grotesque and clown-like, the exultant, celebrating mob.

Suddenly, with a shock that made her catch her breath, she saw what her mind must already have registered unconsciously but which her eyes only now brought into focus.

Standing on one side of the picture, almost as resplendently uniformed as Lafayette himself and waving his hat on the tip of his sword, was Adam Wyatt.

21

She went into the kitchen, boiled some water, and poured it over a sachet of vervain tea. Then she sat nursing her cup and looking at the postcard and debating whether to call Sam and tell him about it. In the end she decided not to; it would be pointless without showing him the picture. She would do it tomorrow.

Although she had been pleasantly tired when she arrived home, her mind was racing now and all thought of sleep abandoned. She rummaged through her desk in search of the magnifying glass she knew was there somewhere.

Enlarged, the face in the painting was even more unmistakably the same as the one sketched by Drew Hearst that hung on the wall of Sam's lab, in the basement that they now called Adam's room. The expression wasn't the same. Here he was animated, caught up in the excitement of the moment, cheering on his hero. But it was the same man.

The most likely explanation, she told herself, was that Drew had seen the picture somewhere and unconsciously reproduced the face when she made her drawing. Yet the drawing had been a committee project. They had all made their suggestions as to how Adam should look, the length of his hair, the colour of his eyes, and so forth.

Like a police artist, Drew had sketched the person they were trying to describe from the picture they had formed of him in their imaginations. It was impossibly unlikely that they had all seen this particular painting or a copy of it and remembered it unconsciously. Certainly, Joanna was sure that she hadn't. And the notion that they had come up purely by accident with a face in a picture they had never seen was too improbable even to consider.

Tomorrow, she told herself, she would start looking for answers. This had to be resolved before she could go any further with the story. She checked the back of the postcard once again for the name of the collection. She would make inquiries, find out everything that was known about this picture – including the names, if they were recorded, of the people portrayed in it.

She drifted at last into a fitful sleep, comforting herself with the thought that she was a journalist and her job was to find answers. There were always answers if you looked hard enough.

Always.

When she awoke at four a.m., she knew at once what was happening. Perspiring and shivering, with an aching head, she had obviously picked up the flu that had been going around her office for the past two weeks. After making her way groggily to the bathroom and taking two aspirin, she dozed uncomfortably until dawn, then fell heavily asleep until almost nine.

She accepted the fact that she was going to feel like this for at least forty-eight hours regardless of any medication she might take. The only thing to do was stay in bed and drink endless cups of herbal tea. Luckily she had a good supply in the apartment. She called her office and told them to forget about her for the next few days. Then she called Sam and told him that she would have to miss that evening's meeting of the group.

Normally when someone missed a session, which had inevitably happened from time to time, the others carried on without them. However, as the whole thing had been set up originally for Joanna to write about, Sam suggested they should cancel and wait until she was better. She hesitated. She wanted to tell him about the postcard, but would rather show him than try to describe it over the phone. Almost as though reading her thoughts, he said he would come by at lunch time. She warned him about catching her bug, but he laughed and said he never caught anything, adding that if she thought of something she wanted him to bring she should call him at the lab.

She slept again until the phone rang. It was the doorman to say that Sam was downstairs. Joanna quickly tried to repair the unattractive image she saw in her bathroom mirror. When the bell rang she hurried to the door and let him take her in his arms, almost crushing the flowers and the carrier bag containing lunch that he had brought.

Before they ate or did anything else, Joanna went to the desk in the annex of her living room where she had left the postcard. She clearly remembered leaving it on her computer keyboard, but now it wasn't there. Nor was it anywhere among the papers on her desk. The rest of her mail was there, including the still unread letter from Australia. But not the postcard.

Feeling annoyed and a little bit strange, she went through to the kitchen where Sam was preparing a salad.

She found him standing with the postcard in his hand, flipping from the picture to the message on the back.

'Where did you find that?' The question came out more sharply than she had intended, almost an accusation.

'I'm sorry, I didn't mean to pry. It was just propped up here and caught my eye.'

She looked at the shelf he nodded towards and frowned. 'I don't remember putting it there. I was trying to find it to show you. Isn't it amazing?'

He looked at her as though he didn't know what she meant. 'Isn't what amazing?'

'The picture. Look!' She pointed to the figure on the left. 'It's Adam – exactly the way Drew drew him.'

Sam stared harder at the picture. 'I suppose there's *some* similarity,' he conceded grudgingly, 'but I can't say I'd have noticed if you hadn't pointed it out.'

She almost snatched the postcard away from him in disbelief. 'For heaven's sake, it's absolutely obvious!' But then she stopped. In all honesty, it wasn't as obvious as it had seemed last night.

He watched her, his concern growing as he saw the puzzlement in her face. 'What's all this about?'

She looked from the card to him and back to the card. 'I looked at this when I got in last night. I was so bowled over that I almost called you. It was Adam to the life!'

'And now it isn't?'

'Well, obviously it isn't. There's a similarity, as you say, but no more.' She put the card back on the shelf where he said he'd found it. 'Is that where it was?'

He moved it slightly to the left. 'Right there.'

'That's really odd.'

'I guess this is where I'm supposed to say it can't have

got there by itself.' He laughed gently as he put his arm around her shoulders and pulled her to him. 'Listen, I think you're getting a little spooked about this. When you got home last night you must have been already starting to run a temperature. Your responses were a little off. You saw this, and after what we'd been talking about all day . . .!'

'I know what I saw.'

'I'm not saying you didn't. But you just admitted you don't see it now. This picture happens to be in one of the books about the revolution that we have at the lab. Even if you don't remember seeing it, you must have done. Next thing, you get this card from your parents and realize there's something strangely familiar about it. Which is where the mind starts to play tricks – especially when there's a flu virus messing with it.'

'That's very rational. I just wish it sounded more convincing.'

'What's not convincing?'

'For one thing, it's quite an odd coincidence that my parents should send this particular card.'

'I don't see why. They know that what we're doing involves Lafayette, they find themselves in some museum . . .'

'All right, all right!' She held up her hands in surrender. 'Let's forget it. "Hysterical woman gets flu and sees ghost." Enough.'

'Seeing a ghost is what we're hoping to do – one that we've created just as you created one in this picture by projecting your mind's-eye view of Adam onto it.'

'I said I'm not arguing, okay? I quit.'

'Sorry, I didn't mean to be a bore . . .'

She held her hands up further, then made a zipping

motion over her lips to indicate that the conversation was at an end. He laughed again. 'Go sit down and I'll bring you some lunch.'

A few minutes later they were sitting by the window with plates on their knees. 'By the way,' he said, 'I've been thinking about it, and if it's all right with you I think I'd like to go ahead with tonight's session.'

'Sure,' she said, 'it's fine with me.'

'After all, we'll have it all on tape, so you won't miss anything. And we've got such a good momentum going I don't want to lose it.'

'You're right. I'll be okay for the next one.'

He reached for the salad bowl as she finished her plate. 'Can I give you some more?'

'Isn't there some rule about feed a cold and starve a fever?' she asked as he served her.

'Old wives' tale,' he said with a dismissive grin. 'Don't believe a word of it. Worst kind of superstition.'

22

Clifton Webb was sitting in his bath, typing up some vitriolic review, and Joanna was telling herself how much he reminded her of Ward Riley. Or was it that Ward Riley reminded her of Clifton Webb? He was younger than the actor and less mannered, but she could imagine him perfectly as the waspish Waldo Lydecker in *Laura*, which she was watching on cable for the fourth or fifth time and enjoying as much as ever.

The sound that exploded in the room made her think that somebody had fired a gun and a bullet had hit the wall. She knew the sound couldn't have come from the television. It had been too real and was still echoing in her ears. Besides, she knew the film and nobody fired anything in that scene.

It happened again. This time she sprang out of bed, tripped on her robe, and stumbled to the safety of a corner where she would not be a target for any idiot firing shots from the street. But she could see, peering cautiously from her window, that there was nobody out there, and no hole where a bullet had pierced the glass.

Shaken, she crossed to where the impact had seemed to come from. There was no mark on the plaster, nothing to explain what had happened.

A hammer blow at the door of her apartment made

her spin with a gasp of alarm. She stood perfectly still, waiting for the next, expecting to hear it burst open. But there was only silence.

She edged around her bedroom door and down the narrow corridor into the tiny hall, where she peered through the peephole. The landing was deserted. If anyone had been there, they had gone.

But she knew that no one had been there, at least not in the normal sense. Some instinct told her that she had just had a visit from Adam.

She noted with interest that the thought left her strangely calm and with none of the alarm she had initially felt.

Sam was there by nine-fifteen. She'd left a message on the machine in his office, and he'd picked it up after the session. He'd called her at once and said he was coming right over with the tape.

It was time-coded in one corner, and she watched the figures flashing by as he fast-forwarded to the point which she already knew was going to synchronize precisely with the time at which she had heard the sounds in her apartment.

'Here it is.' He pressed the remote control and the images on screen assumed normal speed. The group, minus Joanna, were seated as usual around the table, using the ouija board and pointer, which moved around quickly, pulling them by the touch of their fingertips this way and that.

' "Where . . . is . . . Joanna?" ' She heard Sam's voice reading the message as it was spelled out letter by letter.

'Joanna's home sick,' he replied. 'But I'm sure she'll be back next time. D'you have any message for her?'

The pointer drew their outstretched arms to the word 'Yes'.

'What message d'you have for her?' Sam prompted. But there was no further movement.

'Stop!' Joanna reached for the remote control and froze the image on screen, including the time code in the top right-hand corner. It was 7:43 p.m. 'That's exactly when it happened,' she said. 'I leapt out of bed and stood over there in the corner, thinking somebody must be shooting out in the street. I don't know why, but I looked over at the clock, and it was 7:43. Then there was a crash at the door.'

'Looks like you guessed right,' Sam said. 'It was Adam saying "Hi!".'

'You know the weirdest part of this?' she said after a moment. 'It's the way I'm just taking it all for granted. If you'd told me six months ago that I'd react to some disembodied banging on the wall with, "Oh, that's just Adam, some ghost we made up," I'd have told you to your face that you were nuts. Now that's exactly what I'm doing, and I don't know why. What's happened to me?'

'Your horizons have broadened a little, that's all. You had a mind-set that said everything claiming to be para-normal had to be by definition phoney. Now you've seen that it isn't. On the contrary, it's really kind of ordinary.'

'I still think there's something weird about it all some-where. In fact I'm beginning to get confused about what I really think.'

'You're not the only one.' She sensed an unaccustomed

tiredness in his voice as he reached for the remote and pressed play.

'I don't think he has any message to give us for Joanna.' It was Sam's voice again, from the TV speaker this time.

'I'm sure he'd rather deliver it to her personally,' Roger said with a chuckle, 'like any sensible fellow.'

Joanna and Sam exchanged a look, but neither made a comment.

'All right, Adam,' the on-screen Sam was saying, 'you're starting to repeat all your old tricks and we're starting to get bored. Wouldn't you like to try something new?'

The pointer moved again, tugging their fingers around to spell out, 'SUCH AS?'

'Well, for instance,' Sam said, 'we're hoping to see you at some point. Can you manifest yourself to us?'

There was a pause. Then the pointer slid firmly across to 'NO'.

'Is there any particular reason why not?'

The question came from Ward Riley. The pointer pulled back just far enough to take another stab at 'NO'.

'Is there anything you can do to impress us?' Barry asked with good-natured impatience, and flashed a look of amused anticipation around the table.

The pointer moved with stately slowness back to the centre of the table, and there remained still. They waited. Joanna could sense that they were wondering whether to stay as they were or sit back or say something, or take it as a sign that the session was over, or whatever.

As the indecision lengthened, there was a sudden bump from underneath the table as though someone crouching there had tried to stand up. It jolted them. They drew back sharply, and the table moved again. Nobody was touching it as, very slowly and steadily, it began to rise from the floor.

Joanna's eyes didn't leave the screen as the table rose, the upturned faces of the group following it. Impressive though the image was, she couldn't help thinking of remarks that both Sam and Roger had made at different times – about how nothing on film or tape could ever look wholly convincing. Decades of cinematic special effects had made people blasé. Everything was possible because nothing was real. She thought of the faded sepia photographs from around the turn of the century that she'd seen, usually showing a trance medium surrounded by 'spirit faces' and even fairies. To a modern eye the pictures were such patent frauds as to be laughable. Now, paradoxically, only the truth was laughable. True miracles had been rendered impossible by technology. Only the people sitting around the table she could see on screen, and she watching them, would ever believe that what was happening was real. It was an impasse from which there was no escape. Suddenly she realized with utter clarity that whatever she wrote about the Adam experiment would amount to no more than another curiosity, a footnote amid the endless chatter about the great unsolved, and probably insoluble, mysteries of existence.

She glanced sideways at Sam, and saw the weariness she had detected in his voice reflected in his face. She knew that he was thinking at that moment the same thing she was thinking. And it wasn't telepathy that told her that. There was no need of it. It was too obvious.

Meanwhile the table rose until its feet were level with the heads of those around it. Then it revolved slowly in the air – a full hundred and eighty degrees, until it was totally inverted.

As though of one mind, everyone around the table pushed back their chairs and got to their feet – not just because what was happening was so breathtaking, but because the heavy ouija board and pointer were still on the table and must surely fall.

But nothing fell. The ouija board stayed where it was, as though glued in place, as the table continued to rise until its four feet were planted firmly on the ceiling in a grotesque and surreal defiance of gravity.

No one spoke, no one moved – until Maggie, out of some impulse that she herself perhaps neither understood nor anticipated any more than she could control, made the sign of the cross over herself.

As though a magnetic current had been turned off, the ouija board and pointer fell from the table top and hit the floor with a clatter. The table itself followed. But it didn't fall. It shot down, as though pushed by some violent force, and smashed into the floor and shattered into fragments. The last image was of the members of the group leaping to safety and turning their backs against a lacerating spray of wood splinters. Then the screen abruptly went blank.

'A chunk hit the camera,' Sam explained, stopping the video. 'We'll have to replace it. Luckily nobody was hurt. Spectacular, hm?' He looked at her and waited for a reply. She realized that his question was more than rhetorical; he needed to know what she thought.

'What do *you* think happened?' she asked.

'Oh,' he made a sweeping, open gesture with his hand, a gesture almost of self-parody, 'I think it's obvious what happened. We lost our collective nerve. We made the damn thing float up to the ceiling and turn upside down, and suddenly the rational side of ourselves said, "This is physically impossible, it can't be happening," and so it stopped.'

'What about Maggie making the sign of the cross like that?'

He shrugged. 'We talked afterwards. She couldn't explain it, said it just came out of her.' He paused, looked grave. 'She also says we ought to discontinue the experiment. She can't explain why she feels that way, either, but she says it's been building for a while. She says she won't come to any more sessions unless their purpose is to dematerialize Adam and start again. She thinks he's evil.'

Joanna looked at him steadily. 'What do you think?'

He hesitated, like a man who has thought about some problem for a while and has made a carefully balanced decision, but one which he has not yet announced to anyone else and isn't sure how it will be received.

'I think,' he said, 'that Maggie was a bad choice for this experiment. It may be better if she goes.'

23

Sam left for Riverside Drive about eleven. It wasn't just Joanna's flu that muted their enthusiasm for sex; their hearts and minds weren't in it either. When they kissed and his hands stroked the warmth of her body through the layers of cotton and nylon fibre she was wrapped in, she felt a rush of adrenaline that miraculously cleared her sinuses and quickened her breathing. But there was too much on both their minds to sustain the moment. He kissed her a last time at the door.

'Are you sure you wouldn't like me to just, you know, stay?' he asked.

She shook her head. 'I'm fine. If you've no objection, I'm going to call Maggie in the morning and get her side of all this.'

'Sure – it's your story. Write it the way you want.'

She locked the door after him, then went back to bed and replayed the tape that he'd left with her. Occasionally she jotted down a note as some thought struck her that she might use in her piece. It was after one a.m. when she drifted off into a surprisingly dreamless sleep. She awoke at seven and went immediately to her computer, where she spent over an hour getting her material into order and sketching out an introduction to the story. Afterwards she realized that not only had the flu symptoms almost vanished, but she felt as energized as if she'd had a week's total rest instead of just a day's illness. She breakfasted on coffee, juice and cereal, then took a leisurely bath, got dressed and put on a little make-up. She looked and felt herself again. Then she dialled the home number that she had for Maggie.

The phone was picked up on the second ring. The voice that answered wasn't Maggie's. It belonged to a younger woman, and there was a hesitancy in it that told Joanna that something was wrong. 'Is this Maggie McBride's number?' she asked.

'It is.' The voice broke slightly.

'Could I speak to her, please? This is Joanna Cross.'

'I'm afraid that isn't possible, Miss Cross. My mother passed away during the night.'

Heather McBride was in her mid-thirties, slim and some-what severely elegant in the way that career women in New York, and especially on Wall Street, tend to be. But there was also, Joanna recognized at once, a gentleness about her that made her Maggie's daughter. It was oddly moving to sit with this composed but clearly heartbroken woman in Maggie's spotlessly tidy living room at the back of the vast apartment on Park Avenue where she had been housekeeper.

'My mother had suffered from a heart condition for ten years,' she said. 'She'd come to terms only recently with the fact that she was going to need open heart surgery in the near future. But she was on medication, and her doctors didn't think there was any immediate danger.' She paused, drawing in a slightly unsteady breath. 'Obviously they were wrong.'

163

'Will there be an autopsy?'

Heather McBride shook her head. 'I've spoken to my brother, and we don't think it's necessary. He's on his way now from Portland, Oregon,' she added, as though feeling the need to explain why he wasn't present with them as they spoke. 'May I ask, Miss Cross,' she said after a moment's hesitation, 'just what your involvement with my mother was? I don't recall her ever speaking of you?'

Joanna told as much of the story as she felt she had to, and as little as she thought she could get away with. Heather McBride listened, gazing mostly at some point on the carpet in front of her chair, occasionally nodding thoughtfully. 'I know my mother was interested in that kind of thing,' she said when Joanna had finished. 'I'm afraid it's all rather alien to me. We never discussed it much.'

There was a ring at the small door at the back of the apartment which was Maggie's private entrance. It had taken Joanna some time to find it even after Heather's careful instructions over the phone.

Heather got up to answer it, returning a moment later with a tall, thin-faced man in his forties wearing the black suit and stiff white collar of a priest. 'This is Reverend Collingwood,' she said, 'minister of the Unitarian Church here that my mother attended.' She introduced Joanna as a friend of her mother's and they shook hands.

'I have to say, Miss Cross, I've heard your name,' he said. 'As recently as last night, in fact, when Mrs McBride came to see me.'

Joanna sensed Heather's interest pick up as sharply as her own. 'Last night?' she said. 'D'you mind if I ask what time that was?'

'She telephoned around nine and asked if she could come to see me. I could tell that there was something worrying her. It was unlike Maggie to make a drama out of nothing, so I invited her to come over right away. She arrived fifteen or twenty minutes later.'

'Can you tell us what she wanted?' Joanna asked, then immediately darted an apologetic glance in Heather's direction. 'I'm sorry, it's really not my place to ask these questions.'

Heather McBride made a brief dismissive gesture. They were questions she wanted answers to herself. 'That is if you're able to tell us, Reverend,' she added.

He smiled thinly. 'We're not a confessional religion. We have no strict rules on these matters. Confidentiality is respected if requested and when appropriate. Your mother made no such request last night, and I see no reason not to answer your question.' He turned his gaze on Joanna. She sensed an element of accusation in it that made her uncomfortable. She could see the suspicion building in Heather McBride's face that she, Joanna, bore some responsibility in Maggie's death that she had failed so far to be open about. She was acutely reminded of the sense of responsibility for Murray Ray's death that she had even now not wholly thrown off.

'Maggie told me all about your experiment to create a ghost, Miss Cross. I must tell you that in my view it is a misguided and possibly a dangerous endeavour. Maggie, too, had been coming to think of it that way for some time, so she told me. The events of last night, which I imagine you are familiar with, only confirmed her in that belief.'

Joanna held up a hand. 'Can I say something before we start making any accusations? Maggie was a willing

165

volunteer and knew exactly what she was doing. I'm more sorry than I can say about what's happened. I was very fond of Maggie. The whole group was. But this was a properly run and monitored experiment, and anyone was free to pull out whenever they liked. In fact, although I wasn't there myself last night, I understand that this was what Maggie had decided to do.'

'Miss Cross, I'm making no accusations. Maggie's death appears to have been from physical causes arising out of a known clinical condition. But if you will allow me to say so, I think she and the rest of you involved have got yourselves into something deeper than you'd bargained for. If you'll take my advice you'll stop now, before anything else happens.'

'I'm sorry, I have to be clear about one thing.'

They both turned to Heather McBride, who had spoken.

'Are you saying that my mother's death was from natural causes brought about by this "experiment"?' She gave the last word an emphasis that made it both suspect and somehow preposterous.

'I am saying,' said the Reverend Collingwood, picking his words with ponderous care, 'that she believed something had been started which had to be stopped. She also believed that she was the one who was going to have to bear the main burden of doing that.'

'But why, for heaven's sakes?' Joanna protested. 'There were eight of us.'

There was a lugubrious piety in Collingwood's long face as he turned to look at her.

'She didn't believe that the rest of you were prepared to take the danger as seriously as she.'

166

24

Sam phoned around the members of the group to tell them of Maggie's death. Their weeks of sessions together had created a sense of family intimacy which left them all deeply affected by the news. When they met again three days later, it was a sense of personal loss that remained uppermost in their minds more than any thought of Adam or the rights and wrongs of the experiment. Drew and Barry both shed a tear when they entered Adam's room and saw the group there minus Maggie. Even the normally reserved Ward Riley was visibly moved.

A new wooden table had been furnished to replace the broken one. When they were all settled around it Sam addressed them soberly. 'Obviously I've written to Maggie's son and daughter expressing our sorrow. I have to say there was a hairy forty-eight hours when it looked as though the university might become the subject of a court action. Maggie's son, pushed by her local pastor whom she'd talked with the night of her death, wanted to hold us liable. But the daughter, thanks largely to Joanna's persuasiveness, would have no part of it. So the only thing we have to face now is the question of whether we go on with the experiment or not. If any of you have any thoughts, anything you want to say . . .'

Joanna cleared her throat. 'I'm the only one who missed that last session, but it looked pretty astounding on tape. It was also clear that Maggie was deeply alarmed at what was happening, and there's no escaping the fact that it almost certainly played some part in her death. On an emotional level, part of me says okay, that's far enough, let's just drop this whole thing right now. The experiment was set up for my benefit to give me something to write about, so I feel a personal responsibility . . .'

'But you shouldn't,' Sam interrupted her. From the murmurs of agreement around the table it was obvious that the others all felt the same way. 'The experiment was set up as part of the research programme of this department,' Sam continued. 'If we hadn't done it now with this group, we'd certainly have got around to doing it sooner or later with some other group. If there's any responsibility, it's mine. If I'd known Maggie had a weak heart, I'd have dissuaded her from taking part in the experiment. Unfortunately she never told me, nor did I ever think of asking. But there's no point at this stage in breastbeating and crying *mea culpa*. Maggie's dead and that won't bring her back. What all this *does* bring us face to face with is a question which is central to a great deal of what we're trying to do in this department. That question is: What are we to make of phenomena that defy our criterion of rationality? We've all seen things in this room which do that. My belief remains firm that these phenomena are created by our own minds and by nothing else. Maggie, it appears, had become convinced that there was some outside agency at work. What I'd like to ask is do any of the rest of you feel this way?'

There was silence as he looked around their faces one

by one. Barry shook his head as though summing up the feeling of the whole group. No one dissented.

'You know what might be interesting?' Roger said, pulling thoughtfully on one side of his moustache. 'Why don't we talk to Adam – find out what he thinks about all this?'

Sam gave a faint smile. 'It's what I was going to suggest, but I'm glad somebody else came up with it first.' He looked around the table again. 'Everyone agreed?'

There were nods and murmurs of accord.

'All right. Adam, are you there?'

There was silence. Joanna noticed that they were all sitting with their hands in their laps, with the exception of Sam who was leaning on the table, and Barry, who had one hand resting on it curled into a loose fist. Sam became aware of the same thing simultaneously. 'Maybe we need to go back to square one,' he said, 'everybody hands on the table, palms down.'

Everyone did so. Then Sam said, 'All right, let's try again. Adam, are you there?'

The silence lengthened until Pete said, 'Maybe he can't hack it with the new table.'

'Adam, we'd like to talk with you,' Sam said. 'Please respond this time. Are you there?'

They all felt as well as heard it: two sharp raps for 'No'.

'In my neighbourhood that's what they used to call a Polish yes,' Barry said, looking around the table. 'No offence to anyone of that extraction.'

Ward Riley frowned thoughtfully. 'Perhaps it means that someone's there, but not Adam.'

Joanna saw Roger's eyes dart from Ward to Sam, who was careful to avoid their gaze. She knew what he was

169

thinking, what they were all thinking. Because she was thinking it too.

'Is that right?' Sam said quietly. 'Someone's there, but not Adam?'

A clear, firm rap for 'Yes'.

Keeping his voice deliberately calm and seemingly casual, the way she'd seen him do all along when things got tense, Sam asked, 'Can you tell us who you are?'

The scratching noise that came from the table wasn't like the one they were used to. It was lighter, the product of a different wood fibre. But it came, they recognized at once, from within the wood itself, not from anywhere on the surface, neither on top nor underneath. It was the sound that Maggie had correctly identified as Adam wanting to write. Now someone else wanted to do the same.

'We should have thought of this,' Sam muttered. 'The ouija board's in pieces and we haven't got a replacement.'

'I'm on it!' Pete was already out of his chair and heading for the table by the wall. 'This worked when I was a kid,' he said. 'No reason why it shouldn't now.'

He took a sheet of paper and wrote out the letters of the alphabet with a felt pen. Then he took a pair of scissors and cut them into squares. He cut another piece of paper in two and wrote 'Yes' and 'No' on the separate halves. Then he arranged them around the table just as they had been on the ouija board. For a pointer he brought over an empty water glass, which he turned upside down and placed in the centre.

Nobody had spoken throughout the operation, almost as though they feared that by uttering the wrong word they might break some kind of spell. Pete resumed his chair and they all, without having to be prompted, placed a fingertip lightly on the upturned glass.

'Please tell us your name,' Sam said.

The glass began to move. There was a kind of inevitability about its progress that made Joanna think of Greek tragedy, when you know what's coming but the fascination lies in watching it unfold. With a steady and precise movement, barely pausing to register its choice of each successive letter, the glass spelled out 'M – A – G – G – I – E'.

Drew's breath came in a ragged gasp. Her hands rose to cover the lower part of her face in a gesture oddly reminiscent of Maggie when she was taken by surprise or alarmed by something. The rest of them sat silent, wondering what there was to say and who would say it first.

'Keep touching the glass,' Sam said, maintaining his tone of professional calm, like a surgeon demanding a fresh instrument in the operating theatre. Two or three wavering fingertips returned to renew contact, Drew's last of all.

'Please tell us,' Sam said, 'why you call yourself Maggie.'

The glass shot out from under their hands as though fired from a gun. It missed Sam and Roger by inches and shattered against the wall. The whole thing happened so fast that they didn't have time to react, just sat in a frozen silence broken only by a ringing echo of the impact.

A guttural rumble came from Pete's throat as he slumped in his chair and his head fell forward on his chest. At first Joanna thought that he must have been hit by a shard of flying glass. But there was no blood, no sign of any wound. She realized what was happening. It was an almost exact replay of the grotesque performance put on by Murray Ray that day at Camp Starburst when he'd pretended to receive telepathic knowledge of the death of the husband of that poor woman in the audience. But this, Joanna knew, was no performance.

Pete's head rolled on his shoulders and he moaned loudly. They all erupted in movement. There were shouts of alarm.

'He's having a fit. Call a doctor!'

'No!' The word came from Sam as an order. 'That's no fit. Wait.'

He moved closer to Pete and reached out to touch his shoulder gingerly. 'Pete . . .?'

The head snapped back and the face that leered up at Sam was no longer Pete's. The eyes had rolled back half into their sockets, and the lips were drawn back over his teeth in a rictus grin.

Two chairs went over, then a third, as everyone jumped back to put some distance between themselves and this thing that had appeared in their midst. There were gasps of shock, muttered blasphemies. Joanna saw Drew cross herself the way she'd seen Maggie do on the video. Only Sam remained fully in control of his responses, not letting go Pete's shoulder as though the contact somehow grounded them both in a shared reality. 'Who are you?' he said.

The rolled-back eyes focused up at him, and the teeth parted slightly. But the sound that came through them had nothing of Pete's voice in it. Nor was there any movement of his lips or jaw coordinated with the words. It was as though his body had no more life than a ventriloquist's dummy, its words projected from some hidden source elsewhere.

'She will not destroy me . . . not her . . . not you . . . not anybody . . .'

The moment the words were uttered, his eyes closed and he fell slackly sideways. He would have hit the concrete floor if Sam hadn't caught him. He came to with a start, like someone who had momentarily fallen asleep and hoped that no one else had noticed. But he found himself ringed by anxious faces.

'Hey, what's up?' he asked, looking from one to another. 'I'm sorry, I guess I dropped off there for a second. Did I miss something?'

Sam strode over to one of the two video cameras and pressed a switch to eject the cassette. Nothing happened. He tried again. Still nothing. Frowning, he traced the cable from the camera to the transformer.

Pete came over, curious, and saw the problem right away. 'Somebody's pulled the plug out of the wall, for God's sakes . . .!' He replaced the plug in its socket. A handful of indicators glowed as power returned to the system. 'How in the heck did that happen? I checked that plug myself before we started.'

25

Pete looked around the group like somebody who still half suspected that he was the victim of a practical joke. Sam had told him what had happened and the others had corroborated every detail. The fact that there was no video or sound recording was something that none of them could explain. Pete had to take their story on trust.

'Joanna, would you do me a favour?' Sam asked. 'Go upstairs and see if Peggy or any of the others are still there. I'd like to bring them in on this.'

But the lab was empty, most of the rooms dark. She went back down the steps to the basement. Pete was sitting at the table with his head in his hands, still shaken.

'I believe you,' he said. 'Of course I do. It's just that – wow! – the idea takes some getting used to.'

Sam glanced questioningly at Joanna as she came in. She shook her head to indicate that they'd all left upstairs. He looked at his watch. 'Listen,' he said, addressing everyone, 'it's a quarter past nine. Normally we'd have packed up and gone home by now. I don't know how you all feel about this, but I think it might be worthwhile going on.'

'To achieve what, exactly?' Roger asked.

Sam spread his hands to suggest that he was open to

anything. 'To see what happens. I think we're at a very interesting point in this whole process.'

Drew's soft voice pierced the brief silence with complete clarity. 'I think Maggie was right. I don't know what it is or how we've done it, but I think we've come up with something bad. And now we have to get rid of it. You always said, Sam, that we could dematerialize this thing if we had to. I think now's the time.'

Sam accepted her opinion with a shrug of qualified acquiescence. 'I think dematerializing something before it's actually materialized may be putting the cart before the horse. But, if that's how you feel...' He looked around the others. 'How about the rest of you? Do you all agree with Drew?'

'I have to say I do,' Barry said. 'If I'm honest, I don't like what's happening. You know what it makes me think of? Did you ever see that film *Forbidden Planet*? Where this whole race of geniuses gets wiped out by a machine they've built to cater to their every whim? Only what they didn't bargain for was that it would respond as much to their collective id as well as to their ego. So they got wiped out by monsters that the machine created out of the dark side of their own minds? I think maybe what's happening here has something to do with the dark side of our minds.'

Ward Riley's mouth twitched disapprovingly at the corners. 'I saw that film years ago and wasn't much impressed by it. The idea that a people of such brilliance could have overlooked such a possibility and made no provision for it was deeply unconvincing. I think we should beware of looking to Hollywood for any kind of intellectual guidance.'

'So what's your take on all this, Ward?' Sam asked him.

Ward stroked his chin and pursed his mouth a moment. 'I think Maggie's death was natural, but we've been caught up in a collective response to it that owes more to superstition than to reason. I believe that's what is behind the phenomena we've been experiencing.'

Sam turned to Joanna. 'How about you? Any thoughts?'

It was a hard one to call. 'Speaking as a journalist, I've got enough material and more for a story. Speaking as one of the team, I don't know. I don't know if I want out, or if I want to see what happens next.' She paused. 'I think maybe I want to see what happens next.'

She registered an almost subliminal twitch at the corner of Sam's eye. She could barely believe it, but he had given her a wink of complicity. She had to stop herself from laughing out loud. The gesture was in such bad taste in the circumstances, so wholly inappropriate, that it was hysterical. But then she realized that, of course, he hadn't winked at all. She had read something that simply wasn't there into the involuntary movement of a facial muscle. A wave of alarm swept over her. She was coming adrift from reality, losing all sense of proportion and perspective. She also felt suddenly vulnerable, as though everybody in the room must have seen her mistake and now knew what was happening to her. Just as quickly she realized that nobody was paying her any attention. They were all too fixed on the dilemma before them.

Sam turned to Roger. 'What do you think?'

Roger hesitated for a moment, then spoke with a solemnity that Joanna had not so far seen in him. 'I think that whatever this phenomenon is that we've started, the best thing we can do now is stop it.'

His words hung in the air with a quiet authority. Even Sam was impressed by the tone in which they'd been spoken and the feeling behind them. Roger looked at him, aware of his response.

'I imagine that surprises you. The thing is, Sam, I think there's a distinction to be made between exploring an idea and following all of its consequences to their conclusion. Exploring the atom was an idea. The bomb was one of its consequences. It didn't have to happen. There were many other things we could have done with the idea – that we did do, and will do yet. But the bomb happened. And I have a feeling that this is another of those dark tributaries.'

Ward spoke. 'I have to say, listening to Roger, I'm on the whole inclined to agree with him. It doesn't mean we shouldn't try again. In fact I want to. But I'm not easy with what's happened here, and I think we should end it.'

'In the church, we call it exorcism,' Drew said quietly.

Roger looked at her with a gentle smile. 'Exorcism, dematerialization – in physics we call that the principle of complementarity, the same thing described two different ways.'

Sam looked at Pete, who nodded. 'Let's get rid of it – now.'

'You're sure you feel up to this, Pete? You don't have to.'

'I think it'll take all of us. Except for Maggie, of course.'

'Well, it looks like we have a majority,' Sam said, and started to pull up chairs and put them in place. 'I'm not sure I agree with your verdict, but I understand it. And if we don't function as a group, we don't function at all.'

'Talk us out of it if you want to,' Roger said, openly inviting him to try and implying his own willingness to listen.

Sam shook his head. 'I'm not sure I want to. We've all been affected by Maggie's death. It's probably best if we make a new start – those of us who'd like to.'

'Sam, can I say something?'

'Sure – go ahead, Barry.'

'Would it be all right if we put Maggie's chair in place as usual?'

Sam looked around the group, but could read nothing in their faces, aside from the fact that they were all awaiting his response.

'What purpose d'you think that would serve, Barry?'

Barry shrugged awkwardly and looked a touch embarrassed. 'I don't know. Maybe we'll just feel more . . . complete that way.'

Sam thought a moment. No one spoke. 'Why not?' he said eventually.

Pete picked up an extra chair and placed it where Maggie always sat. They took their places. Instinctively Barry placed his hands on the table before him. Drew did likewise. Then everybody followed suit, including Sam.

'There's no formula for this,' Sam said. 'All we're going to do is affirm in a clear and positive way that we invented Adam, and that the experiment is now over. We know that it's been at least partially successful and we've proved our point – that a concentrated thought-form can become manifest in different ways. But Adam was an idea belonging to all of us. There was a little bit of each one of us in him. Now we're each taking back the part of ourselves that was in him. We're dismantling the structure we created. Our thoughts about Adam are no longer held in common between us. Now we have only individual memories of him. They will fade with time, as they're beginning to fade now. Adam was an illusion. A trick of the mind. But it's over.'

For a long time nobody spoke. Drew had closed her eyes. Joanna couldn't see whether Barry had closed his too, or whether he was simply staring down at his hands. Roger was looking at the table top. Ward, too. Sam was looking across the room. Following his gaze Joanna saw the glowing red lights which meant the sound and video equipment were running.

Drew's voice broke the silence in a flat, defeated monotone. 'It's not going to work.'

Everyone looked at her. Her eyes remained closed.

'What makes you say that, Drew?' Sam asked.

She opened her eyes and looked directly at him. 'Because he's part of us all now. Like a child. You create them out of what you are, then they become themselves. But whatever happens, they never really leave you.'

As she finished, her face contorted from within to form a terrible image of unbearable pain. She began to weep silently, as though an anguish bottled up for years was finally coming out of her. Barry put his arms around her and tried to comfort her, but she only wept more bitterly, her sobs arising from the depths of a long-buried heartbreak.

The others looked on helplessly, embarrassed and moved in equal parts. Pete turned away and stared down at his hands spread out on the table top. 'Don't, Drew,' he said, his voice tight with nerves. 'You're bringing him back. You have to stop.'

As though the truth of his barely audible words had pierced her consciousness, she nodded vigorously and took the handkerchief that Barry had been offering her. She dried her eyes, blew her nose, and quickly pulled herself together. 'I'm sorry . . . I'm all right now . . .'

'Drew alone can't bring him back,' Sam said. 'The rest of us have already destroyed him. He's already gone.'

The two strip lights on the ceiling exploded in a shower of sparks and glass. The sudden darkness that enveloped the closed basement room was absolute, and the cries of its occupants were swallowed in a howling blast of wind that came from nowhere, as though the walls had dissolved and they found themselves transported to some icy mountain top. The howl of the wind became a roar no longer made by any natural element. Whether it came from man or beast, or something in between the two, was hard to say. But it made Joanna fear for something she had given little thought to thus far in her life. It made her fear for her immortal soul.

In that moment she knew with utter certainty that something alien and evil was in the room with them. Among the bodies that brushed past and collided with her in terrified confusion was another presence, one that she sensed by faculties she neither knew she had nor could describe. She knew only that something was among them, something more terrible than death itself.

As abruptly as the whole thing had started, so it ended. A total silence fell, broken only by the moans and whimpers of the terrified group who, for all she knew, could be maimed and wounded, if not worse. Joanna herself, so far as she could tell, was unhurt, but crawling on her hands and knees with no precise memory of how she got there.

'Joanna . . .? Where are you?' It was Sam's voice, close by.

'Here.' She reached out in the dark and touched someone. She couldn't tell who, but they pulled away with a gasp of fear.

'Sam, where are you . . .?'

'Trying to find the door . . .'

There was a scraping sound, then a crash as something was knocked over, and finally a rattling of the door handle and somebody pulling on it as though it was stuck.

It came open suddenly, and the pale light that filtered down the stairs, although no more than a reflection from the campus shining through a window higher up, was enough to show the figure of Sam groping for a light switch. The single bulb on the stairs illuminated a scene of devastation in the room that took her breath away.

The table they had been sitting around had been flung against a wall and lay now with one leg snapped clean off. All the chairs were scattered and upturned, half of them smashed. Roger Fullerton crouched in a corner, breathing hard, eyes wide with terror. Drew was curled into a foetal ball with Barry lying across her for protection. Ward Riley was flat on his back with his arms spread, as though he'd been wrestled to the ground by a more powerful opponent. Pete was picking himself out of the tangled wreckage that was all that remained of their video and recording equipment, all of it smashed beyond repair.

Sam came back in, took her by the arm and helped her to her feet. 'Are you all right?'

She tried to speak, but her mouth and throat were dry. She nodded her head. Only now, when he held her, did she realize how violently she was trembling.

'It's over now,' he whispered. 'Come on, help me with the others.'

Sam went over and helped Roger to his feet while Joanna went to Barry and Drew. When she turned, she saw that Sam and Roger were already helping Ward up. They were all in shock, but nobody seemed physically hurt.

There was a crash as Pete got to his feet, knocking over the twisted remains of one of the camera tripods. He lifted a hand to his face, and Joanna gave a gasp of alarm as he appeared to peel away a strip of soft flesh.

He heard her and turned. 'Wax,' he said. 'Paraffin wax, splashed over me. Doesn't hurt, it's barely warm.'

She saw now that the tub that had contained it lay on its side, also twisted. Then she saw something else lying nearby.

'What's that?' she said.

Sam crossed over and picked it up. It was about two feet long, thick and rounded. He brought it over, turning it to examine it from all sides. There was something sculpted about it.

'Dear God in heaven,' Sam murmured. There was a shocked, almost reverential tone in his voice. 'D'you know what this is?'

It was a wax cast of a man's forearm – bare, with the hand closed loosely in a fist. Whatever or whoever had been in the room with them had, deliberately or otherwise, left an imprint in the wax put there for that purpose.

26

They had moved upstairs to the central waiting area of the deserted lab. Barry perched on the arm of the chair in which Drew huddled, pulling her coat tightly and protectively around her. He offered her a paper cup filled with water from the cooler, but she shook her head without looking at it.

Roger was slumped on a couch along the wall, balancing a glass of whisky on his stomach. Joanna walked across and stood over him. 'How are you feeling?' she asked.

'Better.' He pushed himself up into a sitting position. 'Where's Sam?'

'Through there.' She pointed to a closed door in back of the lab. 'He and Pete are making a plaster cast from the wax impression.'

There was the sound of a toilet flushing, and a moment later Ward Riley emerged from the small bathroom pulling on his jacket. Joanna asked if she could get him anything.

'No thanks.' He nodded towards the door in back. 'How's it going in there?'

'Pete said it wouldn't take long – if it worked.'

Ward settled into an ancient armchair across from Roger, obviously intending to wait for the results. Roger was staring down at his feet stretched out in front of him, turning his whisky glass in his hand. 'So,' he said reflectively, 'was it something coming from us, or coming through us? And is there a difference?'

Ward thought for a moment. 'Hard to say.'

'It's hard to say anything that makes sense in the circumstances.' Roger looked up at Joanna. 'Though Joanna's going to have to. What are you going to say about it when you write your piece?'

'Maybe I won't *say* anything. Just describe it.'

'Probably a wise choice.'

They turned as the door behind them opened and Sam emerged, carrying something. Ward and Roger got to their feet and followed Joanna to get a closer look at the white plaster cast that he now held out to them. 'It came out pretty well,' he said.

Drew and Barry joined them, he supporting her with an arm around her shoulder. One by one, with the unconscious veneration of believers reaching out to touch a holy relic, they ran their fingers over the smooth and still slightly warm surface of the plaster.

'It's incredible,' Joanna murmured.

Sam's expression was faintly sardonic. 'That's just what most people will call it.'

She knew what he meant. 'I guess you're right.'

'There's absolutely no way we can prove that this thing isn't a fake. I can't even prove to you that Pete and I didn't cook this thing up back there just now. Or that I didn't plant that wax mould downstairs.'

'I think we're resigned to being called crackpots or liars, or both,' Roger said with a sigh. 'The issue is no longer what people think of us but what we think of what's happening.'

Ward bent forward to get a closer look. 'Is it holding something?'

'Yes, but I'm not sure what.' Sam turned the cast over and sought out a brighter patch of the not very powerful overhead light. 'The detail isn't perfect. You can see these ridges between the fingers that look like the links of a chain attached to this thing in the palm of the hand – an amulet or talisman, or something similar.'

'Talisman more likely,' Ward said. 'An amulet is traditionally for protection, a talisman confers occult powers on its possessor. I didn't get the feeling that that thing down there was in much need of protection.'

'I don't know,' Sam laughed softly. 'Maybe we scared it as much as it scared us.'

Drew shivered. 'I find that hard to believe,' she said in an unsteady voice, but into which she nonetheless managed to inject a note of humour. Barry tightened his arm around her shoulder.

Ward took the cast from Sam and peered more closely at the design on the thing that it was holding. 'There's some kind of pattern on it – sweeping lines overlaying what look like more lines.'

'Isn't that a triangle?' Joanna asked, pointing.

'Or a compass,' Roger said. 'Which could make it some kind of Freemasonic sign – not that I'm an expert.'

'I'll have Peggy look at it tomorrow,' Sam said. 'She's pretty good on that kind of thing.'

It was after eleven when Sam locked the cast in his office safe for the night. No one had given a thought to dinner, and now found they weren't hungry. They stood for a moment in a little group on the sidewalk just off the campus. They decided that they would all talk with Sam on the phone in the next few days and decide whether or not to go ahead with their next group meeting, which was scheduled for the beginning of the following week. Then they went their separate ways.

Joanna and Sam took a cab to Riverside Drive. Neither spoke. She looked out at the familiar lights and landmarks flashing by in the night. Somehow they seemed slightly less familiar than before. Something had changed. Whether it was in the world or in her she wasn't sure, but there had been some underlying shift in her sense of reality. Perhaps it was just a delayed reaction to shock, an adjustment to the weeks of strangeness which had culminated in the extraordinary evening she had just experienced. The only thing she knew with any certainty, and she sensed it in her deepest being, was that something irrevocable had happened that meant her life would never be quite the same.

She reached out for the comforting touch of Sam's hand in the darkness, and felt his fingers interlace with hers. 'What d'you think we should do?' she asked.

He sighed and looked at her. 'We began the evening by trying to get rid of it, but somehow I don't think that hand we produced was waving goodbye.'

'I notice you say "we" produced. You're still sure that's what happened tonight?'

He looked at her in the darkness of the cab. 'It's still more feasible than any other explanation.'

'I wonder.'

'What exactly do you wonder?'

Her gaze went back out to the city. 'If it was something we created, why would it attack us that way? Why would we attack ourselves?'

He took a moment to reply, as though preparing

himself to hear aloud the thoughts that were turning in his mind.

'I suspect that what attacked us was the part of ourselves that knows it would be a shame and a crime to abandon this experiment now. So it made its disapproval known when we attempted to do so – and left a tantalizing hint of what we might achieve if we go on.'

She turned to him again. 'That's what you want? To go on?'

'Yes,' he answered simply. 'As I said, I'll go on with another group if this one folds.' He paused. 'What about you?'

She too thought a moment, then spoke as if disappointed by her own answer. 'I don't know.'

He nodded and gave her a faint smile of reassurance. It was the answer he'd expected and he didn't blame her for it.

'At least,' he said, 'you can't say you aren't getting a story.'

27

Peggy's office, though even smaller than Sam's, was considerably tidier. She had shifted everything off her desk and onto the window ledge in order to make room for the stack of reference books that she had spent the morning going through. In the midst of them, carefully wedged between a couple of paperweights, was the plaster-cast of the arm, turned so that the thing in it faced upwards. She peered through a magnifying glass at the barely discernible detail on it.

What Sam had described as sweeping lines began to look more like one continuous spiral that coiled into some kind of double vortex pattern. She still wasn't sure what the straight lines running through them represented, if anything, partly because the point at which two of them appeared to join was obscured by the fingertips curled over it. She turned several pages of the largest of the books open on her desk, and reluctantly conceded defeat. Nothing in there even remotely resembled the design on the plaster cast she was examining.

She went down to the basement – Adam's room – where Sam was going through the previous night's wreckage with Pete and Bryan Meade, the engineer. Joanna was with them, taking notes in shorthand to back up what she was getting on tape; she no longer relied on technology as much as she had, especially in this place. Peggy caught Joanna's eye as she entered. The two women liked each other, and it took only the faintest shake of Peggy's head for Joanna to understand that she'd drawn a blank with her research. 'What have they found down here?' she asked.

Joanna told her that according to Bryan there was nothing unusual about the damage to the furniture or electrical equipment. They had been trashed by straightforward physical strength – but strength on a human not a superhuman scale. Nothing had been crushed or bent or broken to any degree that a normal man or woman couldn't accomplish. Nobody examining the debris would have reason to suspect the intervention of any paranormal force. The only inference any reasonable outsider could draw would be that the group members had inflicted the damage themselves in some kind of frenzy.

'Which according to Sam's theory,' Peggy said, 'is exactly what happened.'

'What do you make of all this, Peggy?' Joanna asked. 'Just between us?'

Peggy's hands were clasped in front of her as she lifted her shoulders in a gesture of incomprehension and unease. 'It's the most extraordinary thing I've ever been this close to. I've told Sam I think it's a mistake to go on – at least until we can figure out some safeguards against this happening again. What about the rest of you?'

Before Joanna could answer, Sam looked over and called out, 'Any luck yet, Peggy?'

Peggy shook her head again. Sam came towards them, frowning. 'There's got to be something that'll tell us what that design means.'

189

'Why must it mean anything?' Joanna asked. 'D'you think it's important?'

For the first time he looked genuinely surprised by what she had said. 'Of course it's important. Nothing that's happening here is happening by chance. Believe me, it's important.'

Drew and Barry were planning to catch the six o'clock screening of a movie, then have dinner at their favourite Chinese restaurant. The traffic had been light and they'd arrived early, bought their tickets, and found they had twenty minutes to kill. There was a bar next to the theatre, but neither of them felt like a drink, so they took a stroll around the block to look at the shops.

Barry headed straight for a second-hand bookshop that he knew well. Drew was already absorbed in a display in the window of a fabric shop a couple of doors along, but she saw Barry signalling to her that he was going into the bookshop, and she nodded.

The interior was dark and seemed to stretch way back, with bookstacks from floor to ceiling everywhere, leaving barely room for two people to pass between them. Barry wandered through in search of anything that might pique his curiosity. Subjects were divided into sections which were labelled with faded signs handwritten in ink. He spent a few minutes scanning the Military History shelves, but found nothing of great interest. He went on alphabetically, skipping New Age without even a glance, and barely pausing at Occult; he'd had enough of that for the time being. Philosophy looked more promising. There was a complete set of Bertrand Russell's autobiography that looked almost new. He checked inside the cover; it was a first edition.

He began to read and became engrossed. A couple of times he had to step back or press up against the book-stack to let somebody pass, but the response was automatic and didn't break his concentration. What did was the sound of books tumbling onto the floor as he backed into a pile of them. He looked down and saw an assistant crouched where he had been re-filling one of the lower shelves. Apologizing profusely, Barry bent down to help him clear up the mess.

The assistant was a young man with a wispy beard and gentle manner who told him not to worry, it happened all the time. But Barry was already only half-listening. He straightened up slowly, gazing at the book he had picked up, open at the page where it had fallen.

He recognized the design at once.

When he began to read the text accompanying it, he felt the blood drain from his face.

28

Barry had made the call to Sam's office just before ten the following morning. He was subdued and apologetic, but unshakeable: he and Drew were quitting the group and would play no further part in the experiment. Sam had asked for a face-to-face meeting, but Barry had hedged awkwardly, saying there was no point.

Joanna had been at the magazine when she got the news from Sam. She had called Drew and Barry immediately and asked if she could talk to them – 'Just to help me round off this part of the story. I'm not going to try to change your minds.'

There had been a whispered conversation at the other end of the line, then they had invited her to come by after lunch. They would talk to her – still on condition that their names would not be mentioned.

She took a cab out to the quiet tree-lined street in Queens where they lived. It was a prosperous middle class neighbourhood with houses that would have won no architectural prizes but were large, detached, and comfortable looking. She walked up a redstone path past an impeccably tended lawn and flowerbeds and rang the doorbell. Barry let her in. He was friendly, but subdued. She could sense his underlying tension.

Drew appeared in the living room door. The brightness

of her white trousers and floral blouse only emphasized the tiredness in her face. She looked as though she had slept little, if at all. They took Joanna into a good-sized rectangular living room and invited her to sit in one of the two brocade-upholstered armchairs placed at precise angles alongside a matching sofa. The whole room was arranged with jarring symmetry, every object in a space of its own with no sense of an integrated whole. It was, Joanna reflected, with an immediate sense of guilt at her own snobbery, a home typical of a working-class couple who had made money but never acquired the patina of sophistication that would have moved them up the social ladder. Barry and Drew were what they were, without pretence. They weren't the kind of people she would have spent much time with, if any, outside of their group meetings, but she had liked them and instinctively respected them from the outset.

'Thank you for seeing me,' Joanna said. 'I know you're still pretty shaken up after the other night. So are we all.'

The couple exchanged a look, as though for mutual reassurance. Joanna decided to leave the small tape recorder in her bag and not turn an informal conversation into an interview. She sensed that Drew and Barry wanted to talk, but could easily lose their nerve. They needed encouraging, not intimidating.

'I was just making some coffee, if you'd like some,' Drew said.

Joanna sensed it was an excuse to leave her alone with Barry. 'Thank you, that would be nice.'

As Drew left the room, Barry picked up a book from a table by his chair. It had no dust jacket, its spine was split, and whatever colour it had been had long since faded to a murky brown. 'I came across this last night, quite by chance, in a second-hand bookshop.' He thumbed through in search of a particular page. 'When I say by chance, I mean it literally. It fell off the shelf open . . . right here.'

He handed it to her. She found herself looking at a plain black and white drawing or engraving of some kind. It was circular and contained a long, artfully designed spiral that doubled back on itself to give a strangely three-dimensional effect. There could be no doubt that it was the same design as on the object in the hand of the wax cast. The various straight lines and their relationships to one another were now clearly visible.

'They're alchemical symbols,' Barry told her. 'Some of it's Egyptian, but the spiral is closer to a Tibetan mandala. It's all in the text.'

She flipped to the front of the book. Only one word was inscribed on the title page: *Magick*. She turned back to the diagram. 'What is it?' she asked.

He inhaled before answering. There was a ragged edge to his breathing, as though he was making an effort to hide his nervousness. 'It's something that's supposed to give its possessor the power to place a death curse on his enemies.'

Joanna looked at him. 'A what?'

'If you look upon this and the gaze of its possessor simultaneously, your life is in that person's power.' He shrugged, as if to excuse himself for the absurdity of what he'd said, and also for being tempted to believe it.

Joanna looked down at the book in her hand, skimmed a few paragraphs, turned a page. 'It says this thing belonged to Cagliostro.' She looked at Barry again. 'Wasn't that . . .'

'The guy Ward mentioned,' he finished for her. 'And Adam later confirmed that he'd known him in Paris.'

They were both silent a moment.

'How much do we know about this Cagliostro?' she asked.

Barry walked across the room, passing an impressive-looking sound system with expensive speakers. He reached a wall entirely covered with bookshelves on which rows of volumes were arranged with fastidious care. He ran a finger along them until he found the one he wanted. It was a hardback that was almost as worn as the one he had just shown her. He returned thumbing through the pages in search of something, then handed it to her in silence. She saw that it was open at a chapter headed 'Cagliostro, Count Alessandro (1743–1795)'.

'Whether he was a charlatan or not, nobody knows,' Barry said. 'But there's a report of a meeting he had in 1785 with the highest-ranking freemasons in Paris, who demanded proof of the magical powers he claimed to have. He demonstrated a system of numerology derived from the letters in people's names. That day he predicted a revolution in France in four years' time, and the execution of the royal family and various other people, all precisely named and with the dates on which it would happen. And it did, exactly as he said. He also predicted the rise of Napoleon, and his eventual exile in Elba. All this before an audience of at least a hundred highly educated, respected, powerful men.'

'Did they believe him?'

'Apparently not enough. The following year he was arrested over some financial scandal and was thrown in the Bastille for nine months on the orders of the king, then exiled from the country. He died in another jail in

Rome ten years later – by which time almost everything he'd predicted had come true, and the rest came true soon afterwards.'

He paused to let his words sink in, then gave another apologetically self-conscious shrug. 'Whichever way you look at it, this was an extraordinary man. I don't think I want to go up against him.'

Joanna looked again at the book in her hand. It showed a head and shoulders engraving of Cagliostro – a plump face with heavy features, slightly bulging eyes and full lips. His hair was either white or very fair, swept back and shoulder length. He looked barrel-chested, physically strong, probably not tall.

'Are you saying that what we conjured up wasn't Adam at all, but this man Cagliostro?'

'I don't know what we conjured up,' Barry said. 'All I know is we built a bridge back to a strange place – and I'm getting scared about what's coming over it.'

Drew returned with coffee and three delicate porcelain cups on a tray. 'We both feel bad about letting Sam down,' she said, placing the tray carefully in the centre of a rectangular table in front of the sofa. 'But we talked for a long time last night, and we don't see what else we could do.' She straightened up and fixed Joanna with a direct, unblinking gaze. Her voice was flat and toneless, like somebody in shock and still coming to terms with the event that had caused it. 'This isn't something we've created. We've raised something evil. I beg you to believe me, Joanna. You have to warn the others.'

'If you think this,' Joanna asked, 'why don't you and Barry warn them yourselves?'

The answer was without hesitation. 'They wouldn't believe us.'

'Why not?'

Drew and Barry exchanged a look, as though agreeing which of them should answer this. It was Barry who spoke.

'We know Sam, and he'd never accept this. He'd find a million reasons to explain it away. That's because he's an intellectual. I mean no disrespect, but people like Sam analyse everything till they can't see the wood for the trees any more. Me, I'm just a plumber who's read a few books, but I know when I'm up against something I can't fight. And that's where I am now. And that's why we're out.'

29

'All I can say is that Drew and Barry were ill-matched to this experiment. It's my fault – I chose them.'

Joanna gave a wry smile. 'They said you'd explain it away.'

'That's not what I'm doing,' he protested. 'Explaining it away is saying it didn't happen. I know what happened. All we're talking about is how. Frankly, an eighteenth-century alchemist coming back from the dead doesn't cut it for me.'

They were in Adam's room, she and Sam seated on either side of the new table that had been installed that afternoon, and the lanky form of Pete was leaning in a corner, arms folded, watching them.

'Okay,' Joanna said, 'so give me an explanation that does cut it for you.'

Sam accepted the challenge with an open-handed gesture.

'Barry already had a book about Cagliostro in his library, so he knew about him when Ward first mentioned the name. He says he never saw the design on this so-called magic talisman until last night, but the fact is it existed. He might have seen it and forgotten. Ward might have seen it. Any member of the group could have seen it, but without consciously remembering having done so.

The mention of Cagliostro, however, brought it back into play, so – bingo! – it manifests itself in the way we saw. That's the whole point of what we're trying to demonstrate with this experiment.'

'But what about what happened last night? Why did Barry go into that particular bookshop? Why did that particular book fall open at that particular page?'

'We only have Barry's word for the fact that it happened like that.'

'Oh, come on. Why would he lie?'

'I don't know. People have their reasons. All I'm saying is he could have lied – we weren't there.'

'You're doing exactly what you accuse people of doing to you – rejecting an uncomfortable truth by demanding impossible standards of proof.'

He slapped the table with his open hand. 'I know! Don't think I'm unaware of the irony.' Then he laughed. 'Sorry.'

Pete stirred in his corner, shifting his weight from one foot to the other and re-folding his arms. 'The problem is that some as-yet undiscovered force-field emanating from the human brain is every bit as unverifiable as the malevolent spirit of a dead alchemist.'

Sam cocked an eyebrow in his direction. 'Maybe so. But which sounds the more likely to you?'

'Which sounds more likely,' Joanna said, 'is hardly a scientific test.'

'On the contrary,' Sam contradicted her. 'The principle of Occam's razor: Never impose a complicated explanation where a simpler one will do.'

'I'm not sure,' she said, being deliberately provocative now, 'that a force-field emanating from the human brain *is* a simpler explanation than a dead alchemist coming back from the grave. How does this force-field do what it's doing, anyway?'

'By interacting with other force-fields around it – and matter is a force-field. There's nothing solid in it. It's just a rearrangement of the same force-fields that make up space or the scent of flowers – or the brain itself and the thoughts in it.'

'Why is it we can't identify this force-field – "psi" – when we've identified so many others?'

'I don't know. But I do know that the one sure way to go down in history as an idiot is to proclaim that anything's impossible. Like the professor of mathematics at Johns Hopkins who said that powered flight would never happen – two weeks before the Wright brothers took off from Kitty Hawk. Or the astronomer who said "space travel is bunk" just before the Russians launched Sputnik One. Or the whole posse of distinguished experts who said that electric light was an idiotic idea and that Edison didn't understand the first principles of electricity. And don't forget the admiral who told Harry Truman, "The atom bomb will never go off, and I speak as an expert on explosives".'

'All of which,' she persisted, undeterred, 'means that it could be the alchemist after all.'

Sam shrugged. 'It could be invisible green men from Mars. I'd still want to find out how they did it.'

She looked from one to the other. 'So, what do we do? Quit? Or carry on without Drew and Barry?'

'You know what I think,' Sam said. 'I think we should carry on. But it's up to each member of the group to decide for themselves.'

'What about you, Pete?' she asked.

Pete gave a brief laugh. 'The trouble with pulling out now is we'd be buying into the Frankenstein syndrome.'

'The what?' she inquired.

'You know – that bit in all the old movies where somebody realizes what the mad scientist is trying to do, gives him a meaningful stare and says, "There are some things, professor, that human kind should never seek to know . . ."?'

Sam looked amused. 'I think that's the real reason why Roger and Ward are still open to the idea of going on.'

'Are they?' Joanna asked, mildly surprised.

'They'll go along if the rest of us will.'

Pete looked at Joanna. 'How about you?'

She looked at the wall where Drew's sketch of their imaginary Adam still hung. 'Maybe in playing with this kind of stuff,' she said, 'we just stir up problems for ourselves that we could do without.'

'You've already been cursed,' Sam said, 'so we know you're immune.'

It was meant as a joke, but the way she looked at him told him she hadn't taken it as one.

'Do we?' she said.

He leaned forward, immediately contrite. 'I'm sorry. Look, if you've any doubts at all . . .'

She cut him short with a shake of her head. 'It's okay. I'm a reporter. As long as there's a story, I'll stay with it.'

'Anyway,' he said, reaching over to take her hand in his, 'even if we believe this nonsense, which we don't, we still haven't looked into anyone's eyes and at this,' he jabbed a contemptuous finger at the picture of Cagliostro's talisman, 'at the same time.'

Joanna's eyes flashed between it and the drawing of

Adam and back again, and she felt a prickling sensation on the back of her neck which made her shiver. She freed her hand from Sam's and flipped the book shut.

'Let's keep it that way,' she said, 'just in case.'

30

Drew was alarmed when she awoke to discover that Barry's side of the bed was empty. There was no light visible beneath the bathroom door, which meant he must be downstairs, unable to sleep.

She got up and peered over the landing. She could see no light below. Then a draught of cold air hit her. She realized it was coming from above. She shivered, pulling her robe tighter, and started up the narrow stairs from where a chill breeze blew. On a level that gave access to the loft, she found a window open. It was just large enough for a full-grown man to get through, giving onto a flat roof over a rear bedroom that had been added some time after the house was built but before they bought it. She stepped carefully through the window and called Barry's name.

There was no response, and it took her eyes several moments to adjust to the dark. Then she saw a shape on the very edge of the low coping stone that enclosed the area. It could not have been more than a foot in width, and yet Barry was kneeling on it at one corner, hunched as though in prayer and rocking back and forth with a motion that threatened any second to pitch him head first to the concrete yard below.

She cried out in alarm and ran to him, clasping him

in her slender arms and pulling him back from danger with all her strength. He offered no resistance, just fell onto the sandpapery bitumen that covered the roof. She held him there for some moments, breathless more from shock than from effort.

He offered no resistance, just moaned faintly as though in pain or barely conscious. Half-remembered warnings against too violently waking sleepwalkers ran through her head, but she had no reason to assume he had been sleepwalking. He'd never done it before, so why should he start now?

Eventually she took his arm, whispering encouragement as though to a sleepy child or someone old and very sick. He allowed her to lead him back in through the window and down to their bedroom. By the time they got there he was more or less himself, and he remembered every moment since he had woken in bed.

'It was like a waking dream. I haven't had them often, but often enough to know what they are. You know that you're dreaming. It's like waking into the dream and saying, "I'm asleep and dreaming now," just as surely as you'd say, "I'm awake now, it's the morning and I've got to go to work." I was dreaming about Adam. He'd come into the bedroom and beckoned me to follow him. I knew it was a dream, so there was no reason not to. I wasn't afraid. I told myself it was perfectly natural that he should appear in my dreams after all the time we've spent talking and thinking about him. Actually I felt kind of pleased about it. I thought it could only clarify my thoughts and feelings about what was going on.

'He led me up on to the roof where you found me. He was trying to make me jump. I was fighting him, but

I was losing. If you hadn't come when you did, he would have won.'

They got back into bed and Drew held him in her arms for a long time, painfully conscious of how close she had come to losing him.

'I don't understand,' he whispered. 'Why would I dream that Adam was trying to kill me?'

'It wasn't a dream,' she said with quiet conviction. 'It was a spell.'

Joanna replaced the phone and didn't move. She had been at her desk in the *Around Town* office all morning, polishing a draft of events so far. There was going to be no trouble getting a four-parter out of this, maybe more, which she knew Taylor Freestone would like.

In her narrative she had hidden nothing and invented nothing. As evidence she offered such video and sound recordings as they had, frankly admitting that some people would always choose to believe that trickery was involved. She repeated Roger's quotation of David Hume on miracles, that it 'was more rational to suspect knavery and folly than to discount, at a stroke, everything that past experience has taught me about the way things actually work'.

She also pointed out that Roger Fullerton himself, one of the most distinguished theoretical physicists in the world, was prepared to vouch for the authenticity of what she was describing. Next to this, the fact that she was putting her own credibility as a journalist on the line was of minor significance; nonetheless, both she and Roger accepted that in some quarters they would be called gullible at best and corrupt at worst. Such accusations, she wrote, would merely convince them further of the extraordinary nature of the events in which they had participated.

At this point she felt she was straying into rhetoric a little further than she wished, and pulled back, toning down her protestations, and especially those she found herself imputing to Roger. She reminded herself to stick to the reporter's five-point rule: who, what, where, when and why. That was how these articles would work best: as straightforward factual reports.

Then her phone had rung. It was Sam.

'I'm afraid I've got some terrible news. Drew and Barry have been killed in a car accident. It happened this morning, about eight-thirty. Apparently they were heading out on the Schuykill and their car went out of control and hit a bridge. They were both killed outright.'

She felt strangely paralysed by his words, more precisely by the effort to hold back the flood of questions and implications that lay behind them and her reaction to them, and which threatened to overwhelm her.

'Joanna? Are you there?'

'Yes, I'm here,' she murmured. 'Oh, God.'

'I'm sorry. It's a terrible shock.'

'Do you know where they were going?' she asked.

'I didn't ask. I just got this call from a secretary in Barry's office. She's working through his diary, informing everybody.'

'Can you give me her number?'

'Sure, wait a second . . . I don't know if she can tell you any more than I can . . .' He found the number and gave it to her, 'Why do you want to know where they were going?'

'I'm not sure. I'll tell you later.'

She put down the phone and covered her face with her hands. After a few moments she sensed a presence and looked up. Taylor Freestone was standing in the door of her office looking down at her, concerned.

'Something wrong?'

She nodded, conscious of a stinging wetness in her eyes. 'Two of our group, Barry and Drew, were just killed in a car crash.'

'Oh, my God . . .!' He took a step in, closed the door behind him. 'I'm sorry, truly sorry.' He paused, then added, as though the real significance of what she had said had only just occurred to him, 'Does that mean you'll have to stop the experiment?'

She thought for a moment she was going to throw something at him, but her voice came out flat and resigned. 'I don't know. It's too soon to think about that. If you'll excuse me, Taylor, I have to make some calls.'

'Of course. This is awful. Just awful.'

He went out. She took a deep breath, reached for the box of tissues in one of her drawers and wiped her eyes and nose, then picked up the phone.

31

They all met just after six at Sam's apartment. There had been an unspoken agreement to avoid the lab, and in spite of a cold wind that had brought in a driving rain from the Atlantic, everyone preferred to make the trip to Riverside Drive. Sam offered drinks or coffee, but nobody wanted anything. Without further preamble he said, 'Joanna's found out a couple of things that she thinks you should hear.'

She was sitting on the window seat where they'd huddled together on the first night they'd made love. Gazing out into the darkness over the Hudson, Sam had wondered aloud whether he might conceivably persuade Roger Fullerton to be part of the experiment they were planning. It was only a few months ago, but it seemed a lifetime. Now Roger Fullerton sat in an armchair opposite her, looking drawn and tired and probably wishing, she imagined, that he'd never heard of any of them. Sam leaned against the arm of the sofa on which Ward and Pete sat.

'I talked to the police patrol who were first on the scene,' she began, looking down at the scribbled notes in her hand. 'They have no explanation of what caused the accident. Barry was at the wheel and had an unblemished driving record. Blood tests for drugs and alcohol were negative. An autopsy revealed no medical problems such as heart attack or stroke. The roads were dry and visibility good. There was no skid and apparently no tyre blowout. The car was new and the model has no history of mechanical failure. No other vehicle was involved, but three people witnessed the accident and they all tell the same story. The car was travelling at between fifty and sixty miles an hour, and for no apparent reason it swung across two lanes, onto the hard shoulder, and slammed straight into the concrete support of an access bridge. One suggestion is suicide, because the car seemed to take such a direct aim.'

She paused, put away her notes and went on speaking, but without looking at any of them directly. They, too, avoided making eye contact with her. 'I don't think the suicide theory holds up for several reasons. For one thing I just don't believe it. For another, I found out that Drew and Barry were on their way to see a priest when it happened. His name is Father Caplan. He was Drew's parish priest in Queens before he was moved out to some parish near Ardmore three years ago. Drew had got very close to him when their child died. I spoke with him on the phone and he said that Drew had called him early that morning, around seven, and asked if she and Barry could come out and see him. She said it was urgent. He got the impression that they were both very frightened about something, but she wouldn't tell him what it was on the phone.'

She stopped, and now her gaze swept briefly over the four men in the room with her. 'That's all I've got.'

Sam pushed himself up from the arm of the sofa. He paced a few steps, then cleared his throat and said, 'Anybody have anything to say?'

Roger stroked his moustache and looked down at the floor. Pete sat with his hands between his knees. Ward Riley sat with legs crossed and arms folded, his gaze searching the ceiling.

'I suppose the question in front of us,' Ward said eventually, breaking a silence that was becoming charged with awkwardness, 'is whether we feel we should do something or not?'

'Such as?' Sam asked.

'Should we at least say something – to Drew and Barry's family? The police? Or this priest even? About what's been happening in the group?'

Once again nobody spoke. Then Sam said, 'We can't be sure that what happened in the group was what they were going to see this Father Caplan about.'

Roger gave a grunt of bleak amusement. 'Why don't we just assume it was?'

'All right,' Sam said after a moment, 'let's assume that we all know why they were going to see the priest. There's nothing we can say or do that would change the situation, or throw any light on it – at least not what most people would call light.'

'Can I say something?' Pete's voice was tight and trembled slightly, his chin still thrust down on his chest. 'There's something I can't get out of my mind. I have to say it.' He glanced up briefly. 'I'm sorry, Sam.'

'Say anything you like, Pete. That's what we're here for.'

'A few years ago I met a woman, it wasn't a relationship or anything, just somebody I knew. She claimed she'd been a witch when she was younger, but wasn't any more. She said never underestimate the power of witchcraft. They can kill you just as easily as look at

210

you. No one ever suspects, because it always seems like an accident. You fall down the stairs. Or your horse bolts. Or your car just goes off the road for no reason. What they do is make you see things that aren't there. You follow a road that looks normal, but it takes you over a cliff, or into a wall. Whatever. That's how they do it.'

He fell silent, hunched like a child in defiance of the chastisement he knew was coming. Sam walked behind the sofa and laid a reassuring hand on his shoulder. 'It's okay, Pete. We all feel the same way.'

'Do *you*?' Joanna didn't know that she was going to ask the question until it came from her lips almost as an accusation.

Sam looked at her in mild surprise but without resentment. 'I think there'd be something wrong with any of us if we didn't. It's natural that we're looking for reasons for Drew and Barry's death, and Maggie's. And of course, in view of what's been happening, we're looking in the obvious places. I think it's inevitable. But I think it's mistaken.'

'You think their deaths were just accidents?' Roger asked him. There was a rhetorical edge to the question, challenging Sam to show them just how far he was prepared to press his rationalism in the face of what was happening.

'I think it's clear,' Sam said, 'that Maggie's death was from natural causes, arguably precipitated by stress. But it's the coincidence of these other deaths that makes us look for a connection. And frankly I don't see the evidence for one.'

Joanna felt her patience snap. 'For God's sake, Sam, you're in denial about this.'

He looked at her with a flash of real concern. She felt guilty suddenly, as though she'd betrayed him. 'No,' he said, 'I'm just trying to look at it calmly and rationally. It's my job to look at things like this calmly and rationally. That's the whole point of this experiment.'

'Damn the experiment!' Her anger slipped out of her control only for an instant before she pulled it back. 'I'm sorry. All of it's as much my fault as anybody's – more.'

'It's nobody's fault,' Sam said.

'Whatever. Let's just agree we're going to abandon the experiment.'

Sam turned his hands up in a gesture of surrender. 'I've always said, that's up to each of us individually.' He looked around at them. 'Personally, I still intend to go on – with all of you, or some of you, or with different groups of volunteers. I think we've achieved an extraordinary breakthrough, and I'm reluctant to abandon it easily.'

'I don't think any of us is abandoning it easily,' Roger said quietly.

'But you are abandoning it?'

Now it was Sam pressing Roger to define where he stood.

Roger pushed himself up from the sofa and paced the few steps to the window where Joanna sat. The rain was beating hard and a faint mist of condensation had formed on the inside. He gazed out towards the vaguely discernible lights along the river.

'Do you remember what I said last time we had this discussion?' he asked, his back to the room. 'I said that whatever this phenomenon was that we'd started, the best thing we could do was stop it.' He turned. 'I feel that even more strongly now.'

'Aren't you curious about how this phenomenon works?' Sam asked.

'As a matter of fact, not very. I got involved in this thing for a number of reasons, some frivolous, some less so.' He crossed the room to where a jug of water and some tumblers stood on a tray, and poured himself a drink. 'You probably thought that my main aim was to prove you wrong and crow over your failure to produce any phenomena at all. On the contrary, I was fairly confident that we'd produce something. I was equally confident that it wouldn't make any sense, and that we wouldn't know how we were doing it. All of which is consistent with my view of the fundamental laws of nature – or, more precisely, the lack of them. Because I don't believe there are any fundamental laws, or any final theory. I think the only laws we'll ever find are the ones we impose on nature by the way we look at it.'

'The participatory universe,' Sam said, folding his arms and regarding his old teacher with a measure of ironic detachment. 'We make it up as we go along.'

Roger acknowledged with a dubious nod. 'As nutshells go, that one's a little restrictive. But yes, I do believe there's an argument to be made for that central role of consciousness in the universe.'

'This is all very interesting, but perhaps a little academic in the circumstances.' There was an icy sharpness in Joanna's voice that reflected the anger she suddenly felt towards both of them at that moment, and which she made no effort to conceal. 'What we need now is not some alternative theory of life, death, the universe and everything. What we need is to find out whether this "thing" we've created, or raised from wherever, whatever it is, had anything to do with these deaths.'

Pete cleared his throat. 'Why don't we ask it?'

Joanna looked at him. 'Are you serious?'

'If anybody's got a better idea . . .'

He looked around, inviting offers. There were none.

'The problem is,' Roger said, 'how would we know whether it was telling the truth or not?'

Pete acknowledged with a shrug that he had no answer. 'It's just a starting point. I would like to ask Adam, "Did you or did you not play any part in those deaths?" '

A sound like a hammer blow came from somewhere in the bookshelves behind where Pete sat. He sprang to his feet and whipped around. Everyone was looking at the same spot, but there was nothing to see.

For some moments they didn't breathe or move. Then Pete, almost inaudibly, said the thing they were all thinking. 'One rap for yes.'

Sam turned on him angrily. 'For God's sake, Pete, you of all people can't take this seriously. It's a nonsense – just a reflection of our own fears.'

Ward held up a hand. 'No – let's go on with it.'

'D'you really expect to find out anything like this?' The idea seemed to shock Sam more than anything had shocked him in a long time.

'Perhaps.'

Sam hesitated, then held up his hands to signal that he was backing off from any confrontation. 'All right, if that's how you all feel . . .'

Joanna aimed her question in the general direction of the bookshelves and the space around them. 'Who are you? Are you Cagliostro?'

Two sharp raps came from the same place as before.

'So you're Adam?'

One rap.

Sam turned away, dismissing the whole performance with a contemptuous scything of the air.

'Adam,' Joanna continued, ignoring Sam's disapproval, 'did you cause the deaths of Barry and Drew this morning?'

One rap – sharp, clear, unambiguous.

Shaken, but determined to go on, Joanna asked simply and directly, 'Why?' She realized at once that she had put a question not answerable by yes or no, and started to rephrase it. But Pete had already pulled a few blank pages from a shelf.

'We'll need a board,' he said. 'I'll write out an alphabet, we can improvise. Unless, that is, Sam happens to have—'

'I've nothing here.' Sam saw Pete hesitate, intimidated by the harshness of his tone. 'All right,' he added, 'go ahead, get on with it. Let's just do it.'

'I don't think that will be necessary.'

Something in the way Roger had spoken made them all turn to follow his gaze. He was looking at the window before which he had been standing a short time ago, and where Joanna had been seated until she'd jumped up and crossed the room with the rest of them.

The silvery-grey film of condensation on it now bore the imprint of three words written as though by an unseen finger in a forward-sloping, well-formed script, and followed by an exclamation mark.

'*Joie de vivre!*'

32

Her first impulse had been to run, to put as much distance as she could between herself and those taunting, somehow unspeakably evil words.

But distance, she realized, offered no escape. Physics spoke of a curved space-time continuum, but the thought had been a mere abstraction until now. Suddenly it described a trap, surreal, inescapable and singular, that she and all of them were in.

She looked around at the three men with her. Pete was white and standing with his arms pressed hard against his stomach, looking as though he might pitch forward any second in a faint. Ward Riley stood erect and preternaturally still, scarcely breathing as he gazed in grim silence at the ominous scrawl on the window. Roger Fullerton's shoulders had a slope to them that she had never seen before, reflecting, it seemed to her, a passivity made up in equal parts of shock and resignation, as though things had reached a point where further comment was impossible.

Only Sam reacted with what might, in more normal circumstances, have been called presence of mind. He had crossed the room and grabbed a camera almost before she realized he had moved, and was already clicking off shot after shot of the scrawled message, hopping from one side of the window to the other, moving in and out and shifting focus like some paparazzo ambushing his subject in a restaurant door.

Joanna felt her anger rise again. She wanted to scream at him, accuse him of all the things she had accused him of earlier – only more violently, because it was worse now. *The thing was actually in the room with them, turning their lives and everything they believed in upside down – and all he could do was take photographs, like some fool on a day out at the beach!*

She felt a gentle pressure on her arm. Roger Fullerton had come to her side, and she saw concern in his eyes. She thought how odd it was, funny almost, that a moment ago she had been watching him, and now she found him watching her. She opened her mouth, wanting to say something, make some joke about it; but all that emerged from her throat was a shuddering sound that ended in a sob. She didn't resist as Roger guided her to the sofa and settled her onto it. She looked at him and nodded mutely in thanks for his kindness. He reached out to brush a lock of hair from her face and tuck it behind her ear, a gesture of such tenderness that she felt her eyes sting with tears.

Then Sam was on his knees before her, looking up anxiously into her face. He took her hands in his.

'You all right . . .?'

'I'm fine.'

The words came out clearly, cleanly, their sound somehow filling the void inside her into which for a second she had been afraid she might implode. The worst had passed. Reality, or something approaching it, was beginning to return.

Her gaze moved to the camera that still hung around

217

Sam's neck. He gave a faint smile, sheepish and apologetic. 'I had to get pictures. It's not something you see every day.'

She wanted to laugh, but she didn't trust herself: she was afraid that something else might come out. So she just shook her head and held on to his hands a little tighter.

'Don't be afraid,' he said, 'it's nothing that can hurt us.'

It was the wrong thing to say. The anger she had felt earlier welled up in her again. She snatched her hands from his. 'How can you say that? It's already killed Maggie, and Drew and Barry!'

'We don't know that. We don't know it, and I don't believe it.'

The others were looking at them, but she felt no embarrassment. They were all in this together, and there was nothing that any of them could say that didn't affect them all.

'Then just what do you believe, Sam? Would you like to tell us what's going on?'

'We are doing it. Maggie died of a heart attack, Drew and Barry died in an accident. We are looking for reasons.' He pointed to the words on the window. 'We did that.'

She sat back in impatience and closed her eyes, too weary and frustrated to argue; and too unsure of her ground. Besides, what difference did it make? Things happened; understanding why they happened didn't change them.

There was a silence in the room, broken by Ward.

'*Joie de vivre*,' he murmured. 'It's an everyday French phrase for which there's no equivalent in English. We don't say "joy of living", we use Franglais. *Joie de vivre*.'

Pete too looked over at the window, where the words were still visible, although the condensation was beginning to evaporate. 'You'd have to be pretty much a psycho to use *joie de vivre* as a reason for killing somebody.'

Sam was on his feet again, moving in close to the window for a few last shots, using flash this time.

'Unless in some twisted way,' Joanna began, taking up Pete's remark, 'he saw his joy of living as somehow incompatible with that of his victims.'

Pete looked at her. 'Why would that be?'

'Other worlds.'

The remark had come from Roger, murmured more to himself than in response to Pete's question. He was sitting in an armchair, leaning forward with his elbows on his knees and gazing at his clasped hands.

Joanna said, 'Sorry, Roger?'

He straightened up and looked at them all. 'The world in which Adam exists cannot include a future in which there are people who will invent him. As Joanna says, it's a problem of compatibility.'

Sam turned from the window, removing the finished spool of film from his camera. 'Aren't we getting a little speculative here, Roger? Even by what you used to call the "liberal standards of paranormal research"?'

Roger smiled thinly. 'I was merely offering an idea.'

'One that sounds uncomfortably plausible,' Ward said quietly, 'and all the more reason why we have to terminate this thing.'

'But what are you saying "this thing" is?' Sam persisted, joining them.

'Basically, I share your view,' Ward said. 'Adam is something we've created. A thought-form. Whether he's

219

responsible for these deaths, I don't know. How would we prove it either way? But I do know that he or it – this force – is now beyond our control, and I think we need help if we're going to do something about that.'

Sam looked at him differently. 'Help?' An edge of suspicion had entered his voice. 'What kind of help exactly?'

Ward hesitated, tipping his head non-committally. 'I'd like to talk to some people.'

'May we know who?' The question wasn't put aggressively, but it implied what they were all thinking: that they were in this together and had a right to know who else he proposed involving.

Ward understood, and replied willingly. 'It's really just one person. I suppose you'd call him a guru, or a kind of one.' He gave a slight laugh. 'Although I don't know how many kinds there are. I've known him twenty years. He doesn't have a cult or a following – at least not one where the members know each other. I know a couple of people he's taught, one of whom passed him onto me. I don't know where he's from or where he lives. He travels all the time, can be anywhere in the world, but if you need him you'll always track him down with a few phone calls.'

'What does he do for an encore – sing a duet with himself, or perform a rain dance?' The question came from Roger, and the uncharacteristic sarcasm was jarring.

But Ward took no offence and looked over at him with a kind of dry amusement. 'In view of what we've all been through recently, I'm not about to apologize for anything I say that might sound marginally superstitious. Frankly, I'd have thought we were all beyond embarrassment on that score.' As he spoke his eyes flickered to the window, where the writing was still visible, though drops of condensation were running down the glass now, making dark lines through and underneath the words.

'Like it or not,' Ward said, 'something has taken root in our lives. It makes no rational sense, but we all know it's happened. Whether it killed Maggie, or Drew and Barry, I don't know. Whether it wants to kill all of us, or why . . . I don't know that, either. But I want to talk about it to this man, because he's the only person I can think of who'll maybe make sense of it.'

He crossed to where his overcoat lay on the back of a chair. Nobody spoke as he began to put it on. 'By the way,' he added, almost as an afterthought, 'he cured me of pancreatic cancer twelve years ago – solely through diet and meditation. Of course the medical profession say that's nonsense, it was a spontaneous remission that would have happened anyway, as they do in a small percentage of cases.' He shrugged. 'Who can say? I know what I believe.'

He took a step towards the door, then turned again. 'I'll be in touch in a couple of days, Sam. Three at the most.'

Roger started to follow him. 'I'll walk out with you, we can share a cab.'

He paused to say goodnight to Joanna, planting a kiss on her cheek, then carried on after Ward.

'Look, I didn't mean to belittle the idea. On the contrary, the way things are going in physics, I wouldn't be surprised if somebody discovered a new particle called "superstition" any day now . . .'

Pete left with them. Joanna stayed behind while Sam saw them out. She could not take her eyes off those three mysterious, mocking words daubed across the window

221

pane, their condensation trails suddenly reminding her of trickling blood. Finally, to break their spell, she stepped forward and vigorously wiped out all trace of them, using her hand and the sleeve of her dress. When Sam returned a moment later she was gathering up her things.

'You're leaving?'

She nodded briefly, saying nothing. He saw that the window was wiped clean, but he didn't comment.

'Please stay.'

'I really need to be on my own.'

He seemed to think about arguing, then decided against it and stepped aside to let her pass. 'By the way,' he said, 'your editor called me this afternoon.'

She stopped. 'Taylor Freestone? Why?'

'To offer funding for the department. Or at least a generous contribution. I wanted to thank you, but I haven't had a chance to until now.'

'You've nothing to thank me for. This is the first I've heard of it.'

'He said you'd told him about Barry and Drew. He wanted to offer his sympathies – and, apparently, make sure we stayed in business. He must really like what you're writing.'

'I suppose he must.' She started out again.

'I'm not in denial. You're wrong about that.' He had turned to keep her in view as she moved to the door, but he didn't follow her. 'I'm as disturbed by all this as you are.'

Again she stopped and turned to look back at him. 'But you're not afraid, are you? You're cool and detached. That's what I'm finding a little hard to live with.'

'I'm just refusing to jump to conclusions. I'm sorry if that upsets you.'

The protest in his voice was matched by the impatience of her reply. 'If this "thing" is responsible for those deaths, it's our fault. Why do I feel that doesn't worry you? You just accept it. The only question you ask yourself is how does it work?'

'The only question I ask is what evidence we have for believing that—'

'We don't have any evidence for anything!' Her anger boiled up again, but she controlled it with an effort. 'You said it yourself the other night! We're not a court of law. We're not repeating some experiment and confirming a result. We're caught up in something that none of us understand, and I'm frightened, Sam. Can't you understand that?'

'Of course I can,' he said, his tone conciliatory. 'I am too. We shouldn't be quarrelling like this. There's no reason.' He took a step towards her, but she backed away.

'No, don't . . . not now . . .'

She saw the hurt in his eyes, but there was nothing she could do about it. In a way that she couldn't change or as yet even get used to, she was coming to see him as the opposite of everything she'd thought he was. From being a lone visionary fighting against prejudice he had become a sceptic, splitting every hair and exploiting every loophole until all certainty dissolved into a cloud of doubt and ambiguity. She was weary of it all.

'Perhaps Roger's right,' she said. 'What we believe doesn't matter. There's no final theory.'

'It doesn't mean that what we believe is unimportant . . .'

'Tell me, Sam, what do you believe?'

'Believe?' He looked faintly surprised at the question.

223

'You mean about life, death, the universe and everything?'

She ignored the faint sarcasm in his voice and waited for an answer.

'I suppose,' he said after a moment, 'I believe, like Socrates, that the unexamined life is not worth living.'

'What about good and evil? Do you believe in them?'

'As opposing forces in constant war with one another?' He shook his head. 'No.'

She accepted the reply impassively. 'You know what I can't get out of my head?' she said. 'What Pete said about witches – how it happens.' She paused. 'But you'd call that just superstition, wouldn't you?'

He shrugged and offered another apologetic smile. 'Yes.'

They stood motionless, eyes locked across the space that separated them.

'Stay with me,' he said.

It was a plea, touching in its simplicity. But she shook her head.

'Not tonight. I'm going to take a pill and gamble on eight hours of oblivion making me feel human again.'

They kissed chastely at the elevator, but she refused to let him ride down with her. The rain had stopped and taxis, she insisted, would be plentiful this time of night. It wasn't so much that she wanted to get away from him, just that the need to be on her own was urgent now. She needed to think her own thoughts – or not think at all. Another presence, any presence, would be painful to her raw nerves.

'Christ,' she thought, as she counted off the floors through the gate of the descending elevator cage, 'what a mess. What an ugly, bloody, total mess.'

33

The funeral was three days later. Joanna and Sam went, and Pete with them. Roger was speaking at a conference to which he'd been committed for several months. Ward had left a message on Sam's machine the previous day, saying he was in Stockholm, where he had found the man he was looking for and would be in touch again soon.

Over a hundred family and friends turned out. Father Caplan, a short, plump, totally bald man in his sixties, gave an emotional address. There was a reception afterwards, but Joanna, Sam and Pete didn't go. They cabbed back to Manhattan, saying little.

Their presence at the ceremony had been accepted without question. No one had wanted to know how they had known Barry and Drew or what their association had been. The three of them had agreed beforehand that if they were questioned they would tell the truth. The fact that it didn't happen only strengthened Joanna's uncomfortable sense of being part of a conspiracy, cut off from the world by secrets she could never share.

Joanna got out first, on the corner of the block that housed the *Around Town* offices. She waved briefly but didn't look back as they drove off. She was thinking about the decision she had made that morning, and which she now had to carry through. She had made up her mind to tell Taylor Freestone that she couldn't go on with the assignment. If it wasn't for the fact that he had demanded to see the drafts that she'd already written, and had kept them, she would have destroyed all of them. This was not, she had decided for reasons that she did not fully understand, something that people should read about.

Taylor's secretary told her on the phone that the editor was in conference, but she would pass on the message that Joanna wanted to see him as soon as he was free. Twenty minutes later he walked into her office. It was a habit of his, whenever he wished to be sure of having the last word, to come to people instead of have them come to him. She wondered how he had guessed that this might turn into one of those conversations, and what last words he had carefully prepared to end it.

'I understand you wanted to see me,' he said, regarding her owlishly over his reading glasses.

She took a breath. 'I'm sorry, Taylor, but I want to drop the story.'

He looked at her for a while without expression. '*You* want to drop the story?' he said eventually, injecting a note of mild irony into his voice.

She corrected herself. 'All right – you will decide whether the story is dropped or not. I, however, have decided that I cannot carry on with it.'

'Do you mind telling me why?'

'I should have thought that was obvious,' she said flatly. 'You know what's been happening. Do you mind telling me why you gave Sam that money?'

He shrugged. 'I thought it seemed like a good cause, so I suggested it to the board's charity fund.'

'I just wondered why you hadn't asked me to convey your interest in Sam's work to him personally, since I'm the one who's been working with him. Or at least why you hadn't told me you were going to call him, instead of letting me find out from him. It made me look as though I hardly work here.'

He shrugged his shoulders again, this time apologetically. 'You're right. I really didn't think about it. I just wanted him to know that the magazine was behind him.'

'I suppose you imagine that if you pay him enough, he'll go on with this until we've all been killed? Is that your idea?'

'Let's just say I know a good story when I smell one. I shall ignore the rest of your question as being in morbidly poor taste.'

'Three people dead isn't poor taste, Taylor. It's a statistic that points in a depressingly obvious direction. Aren't you just a little afraid that this thing might reach out and touch you if you get too close? Giving money to keep things going like this,' she sucked in a breath through her teeth, 'you could be tempting fate.'

She saw a flash of uncertainty behind his eyes, suppressed at once, but not fast enough. She gave him a broad smile of triumph. 'But then you're not superstitious, are you, Taylor?'

He pursed his mouth and lowered his eyelids to indicate that he was growing bored with the conversation. 'Look,' he said, 'if you want off the story – all right. I'm not impressed by your professionalism – you wanted this assignment, but I can't force you to finish it. But I'll find someone who will.'

'Who?' It was a prospect that for some reason had not crossed her mind, and she asked the question in spite of every instinct shrieking at her not to, because she knew it gave an opening for Taylor Freestone to start undermining her decision and subverting her will, something for which he had a particular and sinuous gift.

'I don't know yet, I haven't decided. But whoever it is, I can tell you one thing that they'll have to put right.'

'What's that?' There was a note of defensive indignation in her voice that told him she had taken the bait.

'I think it's a mistake,' he said equably, as though discussing nothing more dramatic than some fine point of grammar, 'that you don't mention anywhere that you're going to bed with Sam Towne.'

Although the remark was unexpected, she managed neither to flinch nor blush and only blinked once. 'What makes you think I am?'

'Darling, I know when anybody's having an affair with anybody. It's one of the reasons I am where I am.' He continued to fix her with a languid stare. 'I'm not going to say it's unprofessional, exactly. It's not as though you're a doctor or a lawyer, somebody abusing a position of trust, though there are those who might question your judgement in the circumstances. Anyway, whoever takes over the story is going to have to write about that relationship – and speculate on the role it played on your decision to quit.'

She looked up at him squarely, steeling herself not to be manipulated in this way. 'You don't know what it's like, Taylor. I'm too afraid. I can't go any further.'

He leaned towards her, his hands spread wide on her desk. 'I know exactly what it's like – because you're writing about it brilliantly. What I want to know now is how it feels to come through this thing and out the other side, and I won't ever know that if you quit. More importantly, nor will you, Joanna. And I think you should know. I think you need to see this thing through.'

She gave a brief laugh with a touch of bitterness.

'What's so funny?'

'I was just thinking how true it was, Taylor – there really are good reasons why you're where you are. It's a compliment.'

He nodded thoughtfully. 'I'm right about the two of you, you know. It has to be part of the story.'

He took his hands from her desk and straightened up, folding his arms. 'I mean, when you've got one of the world's leading physicists offering to stand up and cheer for your team, the least you can do is admit you're humping the coach. Otherwise it'll only come out later and make you look dishonest. And that would damage the story – which would be a pity, because I think it deserves a Pulitzer.'

He peered down at her solemnly for another calculated moment. 'Anyway, I'm sure you'd rather write about this relationship yourself than have somebody else do it.'

She didn't say anything, but she must have communicated her acquiescence by body language, or perhaps just by her silence. At any rate, Taylor nodded his approval.

'I thought so,' he said, and went out – then popped his head back around the door. 'You don't have to say how big his cock is, just admit that you've seen it.'

For a while, alone, she just stared at the screen onto which she'd brought up the text. She didn't want to do this, but Freestone's blackmail left her no option. The trouble was she knew that he was right: hardened sceptics of the paranormal would seize on the revelation of this 'concealed relationship' as clear evidence of fraud. If only

229

out of respect for those three members of the group who had died, she was not going to let that happen.

An hour later she read through the changes she had made, which had proved easier than she had expected. Surprisingly, they made the whole thing more accessible, describing how on a human level she had found herself drawn into a sequence of events that she would have dismissed as impossible if they hadn't actually happened to her. The only thing she found difficult was figuring out what to say about the effect of those events on the relationship. The reason for that, of course, was that she didn't know herself. She was still pondering the question when her phone rang. It was Sam.

'We didn't get a chance to talk this morning. I need to see you, Joanna. Can we have dinner?'

'My parents are back from Europe. I'm going out for the weekend.'

'When are you coming back?'

'Maybe Sunday.'

'Meet me Sunday night . . .?'

She hesitated. She knew that her anger with him had been irrational the other night, and still was. It was wrong to blame him for what had happened; making him the scapegoat for her fears would solve nothing. Yet she was doing it and didn't know how to stop.

'Look,' he said, breaking the silence between them, 'nothing's changed in the way I feel about you. I love you, Joanna. I'm asking you not to turn your back and just walk away. At least talk to me.'

The simplicity of his plea touched her. She realized then that she still loved him, but something made it impossible for her to say the words – something impossible to define which only confused and unnerved her even more.

'I don't know what time I'll be back,' she said finally. 'I may stay till Monday. I'll call you – okay?'

'Sure, okay. Give my best to your parents, will you? I hope they had a great time.'

'Thanks, I'll tell them. I'll talk to you. 'Bye.'

''Bye, Joanna.'

She hung up and stared into space. What did she want? What was she looking for?

Of course she knew what she wanted more than anything: she wanted the nightmare to end and her life go back to what it had been before all this. But Sam had not been part of that life; he was inextricably part of 'all this', of what was happening now, and that created an incompatibility that she was powerless to resolve.

She remembered she had used that word the other night in Sam's apartment. Incompatibility. And Roger had agreed with her – that maybe, in some way that remained unclear, Adam's existence had become incompatible with theirs. It was a thought that made just enough sense to be frightening, yet not enough to be taken seriously by a sane person.

Yet she was a sane person, and she took it seriously. Was that just another incompatibility? Was she mad, or was it the world? And anyway, where was the line between the two; herself and the world? Was there any line at all?

A sudden and involuntary shudder ran through her, like one of those moments when you've unknowingly fallen asleep and suddenly tip forward in your chair. But she hadn't been asleep, just lost in the vicious circle of her thoughts. She took a deep breath, grateful for the

231

instinct that had shaken her free, and busied herself with what she had to do. She hit a key on her computer that would send the new draft through to Taylor Freestone. Then she looked at her watch. If she left now, she realized, she had time to go to her apartment and change out of her funeral clothes, and still catch a train before the rush hour started.

She hurried through the office without a backward glance or a word to anyone.

34

Her main preoccupation on the journey was what she was going to tell her parents. Like a teenager with some guilty secret, she knew that the whole truth would be a serious mistake. There would be worry and concern and the weekend would be ruined.

Already on the phone her mother had asked about Sam: were they still seeing each other, how was the project going that they'd been working on? Joanna had managed to avoid giving any straight answers, thereby creating the impression that the relationship had entered a troubled no-man's-land and was better not talked about for the time being. This had the secondary effect of putting the experiment itself, by association, mercifully off limits, something for which Joanna was profoundly grateful.

To Joanna, this weekend was something of a lifeline. It represented the essence of what she was trying desperately to cling to, that unquestioned and indefinable sense of belonging that came only from home and family, and which was so much taken for granted until it was no longer there. Now, with the shifting perspectives that had been happening around her, Joanna was beginning to lose that sense of normality, of belonging. More than anything in the world, she wanted it back. She wanted to wrap her old life around her like a warm blanket, and if she had to lie to prevent it being snatched away, then she would do so.

Her father met her off the train, driving her mother's station wagon, with Skip, their cross-breed terrier, in the back. The dog had stayed with neighbours while they were away, and was overjoyed at the prospect of a full family reunion. He sat on Joanna's knee and licked her face during the short drive home through the gathering darkness. She laughed and hugged and scolded him alternately, all the while keeping up a non-stop conversation with her father about places they'd been and people they'd met and meals they'd had.

As they pulled in through the gate the car's headlights swung over the shrubberies, herbaceous borders and plant-covered pergolas that surrounded the rambling clapboard house. The garage door swung open automatically, and closed behind them with a comforting, familiar thunk. Skip was already out of the car, turning in circles and yelping to celebrate their arrival.

Joanna hurried down the short passage to the house proper. Her mother opened the connecting door before she reached it, and they threw their arms around each other. Joanna closed her eyes and let it all flow over her – the warmth, the rich smells from the kitchen, a Mozart flute concerto coming from a radio somewhere in the distance. It was all as it should be, as she remembered it, as she always wanted it to be.

Moments later she was watching her mother check the slowly roasting chicken while her father handed her a glass of wine. The three of them drank to each other, to being together, to being who they were.

Her parents talked some more of where they'd been

and what they'd seen and done. 'We took some wonderful videos,' her mother said. 'We'll show you them after dinner.'

'Come back and watch our holiday movies – we'll pay you!'

Her father shot the words out of the side of his mouth. It was an old joke in the family, and Joanna whooped with laughter – perhaps too loudly in her anxiety to embrace all that was familiar and reassuring, because her mother stole a quick glance in her direction. She didn't break the rhythm of what she was doing or change the expression on her face, but Elizabeth Cross had sensed something, and Joanna knew it.

When they sat down to dinner, candlelight flickered on silverware and the polished table top, and the whole dining room was reflected in the long window that looked out upon impenetrable blackness, but where tomorrow the well-kept lawn, the flowerbeds and the bank of trees that dipped towards the river below would be visible.

They ate and drank with non-stop companionable chatter, enjoying being together in a way that Joanna knew few families were lucky enough to share. Despite that look of her mother's in the kitchen, there was no obvious strain, no sense of certain subjects being carefully avoided while guesses were made and conclusions discreetly drawn under cover of a blameless conversation. She knew that there would be a moment tomorrow, probably in the morning when she went shopping with her mother as she usually did, when questions would be asked and she would have to deal with them. But she was ready for that. She'd worked out a strategy. Nothing was going to spoil these precious few days.

'I'm sorry . . .!'

The apology came from Joanna's mother. She hadn't noticed Joanna's purse lying flat at one end of the sideboard, and had knocked it to the floor as she pushed the cheese board to make room for an empty salad bowl.

Joanna was also on her feet, clearing away plates. 'I'll get it,' her father said, sliding from his chair and down on one knee. Joanna thanked him, but didn't give the incident a second thought. There was nothing breakable in the purse, nothing of value to be lost or damaged.

Then she became aware of her father holding something that he was looking at with a troubled frown. She took a step closer, and recognized the folded white card with the unmistakable black border. Her heart missed a beat. Like a fool she'd left the printed funeral service from that morning in her purse.

'Somebody you know died?' he asked. 'It's today's date.' He looked up at her, concerned. 'You been to a funeral, Jo?'

'Oh, daddy!' She felt a burst of anger, banged down the plates she was carrying and snatched first the card and then her purse from him.

He was taken by surprise, a little shocked. 'I'm sorry, I didn't mean to pry. It just fell out.'

'I know, it's all right,' Joanna tried to sound contrite, but her manner was too brisk. She was trying to brush the incident aside, move on to other things.

It was not going to happen.

'Darling, who died?' Her mother's voice was full of sympathy, but the question was impossible to ignore.

Joanna gave her head a little shake, as though she didn't want to talk about this but was deferring to their interest. 'Drew and Barry Hearst,' she said, avoiding their eyes, 'two of Sam's group that I was working with. They were killed in a car crash a few days ago.'

'But how awful! And here we are chattering about our holiday . . .' Elizabeth Cross moved a few steps towards Joanna and took her daughter's hands in her own. 'I'm so sorry, darling, I feel awful.'

'You mustn't. That's why I didn't mention it. I didn't want to spread a cloud over the evening.'

'But were you close to them? Had they become good friends?'

'Not really. I was fond of them, of course, but I didn't really know them. I'd only been to their house once.'

Her father stood by awkwardly. 'I'm sorry, Jo. It was thoughtful of you to keep it to yourself, but you don't have to hide things from us, you know – not anything.'

Joanna felt suddenly ashamed. She should tell them the truth. She owed them that much. 'I know,' she said. 'I'd have mentioned it later.'

Another lie, and her mother sensed it. Behind the genuine concern in her voice Joanna detected a note of suspicion. Something didn't sound right to Elizabeth Cross and she wasn't ready to let the matter drop.

'But why didn't you say anything on the phone yesterday?'

'You were so excited and full of your vacation, it just seemed somehow not the time.'

Her mother moved her head to one side without shifting her gaze. It was a gesture that said, 'All right, what's really going on?'

Joanna felt a flutter of irrational panic, like a child caught in a lie. Then she thought angrily, I'm too old for this. I can do whatever I want. I don't have to answer to anybody.

'It was such a shock, especially after losing Maggie McBride, I just didn't want to talk about it.'

Why had she done that? She heard the words as though she hadn't spoken them. What strange combination of emotions had made her say that?

'Maggie McBride?' her mother echoed.

Too late now. She must go with what was happening, defy her own fears, drag them out into the open, expose them to the cold light of common sense. Her parents had made the dragons in her closets and the monsters under her bed disappear when she was a child, why shouldn't they do the same now?

'You remember – that lovely Scottish woman I told you about, I'm sure I did.'

'She's dead?'

'While you were away. Apparently she'd had a heart condition for some time.'

'When did she die?' This from her father, putting things together in his masculine, engineer's way, and looking at the bottom line.

Joanna glanced at him briefly, then tried to pretend she hadn't. She was caught. There was no way out now.

Her father repeated the question. 'When did Maggie die?'

'Last week. Friday.'

There, it was said. It was out of her hands now.

The frown of concern deepened on her father's brow. 'My God, Jo, that's three out of a group of ... how many?'

'Eight.'

'Three ... in one week?'

She suddenly realized it was still up to her. They weren't going to make it go away. She'd been right in the first place – she was the one who would have to protect them. The thought renewed her confidence, the way knowing that the worst has happened can give you strength because there's nothing else to be afraid of. What she had to do now was clear; simple, even.

'Obviously we're not going on. I mean we could, but out of respect – and we're all too upset.' She spoke boldly, in charge, putting everything into a sensible perspective. 'Mind you, we weren't getting very far. We were about to call it quits anyway.'

The lie was growing easier and more fluent as she developed it. She hated the feeling of driving a wedge between herself and the two people in the world whose closeness and support she most wanted at this moment, but she knew she had no choice. There just wasn't any other way to handle this.

'You say you weren't getting very far?' her father asked, wanting more detail.

Joanna made a gesture – open, dismissive, suggesting that the whole thing had turned out to be no more than a frivolous enterprise.

'Nothing aside from a few bumps and table knockings – which are actually far more common than you'd imagine. I've got enough for an article – at least, enough to work up into something readable. But I'm afraid it won't amount to anything very spectacular.'

That was a lie that would be brutally exposed when her article was eventually published, whether it was under her own byline or somebody else's. But she would worry about that later. For now all she cared about was protecting the brief sanctuary of these few days from the madness that surrounded her.

They stood facing each other across the room, she on one side of the table, her parents opposite.

'All the same,' her mother said in a voice filled with unspoken disquiet, 'three people dead . . . in just a few days . . .'

'Oh, come on, mom!' Joanna managed to force a kind of shocked, dismissive laugh that didn't sound too artificial. 'You're not trying to make something sinister out of that, are you? I mean, a heart attack and a road accident. It's a coincidence, and tragic – but nothing more.'

Stop now, she told herself, leave it there, you've said enough, any more will simply fan suspicion. 'Why don't I go make the coffee?' she said. It was something she often did at the end of a family dinner, her inestimable contribution, as she jokingly put it, to the evening. 'Then we can watch those videos. I really want to see them – and I swear you won't have to pay me!'

They sat in near silence as the bridges of the Seine, the Thames and the Tower of London drifted before them, and the intricately woven streets of Rome opened into their sudden, unexpected vistas. Joanna gave a whoop of recognition every time one parent or the other appeared on screen, applauded every well-framed shot, recalled some anecdote or character whenever a place she had visited with her parents in the past came into view.

It was a good performance, but a performance nonetheless. And she knew that her parents, from their own subdued response to her enthusiasm, recognized it as such.

But there were no more questions, and no awkwardness. Just a moment, alone with her mother, as they kissed goodnight, when Elizabeth Cross looked into her daughter's eyes with the intense and loving tenderness that only a parent can feel for a grown-up child out in the world alone, independent and beyond protection.

'You are all right, darling, aren't you?'

'Of course I am, mom. I'm fine, truly.'

'Because if anything happened to you, I don't think I could bear it.'

35

Joanna was surprised in the morning to realize how well she had slept. She opened her eyes just after eight, and pulled her blinds to reveal a perfect late fall day. She and her mother drove into town and parked by the Farmers' Market at the end of the high street. The bare branches of the trees around the parking lot were bleached almost white against a clear blue sky.

Inside the covered market Joanna sensed something festive about the crowd that morning, although it wasn't yet the holiday season. She followed her mother through the busy shoppers and the strolling couples and the family groups on their weekly outing.

Elizabeth Cross was brisk and businesslike, darting from vegetable to cheese to fruit stall, loading the cart that Joanna pushed. They only had a light lunch to think about because that evening they were dining with friends. There had been no mention of last night's conversation by either of her parents, for which Joanna was deeply grateful. It meant that she didn't have to put on a performance any more; the subject had been aired and got out of the way. She was beginning to feel that maybe she really could put these last weeks behind her and get her life back on track. Was that all it took? A change of air and some home cooking? It was hard to believe, but maybe if she tried hard enough to believe it . . .

'Why don't we save time?' her mother said, interrupting her thoughts. 'I can finish here while you go over to Clare Sexton's and pick up a couple of cushions I've been having made up. They're paid for, you just have to ask at the desk.'

Joanna relinquished the shopping cart to her mother and they agreed to meet in the parking lot in twenty minutes. Clare Sexton's was a fabric store that had been there for as long as Joanna could remember. She walked the three blocks to it, passing several people she knew well enough to exchange a friendly smile with or wave to through a window. It was a small town, in a way just a village. Nobody famous or fashionable lived there, but it was comfortable and well cared for. It wasn't a life that Joanna wanted, but she was glad that she came from it. These were decent people who wished no one any harm – on the contrary, who would help out if they could.

Clare Sexton's was in a row that had a couple of craft shops, a book store, and a new place decked out to look Victorian which sold imported soaps, perfumed candles and aromatic pot-pourris. The fabric store had a single bow-fronted window with fake antique glass, behind which materials of every kind and conceivable colour were arranged in a display of flamboyant theatrical flare.

Inside, the place was as bustling as everywhere else seemed to be that morning. The girl at the desk was busy wrapping several lengths of material for a couple who seemed thrilled with what they'd found. Clare Sexton herself, a slim, capable-looking woman with short blonde hair, waved at Joanna from a corner where she was occupied with another customer. Joanna mimed back that there was no hurry, and prepared to spend a few minutes looking around.

'What d'you think?' said a man's voice over her shoulder, so close that it almost made her jump. She turned to see a dark-haired man in his mid-thirties, wearing green corduroys and a stylish wool jacket. He was holding a piece of painted cardboard in one hand and a length of material in the other. 'Do these match, or am I colour blind?'

'I'd say,' she said, stepping back to evaluate them in a better light, 'that they match very well – assuming that's the colour you're painting your walls and you're looking for curtains.'

'Right first time,' he said with an amiable, slightly self-deprecating grin. He had a nice face, she thought: intelligent, like someone you could talk to.

'While we're on the subject, would you call this a yellow or an ochre?' He pointed to a stripe in the fabric. 'Silly, isn't it? I know they're different, but I never know where you draw the line between them. I think it's the visual equivalent of being tone deaf.'

'Definitely ochre,' she said firmly. 'Far too rich for yellow.'

'Okay,' he said, 'if you've got this in something plain, no pattern, I'm going to need quite a lot. I'm not sure how much, but maybe you can figure it out if I tell you . . .' He broke off because he could see she was waiting to interrupt him with an amused look on her face.

'I'm afraid I don't work here,' she said. 'I'd be very happy to help you, Clare's a friend of mine, but I don't know what they happen to have in right now.'

Colouring slightly from an embarrassment she found oddly endearing, he stuttered an apology. 'I'm sorry . . . silly of me . . . I don't know what made me think . . .'

'It's all right. I wish I could help.'

'Oh, you have. At least now I know what colour I'm looking for.'

'Where's the house you're doing up? Somewhere out here?'

'No. I rent a place out here, just a cabin, really. But I've just bought a house in Manhattan, a brownstone. Far too big, really, but it's the first place I've owned and I'm kind of enjoying myself.'

Looking past his shoulder she saw that the girl at the desk was free. Also, seeing the clock on the wall, she realized she would have to hurry if she was to meet her mother. 'I have to go,' she said. 'I hope you find what you're looking for.'

'Thanks, I'm sure I will. By the way, I'm Ralph Cazaubon.'

'Joanna Cross.'

They shook hands automatically.

'Cazaubon? Is that a French name?'

'Huguenot.'

He thanked her again for her advice, then she hurried to the desk before anybody else got there. Her mother's cushions were ready, and in a moment they were wrapped in tissue and slipped into dark green plastic bags. Clare came over just as Joanna turned to go. They kissed cheeks and exchanged greetings.

'It sounds like your parents had a fabulous time in Europe – how I envy them!'

'You're not the only one – but we can't all work for an airline.'

'Promise you'll call me before you come out next time – I want to arrange a dinner party.'

'I will. Got to rush now – mom's waiting. By the way, there's a rather nice man over there, needs help with his curtains.'

'Oh, where?' Clare turned to look, bright with anticipation.

But the man Joanna had been talking to was no longer there.

'He was just . . .' She looked around among the shifting groups of shoppers, but there was no sign of him.

'I guess he slipped out when my back was turned. You must've seen me with him – woollen jacket with a shawl collar, dark hair.'

Clare shook her head. 'Mind you, on mornings like this it's all a blur.' A woman across the shop fingering a silvery brocade caught her eye. 'Got to go. Don't forget – call me.'

'I will.'

As Joanna reached the car her mother finished packing things into the boot. They drove home chatting happily about nothing in particular. In the kitchen Joanna made another pot of coffee while her mother prepared a salad. Bob Cross returned from a game of golf full of stories about old friends he hadn't seen in a while. Lunch was pleasant and relaxed, after which Elizabeth Cross disappeared to a committee meeting for a fund-raising event she was involved with. Joanna left her father pottering in the garden and went over to see Sally Bishop, who she'd been at school with and who'd just had her third baby.

Shortly after seven-thirty that evening she and her

parents arrived for dinner at Isabel and Ned Carlisle's house, which was only a short drive down quiet lanes. Two other couples were already there, which made Joanna the odd one out, ninth in the party. The idea didn't trouble her at all, though when she glanced into the dining room she saw that the table was set for ten.

It crossed her mind that it would be an extraordinary coincidence if the tenth guest turned out to be Ralph Cazaubon. The thought had barely flashed through her consciousness before she dismissed it as absurd, and then reproached herself for entertaining the idea at all. Why had she thought of him? She didn't know him, and probably never would. And even if she did, there would almost certainly turn out to be something about him that she couldn't bear.

She remembered with an uneasy sense of *déjà vu* that she had thought the same way about Sam before getting involved with him. Was it some kind of mental process she went through before admitting to herself that she found someone attractive? Had it always been like that? She thought back to previous affairs, and couldn't find a pattern.

Anyway, why was she even thinking like this? In spite of all that had happened, she knew it wasn't over with Sam. The thought of him brought a fond smile to her lips. It had done her good to get away from everything, but she realized now how much she missed him and wanted to see him again.

It was a relief when the doorbell rang and Ned showed the tenth guest into the room, a retired interior decorator called Algernon, a sweet gay man she had known for years.

All the same, she found herself asking Isabel Carlisle

247

if she had ever met a man called Ralph Cazaubon in the neighbourhood. Ned and Isabel were very sociable and knew practically everyone. Isabel frowned.

'Cazaubon? No, I'm sure I'd have remembered an unusual name like that. Are you sure he lives here?'

'He rents a place. I don't know how much time he spends here.'

Isabel thought a moment more, then shook her head. 'I'm afraid it doesn't ring a bell at all.'

36

Sunday morning was as crisp and bright as the previous day, but with a few tufts of white cloud drifting high across the sky.

Joanna called up her old friends Annie and Bruce Murdoch who ran the riding school to see if they could fix her up with a horse for a couple of hours. It was no problem. She pulled on jeans and a couple of sweaters and drove over in her mother's car. Twenty minutes later, after cantering up through forest, she broke into a gallop on the long grassy ridge that led towards a dramatic outcrop of rock that seemed about to swoop out over the valley, and which was aptly named Eagle Rock.

It was there, still at full gallop, that she became aware of another rider converging at an angle. It was obvious that they were both headed for the same spot. Then, as they drew closer together, he waved. She recognized Ralph Cazaubon. They slowed to a trot and rode side by side.

'Fine horse,' she said, with a nod towards the impressive stallion he was riding. 'Is he yours?'

'Yep!' He patted the gleaming chestnut neck. 'This is Duke.'

'Where do you keep him?'

'Oh, he's looked after on a farm near me. Has a fine, easy life, don't you, Duke, old boy?'

The horse tossed his head as though in acknowledgement.

'What farm?' she asked. 'Maybe I know them.'

'I doubt it. Family called Waterford?'

She shook her head. 'You know, you're something of a mystery man,' she said. 'First of all you disappear yesterday morning just as I wanted to introduce you to my friend Clare Sexton – who'll find you all the yellow ochre you want, and more. Then last night I asked Isabel Carlisle if she knew you, and she didn't – and Isabel knows everybody within a twenty-mile radius, and their family histories.'

He laughed. 'I told you I just rent a place. And when I'm here I'm not very sociable.'

'What do you do? Lock yourself in your cabin and write poetry?'

'Close. Actually, I write music.'

'You're a composer? How interesting. What kind of music do you write?'

'Unperformed operas, mostly.' He gave a wry grin and looked over at her. 'Would you like a cup of coffee?'

She was surprised by the question, but he pulled a thermos from his jacket like a conjuror producing a white rabbit. They dismounted in the lee of Eagle Rock, protected from the wind. The thermos had a double top and he filled both cups. The coffee tasted good, and they sipped it enjoying the freshness of the air and the silence broken only by the wind and the chink of their horses' harnesses as they grazed on the short, fibrous grass.

'So,' she said, 'I suppose these unperformed operas are subsidized by TV jingles, movie scores and stuff like that.'

He laughed apologetically. 'Not exactly. To be honest, I'm kind of indulging myself. I inherited a little money, got lucky in the market, and now I do the one thing I really enjoy. But I'm hoping to make it pay some day. How about you?'

She told him briefly about her job on the magazine, the kind of thing she wrote, although she didn't mention Camp Starburst or anything about the Adam story. He knew of *Around Town*, though he didn't read it, but he said he'd make a point of picking up a copy soon and looking for her byline.

After that they were silent for a while, looking out over the valley as they finished their coffee. It was a desolate, dramatic spot, with few signs of civilization, just a scattering of farms, some isolated houses, and a small stone church on a hillside opposite.

As they watched, a congregation of no more than twelve or fifteen people emerged and got into the handful of vehicles parked by the churchyard gates. The priest came out after them, tall and thin in his black cassock, and climbed onto an ancient motorbike that popped and sputtered down the track and out of sight.

'That's a little unusual, isn't it?' Ralph said thoughtfully.

'A priest on a motorbike? Not specially.'

'No – I mean a church made of stone in this part of the world.'

'You'll find them, not that many.'

'Do you know that church?' he asked.

She shook her head. 'I've ridden past it, never paid it much attention.'

'Me neither. I'd be curious to take a closer look. Do you mind?'

'Not at all.'

They re-mounted, and twenty minutes later, having descended steeply to a stream and climbed the far side, they cantered to the gate of the now empty churchyard, left their horses, and strolled to the tiny building's wooden doors. It was even smaller than it looked from a distance, hardly more than a chapel.

'Mid-eighteenth century by the look of it,' Ralph said as they entered. 'Yep, there we are – 1770.' He pointed to a carving on the inside lintel.

After a few moments Joanna wandered back outside, while Ralph remained interested by some of the interior details. She looked around at the graves, on the whole remarkably well kept, but with their headstones tilted to odd angles as the earth that they were planted in had settled over the years. The inscriptions were all well worn, some of them impossible to decipher. It struck her as odd that so few people seemed to have been buried there in recent years. Then she saw that there was another part on the far side of a dividing wall, empty but for a handful of new graves at one end. The part that she was in, the older part, was long since full.

She became curious about just how far back the earliest graves went. The inscription in the church said 1770, but she had already noticed one headstone bearing the date of death as 1753 or 8; it was too worn by the elements to be sure, but suggested that there might have been a previous even smaller church on the site before the present one.

The oldest graves were all arranged along one side of the yard. At least a dozen of those headstones were totally illegible, but as she worked her way along she found the names and dates beginning to emerge as though from the mists of time. They were all carved from the same stone, and little prior to 1760 had survived two centuries of wind and rain.

It was then that she saw a name that stopped her in her tracks and took her breath away. Faint but unmistakable beneath a grey-green mossy growth were five letters that spelt 'Wyatt'.

Without taking her eyes from the word, she approached cautiously, as though it might be some kind of trap. Cautiously she reached out and dusted some of the encrusted deposit from the stone.

JOSEPH WYATT
1729–1794

Beloved Husband of Clarissa

Below that, obviously added later, she read:

CLARISSA WYATT
1733–1797

Wife of Joseph Wyatt

There was another line, obscured by dirt and grass in need of trimming. Her heart was in her mouth as she wiped it clean, and the words appeared:

Mother of Adam

The whinny of a horse a few yards away made her spin around. Both animals were suddenly restless and stamping their feet as though something had disturbed them – a rabbit or hare breaking cover, perhaps. There was nothing she could see.

She turned back to the grave, but her gaze fell, as though by chance but with such certitude as made her feel it had been guided there, upon another. How she could have missed it before was inexplicable. It seemed, now that she saw it, to obliterate all else in her field of vision.

It had a carved and bevelled tombstone running the full length of the grave. The stone itself was darker than the others, a kind of slate-grey, finer grained and more resistant to the weather. More than just a simple grave, it was a monument to its occupant. The inscription on the side was simple and plain to see.

ADAM WYATT

1761–1840

'Joie de Vivre'

She felt a sudden weakness in her legs and fell leadenly to her knees. Her hand reached out, unable to trust the evidence of her eyes until her fingers touched the lettering in the stone.

As they did, something happened inside her. It was as though a void had opened up at the centre of her being and she had disappeared into it. She lost all sense of who she was or why she was there, even of what had just happened. It was a kind of instant, but total and petrifying amnesia.

It was shock, of course. Just shock. The word pounded in her mind until she grabbed onto it and used it as a lifeline to haul herself back up from the abyss she had plunged into.

Only then did she become aware of Ralph kneeling at her side, peering into her face, concerned at what he saw there. She had not heard him approach, and now she realized he was trying to ask her something, but his words made no sense. Slowly her eyes focused on him, and with an act of will she spoke.

'I'm sorry . . .'

The words came out suddenly, as though she was apologizing for something she'd done, though she wasn't sure what. She struggled to get up, and he helped her to her feet. She brushed her clothing automatically and pushed her hair back from her face.

'Something's wrong,' he said. 'Tell me.'

She shook her head. It was less a refusal to answer than a plea that he not press the question. She was too confused, she couldn't think.

'I'm sorry,' she said, 'I have to go. I have to go now. I'm sorry.'

'Look, if there's anything I can do . . .'

But she was already striding swiftly from the grave-yard. He watched as she mounted her horse, wheeled about and rode off at a gallop. She didn't look back once.

It was almost, he thought, as though she was afraid to.

37

She didn't have her mobile with her, so she stopped off at a pay phone on the way back from the stables. Sam wasn't home, but she left a message on his machine saying that she had to see him urgently. She told him which train she would be on and asked him to meet her at the station if he could.

Fortunately she had told her parents that she would be returning to Manhattan on Sunday evening, so it wasn't a big problem explaining why she'd have to leave a little earlier than anticipated. She made up some story about having work to finish for an editorial conference in the morning.

Somehow she managed to keep the performance going through lunch, which was just herself and her parents. She talked a lot to avoid having them ask questions, any kind of questions. She didn't refer to the morning except to say that she'd ridden well and 'blown the cobwebs away'. She didn't mention her meeting with Ralph Cazaubon and only hoped that neither of her parents would run into him by some perverse chance and learn what had happened. She felt that her mother still suspected, as she had on the Friday night when she arrived, that something was not quite as it should be, though she had chosen not to pry. But there was a special warmth and a kind of anxiety in her embrace when they parted later.

'Look after yourself, darling. Come back soon, won't you?'

'Of course I will. It's been lovely. And I'm glad you had such a good time in Europe.'

She picked up her bag and turned to go. Her father was waiting in the car to drive her to the station. She could see him through the open door, but she couldn't get to him because Skip was suddenly there, barring her way by jumping and circling and barking hysterically.

'Skip, what is it, what's the matter?' She reached down to stroke him. He wagged his tail at the contact, but he wouldn't be consoled. Still he barked and jumped and blocked her path whenever she tried to pass through the door.

'Stop that! Come here! Skip!'

The dog ignored Elizabeth Cross's order.

'Skippy,' Joanna laughed, setting down her bag and catching the prancing dog's paws in her hands, 'what's wrong with you? I'll come back soon, I promise.'

Her father was out of the car now, holding open the door. 'Come on, Skip, you can come with us. Come on – in the back.'

But the dog didn't want to get into the car – didn't want anything, apparently, except to prevent Joanna leaving the house. Finally he had to be pushed back and forcibly shut in the hall. Even then he continued barking and scratching at the door.

'Separation trauma,' Joanna suggested as she drove off with her father. 'He's afraid we're all going to go away and leave him with the neighbours again.'

'Nonsense,' Bob Cross snorted. 'He had a better time

with George and Naomi and the children than he does at home. I'm having a labrador next time, all terriers are nuts.'

When they reached the station, her father got out of the car and walked her to the barrier, carrying her bag the way he always did. When they parted, he looked at her solemnly for a moment and said, 'You take care now.' Then he kissed her.

She hugged him, told him she loved him, thanked him for everything, and hurried to her train which was already waiting at the platform.

As soon as she got off the train at Grand Central, she saw Sam waiting for her at the barrier. They kissed, he took her bag, and they walked to where he'd parked his car, which he only ever used in Manhattan on weekends.

'So,' he said, 'what's the story?'

She sighed, rested her head against the back of her seat, and told him what had happened.

He listened in silence. By the time she'd finished he was pulling into Beekman Place, where he found a spot and parked. He switched off the engine and they sat in silence for a while.

'Well?' she said eventually, looking at him for some response.

He stared straight ahead through the windscreen. 'You're going to accuse me of being in denial again.'

'Go ahead,' she said, 'I'll live with it.'

'Let's go inside. I wouldn't turn down a large vodka on the rocks.'

Five minutes later he clinked the ice in his glass and stood by the window, gazing out as he brought his thoughts into focus.

'There's a couple of things strike me. First, you say

you've never been in that churchyard before. But you've lived around there all your life, or most of it. Who can say there wasn't some time in your childhood, an Easter service or a family picnic or whatever, something you've forgotten about – at least consciously?'

'But that means I would have had to invent Adam on my own, whereas in fact it was a group thing.' She leaned back on the sofa and twirled a glass of tonic in her hands.

'Well, maybe this hidden memory of yours was communicated telepathically or by some kind of suggestion to the rest of the group.'

She lifted a sceptical eyebrow. 'Okay. Next idea?'

'Maybe Adam Wyatt was a real historical figure that we'd all heard of but forgotten about, until he came up from our subconscious when we needed somebody.'

'But we checked and re-checked in every possible reference book. There was no mention of an Adam Wyatt anywhere.'

'Not in connection with Lafayette and the French Revolution. Maybe we made that connection.'

'The French connection – because he went around saying *joie de vivre* all the time, I suppose!'

Sam looked down into his drink, as though half hoping to find an answer there. Failing, he was gracious in defeat. 'You're right – I'm in denial.'

She smiled, and tipped her head towards the space on the sofa next to her. He sat down, then leaned over and kissed her.

'I'm glad you're back,' he said.

'So am I.'

They kissed again. Then he leaned back alongside her, his head next to hers, both of them staring at the ceiling. After a while she said softly, 'Sam . . .?'

'Yeah?'

'What the fuck have we done?'

'What we've done,' he said quietly, 'is create something – someone – in the past who didn't exist until we thought of him.'

There was a silence, as though he had thrown down a challenge and was awaiting her response.

'You know something?' she said. 'Even if it's true I don't believe it.'

He gave a thin smile and pushed himself up from the sofa. 'Don't take my word for it. "The existence of things consists of their being perceived." That's Bishop Berkeley, talking philosophy three hundred years ago. "The stuff of the world is mind stuff." That's Arthur Eddington, talking quantum physics this century. "The past has no existence except as it is recorded in the present." That's another physicist, John Wheeler, one of Roger's generation. "The universe is an inextricably-linked loop." That's the astronomer Fred Hoyle. They're all saying the same thing – that there's a connection between consciousness and whatever it's conscious of. When we look at something, we're looking at something we've partly created.' He was standing across the room now, looking at her, nursing his drink.

She lifted an eyebrow the way she always did when she wasn't convinced by something she was hearing. 'That sounds like a pretty smart way of keeping ourselves at the centre of everything.'

He gave a brief laugh. 'The trouble is that's where we seem to belong, and there's nothing we can do about it. Without consciousness at the centre, there is no universe. If consciousness had not evolved and become aware of everything around it and from which it had sprung, there

260

would have been no Big Bang, no galaxy formations, no suns, no planets, no earth, no fossils ... and finally no consciousness. A loop.'

'Then why doesn't it happen all the time? Why isn't everybody going around re-inventing the past, creating people who never existed?'

'Maybe that's exactly what's happening. Maybe we do it all the time, and that's what the past is.'

She thought about this for a moment. 'Maybe,' she said, getting to her feet, 'I'll have some of that vodka.'

She went through to the tiny kitchen and got some ice cubes from the fridge, then tipped a shot of alcohol over them and listened to them crack. She took a sip, letting the sensation brace her, enjoying the instantaneous sense of well-being that it gave, no less welcome for being illusory.

'If that's what we've done,' she said, crossing back into the sitting room, 'if we've created someone who never existed before we thought of him,' she looked at Sam, an odd smile playing at the corners of her mouth, 'then it's rather appropriate that we called him Adam, isn't it?'

'Maybe we knew what we were doing.'

'Oh, no!' She held up a hand in protest. 'I can swallow anything except the idea that we knew what we were doing!'

She took another sip of her drink. 'At least,' she said, 'we've finally got some concrete proof that paranormal phenomena exist.'

There was something in the way he looked at her that made her think he was about to burst into laughter. But he just shook his head, and gave a resigned smile. 'No, I'm afraid not.'

261

She frowned. 'How come?'

'Think about it. To anybody outside our group, who finds out about Adam now, it will seem that he must have always existed. How can we prove otherwise?'

Joanna's blood ran cold. She saw so totally the logic of what he had just said that she didn't even for a second question it.

'That's what that old woman said. *You're on your own now.* Maybe she really did put a curse on me, and this is all part of it.'

'Well, she didn't put a curse on me. Or Maggie, or Drew and Barry, or any of us in this thing with you. So I don't think that hypothesis stands up.'

'Good,' she said, 'I'm glad to hear it.' She took another sip of her drink, and was surprised to find that she'd already finished it. 'Have you heard any more from Ward?' she asked.

'I forgot to tell you with all this other stuff. He gets in tomorrow morning. I'm meeting him at his apartment at midday – can you make it?'

'Sure.'

'He wouldn't tell me what he's got, but he sounded excited – at least for Ward.'

38

They ate round the corner in a popular and noisy fish restaurant. Over a bottle of Chablis, they turned over what they'd been talking about a few more times and speculated about what Ward might have come up with.

'The first thing we do tomorrow,' Sam said, 'is start researching who exactly the Adam Wyatt in that grave was.'

'I'll get onto it. I've got some great people for fast research.'

She linked her arm through his as they walked slowly back to her apartment, heads down, each lost in private thoughts. They undressed and shared her tiny bathroom like a couple long familiar with each other's habits. It was only once they were in bed and their bodies touched beneath the sheets that the responses of the past few months were reawakened. To their surprise and mutual delight, they lost themselves in sheer physicality for what seemed half the night, falling at last into a sated and more contented sleep than either had imagined possible.

'So tell me,' he said over a hurried breakfast of cereal and coffee, 'have you decided yet what you're going to do about the story?'

She had told him over dinner about Taylor Freestone's ultimatum.

'I'm going to stick with it,' she said. 'I've come too far with it to quit. We all have.'

'I think it's the right choice,' he said, 'I'm glad.' He glanced at his watch. 'Gotta go. See you at twelve.'

He reached for his coat, they kissed, and he was gone. From her window she watched his car pull out of its space and head around the corner towards the dense traffic of First Avenue. As he disappeared from sight, her phone rang. She crossed to her desk and picked it up.

'Joanna?'

'Yes.'

'This is Ralph Cazaubon.'

She was surprised by the call, but even more by the strange sense of guilt that it provoked in her, as though just by talking to him she was somehow betraying Sam. It was absurd, of course, an irrational response that reminded her of what Sam had said about superstition the first time they met.

'Hello? Are you there? Don't tell me you've forgotten me already.'

'No . . . I'm sorry, I just wasn't . . . it's just a surprise.'

'I hope this isn't too early, but I wanted to catch you before you left for the office – that is if writers work in offices.'

'Sometimes. Not today, though.'

She wanted to ask how he'd got her number, then she remembered she was listed: Cross, J.E. Had she told him she lived in Beekman Place? She couldn't remember.

'I was a little worried about you yesterday. You rushed off so suddenly I was afraid something had happened.'

'No . . . not really . . . not *happened* exactly. I'm afraid it's something I can't explain.'

Which was truer than he knew, she thought.

'Well, as long as you're all right . . .'

'I'm fine.'

She was grateful that he didn't probe further.

'I was wondering,' he said, as though coming to the real point of his call, 'whether we might meet some time. Is lunch or dinner good for you this week?'

She hesitated. Not about whether to accept, but how to answer. 'I'm afraid not,' she said. 'It just isn't possible at the moment.'

Why had she said that? *At the moment?* Was she hedging her bets? She hated herself for the thought. She had spent the night with Sam, she loved him. And yet there was something about Ralph Cazaubon that was curiously intriguing. He was attractive, undeniably; but it was more than that, something that she couldn't put her finger on.

'I understand,' he said.

He didn't, of course, she told herself. How could he? But again he didn't ask questions or try to insist. He was respecting her privacy, while carefully leaving the door open.

'Can I give you my number . . .?'

He gave it without waiting for an answer. And she wrote it down on the pad she kept by her phone. As an afterthought he added his address – a few blocks up on the east side, between Park and Lexington. She knew the street well, full of large and very expensive brownstones.

'I'll be giving a party soon – when I've finished buying curtains and sorting out colours. Maybe you'll be able to come. I'll send you an invitation.'

'Thank you, I'd . . . I'd be happy to if I can.'

That was all right, wasn't it? She felt oddly

disconcerted. Not shy, exactly, not that teenage tongue-tied thing. There was just something about him, about this call, that wrong-footed her. It wasn't him so much as her. But what? Again it was something she couldn't pinpoint, something she would need to think about.

'Well, I'm sure you're busy,' he said. 'I won't keep you.' He sensed her awkwardness, she knew, and was trying to put her at ease. 'I'm sorry again if this was a little early. But I did want to be sure you were, you know, all right.'

'Thank you. I'm fine, really. You're very kind.'

When she hung up she made an effort to put him and the banal little conversation they'd just had out of her mind. She was angry with herself for being so distracted when she had important things to do. She picked up the phone and dialled a number that she knew by heart. A woman's voice answered sleepily.

'Ghislaine? You sound like you're still in bed.'

'I was working half the night. Had a deadline.'

'Good – I hope that means you're free to start something for me.'

Ghislaine Letts was the best researcher Joanna knew. An academic high-flyer with an IQ off the charts, she lacked the discipline or aptitude to hold down any kind of routine job. By rights she ought to have been writing learned tomes or directing the fortunes of mankind in one arena or another; instead she was living in a cramped apartment in the Village and fighting an eating disorder that kept her weight seesawing between stick-thin and hopelessly obese, and which would one day kill her if she didn't get on top of it. Meanwhile, she was Joanna's friend and secret weapon whenever she needed to find out something that seemed beyond the limits of human ingenuity to discover.

'Shoot,' said Ghislaine, stifling a yawn.

'All I've got is a name, dates, and a graveyard . . .'

39

Ward Riley, Joanna realized as she entered his apartment for the first time, must be a very rich man indeed. He lived in the Dakota Building, a neo-Gothic pile on Central Park West, built towards the end of the last century and one of the most prestigious addresses in Manhattan. It was famous as the place where John Lennon was shot, and also as the location for the film *Rosemary's Baby* in the sixties. And to people like Joanna who liked to read occasionally, it was also the setting of Jack Finney's marvellous novel about time travel, *Time and Again*. A place, as she said to herself, with interesting associations.

A Chinese manservant showed her into a sitting room which was high-ceilinged and light with a commanding view over the park. The place had a distinctly oriental flavour, with everything in it – antique bronzes, carvings, lacquered work and delicately coloured paintings – giving the impression of having been chosen with fastidious and exquisite care.

Ward and Sam were already in conversation. They rose to greet her. Ward, with his usual formal courtesy, shook her hand and asked if she would like coffee, which they were drinking, or anything else. She said no thank you, and sensed rather than saw the manservant discreetly withdraw, leaving them to talk in private.

'Well,' she said, taking a seat on a long sofa with her back to the light, 'I gather you were in Sweden. Did you find the man you were looking for?'

He nodded almost imperceptibly. 'As I said, he's never hard to find when you need him. He was holding a symposium for a group of bankers and industrialists in a castle near Stockholm.'

'Just your average group of pilgrims on the hard road to enlightenment?'

The remark was more ironic than malicious. Ward smiled faintly.

'Shahan says – that's his name, Shahan – Shahan says that self-denial has no meaning once the self is properly understood.'

'Well, maybe he's right,' she responded equably. 'I wouldn't want to give him an argument right now.' She glanced at Sam. 'Did you tell Ward about the grave?'

'Yes. But only just before you arrived.' He looked at the older man. 'I'm not sure yet what his reaction is.'

Ward answered cautiously. 'I'm not sure yet myself. It's not inconsistent with what's known of these phenomena.' He looked at Joanna. 'I shall be curious to see what your research into this grave turns up.'

'Was Shahan familiar with "these phenomena"?' she asked.

'Indeed, yes. He has no personal experience, but he quoted texts on the subject written nearly three thousand years ago. As I think we were all aware, the phenomena are as old as recorded time.'

'And did he think,' she continued, 'that Adam could have caused the deaths of Maggie, and Drew and Barry?'

Ward again hesitated over his reply. 'Caused, perhaps, is too strong a word. The phenomenon is powerful, and potentially destructive. But it's a destructiveness more of the kind that you and Roger talked about – an incompatibility more than outright malevolence. It's a thought-form, made of energy – our energy. And energy is finite. It can't be in two places, doing two things at once. In the end either the *tulpa* will exist, or its creators will. But not both.'

There was a silence as they absorbed the implications of Ward's somewhat apocalyptic statement. Sam sat staring into space, hands cupped beneath his chin in an attitude almost of prayer.

'What I'd like to know,' he said, 'is why this has happened. To us. This group. This experiment. Why didn't Adam just fade out when we wanted him to? What's made him hang on to his existence like this?'

'I get the feeling he's not just hanging on to it,' Joanna said quietly, 'he's fighting back.' She turned to Ward. 'Did Shahan think there was anything at all we could do?'

Ward pulled a long white envelope from inside his jacket. Even though he had stepped off an international flight only hours ago, he wore as usual an impeccable suit, silk shirt and tie.

'In here,' he said, 'I have a mantra. It's a very particular form of mantra, called a *paritta*: a protective rite. They're used widely throughout Tibet and eastern Asia to ward off danger and disease, and exorcize evil spirits.'

Joanna watched Sam as he listened to Ward. She could see that he was torn between the belief he wanted to have and the doubts he instinctively felt towards formal ritual.

'*Paritta?*' he said. 'It sounds like something you might get in a Mexican restaurant. D'you think it can work in New York?'

'Why not?' Ward said. 'New York is where Adam was created.'

Sam pursed his lips and shrugged. 'I'm open to anything . . .'

The ghost of a smile passed over Ward's face. 'Fortunately this isn't something you have to believe in to make work. You simply have to perform the ritual in the correct way at the appropriate time. But there must be no deviation from the form laid down.'

'So what is this mantra?' Sam asked, glancing at the envelope in Ward's hand.

'I can't tell you – yet. After he wrote it down, Shahan sealed this envelope himself. It must not be opened, and what is written down must not be spoken, until all five of us are gathered in the place where we created Adam. Otherwise,' he returned the envelope to his inside jacket pocket, 'whatever force the *paritta* has will be lost, and with it quite possibly our struggle against Adam.'

Sam spread his hands in a way that implied he would go along with whatever Ward wanted, regardless of his personal reservations. Ward inclined his head in acknowledgement.

'I'm sorry if these restrictions seem irritating or even naïve, but I'm afraid they're an important part of the ritual. I've taken the liberty of calling Roger. He can get in from Princeton by six. If it's agreeable to both of you, and of course Pete, I suggest we meet in Adam's room at the lab.'

The phone in Joanna's purse buzzed. She excused herself and answered it. It was Ghislaine.

'You said this was a rush job, so I thought you'd like to hear what I've come up with so far.'

Joanna covered the mouthpiece and whispered to the

two men watching her, 'It's my researcher. She's got something.'

Ghislaine's voice continued in her ear. 'It's just what I've been able to pull from various sources, mainly ones I can access on the net. I'll have something fuller in a couple of days.'

'It's okay, just give me what you have.'

'It's probably easier if I e-mail it. Where d'you want me to send it?'

Five minutes later the three of them were gathered around the PC on the glass-topped desk in Ward's study. They watched as the words scrolled up the screen and were simultaneously printed out alongside.

ADAM WYATT – Colourful adventurer who won patronage of Marquis de Lafayette, commander of French troops assisting rebel colonies in American War of Independence. Returned to France with Lafayette, where he married into aristocratic family – his wife was member of Queen Marie-Antoinette's inner circle at court. Ultimately fell foul of the revolution, and he and his wife were sentenced to death. Wife apparently executed, but for reasons not entirely clear Wyatt given last-minute reprieve and went free. Settled in England, where he made a second marriage to wealthy heiress in 1795. After her death in 1799 he returned to America a rich man, made a further large fortune in banking, married a much younger girl (surprise, surprise!) who bore him five children and survived him by several years.

That's the digest. Now here's the interesting part that I'm still following up. There were suggestions in various quarters that Adam Wyatt was not entirely what he appeared to be. Two men claimed he staged the incident that won him Lafayette's approval – something about a runaway horse that threatened to give away strategic positions the night before Yorktown. If true, that means he deliberately risked American and French lives, and maybe the battle, in order to get in solid with Lafayette. Apparent motive seems to have been, in part at least, usual one of pregnant girl back home and brothers with shotguns. Truth of allegations unknown. All that is known is that remaining accuser still alive on Wyatt's return in 1799 was murdered shortly after.

It also seems that Wyatt forfeited the support of Lafayette some time after reaching Paris. Having married into a family with which Lafayette was connected, he proceeded to have many affairs and get into very questionable company – hints of black magic among other things. His name is coupled in a number of references with the Marquis de Sade, the mysterious and almost equally weird Count de Saint-Germain, and in particular with an old swindler called Cagliostro, supposedly an alchemist and magician, who got thrown into jail over a famous scam called the Diamond Necklace Affair.

The bones of that affair are that Wyatt and Cagliostro persuaded a certain Cardinal Rohan, who needed a political alliance with the queen, that they could arrange it for him. All he, the cardinal, had to do was purchase a very expensive diamond necklace on behalf of the queen that she thought it would be indiscreet to purchase herself – on account of such extravagance being bad PR with people starving in the streets, etc. The cardinal fell for it, and handed the necklace over to some mistress of Wyatt's who impersonated the queen in a secret meeting. There is a suggestion that Rohan might have been either drugged or hypnotized by Cagliostro to fall for this imposture. Needless to say, the necklace was never seen again.

The idea had been that the cardinal, who was thought to be wealthy, would write off the money rather than look a fool. But it turned out he was broke and couldn't pay the jeweller. When the shit hit the fan, Wyatt somehow got away scot-free, while Cagliostro took the fall and went to jail. It may be they made some deal, with Wyatt using his (or his wife's) influence at court to get Cagliostro's sentence commuted to banishment. Thereafter Cagliostro went to Italy, and Wyatt stayed on in Paris with his long-suffering wife, until the revolution and her death.

There is a suggestion, which I'm going into, that he might have murdered his English wife, and possibly her brother, before returning to America. But nothing was ever proved.

This guy sounds like the original all American hero – right? Incidentally, if you're planning to write about him, it might be interesting to find out where his descendants are now and what they're called – and whether any of that fortune still exists. I'm having Jenny Sterns, who sometimes helps me out, do genealogical checks – assuming you're not going to nickle and dime me on this as you're in a hurry. Will keep you informed.

Love,
G.

Ward had his manservant prepare a lunch of omelettes and salad. Sam talked about the work of a researcher called Helmut Schmidt, who had used pre-recorded random events in the kind of experiments that Joanna had seen demonstrated in the lab when Sam first showed her around. According to Schmidt's results it appeared that subjects were able to influence those random events retroactively: patterns generated months earlier appeared to correspond to an influence exerted only after, sometimes long after, they had been recorded. If true, Sam argued, such results mirrored in a small way what seemed to have happened with Adam.

'There's an essay on time by the Buddhist writer Alan Watts,' Ward said, 'that reflects this whole notion. He says that we tend to think of everything, including ourselves, as creations of the past, driven along by events that have already happened. But that's an illusion. It's not the present that comes out of the past, but the past that comes out of the present. We see it every day. For example, if I say, "The bark of a tree," you don't know what "bark" means until I get to "tree". It could have been the bark of a dog. Or take a line of poetry: "They went and told the sexton, and the sexton tolled the bell." You don't know what the first "told" means, or even how it's spelled, until you get to "sexton". And you don't know that the second "tolled" is any different until you get to "bell".'

'But the Adam we created in the present was a decent man,' Joanna protested, 'so it was the past that changed him.'

'We created someone who had to survive in the time and place we put him in,' Ward replied, 'and we showed him how to do it.'

'We didn't exactly teach him how to steal and kill,' she said.

Sam put down his fork and leaned back, obviously

having little appetite. 'Don't you remember Maggie's unease about involving our nice, clean-living young Adam with undesirables like De Sade and Cagliostro? It looks like she had a point.'

'My fault, I'm afraid,' Ward said. 'I was the one who brought their names up.'

'But that's just it,' Joanna said impatiently. 'They were only names. How can names have that kind of power?'

Ward gave another of his faint smiles. 'It's been said that the heart of all magic is knowing the true names of things. If you know the true name of your enemy, you have power over him. And if you know the true names of the gods, they must lend you their power.'

Joanna had placed her phone on the table next to her. Now it rang and she reached for it. Ghislaine's familiar, rapid-fire voice launched straight into the subject without preliminaries.

'Okay, that family tree we talked about – Jenny's come up with some interesting names. One in particular. Very respectable, very old money.'

Both men saw the colour drain from Joanna's face as she listened, barely saying a word. When the conversation ended, she put the phone down and sat in silence, staring at her half-eaten omelette, saying nothing.

'Joanna . . .? Darling . . .?'

When she didn't respond, Sam reached out for her hand. She jumped at his touch.

'What is it?' he asked, concerned.

'I'm sorry . . . I'm all right . . . it's just . . .'

She turned her face to him. He could see shock in her eyes. And fear.

'Tell me.'

'Adam's granddaughter – one of them – married into

a family called Cazaubon. It cemented the merging of two very powerful banking families.'

'Cazaubon,' Ward murmured. 'I know that family – well, one branch of it, anyway. Huguenots originally, fled from France in the late seventeenth century to escape persecution by the Catholics.'

She turned her head and focused on him. 'D'you know a Ralph Cazaubon?'

'Ralph Cazaubon?' Ward thought for a moment, then shook his head. 'No, I don't believe I do.'

'In his thirties, obviously has money – it must be the same family.'

'Who is this Ralph Cazaubon?' Sam asked, a note of suspicion in his voice now.

Joanna turned back to him, oblivious of anything except the chilling sense of unease that had been creeping over her since Ghislaine spoke the name.

'He was at the grave,' she said. 'I'd met him the day before, quite by accident. But the next day, Sunday morning, he was there when I found Adam's grave.' She continued to stare at Sam, though no longer really focusing on him as the implications of what she was saying compounded in her mind. 'He even phoned me this morning.'

'Phoned you?' Sam echoed. 'What for?'

'He wanted to . . . say hello.' She made a vague gesture, feeling guilty suddenly, as though she was hiding something. 'He asked if we could have lunch . . .'

She was going to say that she'd refused, but Sam spoke before she could get the words out. 'D'you have his number?' he asked.

'No, I . . . it's in my apartment.'

'He must be listed.' He reached for her phone. 'May I?'

'Go ahead.'

He dialled inquiries, gave the name and the street and the number of the house, which Joanna found she could remember. There was nobody of that name listed at that address. He put the phone down.

'Maybe it's listed under a different name,' she said. 'He's only just moved in.'

Sam thought a moment, then got abruptly to his feet. 'I'm going over there.'

'I'll come with you.'

They gathered up their things quickly, thanked Ward for lunch, then asked almost as an afterthought if he'd like to accompany them. Sensing perhaps that it would be better if they did this alone, he said he needed to get some rest before the evening. They confirmed that they would all meet at the lab at six.

Fifteen minutes later they got out of a cab on Park Avenue, preferring to walk the last few yards rather than make a slow crawl around two blocks in the one-way system. They looked for numbers to work out which side of the street the house must be on. Having determined that it must be on the south side, they moved to the edge of the sidewalk and waited for a break in the traffic. Just as they were about to step off the kerb, Joanna grabbed Sam's arm hard enough to make him almost lose his balance.

'What on earth . . .?' he started to say, but then saw she had a hand to her mouth as though to stifle a gasp and was staring at something across the street.

He followed her gaze, and saw an elderly couple getting into a smart black town car while a driver held open the door for them. They were both short, the woman wearing the kind of expensive fur coat that would draw stares of disapproval and even open hostility in many places these days, and the man a camel-hair coat and black fur hat. They were glimpsed for only a second before they disappeared into the car's interior.

Perplexed by Joanna's reaction, Sam turned to her, intending to ask again what was wrong. But her gaze was so strangely intense that he remained silent, watching with her as the car drove off. As it passed them, he discerned two vague silhouettes gazing impassively ahead; then it was swallowed up into the flow of traffic going west towards the park.

Still she clung on to him in fear, her eyes fixed on the disappearing car. He had to speak her name twice before she looked at him.

'Joanna? Joanna, what is it? Who were they?'

'Ellie and Murray Ray.' Her voice was flat, like someone in shock, unable to connect with what was happening.

'Ellie and Murray Ray? The couple from Camp Starburst?'

She nodded, mute.

'But you told me he was dead.'

'Yes.'

He paused, taking in what he'd just heard. 'So obviously she lied to you. That first day we met, you and I, the old woman had just told you he was dead. Obviously she lied.'

Joanna shook her head. 'I checked. I had someone call the hospital.' She looked at him, her eyes seeming to search his face, yet unable to focus. 'Murray Ray died.'

They continued looking at each other, neither knowing what to say.

'Then that wasn't him,' Sam said, suddenly and

decisively. 'We were ... how many yards? Twenty? Thirty? It probably wasn't her either. You couldn't be sure of recognizing anybody at this distance. You saw two people who looked a little like them, and you imagined it was them.'

She was silent, still pale and clearly shaken, but he felt her grip slacken on his arm.

'Yes, you're right,' she said, her voice little more than a whisper. 'I must have been mistaken. It was just so weird for a second.'

He put his arm protectively around her, and they crossed the street. They walked briskly past the spot where they'd seen the couple getting into their car. Joanna turned to look, as though the ghost of the event somehow still lingered in the air. Sam's attention was on the houses they were passing, calculating which one up ahead must be the number they were looking for.

'One-three-nine ... right here,' he said. They slowed outside a big brownstone similar to all the others in the street – except that the windows of this one were shuttered, the paintwork drab and peeling, the whole place exuding an air of neglect as though it hadn't been lived in for years.

'This can't be it,' she said.

'It has to be. There's one-three-seven on one side of it, one-four-one on the other. Are you sure it was this street?'

'Positive.'

'Well, if anybody's living here, they want to keep it a secret.'

There was a clatter from the basement area. Two cats scuttled out of a garbage pail that lay on its side amidst an accumulation of debris that nobody had cleaned out for a long time. The basement window had bars set into the wall and wooden shutters inside like the rest of the house.

'I told you,' she said feebly, 'he's just moving in. When I met him on Saturday he was buying curtains.'

Sam looked up at the house, its stonework streaked and stained from long neglect, its windows grimy and unwashed. 'It's going to be a while,' he said, 'before anybody needs curtains for this place.'

41

'Is this going to be a long business?' Roger asked. He was subdued, more so than Joanna had ever seen him.

'Not much more than an hour, I should think,' Ward said.

They were in Adam's room in the basement of the lab, all of them except Pete, who was out apartment-hunting. He had promised to be there by six, but it was now ten after.

Roger had listened to the story of the grave, sitting impassively on the old sofa with his arms stretched out along the back. He made no comment apart from a nod of acknowledgement. Nor did the coda about the empty house provoke a response. He seemed resigned to any and whatever fresh absurdities were thrown up by the situation they were in.

'So now we try exorcism,' he said, and gave a loud sniff – whether out of disapproval or the beginnings of a cold was hard to tell, but he produced a green and white spotted handkerchief and blew his nose loudly.

'D'you remember what you said when Drew talked about exorcism?' Joanna asked him. 'You said something about complementarity – two ways of describing the same thing.'

'Yes, I do remember,' Roger said quietly, tucking the

handkerchief back in the breast pocket of his old but immaculate tweed suit. 'I remember very well – though I'm beginning to think that limiting ourselves to only two ways of describing what's happening here may be unduly modest.'

Sam looked at his watch. 'Time Pete was here. He swore he wouldn't be late.' He walked over to where new video and audio equipment had been set up – paid for, Joanna reflected, by *Around Town* magazine – and began to check it over.

'By the way,' he said, almost as an afterthought, 'I'm proposing to record this – it's still a legitimate part of the experiment. Ward has no objections. I trust neither of you has.'

Roger waved a hand indifferently. Joanna said of course she hadn't. She watched Sam as he bent over plugs and switches and control units with tiny flickering lights. There was a hunch to his shoulders, a concentrated smallness in his movements, like a man driven in on himself by circumstances but determined to fight back. She felt a sudden surge of tenderness for him, an impulse to put her arms around him, to tell him she believed in him and loved him. But she held back. It wasn't the time.

Sam looked at his watch again. 'Almost twenty past. Where the hell's Pete?'

A phone rang harshly, close enough to where Joanna stood to startle her. It was an old-style wall phone which had always been there, but which she had never seen used. As she was the person closest to it, she instinctively reached out to answer it. Then, equally instinctively, she checked herself and looked over towards Sam in case he preferred to answer it himself. When he made no move, she picked up the handset and said hello.

There was bad static on the line with a voice behind it that she couldn't make out.

'I'm sorry,' she said, 'I can't hear you. Maybe you should call back.'

The static cleared slightly. She thought she recognized Pete's voice, but couldn't make out what he was saying.

'Pete? Is that you? Where are you?'

She glanced at the others in the room, all watching her, and gestured that she still couldn't hear.

'What?' she said into the mouthpiece. 'Say again.'

His words came more slowly now, carefully formed, deliberate. Yet still she couldn't understand them.

'My what . . .?' she said, then repeating what she heard, 'my . . . a tam . . . can . . . I'm sorry, Pete, I just can't . . .'

Suddenly Sam was at her side, taking the phone from her. In his other hand he held a small cassette recorder like the one she used for interviews.

'Pete, this is Sam. Just say it, Pete. Say what you're trying to say.'

He started the recorder and held it to the earpiece as he listened. The others watched with an odd fascination, sensing that something strange was happening but having no idea what. Even Joanna, though she was almost as close to the phone as Sam, couldn't hear anything beyond an incoherent murmur coming through the static.

Sam kept the phone and the recorder close to his ear until it seemed that what he had been listening to had ended. 'Pete . . .?' he said. 'Pete, are you still there . . .?'

He waited a moment more, then switched off the recorder and hung up the phone.

'What did he say?' Roger demanded when Sam didn't move or speak. 'Where is he?'

284

Sam rewound the tape. They all heard the high-pitched twittering of a voice in fast reverse. When it came to a stop he pressed play, and turned up the volume.

The static was still there, all but drowning out the voice. But it was undeniably Pete's voice, or one very like it. And the words were clear, though ostensibly nonsense.

'Maya . . . tan . . . kee . . . noh . . . maya . . . tan . . . kee . . . noh . . . maya . . . tan . . .'

Joanna saw Ward Riley's face grow tense and the colour drain from it as he listened. It seemed as though an understanding of what he was hearing was slowly dawning on him – not certainty, perhaps, but a terrible suspicion. His hand went to his pocket and was visibly unsteady as he withdrew the envelope he'd shown them at lunch.

While Pete's thin and tinny voice continued to chant out the strange sounds from the tape recorder, Ward tore open the envelope and unfolded the piece of paper it contained.

His eyes ran over the lines written on it several times. Then he swayed slightly. Joanna thought he was about to faint, but he got a grip on himself, took a deep, unsteady breath, crumpled the piece of paper he was holding, and let it fall to the floor.

Without a word he started for the stairs, walking like a man – it was the only comparison that came into Joanna's mind – who had just received a sentence of death.

'Ward . . .?'

He paid no attention to Sam's voice.

'Ward, what is it . . .?'

This time he paused, turning to look back at the three

of them. He threw out his arms slightly and let them fall back to his sides. It was a gesture of despair.

'There's no point,' he said, 'not now. It's over. I'm sorry.'

He turned away and continued up the stairs. No one called him back or tried to stop him. There was a terrible finality in the moment.

Sam picked up the crumpled piece of paper. Roger moved across and peered over his arm at it.

'What does it say?' Joanna asked.

Sam read the words woodenly, without expression. They made no sense and she didn't know how they were spelt. All she knew was they were the same words that Pete had spoken over the phone.

'Not even Ward knew what was written on that paper,' she murmured. 'How did Pete know that?'

In reply, Sam picked up the wall phone and handed it to her. 'Listen,' he said.

Puzzled, she put it to her ear. There was no dial tone. The line was dead.

'To my knowledge that phone's been disconnected for two years,' Sam said. 'It just stayed on the wall because . . . well, because nobody bothered to take it off.'

It took only an instant for the terrible suspicion that had already seized Sam to strike its chilling logic into Roger's and Joanna's minds.

Pete was dead.

The next few minutes, when she tried to sort them out later, remained a blur. She couldn't be sure in what order things had happened. Whether she'd heard Peggy's voice calling down. Or seen the faint reflection of blue light sweeping the cellar walls. Or simply guessed, then known intuitively and for sure what had happened.

Sam was the first up the stairs. She followed, and then Roger. They could hear the chatter of a police radio now, coming from the patrol car parked outside the window. The flashing blue light gave a sickly, stroboscopic pallor to everybody in the room. Peggy's hands went to her face, horrified at what she'd just been told. The movement had an unreal, silent-movie quality about it. Next to her Tania Phillips and Brad Bucklehurst stood rooted where they were, in shock.

Sam was talking to two men in NYPD uniforms. One of them, Joanna noticed, wore a hat, the other not. It was an unimportant detail and she had no idea why she'd registered it – unless perhaps to distance herself from the words she could hear being spoken in that flat, emotion-less, follow-the-regulations tone of a cop.

'The body was discovered at ten after five, in an alley off Pike Street near Cherry. All he had to identify him was a campus ID card, which is why we're here. Cash, credit cards, if he'd been carrying any, were all gone. Likewise watch and any jewellery he might have had. Multiple stab wounds – we'll have to await the coroner's report for an exact cause of death. Meanwhile I'll have to ask you to accompany me to the morgue for a formal identification.'

42

She walked with Roger to a bar just off the campus where they'd been a couple of times before. Sam said he'd meet her back at her apartment as soon as he could – probably an hour, maybe two. Roger had offered to accompany her and wait, but she'd said she needed people around her, some semblance of normal life. And a drink.

All the tables were busy, so they sat on stools at the bar.

'It's strange,' she said, 'I can't even cry. I'm not in shock, it's worse – something in me just accepts it.'

Roger took a long pull on his scotch and water. 'I liked Pete a lot.' There was a tremor in his voice that he suppressed by clearing his throat. 'Nice kid. Smart. Straightforward.'

They were silent a while. Then Joanna said, 'What are we going to do?'

When he didn't offer a response, she essayed one herself. 'Maybe if we just walked away, gave up trying to destroy him, forgot about him . . .'

Roger gave a short, faintly sardonic laugh. 'Forgetting about Adam Wyatt sounds as easy as not thinking about a rhinoceros for five minutes.'

Again they fell silent amidst the busy early evening life going on around them.

'So,' she said eventually, 'we just sit here waiting to see who's next. Is that all we can do?'

He drained his glass and signalled the barman. 'What I'm doing is having another drink. You?'

She shook her head.

'The trouble was,' he said, clinking the fresh ice in his newly topped-up glass, 'we wanted proof.'

She turned to look at him. 'Proof?' she asked, waiting for him to expand on the remark.

'We invented somebody who never existed. There's nothing new in that – writers, artists, children do it all the time. But they don't pretend it's any more than that. We did. We looked for proof that this Adam Wyatt we'd dreamed up was real. We made him talk to us, prove he was real.'

'That,' she said, 'was the point of the whole experiment.'

He took another long sip of his drink, then kept the glass in his hand, moving it slightly to emphasize a word here and there.

'Every scientist worth his salt knows that if you look hard enough for a proof of something, or even just evidence, you'll find it. For example, we cannot put our hands on our hearts and swear that we're observing sub-atomic structure in high-energy accelerators and not creating it by looking for it. We start with equations and theories suggesting that certain particles may, sometimes we even say must, exist. Then, because we'll never see these particles – they're not seeable – we look for their tracks in the collision chambers. And sooner or later we find them – like footprints in the snow which people who believe in the yeti say must have been left by the yeti, so that proves the yeti exists.'

He took another long pull on his drink, then looked at her. 'We like to pretend that what we observe determines our theory, but it doesn't, not really. Einstein said that in reality it's the theory that decides what we observe. So what are we doing, we scientists? Are we chipping away at a block of stone and discovering some fossil of truth hidden inside it? Or are we carving it like a sculptor? Is the shape we end up with something that's been in the stone all along, or has it come from our imagination?'

He tipped his head back and finished his drink, then looked thoughtfully at his empty glass. 'And anyway, what's the difference?'

He caught the barman's eye for another re-fill, and glanced at her. 'How about you – ready yet?'

'No, thanks.'

She watched as he ordered a double, then she said, 'Tell me something, Roger . . . I've never really understood why you got into all this in the first place, or why you agreed to let your name be used.'

He sipped his fresh drink thoughtfully. 'Something interesting has happened to scientists this century. We started out as the champions of reason and logic. We believed that if we just worked diligently enough, observed and measured carefully enough, nature would in the end be forced to yield up her innermost secrets. And they would be logical and rational. They would make perfect sense, because the universe, we believed, made sense. Anything that went against that belief was dismissed as mere superstition. Well, the trouble started right there. The more we learned about nature through

290

the application of this process of reason and logic, the more we found ourselves being forced to abandon the idea that nature makes sense at all.'

She became aware that he was watching her as he paused, checking that she was listening and not growing impatient as she had the other night after Drew and Barry died.

'The idea that we can uncover the truth and find out why things are the way they are goes against all the accumulated evidence of science, of which there's now a great deal. It's not that we can't see what's going on. We can observe and measure with extraordinary precision – enough to calculate the distance between New York and Los Angeles to the thickness of a human hair. That's an example that Dick Feynman liked to use. He also said, repeatedly, that nature was absurd. Even though we know how it behaves, and can predict its behaviour accurately enough to use it and accomplish some mightily impressive things with it, we have no idea why it behaves that way. It doesn't make any sense. We know that this happens if we do that. But the idea that there's a logical reason for it turns out to be the biggest superstition of all. In fact it looks more and more like just a childish emotional need to believe that our world has order and meaning and that we're secure in it.'

She thought about this for a while, then said, 'I suppose that's why Sam says everybody's superstitious.'

Roger gave a wry smile. 'He's right. When we cross our fingers or touch wood, we're reaching out for some place where things happen the way they're supposed to, where there's order and rules you can play by – the way scientists thought the world was until they looked at it more closely.'

He took another long pull on his drink. Joanna noticed that he'd almost finished it already, his third since they arrived. His thought processes seemed perfectly lucid, but he was starting to slur his words a little.

'So what are scientists?' he asked, giving the question a rhetorical flourish. 'Surveyors? Stocktakers and clerks? Measuring and recording – ingeniously, I grant you – but nothing more?'

He threw back his head to finish his drink, then banged his glass down on the bar a little harder than necessary. 'I suppose,' he said, swivelling to look at her full on, 'I suppose that's the reason I signed on. To find out if Sam had anything new to offer. And also because you have terrific legs.'

He flashed her a rakish smile, his spirits revived by the alcohol. 'Now,' he said, 'how about that other drink that you've been putting off?' He looked around for the barman.

'I have to go. And Roger, I don't want to sound like your mother, but I don't think you should have much more . . .'

'There I'm afraid I must disagree with you . . . Bar-man . . .!'

'All right, if you're determined to get drunk, I'll stay.'

'If that's blackmail, you win. Stay right where you are.'

The barman appeared, smiling, awaiting Roger's order.

'Another large scotch and water, if you will. And . . .?' He looked questioningly at Joanna.

'No, really, nothing.' She looked at her watch. 'Oh, God, I really have to go. Look, Roger, at least let me organize a car – on the magazine – to take you back to Princeton.'

'Whatever you say, my dear. And don't worry – you're not a bit like my mother.'

She took out her phone and called the car service with which the magazine had a permanent account. If Taylor Freestone queried the expenditure later, she'd pay for the damn thing herself, but she didn't imagine for a second that he would.

'There'll be a car outside in twenty minutes,' she said when she'd finished, and slipped off her stool. 'I don't care how blasted you get now, at least I know you'll get back safely – all right?'

'All right, my dear,' he said, planting a kiss on her cheek.

She gave him a hug. 'Take care, Roger. See you soon.'

'You bet!'

When she reached the door she paused and looked back. He was watching her and waved cheerfully across the crowded room. She blew him a kiss, and stepped out into the night.

43

Fifteen minutes later she paid off the cab that dropped her in Beekman Place. She noticed that the doorman wasn't on duty, which meant he must be doing some chore in the building, so she tapped in the code that admitted her to the lobby, and took the elevator to her apartment. She deliberately drew the blinds before putting on the lights, aware that it wasn't something she normally did. What, she asked herself, was she hiding from?

She wondered what Roger was doing, hoping he'd had only one more drink and was already on his way home in the car she'd provided. Then she wondered how to occupy herself until Sam arrived. She didn't want to talk to anybody on the phone, couldn't concentrate to read, listen to music or watch television. She felt the kind of awful restlessness that needed to be worked off in a long walk or a vigorous physical sport. Yet she didn't want to be outdoors, exposed, unprotected. Here, in familiar surroundings, she felt at least relatively safe. She made herself a cup of herb tea and stretched out on the sofa with that morning's *New York Times*, which she hadn't opened, willing herself to make sense of the words that swam before her eyes.

After a couple of minutes her entryphone buzzed. She

got up quickly and crossed to answer it with a sense of relief, expecting to hear Sam's voice.

'Joanna, I'm downstairs. There's no doorman – can you let me in?'

It wasn't Sam's voice, it was Ralph Cazaubon's.

'Joanna? Are you there? Hello?'

She froze, unable to speak.

'Joanna, it's me, Ralph.'

She hung up. But she missed the cradle and the handset clattered noisily down the wall, bouncing at the end of its cable. She could hear his voice still coming thinly and distantly from it, like the sound of Pete's voice earlier. She reached out for the thing, hesitating as though half afraid it would give her an electric shock, finally snatching it and slamming it back in place.

This time it didn't fall, but it buzzed again, insistently, repeatedly. She backed away, her gaze fixed on it, struggling to control her mounting panic. Thoughts chased each other through her mind, each one wilder than the last. Wildest of all was the one insisting there was nothing to be afraid of – that there was just a man downstairs who had stopped by to see her, and she was behaving hysterically.

Yet she had met him only two days ago. Nobody in a city like New York went to the home of somebody they barely knew and expected to be let in just casually. Maybe there was some special reason. She hadn't even asked. What was so terrible about a man ringing her doorbell in the early evening, a man she had met and who had been perfectly charming and courteous and normal in every way? Was she going insane? Would she be running in fear from her own shadow next?

Yet nothing on earth would have persuaded her to

pick up that entryphone again and speak to him. She stepped around and past it like someone skirting a chained but vicious dog, its continuing, staccato, ear-jabbing buzz growing more unbearable each second.

She ran to the door and checked the locks. She was safe, but trapped. What could she do? She could call down to the lobby and see if the doorman was back from whatever he'd been doing. Or call the police? And say what? She would worry about that if and when she had to – she had no sane reason to call the police yet.

Call Sam? Yes, call Sam – that made sense. Sam would understand why she was terrified. She began to dial the number of his portable and prayed that he was carrying it. Maybe he was on his way to the apartment now and would arrive any minute. She must warn him of possible danger from whoever or whatever was down there waiting in the street.

The noise from the entryphone stopped. In the silence she could hear only her own breathing and the sound of her heart beating. She realized she was halfway through Sam's number, but forgot how many digits she'd dialled, and hung up.

She listened to the silence. Had he gone away? He knew there was someone in the apartment because she'd answered, but she hadn't spoken. It could have been a friend, a colleague, a cleaner – anyone – who had picked up the phone.

Cautiously she moved to the edge of one of her windows, pulled back a drape and peered out. There was no sign of anybody in the street. She couldn't see the door from where she was, so he could still be there, but at least he'd given up trying to get in.

Unless, of course, the doorman was back and had

opened it for him. But the doorman wouldn't let him up without calling. That was the rule, stated plainly on a sign in the lobby: 'All Callers Must Be Announced.'

'Joanna . . .?'

She spun around with a cry of alarm. The voice had come from just behind her. His voice. In the room with her.

For a second she saw nobody, and told herself she had hallucinated it. Then a shadow moved in the hall beyond the open doorway of her living room. Ralph Cazaubon stepped into view.

'Joanna, will you please tell me what's wrong?'

His expression was earnest, his tone of voice concerned. Except for the fact that he was dressed more formally now, he looked exactly as he had the previous day. Yet something in his manner had changed. There was a familiarity in it, an intimacy even, that had no place between them.

'How did you get in here?' she managed to gasp in a shaky voice.

His frown of consternation deepened. He took a step towards her. 'Joanna, what's wrong . . .?'

She backed away. The corner of a table jabbed into her hip, a lamp tipped over and crashed to the floor. 'Don't come near me!' Her hands groped behind her, whether to find something to defend herself with or to avoid further collisions she wasn't sure.

'Will you stop this, please!' There was a note of anger in his voice now, and in the way he reached out to grab her by the shoulders, as though wanting to shake this nonsense out of her.

She spun away from him and over to her desk. There was a paperknife somewhere there, a long, steel blade sharpened to a point. Her fingers scrabbled among the scattered books and papers until they closed on the carved ivory handle. She held it out before her like a dagger.

'Don't come near me. I'll use this if I have to.'

He looked alarmed now and held up his hands. 'All right, all right . . . I'm not moving, calm down . . . Just tell me what's the matter and let me help you . . . please, Joanna . . .'

Her breath was coming raggedly in gasps, breaking, close to turning into sobs. She made an effort to control herself, fight back the fear, stay in control. Keeping the knife out and ready to thrust, she began moving sideways, edging crab-like towards the tiny hallway, not for a second taking her eyes off him.

He turned, following her movement, his hands still up, but less in surrender now than in a readiness to defend himself, even attack her if he saw a break in her concentration.

But there was no break. She wiped her free hand across her face and discovered she was bathed in perspiration. She blinked and then stretched her eyes wide to clear the cloudiness from them. And all the time kept moving, one careful step after another, towards the door of her apartment and escape. When she began to walk backwards the few last steps, he followed her, but held back when she raised the knife a threatening inch or so.

'I warned you – don't come near me.'

She had to transfer the knife from one hand to the other in order to undo the locks. First the main lock, then the lower one. They were locked just as she had left them when she came in.

Her eyes flickered sideways for a second as she sought

the handle to pull the door open. Out of the corner of her vision she saw him move.

'No!'

He froze. 'Joanna, please, this is insane. What's happened? Are you ill? How could you imagine that I'd want to hurt you?'

Her fingers found the handle and pulled. 'How did you get in here?'

'The same way I always do. What's wrong with you?'

She didn't answer or argue or press the question further, just pulled the door open and stepped through. She slammed it shut and ran the few yards to the elevator. She pushed the call button, but saw that the 'in use' light was on. In the distance she could hear the hum of machinery. It stopped and the elevator doors slid open.

Not thinking how she might look to an outsider walking into the scene, she kept her eyes on her apartment door, which remained closed, but suddenly became aware of a figure stepping from the elevator. Before she could turn to look, she heard, 'Jesus Christ, Joanna, what's going on?'

She spun around. Sam jumped back to avoid the blade of the paperknife, but when she saw it was him she fell into his arms. The fear and tension she'd been holding in burst from her in a long and shuddering sob.

'What is it? What's happened? Tell me.' He took the paperknife gently from her fingers.

She pointed shakily to her apartment. 'He's in there.'

'Who?'

'Ralph Cazaubon.'

'What—?' He started for the door, but she pulled him back.

'No, wait. Get help.'

'There's no time for that!'

Then she realized, 'I haven't got the keys. We can't get in.'

He thought a moment. 'Does the doorman have a set?'

She nodded. 'Yes.'

'Go get them. I'll wait here.'

'No, I don't want you to—'

'Just do it, *please*, Joanna.' He held up the paperknife. 'Don't worry, if he's in there he won't get past me.'

The elevator had already been called to another floor. She could see from the indicator it was going up, so she took the stairs, running down the three flights to the lobby. She found Frank Flores sitting at the desk where there'd been nobody when she arrived. He looked up as she ran in and registered surprise at her distraught appearance.

'Frank, there's somebody in my apartment, you'd better come up. Give me the spare keys, please.'

He reached beneath his desk. 'Somebody in your apartment? Mr Towne just went up. Did you see him?'

'Yes. Did you see another man go up earlier? Tall, dark hair.'

'Nobody's gone up while I've been here. I was down checking out the furnace a while back, but the street door was locked. Nobody would've got in unless they had a key or someone buzzed them in.'

He handed the spare keys over to her. 'You want me to call the police?'

'I don't think so. Just come up with me.'

They took the stairs. Frank, who was a big man, muscular but overweight, was out of breath when they arrived. Sam was still there. He gestured that nothing had happened.

300

'Okay, you'd better tell me what's going on,' Frank said, asserting his role as the man responsible for the building's security. 'Is somebody sick in there, or drunk, or intent on causing bodily harm or damage?'

'No, I don't think any of those things,' Joanna said.

'Is this person known to you?'

'To me, yes – slightly,' she said. 'Mr Towne doesn't know him at all.'

'I see,' Frank said, thinking he did, and casting a speculative glance in Sam's direction before turning back to her. 'And you've asked this person to leave – is that correct, Miss Cross?'

She said it was.

'And he has refused?'

'Yes.'

Frank rubbed his chin. 'Is this man armed as far as you know?'

She looked surprised by the question. 'No . . . no, I'm sure he isn't . . .'

'Any weapons in the apartment? A gun, knife?'

'Nothing at all. Except . . .'

Frank followed her gaze to the paperknife in Sam's grip. 'I'll take that, if you don't mind, Mr Towne.'

Sam hesitated.

'It's okay, sir – I'm a vet, I can handle myself.'

Sam glanced at Joanna as though unconvinced, but handed the knife over anyway.

'Do you want to give me those keys again, Miss Cross?' Frank said, tucking the knife into the leather belt of his uniform.

She handed him the keys he had given her downstairs, pointing out that the one for the main lock was all he'd need. Gesturing them both to stay back, he opened the

301

door with a swift, firm movement. Positioning himself on the threshold and to one side, so that he had a clear view through to the lighted living room, he called out, 'Security. Would you step into view, please, sir?'

There was no sound or movement from the apartment. Sam noticed that, although Frank carried no gun, his hand hovered near the nightstick attached to his belt.

Frank looked at Joanna. 'Are you sure somebody's here, Miss Cross?'

'Somebody was,' she said, feeling increasingly uneasy.

'Okay,' Frank said, directing his words into the apartment, 'I'm asking you to come out now, or I shall be obliged to call the police.'

'The hell with the police,' Sam said, losing patience and pushing past him. 'If he's in here, I want to see him.'

'Please, Mr Towne, let me handle this . . .'

Frank's protest was futile. Sam strode into the apartment, moving rapidly from room to room.

'Cazaubon . . .? Ralph Cazaubon, I want to see you! Where are you . . .?'

A couple of minutes later they all three stood in the middle of the living room. It was clear that there was nobody in the apartment other than themselves. The only sign of anything abnormal was the lamp that Joanna had knocked to the floor. She picked it up and put it back in its place.

'Everything seems all right now, Miss Cross,' Frank said, looking at her doubtfully.

'So it seems. He must have slipped out between my going and . . . and Mr Towne arriving.' She looked at Sam. 'He would have just about had time, wouldn't he?'

'I guess,' Sam lied.

302

'Then he may still be in the building,' Frank said, with renewed urgency. 'I'll check.'

Neither of them tried to persuade him that the effort would be worthless. Joanna thanked him for his trouble, and shut the door after him. When she returned to Sam he was standing at her desk looking down at something.

'He *was* here,' she said, as though fearing he wouldn't believe her.

Sam tore a leaf from the notepad by her phone. 'Here's his number and address that you wrote down this morning.' He picked up her phone and dialled, waited a while, then shook his head. 'No reply.' He hung up and slipped the piece of paper into his pocket. 'I'll get this number checked out tomorrow.'

She took a step closer. 'Sam, tell me you believe me. Tell me you believe that he was here.'

He took her in his arms. 'I believe you,' he said. 'Of course I do.'

44

They checked into a hotel a few blocks away from Beekman Place. It was illogical, they knew, but they both felt safer surrounded by its bland, impersonal trappings than they would have in either Joanna's or Sam's apartment.

Although neither had much appetite, they decided that having dinner would help them get through the evening, so they walked over to the Chinese place on Third where Joanna had been a regular for years. Its familiarity and cheerful service were reassuring.

She recounted her conversation with Roger, Sam nodding thoughtfully, managing a faint smile from time to time.

'It's quite rare that Roger drinks like that,' he said, 'and it's usually when he's trying to get his mind around some puzzle – like one of Sherlock Holmes's "three-pipe problems".'

'Yeah, well, it's at least a three-pipe problem we've got here.'

They turned things over for a while, eventually falling silent in tacit acknowledgement of how little what they said mattered any more. Events had run away with them, and Sam knew no better than she what they should do now or what might happen next. They walked back to the hotel through the damp November air. Joanna had brought some sleeping pills from her apartment. They both took one, and curled up in each other's arms in the comfortable, queen-size bed.

In the morning they woke early and had finished breakfast in their room by eight. Joanna called her machine for messages, and he checked his. There was nothing of importance.

'I wonder if it's too early to call Roger,' she said, 'just to make sure he got back all right.'

'If he's got a hangover, he won't appreciate it.'

'I'd like to anyway,' she said. 'I don't know why, but I'm worried about him.'

She dialled his number. The phone rang several times, then a man answered whose voice she didn't know. The moment reminded her immediately of the morning she'd called Maggie and spoken to her daughter and her heart at once began to beat faster.

'I was calling Roger Fullerton,' she said, her voice faltering slightly. 'Is he there? Could I speak with him, please?'

'Could I ask who this is?' said the man on the other end, his tone grave.

Sam saw from her face that something was wrong and hurried to her.

'I'm a friend of Roger's,' she said. 'Joanna Cross.'

She could hear the man at the other end speaking to someone else, but as though his hand was over the phone so she couldn't make out the words.

Sam took the phone from her. 'Hello?' he said insistently. 'Hello? Who am I speaking to, please?'

The man on the other end gave his name. Sam recognized it. He was a senior member of the university

305

administration. Fortunately the two had met on more than one occasion, and he was more prepared to talk to Sam than he would have been to Joanna. As he listened, Sam lowered himself to a sitting position on the edge of the bed, and reached for Joanna's hand.

They took a train from Penn Station and were at Princeton Junction before ten. Instead of waiting for the shuttle they took a cab and were on the campus minutes later. By the time they approached the building in which Joanna had first met Roger many months ago, she knew as much about his death as Sam did.

Apparently there'd been a fire in his room. It had not spread but had remained confined to the room and had died out of its own accord. His body had not been found until morning, less than an hour before Joanna's call.

A fire engine was parked on the grass and a handful of firemen stood around with a faintly puzzled air, as though not sure why they were there. The entrance to the building was guarded by campus security and two members of the Borough Police Department, who were keeping curious onlookers back, but they let Sam and Joanna through when Sam gave his name.

The man they had both spoken to on the phone was called Jeffrey something – she didn't catch his full name. He was tall and wore a grey suit with a blue shirt and tie and had thinning hair brushed straight back. He was clearly badly shaken by what had happened, and glanced anxiously at Joanna as though to suggest this was no place for a woman.

'You can go in,' he said. 'The medical examiner's still

there, and the police. It's the strangest damn thing you've ever seen.'

Sam turned to Joanna. 'Are you sure you want to do this?' he asked her quietly. 'I can go in first, tell you how bad it is.'

She shook her head. 'I'd rather do anything but go in there, but I think I have to.'

He slipped his hand under her arm. Someone in a uniform opened the door for them.

The room was exactly as she remembered it – the congenial clutter of books and papers, the photographs and pictures at odd angles on the panelled walls, the computer on the table by the stained-glass window. Everything was the same, including the leather armchairs they'd sat in that afternoon, empty now – except for Roger's.

As it had been then, it was angled so that a reading lamp stood over it and there was a table at one side on which were books, a box of the cheroots he smoked occasionally, and a half-finished glass of what looked like whisky.

But sitting in the chair was a thing beyond description. Charred black from head to foot, it was a hellish effigy of what was once a man. Only one hand and part of an arm, resting loosely on the table by the armchair's side, had escaped the incinerating fire. The material of the sleeve was part of the suit that Roger had been wearing when Joanna last saw him.

She wanted to scream, run, or even faint. But she was frozen by the horror. Her feet wouldn't move, nor would her throat make a sound. She became aware of Sam's arm around her, and her own hands clutching at him as she fought to drag her gaze from the hideous sight before her.

Two forms moved – one that had been kneeling by the corpse, another standing by the wall in shadow, now suddenly outlined against the window. She heard a strange noise, and realized that it came from herself. She hadn't breathed since she entered the room, and now she was gasping for air.

'I'm all right,' she managed to say, letting go of Sam to show that she meant it and could stand unsupported. 'I'm all right. What happened to him?'

The man at the window came towards her. 'That's what we're trying to figure out. Lieutenant Fraser, Borough Police.'

They introduced themselves. 'Roger Fullerton was my old physics professor,' Sam said. 'We'd remained close friends. We saw him yesterday. Joanna – Miss Cross – saw him after me. They had a drink together, then he came back here.'

'I arranged a car for him,' she said. 'It must have been around seven, seven-fifteen when I left him.'

The detective nodded and made a note. 'Sounds about right. I was told he was seen back here by nine.' He looked at them both. 'Anything you can tell me? Anything unusual? Any particular state of mind he was in?'

Sam shook his head. 'I don't think you're going to find this is suicide, if that's what you mean. Do you mind if I take a closer look?'

'Go ahead.'

He stepped forward. Joanna stayed where she was. The medical examiner looked up at him. He was fifty-ish, his face round and pale. There was fear in it.

'Did you ever see anything like this before?' Sam asked him.

'Not in all my born days.'

Sam moved around the back of the chair, then reached out and touched part of the unburned leather near the corpse's shoulder. 'No residual heat,' he said. 'Did anybody actually see this fire?'

'Nothing was reported until cleaning staff came in this morning,' the man called Jeffrey said from the door.

Sam looked over at him, then back to the medical examiner. 'Have you ever heard of SHC – spontaneous combustion in human beings?'

The other man put a hand on his knee and pushed himself to his feet. 'I've heard of it, but I don't believe it. People don't just catch fire for no reason.'

'You should read some of the case histories,' Sam said. 'This has all the signs.'

He walked around the far side of the table on which the corpse's arm still rested, coming to a stop in front of the chair, looking down on it and its hideous occupant.

'I don't need to tell you the kind of heat it takes to burn a human body this badly,' he said. 'At least three thousand degrees fahrenheit. And look,' he pointed, 'the chair's only burned for a few inches around the body. Nothing on the table caught fire, the carpet isn't even singed.' He looked up. 'There's some soot, a thin film, high up on the wall and ceiling. And have you noticed something else? There's no odour. A human body burns like this, there should be a distinctive smell. There's no trace. It wouldn't have evaporated yet.'

'You're only telling me what I know,' the medical examiner said. 'I'm sure we'll find some combination of circumstances that'll explain this incident in time. Until then, forgive me if I don't join you in jumping to any unjustified conclusions.'

'Spontaneous human combustion,' Sam murmured softly, as though to himself. 'Sometimes known as fire from heaven.'

Lieutenant Fraser ran a hand over his face and rubbed his chin. 'If this fire came from anywhere, it wasn't heaven, Dr Towne. It was some other place.'

They sat together in a corner of the near-empty carriage as it rattled back to Penn Station.

Sam glanced at his watch. 'Lend me your phone again, will you?' he said.

She handed him her portable and he tapped in a number; it was the third time he had tried to call Ward Riley since leaving the campus. Still no reply, and no service or answering machine.

'I'll try again when we get in,' he said, handing the phone back to her. 'If there's still no reply we'll go straight up there, find out what's happening.'

They had said nothing to Lieutenant Fraser about Adam Wyatt or the experiment in which Roger had been a participant. It would come out later, they knew, and there would be questions about why they had stayed silent. But time enough for all that then. Getting entangled now in a slow-moving police inquiry was the last thing they needed, though what precisely they intended doing next, aside from telling Ward what had happened, they didn't know.

SHC, Sam had told her when they were clear of the building, was thought by some, including Sam himself, to be a form of poltergeist phenomenon: there were many recorded cases of people, children and adults, unconsciously causing fires of extraordinary intensity that caused injury or death to others or to themselves.

'The facts are there, people just have to look at them,' he said. 'This is one of those times they're going to have to.'

Joanna shuddered involuntarily and looked out of the window, trying to escape the appalling image that kept flashing in merciless detail into her mind. Sam knew what was happening and took her hand.

'I don't think I'll ever sleep again,' she said.

'You will,' he said. 'I promise.'

She leaned her head against his shoulder, but dared not close her eyes.

When they stepped off the train at Penn Station, Sam stabbed Ward's number into the portable again. This time it was answered almost at once. The Chinese manservant's voice was high-pitched and distressed.

'You better come, Dr Towne,' he said. 'Mr Riley leave message for you – and Miss Cross. Come quickly, please.'

45

The Chinaman was waiting at the door of the apartment
as they stepped out of the elevator, their footsteps sound-
less on the thick carpet. They did not speak until they
had entered the hallway of Ward's apartment with its
polished wooden floor, and the door was closed behind
them.

'What's going on?' Sam asked without preamble.

The manservant spoke quickly in his light voice,
rocking slightly from the waist, his hands clasped before
his chest.

'Last night I see Mr Riley when he return – this shortly
before eight. He say he go to bed and not to be disturbed.
I spend morning visit friends, do shopping, but when I
return, still no Mr Riley. I begin to worry if he sick. Mr
Riley *never* this late in morning. So I knock on Mr Riley's
door, but there is no reply. I open door, find his bed not
slept in. This note on it.'

He produced a card bearing a few lines in Ward's neat
and uniformly slanting hand. It read: '*Allow Sam
Towne and Joanna Cross into my quiet room. Nobody
else. W.R.*'

Sam looked from the card to the manservant. 'His
"quiet room"?'

'I show you.' He led them down a corridor and

312

through a double door into a spacious bedroom furnished with the same eastern influence as the rest of the apartment. Joanna sensed something odd about the place at once, and realized that it had no windows. She glimpsed a tiled and mirrored bathroom through open doors, then followed the manservant to a far door that was virtually invisible in a dark, wood-panelled wall containing built-in drawers and closets.

'Nobody allowed in here ever,' he said. 'Mr Riley even clean this room himself. I leave you now.'

He gave a stiff little bow and retreated the way they had come. Sam turned the door handle. They found themselves in a space about the size of a closet, bare walls and nothing in it except another door on the far side. They exchanged a look, and Sam opened the second door.

A wall of cold air hit them. The room was medium-sized with a floor-to-ceiling window running the whole of the far side and overlooking the park. Three sliding glass panels had been opened as far as they would go. There was no furniture other than a few bookshelves and several pictures and statues that looked as though they had religious or iconic significance.

In the centre of the floor was a mat. Ward Riley sat on it in the classic cross-legged meditation pose. He was barefoot and wore only a simple robe of thin cotton. His eyes were closed and his skin waxy pale.

'Is he dead?' Joanna whispered, falling to her knees and reaching out to touch him. He was ice cold.

There was a slamming sound behind Joanna. She turned to see Sam sliding the windows shut, then he came and knelt on Ward's other side.

'I can see a pulse,' he said, 'in his neck, very slow.'

'Thank you for coming, Sam . . .'

They both jumped as Ward's voice came out of nowhere, filling the room.

' . . . and Joanna. It is good that you are here, that we are together now.'

They exchanged a look over Ward's head, both unnerved by the familiar yet strangely disembodied voice.

'By the time you hear these words I will have reached a place from which I shall neither wish nor be able to return.'

'It's coming from his throat,' she said. 'His mouth isn't moving, but the sound is coming from his throat.'

'I want to help you,' Ward's voice continued. 'It is too late for you to take the path that I have taken – it involves long preparation. But do not fear the void before you. Enter it as you would the light . . .'

'Look,' Sam said suddenly. She followed the direction he was pointing and saw a small sound system on a shelf to Ward's right. A cassette was turning in it. 'We must have triggered it when we came in.'

As he spoke she saw what looked like an electronic eye, positioned so that anyone entering the room would break its beam.

'Our world has changed,' the voice continued, 'and there is no going back . . .'

The voice stopped as Sam impatiently yanked a plug from the wall. 'Go find that manservant, Joanna. Get some blankets. And have him call Ward's doctor, or emergency, right now.'

She hesitated. She did not know why she hesitated, except it came into her mind that Ward did not want them to do this. He had made his choice, and it was not for them to interfere with it. But she pushed the thought aside as swiftly as it had come. She did not, on the whole, regard the right of self-destruction as inalienable; and what Ward had done looked very much like attempted suicide.

She ran through the apartment calling out, 'Hello? Where are you?' because she did not know the manservant's name. There was no sign of him in the hallway or the main reception room where they had sat with Ward the day before. She tried a door that led to guest rooms and extra bathrooms. She called out again, but there was no response.

A couple of doors were visible on the far side of the reception room. She guessed these probably led to the kitchen and domestic quarters – the 'butler's pantry' as she supposed it might be called in a building like this. She tried one of them and found herself in a maze of corridors between laundry rooms and storage areas, then she pushed through a swing door that led into a large and ultra-modern kitchen, all white walls and stainless steel. Still there was no reply when she called out.

Another door brought her into a dining room with a long table and places for about twenty people. It, too, was empty and immaculate, with a barely-ever-used look. The door she pushed open on the far side took her back into the reception room, still as empty as it had been two minutes ago. Another door to her right opened into a corridor that she hadn't noticed before, although it connected with the main hallway which she could see in the distance to her left. She looked to her right for signs of further hidden rooms and recesses, but as she did so she caught sight of a movement in a mirror on the wall.

She turned to her left just in time to see someone disappearing, evidently in a great hurry, out of the main door of the apartment – someone wearing a raincoat the same colour as Sam's.

'Sam!' She called after him, but there was no response. She ran towards the hallway where the door was still open.

As she stepped out into the corridor she saw him disappearing around the far corner – again just a glimpse, running, the light-coloured raincoat flying out behind him.

Joanna ran after him. She didn't think about it, didn't even close the door behind her. All she wanted was to know what was happening. Was he running from or after something? And why?

By the time she reached the corner where she'd seen him, he had disappeared again. The only movement was a door swinging shut. She ran towards it. A sign on it said 'Emergency Only'. She pulled it open.

She found herself in a stairwell with an open staircase made of steel that twisted down in sharp, one-eighty-degree turns like a fire escape. She couldn't see Sam, but she could hear the clatter of his feet descending.

Twice she called his name, but there was no response. She supposed he couldn't hear her above the echo coming off the bare, grey-painted walls. She started after him.

Glancing down as she descended, she saw brief flashes of his arm as he grabbed the handrail to swing himself around each turn in the stairs. She tried calling again, but it was futile. In fact, as she continued after him, it seemed increasingly pointless to be chasing him at all: she had no chance of catching him. Yet she wanted desperately to know what had provoked this flight without a word or even apparently a thought for her.

She slowed, beginning to feel foolish for having even

tried to follow him. It was obvious that there must be some reason for his behaviour, and it was probably to be found upstairs in the apartment rather than down here in this strange limbo of a place. Most likely the manservant had shown up in Ward's room while she was still looking for him. It didn't explain why Sam should make this mad dash out of the building, but there must be some good reason. If there'd been any danger he would certainly have warned her and made sure he took her with him. Of that she was certain. Running after him like this was in itself a kind of betrayal, a refusal to trust him. She should have gone back to Ward and the Chinaman, where she would have learned that Sam was dashing down to a pharmacy, or to some doctor on another floor – needing something so urgently that he couldn't even wait for the elevator. Of course that must be the explanation. She had been silly to react as she had. She must go back up and see what she could do to help.

Yet she had come so far now that she was nearer to the bottom of the stairs than where she had started. Ward was on – what, the fifth, sixth floor? The sensible thing was to carry on down and take the elevator back up. She would do that.

Giving up all thought of catching Sam, she continued on down at her own speed. It occurred to her that she need not go all the way; if she took the emergency door to the next landing – it would be the second or third – she could take the elevator back up from there.

The door was set back some way into a deep wall. She was lost in thought, paying little attention to her immediate surroundings, when she turned off the stair-case and into it. She reached for the handle, or rather where she thought the handle would be in the dark recess . . . and touched something soft.

She gave a small cry – of surprise more than alarm. Because she had already registered the colour of the coat. Sam's coat. But as her eyes travelled up to the face she expected to see, her blood turned cold. The man standing there, waiting in the shadows, was Ralph Cazaubon.

'Don't let it end like this,' he said, his voice soft, breaking slightly. 'I don't know what's happening to us, Jo. Don't let it end like this.'

46

Sam stood in the middle of the main reception room. 'Joanna?' he called out for the third time. There was no reply.

Puzzled and becoming concerned, he returned to the hallway. The door of the apartment still stood open just as it had when he came out to look for her. He was about to step outside when something moved on the edge of his vision. He stopped and looked to his right, but it was only his own reflection, the whiteness of his raincoat caught in a mirror at the far end of a dark corridor off the hallway.

'Mr Towne, sir...?' The Chinese manservant appeared from somewhere behind him. 'Can I help you, sir?'

'Have you seen Miss Cross? She was looking for you.'

The manservant frowned. 'Miss Cross? No, sir, I no see Miss Cross.'

'I just came out of the bedroom and found the apartment door open. Why would she...?' He stepped out into the corridor and looked both ways, but there was no sign of her. He came back in. 'Why on earth would she disappear like that?'

The Chinaman bobbed his head to confess that he had no answer. 'I'm sure she come back, sir.'

'Let's hope. Meanwhile, get some medical help up here, and find me some more blankets – before your employer dies from hypothermia.'

She had tried to scream, but the sound was choked off in her throat by sheer terror.

Ralph Cazaubon made no move. There was nothing overtly threatening about him. On the contrary, there was a sadness in his face, a tenderness even.

All the same she turned and ran for her life. She looked back once to see if he was following, and saw him unhurriedly, almost casually, descending the steps after her.

At the ground floor she wrenched open a door and found herself in a corridor with green-painted brick walls and no way out except by a double door with a push bar across it at the far end. She sprinted towards it, again looking back over her shoulder. Ralph still followed her in the same relaxed fashion, as though confident that there was no way she could escape him.

Praying it would work, she slammed both hands down on the bar. The door sprang outwards, and she found herself in a kind of courtyard in the centre of the building. She looked around for a way out, and saw a gap that seemed to lead to the street. But there were gates – which was all right, because this was a secure building, and that meant guards.

She ran on, glancing back just once, and being surprised to see that Ralph had not emerged yet. Did he imagine she'd go back in there with him waiting for her?

Or had he really been there at all? Was it possible she'd imagined him? Had he been some kind of illusion, some projection of her mind, like his ancestor Adam Wyatt?

But why was he wearing Sam's coat, or something very like it? Was he becoming somehow confused in her head with Sam Towne? Why should that be? What was happening here? She had gone too far in this peculiar adventure to doubt that there was a pattern in events, a meaning and a purpose, however indiscernible.

The armed guard on the gate accepted her story about getting lost in the building; at least, he looked at her less suspiciously when she said she'd been visiting Ward Riley. He unlocked the gate and told her the best thing was to take a right and right again, then go in the main entrance and take the main elevator back up to Mr Riley's apartment.

She walked briskly along the sidewalk, keeping close to the building, reassured by the noise and energy of normal street life. She turned right at the corner as she'd been told to . . . and stopped.

Ralph Cazaubon was standing between her and the entrance, casual, hands in the pockets of his raincoat, watching her.

'Have you got those extra blankets yet?' Sam stepped out of Ward's bedroom and looked around impatiently for the manservant.

'Right here, sir. Got them right here.' He hurried up the dark corridor where Sam had glimpsed his own reflection earlier. 'And paramedics on way.'

'Good. His pulse is a little stronger – we may be just in time.'

He grabbed a couple of the blankets and ran back

through Ward's bedroom and on into the meditation room where he had left him. The manservant was right behind him when they got there, and they both stopped.

The room was empty, and one of the windows had been opened.

'Oh, no . . . Oh, my God . . .!'

Sam let the blankets drop and ran to look out. Before he got there his fears were confirmed by a screech of brakes and the sound of vehicles colliding in the street below. People screamed. He peered down over the stone parapet beyond the window.

Ward Riley's body lay spreadeagled on Central Park West.

She had crossed the road quickly, dodging traffic, and was hurrying now in the direction of Columbus Avenue. At the corner she stopped and looked back. There was no sign of him. She debated whether to return to the Dakota, but some instinct warned her otherwise. As though in confirmation of its rightness, she suddenly spotted his light raincoat on the far side of the street. He was strolling, casually as ever, but looking in her direction, watching her. She turned left, heading south, walking as fast as she could without breaking into a run.

Sam, she knew, would be worried, wondering what had happened to her. She must talk to him, tell him how she had been tricked, ask him what she should do now. It was absurd that they had been separated in this way. Had that been the purpose of this whole thing?

But why? And was she now running from something, or being driven towards something?

She stopped and reached into her coat pocket. To her

relief her portable phone was still there. She didn't have Ward's number in her head, but the phone would automatically redial the last number called, which had been Ward's. She stepped into the recessed doorway of a building and tried it.

Nothing happened. She tried again and held the phone to her ear. There was a faint crackle of static, but nothing more. When she looked at the tiny display panel it bore the words 'CODE NOT RECOGNIZED'.

What the hell did that mean? She tried again, with the same result. 'CODE NOT RECOGNIZED.'

She experienced the surge of impotent fury she always felt whenever some dumb machine refused to function the way it was supposed to. Resisting an urge to shake it or bang it on the wall next to her, she tried again.

'CODE NOT RECOGNIZED.'

If the damn thing wasn't working, she would have to use a pay phone. It was only then she realized that her purse, with all her credit cards and money, was in Ward's apartment. She didn't have a cent with her. That meant she had no choice: she would have to go back.

Or perhaps not. She became aware that the building she was standing in front of was a bank – the same bank, though not the branch, that she used. But they could check out her name and account number and give her some money.

A minute later she was seated before the desk of a pleasant young woman who said she would see what she could do, although it was unfortunate that Joanna was carrying no identification whatsoever. But when Joanna mentioned the names of two people with whom she dealt regularly at her bank and who she was sure would be willing to identify her over the phone, the young woman made the call.

One of the people Joanna had mentioned was, it appeared, off sick. The other was called to the phone, and Joanna waited patiently while the young woman before her explained the problem. Joanna watched as her face clouded with concern.

'I'm sorry,' the young woman said, covering the phone with her hand, 'he says he doesn't recognize your name.'

'That's impossible. Can I speak to him, please?'

She held out her hand for the phone. 'Hello? Is this Ray? Ray, it's Joanna Cross.'

His voice was hesitant. 'Joanna . . . Cross?'

'Is this Ray Myerson?'

'This is he.'

'Well, for heaven's sakes, Ray – it's me! I need some cash.'

'Could you give me your account number, Miss Cross?'

She supposed that his formality was part of some kind of security procedure. Luckily she knew her account number by heart and gave it to him without hesitation. There was a pause.

'I'm sorry, Miss Cross, but none of this appears on my computer. Are you sure you have the right bank?'

'Of course I'm sure. Look, Ray, I don't know what's going on here, but I need you to help me out.'

He asked to be handed back to the young woman who had called him. Joanna gave her the phone, then watched with growing unease as the young woman listened for several moments, nodding her head and saying 'Yes' and 'Mm-hm' while carefully avoiding eye contact with Joanna.

She began to have a hollow, guilty feeling, as though she had attempted something improper and had been found out. At the same time she was angry at Ray Myerson's and the bank's obtuseness in making such heavy weather out of such a simple request.

The young woman finally hung up and turned to her with a mixture of sympathy and suspicion in her face. 'I'm sorry, Miss Cross, there seems to be some mistake. There's no record of any account in that name at the bank, nor in fact any account of that number.'

'That's impossible.'

The young woman gave a nervous shrug, as though half afraid that Joanna might turn out to be some kind of dangerous lunatic despite her respectable appearance and apparent normality.

Whatever the reasons for this farce, Joanna realized there was nothing to be done. 'Okay,' she said, 'forget it. Thank you for trying, I appreciate your help. Would you mind if I ask one more favour? I need to make a phone call. I've left my purse and everything in a friend's apartment, and I need to talk to them.'

'Please – go ahead.'

'I'll have to call four-one-one for the number.' She did so, praying that Ward was listed. He was. A moment later she was listening to the phone ring unanswered. She hung up. 'They must have left. Thanks anyway for your help.'

She got up and started out, half fearing now that she would be stopped before she reached the door and accused of some kind of attempted fraud. She felt the young woman's eyes on her back all the way, but nothing happened.

On the street she looked both ways in search of Ralph.

There was no sign of him. She debated returning to the Dakota, but quickly decided against it. If, as seemed likely, Sam and the Chinese manservant had accompanied Ward to the hospital, she wouldn't even be able to get into the apartment. And above all she didn't want to risk running into Ralph Cazaubon again.

She had decided to walk to the *Around Town* office, which would take about half an hour, when her fingers closed on something that felt like coins in the bottom of her coat pocket. She pulled out a couple of subway tokens.

For the first time in a while, she felt lucky.

47

She emerged from the elevator and turned right, towards the glass double doors with *Around Town* engraved on them in the same lettering as on the cover of the magazine. She passed through them and headed diagonally across the lobby, passing the reception desk and giving a somewhat abstracted nod of greeting to Bobbie and Jane behind it. She was about to go through the pale wooden door that led back to the part of the floor where her office was situated, when she heard, 'Excuse me, can I help you?'

The words were spoken in the officious and slightly indignant tone of someone whose presence has just been deliberately and insultingly ignored. She turned to see Bobbie, a slim and efficient woman around forty whom she'd known for several years, glaring at her.

'I'm going to my office.'

Bobbie continued to glare, and now rose to her feet. 'You're going where . . .?' She narrowed her eyes and tipped her head to one side as she asked the question. It was a challenge that demanded a response.

'Bobbie, what's the matter? Why are you looking at me like that?'

'I don't know how you know my name, but I'm afraid I don't know yours. If you don't mind, it's customary for visitors to come to the desk when they enter this office, and not just go barging on through. Who are you here to see?'

Joanna remained where she was for a moment, one hand on the door she had been about to push open. She withdrew it and took a couple of steps towards the desk, focusing on the two women behind it.

'Bobbie . . . Jane . . .' She looked from one to the other. 'What is this?'

The two women exchanged a look. There was a hint of alarm in Jane's eyes, puzzlement and distrust in Bobbie's as she turned back to Joanna. 'I'm sorry, is there some reason we should know who you are?'

Joanna stood before them. Her mouth worked as though she was about to speak, but she said nothing. She shook her head slowly, as though the movement could somehow make the situation go away like a bad joke that had outstayed its welcome.

'Don't do this to me, please. I don't think I can take this just now – all right?'

But it wasn't all right, and she could see in their faces that this was no joke. 'Oh, my God,' she murmured. 'Oh, my God . . . Oh, my God . . . no . . . no, this can't be . . .'

She turned and slammed open the door she'd been about to go through and ran down the corridor, barely hearing the angry shout of 'Hey!' behind her. People she passed looked at her curiously, but she paid them no attention and ran on, turning right and left, past conference rooms and offices until she reached her own.

A man she'd never seen before sat at her desk. He looked up from the computer he was working at, frowned, and seemed about to ask a question.

She spoke first. 'Who are you?'

'That's what I was going to ask you.'

'You're in my office. Do you mind telling me what you're doing in my office?'

'Now wait a minute . . .' He leaned back, looking at her more searchingly now. 'I don't know what the problem is here, but this is *my* office and you're in it. Now if there's any way I can help you . . .'

He stopped. She had bunched her hands into fists and raised them to her temples as though to prevent her head from splitting open.

'This is insane . . . this can't be happening . . . I'm going mad . . .!'

The man got up from his chair, concerned now. 'Look, maybe you'd better sit down. Can I call someone for you . . .?'

His tone was kindly, but when he reached out to guide her to the chair across the desk from his, she screamed. 'Don't touch me! Get your hands off me!'

She turned and ran, this time wildly. People got out of her way, backing against walls to avoid collision or contact of any kind with her. Startled faces peered out from their offices to see what the commotion was about. Suddenly up ahead she saw Taylor Freestone about to go into his office. He was reading something and didn't register her presence until she was almost on top of him.

'Taylor . . .!' She was breathless, her hair wild, confronting him with her feet planted firmly apart and arms rigid at her sides. 'For God's sake, Taylor, tell me you know me. Tell them who I am!'

He turned totally white. His eyes flickered nervously over the people who were gathering to observe them.

'What's all this?' he asked. 'What's happening here? What's this about?'

'I'm Joanna Cross! I work here!' She screamed the words, as though by sheer volume she could force everyone to acknowledge their truth.

'You *what* . . .?' he said incredulously.

She made an effort to control the panic that was gripping her. 'Joanna . . . Joanna Cross . . . Why don't you know who I am, Taylor? Why are you behaving like this . . .?'

Without realizing, she had taken a step towards him and seized the lapel of his jacket. His eyes widened in fear and he pulled himself free, stumbling slightly as he did so.

'Somebody get security . . .!'

'They're on their way,' a man's voice called out.

'Now look, Miss,' Taylor Freestone stuttered, 'whoever you are and whatever you want . . .'

'I'm not whoever . . . I'm Joanna Cross. I work for you, I write for this magazine . . .'

'I've never seen you before in my . . .'

'Camp Starburst. My story on Camp Starburst boosted circulation two per cent . . .'

'Camp what . . .?'

'You said the one I'm writing now on Adam Wyatt is worth a Pulitzer . . .'

Taylor Freestone's eyes continued to widen with alarm and disbelief. 'I've no idea what you're . . .'

'Sam Towne! You made a donation to his department at Manhattan University, for the story that I'm doing on the Adam Wyatt experiment.'

She became aware of a movement behind her. Two of

the uniformed security guards who were normally on duty downstairs in the main lobby appeared at her side.

'Just come along with us, quietly now, please,' one of them said.

She felt their hands on her arms and tried to shake them off, but they gripped tighter.

'Wait a minute, let's at least try to find out what's going on here.' The man who spoke was the one who'd been occupying her office. He stepped forward now, prepared to defend her.

'Leave this to us, please, sir,' one of the security guards said.

'I will leave it to you – as soon as I'm satisfied we all know what we're doing.' He looked at her squarely. 'Now who are you? What do you want?'

She realized she had to stay calm, or at least pretend to, let them see she could do it and that she was not demented, not a mad woman but somebody worthy of respect, their respect. 'I'm trying to tell you,' she said, 'I'm Joanna Cross . . . I'm a writer . . .'

'Is that why you've come here?' he asked. There was a strange gentleness in his tone. She realized that despite his gallantry he was still humouring her, doing the decent thing by a troubled woman rather than sensing a truth that he meant to uncover.

'I came here,' she said, her voice trembling, 'because I work here . . . and because I needed money . . .'

'The magazine owes you money?'

'No . . . I found myself on the street with no money . . . I needed . . .'

The man reached into his back pocket and brought out a wallet.

'Don't give her anything,' Taylor Freestone said

331

sharply. 'We have no responsibility here, don't assume any.'

'Giving her a few bucks isn't going to hurt,' the other man said.

He held out some bills. She didn't know how many, she didn't look. She thought for a moment she was going to pass out. The sheer impossibility of it all was overwhelming, and unconsciousness, with its implied promise that maybe she'd wake up and things would be all right again, seemed like the only choice before her.

But some small part of her brain was telling her to hang on, not to let go, not now, not yet. This wasn't a dream and it wasn't impossible, because it was actually happening. She couldn't run or hide. She had to face this thing and see it through.

'Take it,' the man said, still holding out the money. 'I'm sorry we can't help you, but if you need money . . .'

'No!' Taylor Freestone protested again.

'It's *my* money, dammit!' the man snapped back. 'Please take it,' he said to her more gently. 'Please just take it and go – all right?'

Very slowly, realizing there was nothing to be done, knowing that whatever happened, whatever she did next or wherever she went or tried to go, she would need money, she reached out and took it.

'Thank you.' Her voice was barely audible, but she sensed that her action, her acceptance of this stranger's gift, had somehow defused the situation.

'Just get her out of here,' Taylor Freestone said to the guards. 'And make sure she doesn't get back in.'

This time she didn't shake off the pressure on her arm. She let herself be led along the familiar corridors, through the lobby where Bobbie and Jane's silent gaze followed her, out through the glass doors, then into the elevator, and finally onto the street.

There they let her go, and watched until she was safely out of sight.

48

It was only when she asked for change in a magazine store that she realized that the man in her office had given her fifty dollars – an act of surprising generosity that she wished she'd thanked him better for. Better still would have been not needing to thank him for anything.

She found a payphone and tried Ward's number again. Still no reply. Next she phoned the lab. Peggy answered.

'Peggy, it's me – Joanna.'

'Joanna?'

'I wondered if you'd heard from Sam in the last half hour or so.'

'Sam's out right now. Actually I'm not quite sure where he is. Can I give him a message?'

'No, I . . . tell him I'll call back.'

'All right, Joanna, I'll make a note.'

The way she said Joanna didn't sound right. It wasn't the way you'd speak to a friend, or even to anyone you knew. Peggy was using the caller's first name out of politeness, not out of any sense of intimacy. 'Joanna' was just a woman on the phone who could have given any name.

Joanna swallowed, forcing herself to accept what she knew was the truth. 'You don't know who I am, do you, Peggy?'

'I'm sorry, I'm not sure I can quite place you. Would you like to remind me where we've met?'

'It doesn't matter,' she managed to say, and hung up.

The phone was one of a row in the subway at Columbus Circle. Nobody paid any attention to the woman who stood there with her face in her hands, leaning against the inside wall of the booth as though about to collapse. One or two people glanced her way as they passed, thinking maybe she'd just made a call and received some devastating news – the death of a loved one, perhaps, or the diagnosis of some illness more grave than she'd feared. None of them paused or came over to help. No one chose to get involved.

Joanna fished out some more coins and dialled the number she most feared calling. Her mother answered after three rings with her usual interrogatory 'Hello?'

'Mom?'

A pause, then, hesitantly, 'Joanna? Is that you?'

Joanna didn't realize she'd been holding her breath until it came out of her in a shuddering sob. 'Mom . . . help me, mom, I don't know what's happening . . . you're the only one who knows who I am . . . I've got to see you . . . I'm coming out there right now . . .'

'Who is this?'

The words cut like a knife through her brain. 'Mom, you just said . . . I said "mom" and you said "Joanna" . . .'

'I said, "Joanna, is that you?" But you're not Joanna. Now whoever you are, this is not a very funny joke. Don't call me again.'

She hung up.

49

It was nearly three hours before Sam was finished with the police. Their questions had been probing and fuelled by a deep suspicion – for which he couldn't blame them, given the circumstances. But they seemed satisfied in the end that Ward's death was suicide or conceivably an accident, but not murder.

He thought it wise not to tell them too much about Adam Wyatt and the whole experiment, saying merely that Ward took an interest in his work and had volunteered to take part in a series of experiments that were essentially statistical. The mention of statistics had deadened their interest sufficiently to let the whole topic of the paranormal slip by unexplored. Sam gave his personal details and said he'd be glad to make himself available for any further questioning.

Before leaving, and with the distraught manservant's approval, he made some calls from the phone in the apartment's main reception room. The first was to Joanna's mobile. He tried three times, each time getting a recording that told him there was some error in the number he had dialled, which was not currently allocated to any subscriber. He knew there was no error, but didn't persist.

He tried her number in Beekman Place, and listened

to the phone ring out – until it was answered by a man with a Bronx accent.

'Fiedler's Deli.'

Sam checked the number with the man. He'd dialled correctly, but this was not Beekman Place and there was no Joanna Cross at that location, only an assortment of sandwiches and salads that could be delivered in the neighbourhood at no extra charge. Sam apologized for troubling the man and hung up.

He called the *Around Town* office and asked for Joanna Cross. The request caused a flurry of excitement; he could hear muffled conversations around the phone, people being called, advice sought. Finally he was put through to Taylor Freestone.

'Who is this?'

'My name is Sam Towne.'

'Sam Towne? That's the second time I've heard that name today. The woman you're asking about, Joanna Cross, mentioned it when she was in here.'

'I'm trying to find her.'

'Well, you won't find her here. I don't know who she is, but security have orders to keep her out if she ever comes back. Who is she, anyway?'

Sam hesitated. 'I'm not sure I can tell you that, Mr Freestone. I'm sorry to have troubled you. Goodbye.'

When he hung up he waited a moment before dialling again. He was too afraid that he already knew what he was going to hear. All the same, he had to face it. If only as a scientist, he had to put his theories to the test. Peggy answered the phone.

'Any messages for me, Peggy?'

'There was a call from Carl Janowitz at that funding board you've been talking with. One from Bob Gulliver in the Dean's office. And one from a Joanna Cross. She seemed to think we knew each other. Has she worked with us at some point?'

'Yes, actually she has, Peggy.'

'I can't quite place her. Anyway, she said she'd call back.'

He thanked her and hung up. He debated whether to try calling Joanna's parents. He didn't have their number, but could probably find it easily enough.

But what would he say? What could he?

There were other things he had to do first, things that would cause no unnecessary distress to others. Above all he had to keep a tight grip on himself and his own sanity, remembering that he was a scientist who must confront the situation he was in with such emotional neutrality and clarity of mind as he could muster, asking questions and not hiding from the answers, whatever they might be and wherever they might lead.

Before leaving, he walked to the window and stood motionless for some moments, looking out. He remembered how the narrator in Jack Finney's story of time travel – he and Joanna had talked about it only yesterday – had stood at a window in this building and looked out on a New York of the past.

Sam knew that what he was looking out on now was something far more alien than the past.

50

It had started to rain while she was on the train. Now, as she emerged from the station, it was pouring hard and the November dusk was closing in.

There was no sign of a cab anywhere, so she took up her place at the head of the rank under cover of the station forecourt, and waited. She felt little except a strange numbness, a detachment from reality that reminded her of the way her mouth felt after a shot of novocaine at the dentist – still there, but mysteriously untouchable.

It was a defence mechanism, she told herself, while marvelling at the fact that knowing something didn't change the way it worked or the effect it had. But if it were not for this strange sense of being there and yet not there at the same time, she knew that the madness hovering on the edges of her consciousness would overwhelm her, and she would disintegrate totally.

A cab swished up and stopped to disgorge a couple who went through to the ticket office, then it pulled around and picked up Joanna. She gave her parents' address and sat back, hoping the driver wasn't the talkative kind. He wasn't.

She tried to analyse her feelings, to observe and define what was going through her mind, but found it impossible. Everything both conceivable and inconceivable seemed to be happening at once in her imagination, but she didn't know what she was actually thinking. That too, she supposed, was part of the defence mechanism that was enabling her to function well enough and long enough to reach her destination. What would happen when she got there was another question – one which she found herself unable even to contemplate.

The gate to her parents' drive was shut, so she paid off the cab and walked to the house. There was a wind getting up, driving the rain at an angle into her face. She lowered her head and pulled up her collar, quickening her pace.

At the door she paused a moment, protected by the small portico, and shook out her hair. For the first time it struck her that maybe they wouldn't be at home. There were lights in the house, but they always left lights on. Then she recognized the thought for what it was – a delaying mechanism to put off the confrontation that she knew was going to be the most painful and traumatic of them all. She rang the bell.

She heard it ring in the distance. Skip began to bark, running towards the door from wherever he'd been – probably asleep by the fire or curled up in his basket in the kitchen. She called his name through the door, but the barking didn't stop and turn into excited whimpering the way it usually did when he recognized someone's voice. She called his name again, but his bark just became more agitated.

A light went on over her head, then her mother's voice came tinnily from the speaker by her shoulder.

'Who is it?'

'Momma, it's me.'

There was a long pause, during which Skip continued to bark, scrabbling at the door now as though trying to claw his way through and attack her. She could hear her mother calling out to him, maybe even coming to get him and hauling him physically away, because his barking became more distant but lost none of its excitement.

She knocked on the door several times and called out, 'Momma? Momma, are you there?'

When her mother spoke, it was through the entry-phone again. She sounded different now, strained and ill at ease.

'Are you the person who called me earlier?'

'Momma, for heaven's sake, it's *me*. Let me in – please.'

She could still hear Skip's barking through the speaker, but distant and hollow-sounding now, as though he'd been locked in somewhere.

'Why are you doing this?' her mother asked. 'If you don't go away, I shall call the police – do you understand?'

'Mother, I'm begging you, open the door, look at me, tell me I'm Joanna – *please*.'

'I am looking at you. And I don't know who you are.'

Joanna turned sharply. She had forgotten about the security camera that her parents had installed a year or so ago after a couple of break-ins in the neighbourhood. She stared into its impersonal gaze.

'Momma, for the love of God, it's *me*. Don't tell me you don't know me! Please, just open the door and face me – that's all I'm asking. Open the door and look at me!'

There was a silence. Joanna waited for the sound of

341

footsteps in the hall, for the sound of a key being turned in a lock, a bolt being drawn.

She waited, but she waited in vain. Then she forced herself to wait some more, biting back the anguished cry that was building in her throat, angrily wiping away the tears that had begun to blur her vision. She waited until she could wait no more, and rang the bell again.

When there was no response, she banged at the door a couple of times with the side of her fist and called out to her mother. When there was still no response, she banged harder. The physical effort dispelled the last vestiges of her self-control and freed the panic so far held in check just beneath its surface. She clawed and kicked and battered at the door like a madwoman trying to escape from her locked cell, or like someone buried alive and screaming for release.

But no one answered. She stopped, exhausted, her throat hoarse. It was then that she remembered the dream her mother had described to her months earlier: she outside, hammering at the door to be let in, and her mother cowering terrified inside. There had even been rain, driving rain like now. It was that dream come true.

'Momma,' she cried, her face pressed against the wood, her fist beating out a relentless, steady rhythm to underline her words. 'Momma, don't you remember? It's your dream. Remember your dream? The nightmare? You told me I was outside in the rain, and you were too afraid to open the door. There's nothing to be afraid of, momma. It's me. Open the door, momma. Please, please open the door . . .'

A beam of light swept over her. She turned, shielding her eyes as a car came up the drive at speed. It stopped with a scrunch of tyres on the gravel. Doors banged. She heard the static of a radio, and realized that the two figures moving towards her were in uniform. Her mother had called the police as she'd threatened she would.

One of them turned a flashlight on her. She threw up a hand to shade her eyes.

'Step away from the door.'

She obeyed automatically.

'Turn and face the wall on your left.'

The second voice was a woman's. It was the female officer who now came up behind Joanna.

'Place your hands on the wall and stand with your feet apart.'

Joanna tried to protest that she wasn't carrying a weapon, but the female officer snapped at her to shut up while she briskly patted her body up and down.

'Okay, turn around.'

Joanna faced the two cops. Rain dripped from their faces, and she could see they were wearing heavy water-proofs which gave them an awkward, semi-inflated look. The man shone the powerful flashlight in her face again, making her squint.

'You got some I.D., lady?'

'No, I . . .' She was about to explain that she had left everything in a friend's apartment in New York, but saw at once it would be pointless. 'No, I don't have any.'

'Who are you and what are you doing on this property?'

'I'm Joanna Cross, and this is my parents' house.'

She saw a look pass between the cops. The man shook his head as though confirming to the woman that this was a lie.

'Get in the back of the car,' he said to Joanna, flicking his flashlight towards the patrol car and indicating she should walk ahead of him. When she was in, he left the door open but stood by it.

Looking past him, Joanna could see that the female cop was now talking to her mother at the front door. Her mother gave a nervous glance in the direction of the pale young woman sitting in the back of the car, and shook her head.

'No,' Joanna heard her say, 'I don't know who she is. I've never seen her in my life.'

'Are you quite sure of that, ma'am?' the male cop said, taking a few steps away from the car. 'I've met Mrs Cazaubon when she's been out here with her husband, so I know this isn't she. But are you sure you haven't some idea who this . . .'

He stopped as another set of headlights swept up the drive and illuminated the rain as if it were long threads of silver twisting in the night. Joanna didn't register her father's arrival rightaway. She was too stunned by what she had just heard and was still struggling to absorb its significance. *Mrs Cazaubon!*

She heard a car door slam, then her father's voice. 'What's going on here? Honey, are you all right?'

Joanna saw her father hurry over to her mother, who, clearly upset, was saying something that she couldn't hear, but which made Bob Cross look over in Joanna's direction, puzzlement written on his face. They gazed at each other across the space between them. There was no recognition on his side, nor any longer the hope of it on hers.

A crash came from the house, and Skip's barking, which had been muffled in the distance, suddenly grew louder as he bounded furiously out of the door. Joanna's father tried to catch him, but he slipped through his hands and began running in circles in the rain, hysterical in the face of all this strange excitement. Both her parents called him furiously, but he ignored them.

Joanna saw her chance. She had hoped that by coming here she would find some haven from the madness that her life had become, but saw now how wrong she was. Her only thought was to escape. She was not yet ready to give up the fight, even though she no longer knew for sure what she was fighting. While both her parents and the cops were distracted by the racing, yapping dog, she slid across the seat of the car and reached for the handle of the far door. She squeezed it gently; it wasn't locked. She was out and running before anybody saw her move.

'Hey, you! Stop right there!'

She could hear both cops coming after her. She didn't look back and she didn't slow down. They could shoot her if they liked; she didn't think they would, but even that would be better than just giving up. She raced through bushes and trees, down slippery rain-soaked paths and hidden places she had known since childhood, and where there was no way they could follow her in the dark.

After a couple of minutes she thought she'd lost them. She stopped, breathless, hearing nothing but the pelting rain all around her. Then she heard Skip's barking in the distance. He was coming after her.

She started to run again, but in a moment the little dog was snapping and snarling at her heels. She turned and tried to hush him. 'Quiet, Skip! Go back! Go back!' But he didn't know her, and his barking grew more frenzied. She knew he would bring the police in a few seconds if she couldn't shake him; she could already see their flashlights angling in the distance through the rain as they tried to figure out where the dog's barking was coming from. She tried running a few steps then turning and trying to chase him off again, but he only redoubled the noise he was making and crouched down, the hair stiff and bristling on his neck, ready to attack her.

Finally she came to a bank of huge old laurel bushes where, as a child, she'd found a secret tunnel through to the woods on the far side. If she could find that again she could probably lose Skip. Like a lot of small dogs he grew less brave the further he was from his own territory; with luck he wouldn't follow her.

She pushed through, her clothes and hair snagging on branches. She tugged them free and pressed on, until suddenly she found herself in a relatively open space.

A soft carpet of moss and leaves cushioned her feet as she ran. With every step the dog's barking and the angry voices of the two cops grew fainter in the distance.

51

Sam walked into the lab and glanced around at the various open doors and lighted rooms beyond. He had prepared himself for this as far as possible, despite his fears of what he might find. He knew only that he was deep into uncharted waters, and reminded himself for the hundredth time that afternoon that, as a scientist, it was his job to chart them. He must hang on to that thought at all cost; it must be his anchor and his sanity.

Peggy looked up from the computer she was working at and smiled a greeting, then paid him no more attention as he crossed to the door that led to the cellar and Adam's room. He tried the handle. It was locked, but the key was in the lock and turned easily. He pulled open the door, felt for the light switch, and went down the stairs.

Despite the fact that he had half expected it, the shock of what he found at the bottom was still hard to absorb. The cellar was the same old junkyard of discarded furniture and obsolete equipment that it had been months earlier when the Adam experiment was first mooted. It was as though the intervening time, and everything associated with it, had been wiped out.

Yet he, Sam Towne, still survived. And so did his memory of what had happened. How could that be? Why? Was there some reason for it, some purpose? Or was he by now merely part of a process that was not yet over but soon would be, leaving him . . . where?

That these were questions without answers was no reason for not asking them. There was some quotation echoing at the back of his mind that he couldn't quite place, about how man must assume that the incomprehensible is ultimately comprehensible – or else abandon all attempts to understand the universe and his place in it. Goethe, perhaps. It didn't much matter. The notion was a simple truth that every scientist lived by, and which he more than most had been brutally reminded of in these last days and hours.

'Are you looking for something?'

He jumped at Peggy's voice on the stairs behind him. 'Not really,' he said, turning to her. 'Just thinking.'

He continued looking at her, then said, 'That name, the woman who called – Joanna Cross – still doesn't mean anything to you?'

Peggy seemed to search her memory for a moment, then shook her head. 'Sorry, I can't place her. Is she one of our volunteers, or something?'

It was impossible to suspect that this was some kind of joke or game that she was playing.

'Yes . . . yes,' he said vaguely, 'she was involved in one of our programmes.'

He started for the stairs. 'Come back upstairs, Peggy. I want to talk to all of you. It'll only take a couple of minutes.'

Tania Phillips, Brad Bucklehurst and Jeff Dorrell were there. Bryan Meade, Peggy said, was off somewhere checking out some new piece of equipment he'd heard about. They all assembled in the open area in the centre of the lab. Sam had already rehearsed in his mind how he was going to do this. On the way over he had decided it would be the second thing that he would do, after checking on Adam's room, as he just had.

'I'm going to ask you all a few questions,' Sam began. 'I'm not going to tell you why or say anything about what's behind them. And I don't want you to ask me.'

'Will you tell us later?' The question came from Brad Bucklehurst. It was just an amiable inquiry, not challenging the rules in any way.

'I may,' Sam said. 'It depends how things work out. The first thing I want to know is whether the name Joanna Cross means anything to any of you.'

He gave Peggy a little sign to say nothing and let the others answer. They all shook their heads, shrugged, murmured, No they didn't think so.

'Okay,' Sam said. 'And Peggy, I know the name still means nothing to you other than that she called up this afternoon – right?'

'Right.'

'Next, how about Ward Riley? Does that name ring any bells for anybody?'

He watched as they exchanged looks, shook their heads, said no they didn't think so. All except Peggy, who said, 'I remember Ward Riley. He made several very generous contributions to our research funds, including a bequest when he died.'

Sam looked at her. 'When did he die?'

She returned his gaze, puzzled. 'You know perfectly well when he died.'

'When, Peggy?' he repeated.

'Spring, early April.'

'How did he die?'

'Sam, what's all this about . . .?'

'Please, Peggy, just do it my way.'

'He jumped from a window of his apartment in the Dakota building. Nobody knew why. You were shocked, you couldn't understand it. We talked about it.'

'All right,' Sam said quietly, 'thank you, Peggy. Now, the next name is Roger Fullerton. Does anybody know who Roger Fullerton is?'

This brought a chorus of response. They all knew who Roger Fullerton was. How could they not, he was world famous? They also knew that Sam had studied under him at Princeton.

'But he died this year, too, didn't he?' Jeff Dorrell asked.

'Aren't you sure?' Sam said, looking at him.

Jeff gave a slight shrug. 'I'm fairly sure. Now that's odd – you'd think I'd be sure whether or not somebody like Roger Fullerton had died. Actually, I know he did – I just can't remember when I heard it.'

Sam didn't pursue the question for the moment. Instead he continued with the list he had prepared in his mind. 'Okay, who knows Drew and Barry Hearst?'

Again there was an affirmative response from everyone. Drew and Barry had been volunteers in a number of experiments, particularly the remote viewing ones with Brad and Tania.

'But they died,' Tania said, looking at Sam with a marked degree of suspicion now. 'They were killed in a car crash about three months ago.'

'Maggie McBride?' Sam said.

Hers too was a name they recognized. Maggie had worked on remote viewing and several of the PK tests. 'But I haven't seen her in a long time,' Tania said.

'And I'm afraid you won't,' Peggy added, her gaze too now fixed on Sam. 'I got a note from Maggie's daughter just recently to say she'd passed away – a heart attack. I know I told you that, Sam.'

He made no comment, just went on. 'What does the name Pete Daniels mean to any of you?'

This too brought a general response. They'd all known Pete.

'What is this, Sam?' Brad Bucklehurst said. 'Some kind of obituary game, or what? Why are you asking about all these people who've died?'

Sam held up a hand. 'Please . . . I warned you I wouldn't say why I was asking. Just tell me about Pete, who he was, when and how he died.'

'He joined us about two years ago,' Brad said. 'Worked as your personal assistant for six, seven months, then got knifed in some street fight. We never did get to the bottom of it. I was here when the police called. You went to the morgue to identify him. You can't have forgotten that.'

Again Sam made no comment. 'Finally, Adam Wyatt,' he said, and looked around at them one by one. 'Does the name Adam Wyatt mean anything to any of you?'

Blank faces gazed back at him, lips were pursed, heads shaken. The name meant nothing.

Sam was silent a moment. Then he pushed himself up off the arm of the chair where he'd been perched. 'All right, that's it – thank you, everybody.'

True to their agreement, nobody asked questions or pressed for explanations. They all went back to what they had been doing, though full of curiosity and speculation among themselves.

Sam walked over to his office. As he turned to shut

the door, he caught Peggy's gaze on him, questioning and concerned. He made an effort to give her a thin smile of reassurance, but he knew she sensed that something was deeply wrong. He closed the door, then slumped into the chair behind his desk.

There was, he told himself, an inescapable if insane logic to the situation. The world in which Adam Wyatt existed was no longer the world in which they as a group had created him. By imagining him into existence they had imagined themselves out of it – at least in the form in which they had previously existed.

It was, as Joanna and Roger had both said, a problem of compatibility. There were mathematical principles, descriptions of the fundamental laws of nature, under-scoring that truth. The Pauli exclusion principle, or Bell's Theorem, could surely apply in some form. Or Godel. Wasn't there something here of closed systems and self-reference . . .?

He pulled himself up short. He was doing the very thing that orthodox science contemptuously accused people like him of, and that he himself strove to avoid in all his work: he was taking the hard-won results of scientific experiment and theory and turning them back into the kind of magic that men believed in before the dawn of reason drove out the crippling superstitions that had governed man's early history.

Or was science itself the dead end? He thought of what Joanna had told him of her last conversation with Roger. Could that really have been what a man like Roger thought? That in the end, as the eastern mystics taught, there was only the eternal dance, with western thought and scientific rationalism no more than one of the forms it took from time to time, no nearer to a final truth than the caveman's belief that the sun rose only because he sacrificed the life of some animal or fellow human being on the altar of his tribal gods?

His hand closed on something in the bottom of his jacket pocket. He pulled out the square of paper torn from Joanna's notepad, the one he'd picked up in her apartment the night before, on which she'd written down the address and phone number of Ralph Cazaubon.

He looked at it a while, and wondered. He'd tried the number last night to no avail. Could there be any point in trying it again? He hesitated only for a moment, then reached for his phone and dialled.

After three rings a man's voice said, 'Hello?'

Sam was aware suddenly of his heart beating in his chest.

'Is this Ralph Cazaubon?' he asked.

'Yes it is. How can I help you?'

'I'm trying to get in touch with someone called Joanna Cross.'

'Joanna Cross.' The voice on the other end repeated the name with a note of curiosity. 'That's my wife's name – or was before we married.'

52

The rain had lightened by the time she reached the road and started walking towards the station. Each time she heard a car approaching she slipped into the trees and hid in case it was the police, but she knew she was going to have to risk hitching a ride sooner or later. Eventually she heard a truck coming up behind her. She turned, blinded by its massive lights, and raised a thumb. It shuddered to a halt with a hiss of air brakes.

She ignored as far as she could all the driver's standard conversational gambits, saying only that her car had broken down and she had to catch a train. He offered to let her use his phone to call a garage, but she said she'd already taken care of that. He looked at her doubtfully, bedraggled and exhausted as she was, but something about her discouraged him from asking further questions.

When they approached the station she asked him to stop about a hundred yards short. He did so, merely nodding his acknowledgement of her thanks as she climbed down from the cab, then leaning over to pull the door shut. He was glad to be rid of her. She was a good-looking woman, and for a moment when he'd seen her in the road back there he'd thought he might get lucky. But something about her had given him the shivers. She felt like bad luck – not, he told himself, that he was a superstitious man.

She approached the station carefully, hugging the fence on the far side of the road where it turned and doubled back on itself and into a narrow, quiet road on a slight hill. Standing there, she could observe the station forecourt without being seen.

Her caution was rewarded when she saw the police car parked right outside the main entrance. These cops were neither subtle nor particularly smart; at least she had that much going for her. Her only worry was that they'd stay there indefinitely and she'd never be able to get on a train. But after a couple of minutes they came out, gave a perfunctory check around the forecourt, then drove off.

She started to cross the road, but stopped as a thought occurred to her. There was every chance that the cops would have given her description to whoever was in the ticket office and told them to look out for her. Luckily she had a return ticket in her pocket and so didn't need to show her face at the window. Also she knew there was a way onto the platform that only the local commuters were aware of – a gate at the far end that was supposedly for freight and heavy goods, but which was a godsend for anyone cutting it too fine and arriving just as their train was about to pull out. She headed for it and waited in the shadows until her train arrived.

Minutes later she was settled in a window seat watching the night rush by outside, and wondering if the wraith-like creature staring back at her could really be her own reflection.

53

Something impossible had happened.

'Darling,' Ralph Cazaubon had said as his wife entered, 'this is Dr Sam Towne of Manhattan University. He's been telling me a rather odd story . . .'

He stopped because Sam had gasped audibly. Both he and the woman who had just entered turned their gaze towards the man who stood with his mouth slightly open and his pale blue eyes staring, unblinking, at her. His face was white and he looked on the verge of passing out.

Sam Towne had not been ready for this. The Joanna Cross who stood before him was the same age and physical build as the one he knew; but she was quite distinctly someone else. Her hair was lighter and worn shorter. Her eyes, too, were lighter – blue instead of the green that he was used to. The contours of her face were subtly changed. They could have been sisters, but they were different people.

'Is something wrong, Dr Towne?'

The question came from Ralph Cazaubon. Sam swallowed and made an effort to pull his thoughts together.

'To be honest, I'm not entirely sure. Your wife isn't . . . isn't quite the person I'd expected.'

She was looking at him curiously, a half-smile of polite anticipation on her face, waiting to hear what this stranger was doing in her house, what he'd been saying to her husband.

'What "strange tale" has Dr Towne being telling you?' she asked him.

'It might be better if he told you that himself,' Ralph replied. They both turned to Sam and waited for him to go on.

'There's a woman who's been involved in some work I've been doing,' he began, a little unsurely, 'who's been using your name – your maiden name, that is. Joanna Cross.'

She frowned. '*Using* my name? Or someone with the same name? I daresay it's not that unusual a name. There must be more than one Joanna Cross in the world.'

'Yes . . . yes, I suppose there are . . . Perhaps that's it,' he finished lamely, not knowing what else to say.

'Is that all?' Ralph said, frowning. 'You seemed convinced when you arrived that there was something a good deal more sinister going on.'

Sam ran a hand across his mouth. He could feel his lips were dry. 'I'm sorry, I didn't mean to alarm you. But the coincidence was, from where I stood, rather strange.'

'You say this woman's been involved in work you've been doing? What kind of work is that, Dr Towne?' Joanna asked.

'Dr Towne is an investigator of the paranormal,' Ralph said with a faintly disparaging smile. 'I have the feeling he suspected there was some kind of doppelganger at work here.'

He caught the flash of response in Sam's eyes. 'Good God,' he said, 'I believe that's what you *did* think, isn't it?'

Joanna spoke before Sam could find a reply. 'Dr Towne

looks as though he has rather a lot on his mind. I think the least we can do is ask him to sit down and offer him a drink.'

'Thank you – your husband has already offered. If you don't mind, though, I will sit down. And with your permission ask a couple of questions. I won't take up much of your time.'

'Please, go ahead.'

Sam resumed his place on the sofa where he'd been when she arrived. 'Can I ask first,' he said, 'if the name Adam Wyatt means anything to either of you?'

'Well, of course it does,' she said, as though mildly surprised that he should ask, but at the same time pleased. She crossed over to a shelf and took down one of several identical white-bound paperbacks. 'Here's a proof copy of my book. It's due for publication in the spring.'

Sam took the book she held out to him. On its cover he read in plain print:

ADAM WYATT

An American Rebel in Revolutionary Paris

by

JOANNA CROSS

Hoping that he was concealing the astonishment he felt, he thumbed through its three hundred or so pages, its print broken here and there by illustrations and portraits reproduced in colour.

'How do you know about Adam?' she asked, happily intrigued by the conversation now. 'I thought he was my

358

secret – at least until the book comes out, then I hope he'll be everybody's.'

'Oh, I . . . I don't know a great deal about him,' Sam lied awkwardly. 'It's just that I've come across several references to him recently . . .'

'There you are, it's what I always say,' she said with a triumphant glance towards her husband. 'When a subject's time has come, it's just in the air, up for grabs. It's simply a question of who gets to it first.'

'To be honest,' Sam said, 'I wasn't sure whether Adam Wyatt was a fictional character or a real one.'

'Oh, he was real, all right,' she said with the brief laugh of someone utterly certain of what she was saying. 'When I started to research him I came up with an extraordinary amount of documentation. He was quite a character. When he was hardly more than a boy during the War of Independence he wormed his way into a friendship with Lafayette – risked the whole Battle of Yorktown to fake an incident with a runaway horse that made him look a hero. Years later he almost certainly murdered the only surviving person who knew what he'd done. Meanwhile he'd persuaded Lafayette to take him back to France, where he married an aristocrat who was a close friend of Marie-Antoinette, and got mixed up in every kind of wickedness you can imagine. Despite all of which he died old, rich, and apparently happy, thereby proving,' she added with another laugh, 'that, as we all know, there really is no justice in this world.'

Sam had been watching her as she spoke. She had an innocent and lively effervescence, quite obviously a spoilt and privileged young woman, but one whose advantages not even the hardest heart could easily resent. Something about her made him say to himself that this was a charmed life. Pain, misery and meanness would somehow never touch her. She would survive them. She was born to be, and always would be, he felt, happy, just as surely as some were fated not to be.

'Do you remember how exactly you came across Adam Wyatt in the first place?' he asked her.

She answered with a slight frown. 'I'm not sure I do now. I think it was a casual reference in some local history of the place where I was born in the Hudson Valley.' She broke again into a bright, enthusiastic smile. 'The amazing thing is he turned out to be an ancestor of Ralph's, on his mother's side. In fact it was Adam who brought us together – literally.'

As she spoke she reached out for Ralph's hand. Sam noticed that they touched each other with an easy spontaneity and total lack of self-consciousness. They looked, he thought, like a couple very much in love.

'My parents still live there and I've always gone up to see them quite often. Ralph was renting a house nearby, but we didn't know each other until one morning we were both out riding, and we met literally over Adam's tomb in this little churchyard. I was there for research, and Ralph was curious about where this notorious ancestor of his was buried . . .'

'Excuse me,' Sam interrupted, 'that was the first time you met? Do you mind telling me how long ago this was?'

Ralph gave a smile and looked at his wife with undisguised adoration. 'Exactly twelve months and three days ago,' he said. 'But may we know why you ask?'

He was relaxed now, apparently over his initial distrust of Sam and untroubled by his questions, but still curious.

'I . . . I just wondered,' Sam said lamely. 'That would

make the date . . .' He did a rapid calculation and confirmed it with them – chiefly to assure himself that he and they were working within the same time frame. They were. Today's date for him was the same as for them. Somehow the meeting between *this* Joanna Cross and Ralph Cazaubon had pre-dated the meeting between *his* Joanna and Ralph Cazaubon by exactly one year.

'Anyway,' she said, 'the coincidence of us both being in that tiny churchyard at the same time and looking for the same grave was so extraordinary . . .' She made a gesture that implied she need elaborate no further. 'It just seemed sort of inevitable.'

'And so you wrote your book,' Sam prompted her.

'I wrote my book with the subject's great-great-several-more-greats-grandson correcting my spelling and making sure I was no more horrid about his family than I had to be.' She gave Ralph's hand a squeeze.

'Had you published anything before?' Sam asked her.

'Heavens, no. I'd been working in a brokerage firm – deathly dull, just a job. I'd always dreamed of becoming a writer, but never had the confidence to start. Now I'm hoping I can make a career of it. I've got a few more ideas for biographies, then maybe a novel.'

'Now come on, Dr Towne,' Ralph said, 'you must tell us something about what's behind all this. Are you working on something about Adam yourself? Or has he come up in one of your psychic investigations? It wouldn't surprise me, he was a pretty dark character – used to dabble in black magic by all accounts.'

'Well, yes, as a matter of fact he has come up in connection with my work – in a way.'

'How exciting! Do tell all,' Joanna said, like a little girl eager to hear the latest gossip from a friend.

Sam hedged delicately. 'I'm afraid it's difficult to go into detail right now. But I'll be glad to tell you whatever I can as soon as I'm able.'

Joanna looked faintly disappointed at his evasiveness, but said nothing.

'Do you think I might borrow a copy of this book?' Sam asked tentatively. 'I'd be happy to buy one, but if it isn't published yet . . .'

'Take that one as a gift,' she said at once, and gestured towards the shelf behind her. 'As you can see, I've got plenty.'

'That's very kind of you, thank you.' Sam got to his feet. 'Now I really mustn't trouble you any longer.'

'Just one thing,' Ralph Cazaubon said, frowning like someone tripping over an awkward detail that he'd briefly forgotten, 'when you got here, you said something about two men dying. What exactly was all that about?'

The question took Sam by surprise. He too had pushed the matter from his mind.

'I'm sorry,' he said, as reassuringly as he could, 'that was rather misleading of me. 'As your wife is plainly not the Joanna Cross I thought she was, none of that applies any longer. I know that sounds obscure, but I can't tell you more for the moment. I don't really know any more.'

'Well, this is all very mysterious,' Ralph said, though not seeming especially perturbed, 'but I can see we'll have to take your word that you'll explain everything when you can. You don't have a card by any chance, do you? Somewhere we can get in touch with you if we should need to?'

'Yes, I should have somewhere . . .' Sam fished out his wallet and found one of the cards Peggy had got printed for him a couple of years ago and that he rarely found use for. He wrote his home number on the back. Ralph took it with thanks and placed it on the mantelpiece.

'You must be sure to let me know what you think of my book, Dr Towne,' Joanna said. 'I'd love to have an academic opinion.'

'I promise I'll call you.'

'And do tell me if there's anything you can think of about Adam that I've left out. It's not too late to add a few footnotes.'

'Yes, of course,' Sam mumbled. Then he looked at them, first one, then the other, and said, 'I assume you're not superstitious, either of you.'

'Superstitious? How d'you mean?' she asked.

'Oh, you know, history repeating itself. I mean, Adam being your husband's ancestor . . .'

'Oh . . .' She laughed as though he'd made a joke, and reached out to ruffle Ralph's hair playfully. 'No, I'm not superstitious in that way. Neither of us is.'

They saw Sam to the door and watched as he walked off into the night.

'Strange man,' Ralph said when they were back inside.

'I thought he was rather nice.'

'All right – nice and strange. But I hope we find out what that was all about some day.'

'Maybe Adam's started haunting somebody – clanking around in chains and uttering low moans. I wouldn't put it past him – he's done just about everything else.'

The phone rang. Ralph went back to the room where they'd been sitting to answer it.

'Hello? Oh, Bob . . .' He gestured to Joanna that it was her father. 'How are you? You want Joanna, she's right here . . .?'

363

He broke off, his face clouding. Joanna, realizing something was wrong, came quickly to his side.

'What is it?'

He gestured her to be patient while he listened. 'You're kidding. When was this?'

He listened some more, then he said, 'That's the weirdest thing. We just had someone here looking for her. It must be the same woman.'

Joanna's patience, never remarkable, was reaching its limit. She was holding out her hand for the phone, expecting him to pass it over any moment, but instead Ralph said, 'No, sure, I understand. I'll tell her. Okay, 'bye, Bob.'

He hung up and turned to her. 'That is quite extraordinary.'

'What? What?'

'Your parents have had some strange woman at the house banging on their door and claiming to be you. It must be the same woman Sam Towne was looking for.'

'Is she there now?'

'No, she got away. Apparently your mother was alone and freaked out and called the police. Who can blame her? Your father got back in time to see the woman, but then she gave them the slip.'

'What was she like? Did he say?'

'Not much – only that she was about your age, dark hair. He said Elizabeth's still pretty shaken, but she'll call you tomorrow. He just wanted to warn us in case the woman shows up here. She must be some kind of weirdo – a stalker or something.'

'Jeez!' Joanna gave an involuntary shudder. 'That's a little creepy.'

Ralph reached out to brush back the hair where it fell

across her forehead. 'Don't worry, the cops seemed to think she was harmless. They said there was a name for it, some kind of syndrome – people who develop an obsession about being someone else. Maybe it'll turn out to be somebody you were at school with, or college. I've heard of that kind of thing happening.'

'All the same, I don't like it.'

He took her in his arms and held her face against his. 'Don't worry, nothing's going to happen to you. I'll make sure of that.'

54

She took the subway from Grand Central and emerged on 68th Street. Minutes later she was on the street that she had walked along the day before with Sam. The house they had seen then had been neglected, closed up and uninhabited. Tonight its windows blazed with light, and its door, painted in a green so dark that it was almost black, bore the number 139 in plain brass characters.

Filled though she was with an apprehension bordering on terror, she stepped up and rang the bell. She heard a lock turn, and the door opened. There was no recognition in Ralph Cazaubon's face when he saw her.

'Ralph?' She spoke his name uncertainly, her voice caught somewhere in her throat.

A look came into his eyes. Not recognition, but understanding of some kind. 'Do you know me?' he asked her.

'Yes. Don't you know me?'

He shook his head slightly, then checked himself. 'Yes, I think I know who you are.'

There must have been some change in her face, some expression of relief or gratitude for the tiny crumb of comfort he had offered her, because she saw it reflected in his. There was a sympathy in the way he looked at her, a kindness that had become in so short a space of time quite alien to her.

'Do you? Do you really know me?'

There was a pleading in her eyes and voice that touched him. He could not believe that this poor, disturbed creature meant ill towards anyone.

'I think you'd better come in,' he said.

As she stepped into the light, he saw that her hair was dank and tangled from the rain that had been falling earlier. There was a red mark on her cheek where she'd been scratched by something. Her clothes were creased and dirty, and her shoes caked with mud that had splashed up her legs.

She looked around, then turned to fix her gaze on him as he closed the door behind her. The words began to tumble out of her.

'Nobody knows who I am any more. Only you. And this morning I was so afraid of you I ran away. I went to my parents' house and they locked me out, they didn't know me . . . and then I heard someone say their daughter's name was Cazaubon, Joanna Cazaubon . . .'

'Come through, in here . . .'

He took her arm and steered her gently through into the drawing room where he had sat with Sam two hours earlier.

'Sit down. Don't be afraid, don't worry about anything. I'll do all I can to help you.'

'But do you know what's happening? Do you understand?'

'I think I do.'

She became agitated suddenly. 'I have to talk to somebody. His name's Sam Towne. I must find Sam, we must call him . . .'

'Sam Towne was here earlier.'

367

She seemed both surprised and reassured to hear this. 'He was here . . .?'

'Two hours ago. He was looking for you.'

'We must call him now . . . Please, I must see him . . . Sam will know what to do . . . we must get him here . . .'

'Yes, of course, I'll call him.'

Just then, distantly, he heard his wife call 'Ralph . . .?' She was coming down the stairs.

The woman with him reacted instantly. 'Who's that?' she asked abruptly, as though the voice she had heard belonged to someone with no right to be there, an intruder whose presence was both an affront and a threat to her.

He didn't answer her question. All he said was, 'Wait here a moment, please.'

'But I have to see her . . .'

'You will. But just sit down a moment, please.'

She sat obediently on the edge of the sofa that Sam had occupied earlier. Ralph started out of the room. At the door he glanced over his shoulder; she was still there, tense and ready to get up and follow him if he gave the word.

'One second,' he said. 'I'll be right back.'

He slipped out and closed the door behind him, then ran up the stairs to intercept Joanna. They almost collided at the first landing.

'I heard the bell,' she said. 'Who was it?'

'It's her,' he said in a whisper, 'the woman who was at your parents' earlier.'

'Where is she?'

'The sitting room.'

She made a move to pass him, but he blocked her.

'No – I think it's better you don't.'

'But I have to see her. I want to find out who she is.'

'Darling, let me handle it – please.'

'Maybe I know her. Like you said, it could be some-body I was at school with . . .'

'She's obviously disturbed, I don't think we should risk provoking some kind of crisis.'

'There's already a crisis if she's going around pre-tending to be me. I want to see her.'

He didn't argue further, just let her pass and followed her down the remaining stairs and into the hall. He made sure he was right behind her as she pushed open the door into the drawing room.

They both stopped and looked around. The room was empty.

She turned to him. 'She doesn't seem to be here now.'

He looked around again, bewildered. 'She was right there, on the sofa.'

'Well, she must have left.'

Ralph quickly checked the room. There was no hiding place. 'She can't have left,' he said. 'We'd have heard the door.'

'Maybe not if she didn't want us to.'

'For God's sake,' he said, 'this is ridiculous. Who is she?'

55

It was almost three in the morning when Sam finally
closed Joanna's book and set it down on the table by his
chair. For a while he didn't move. Then he ran his hands
over his face and through his hair, and got up to pour
himself a large whisky.

As she had told him, it was an extraordinary story –
the more so for being familiar in all but a handful of its
details. It was everything that the group had invented
about Adam, but set out now as historical fact and auth-
enticated by a comprehensive index of sources. Even the
various pictures of Adam, attributed though they were
to portraitists and sketch artists of the period, were
unmistakably of the man drawn by Drew Hearst way
back at the start of the experiment.

But this version of Adam had become a very different
person from the one they had intended to create. This
was a man who had betrayed the trust first of his patron,
Lafayette, then of his wife, and subsequently almost
everyone with whom he had come into contact. In Paris,
during the period leading up to the revolution, he had
consorted with thieves and whores and scoundrels of all
kinds. When asked once by the generous though
despairing Lafayette why he behaved so badly, he

answered insolently, '*Joie de vivre!*' It was the only explanation he ever gave for any of his actions.

The magician Cagliostro became his ally, and together they conspired to defraud the gullible Cardinal Rohan of a fortune in the diamond necklace affair. When Cagliostro was thrown in jail for his part in the plot, he kept quiet about Adam's involvement because Adam, who still had connections at court through his unfortunate and much-abused wife, represented his only chance of getting out.

Cagliostro's silence was rewarded when Adam did in fact secure his release, but in return Adam demanded the magic talisman which had thus far in his life protected Cagliostro against all enemies. It would do so, Adam said, one last time, when he handed it over in return for his freedom and his life and went into exile outside France.

The talisman was shown in one of the book's illustrations. Sam was familiar with the design it bore. It was the design he had first seen indistinctly in the wax impression left on the floor that terrifying night in Adam's room at the lab, then later and more clearly in the book given to Joanna by Barry Hearst.

According to legend, Adam had kept the talisman with him all his life, even having it buried with him in his tomb. Something else he had never abandoned was his strange love of the French term *joie de vivre*, for which no equivalent existed in English, and which he not only had engraved upon his tomb, but also incorporated into the Wyatt coat of arms – a vanity he had acquired in England, along with a second wealthy and aristocratic wife.

His return to America after her suspicious death had

marked the start of the third long period of his life. Rich, and with the acquired airs and graces of a nobleman, he had become an immensely wealthy and successful banker, and finally even a renowned philanthropist. Whenever, as had happened occasionally, some whispered rumour of the dreadful reputation he had left behind in Europe reached across the ocean and threatened the high regard in which he was now held at home, the bearer of such gossip either mysteriously disappeared, or recanted his lies and lived on in comfort as the willing and obedient servant of the all-powerful Adam Wyatt.

Sam found himself gazing out into the night through the very window on which the words *joie de vivre* had mysteriously appeared only a few days ago – that common phrase which Adam had distorted and so strangely made his own.

'Dear God,' he murmured to himself, and instantly wondered if unconsciously he'd meant it as a prayer.

He decided that perhaps he had.

56

The crash woke them both. Ralph reached for the light and swung his feet out of bed in one movement. He grabbed his robe and looked at Joanna, who was sitting up, pale with shock.

'Stay there,' he said, starting out.

'Ralph – be careful. There may be somebody in the house.'

'I doubt it – after making that much noise.'

He ran down the stairs, switching on lights as he went. There was no further sound or movement anywhere. On the floor below their bedroom he pushed open all the doors one by one, including the one to the music room where he worked. There he grabbed his old baseball bat from a corner before taking the remaining stairs to the hall. When he got there he stopped in his tracks.

The antique hat- and coat-stand that normally stood near the foot of the stairs lay some twenty feet away on its side by the front door. There was a gash on the door's paintwork where it had hit, as though the heavy object had been thrown against it like a missile.

He approached cautiously, holding the baseball bat ready to defend himself in case whoever had performed this considerable feat of strength was still hiding somewhere. But there was no sign of anyone, no sound or movement.

Looking around him and keeping his back to the wall so that nobody could take him by surprise, he reached down and hefted the iron stand in one hand as though to reassure himself that it really did weigh as much as it had the last time he'd had cause to move it. The strength that it had taken to fling it this distance would be frightening to confront; the reason why anybody might have wanted to do it was even more alarming to speculate upon. It made no sense.

He stepped over the stand without even trying to haul it upright. The drawing room was in darkness and the door partly open. He approached in a half crouch, both hands gripping the handle of the bat ready to lash out at the first movement. When he reached the door he slammed it with his shoulder, banging it back against the inner wall. At the same time he hit the light switch.

The room was empty, nothing had been disturbed. He went around it, circling the furniture to make sure that nobody was hiding behind anything, bat still in hand and ready to swing. There was nobody, and nowhere in the room where anyone could hide.

As he straightened up, lifting a hand to rub his nose in puzzlement, he sensed a movement in the door behind him. He spun around – and only Joanna's cry of alarm checked his swing before the hard wood smashed into her face. He let the bat fall to the floor and grabbed her in his arms, his fingers digging into the flesh beneath the thick white robe she wore.

'For God's sake, Jo, I could have killed you! I told you to stay where you were.'

'I was afraid.'

He could feel her trembling.

'It's all right, Jo . . . there's nobody here . . .'

'How did the coat-stand get over there?'

'I don't know.'

'Ralph, there must have been somebody here.'

He didn't answer; he didn't know what to say. But he felt her stiffen, felt her scream before the sound even left her throat. She had seen something over his shoulder.

Ralph turned in time to see the big Venetian mirror that hung above the fireplace lurch crazily into space and fly across the room, moving like a playing card tossed by some unseen, giant hand. A corner of it caught the back of the sofa. There was a sound of tearing fabric, then it cartwheeled on, smashing over an antique writing desk and against the far wall.

A moment later, in the sudden unreal silence, neither of them could hear anything except the sound of their own breathing and the beating of their hearts. They clung to each other, conscious of nothing other than the sheer impossibility of what they had just seen.

'I saw somebody,' she whispered, her voice shaking.

'Where?'

'In the mirror. Just before it came off the wall. I saw a woman, standing over there, watching us.'

They both looked in the direction she was pointing. There was nobody.

'Can you describe her?' he said.

'I only saw her for a second. Dark hair, a light coat, about my age. She had a kind of wild look about her, like she was half-crazed or something.'

'It's the woman who was here earlier.'

She looked at him. 'Ralph, this doesn't make any sense. I'm scared.'

'We're getting out of here – now.'

'It's two in the morning. Where will we go?'

'It doesn't matter where we go. Why don't you call that place your parents stay – they know you.'

'Okay.'

'We'll call them from upstairs . . .'

He took her by the arm, his eyes darting everywhere with each step for any threat or hint of movement. In their bedroom they pulled on clothes and gathered up the few things they would need to take with them. They spoke hardly at all, except when Joanna called the hotel to check they had a room and to say they'd be there in fifteen minutes.

A loud crash came from somewhere on the floor below. They froze and looked at each other. She sensed he was debating whether to investigate.

'Don't!' she said.

He started for the door. 'That was the music room.'

'Ralph, leave it!'

He looked back at her. 'Stay here, finish packing. I'll only be a second.'

She watched him disappear down the stairs, wanting to call him back, but saying nothing. Instead she picked up the overnight bag she had already half filled and went into the bathroom. She grabbed a toothbrush, comb, a few cosmetics . . . and heard the door click softly shut behind her.

Her first thought was that she mustn't think at all. A door closing by itself was no mystery: a draught of air, or perhaps she'd caught it coming through and caused it to swing shut slowly after her. It was nothing to worry about, even now after what had been happening. She would simply walk over and open it again.

It wouldn't budge. The handle turned, but when she pulled it the door didn't open. It wasn't locked, it was sealed shut by some force, some power, that didn't want her to leave.

She banged it with her hand, held flat, her palm slapping the smooth surface, and called out for Ralph. There was no answer, no footsteps coming to help her. She waited, then she banged the door again, with her fist this time, then both fists. And she called out, louder. She hammered with her fists and cried out for Ralph, until she realized that her hands hurt and her throat was sore.

Fear stole over her slowly, stealthily, like delayed shock. She became aware that she was fighting uselessly to hold it back, a Canute-like struggle that she couldn't win. Fear, like pain, she knew, would always overwhelm you in the end. You had to let it, but find something to cling onto while it passed – even if no more than the idea that it *would* pass in the end.

But suppose it didn't? Suppose the fear stayed, became a permanent, eternal, tortured scream with no escape?

No! That was panic, it wouldn't last. Just the first wave . . . a wave, a wave . . . a wave by definition couldn't last for ever . . .

A sound came from the wall as though a small explosive charge had detonated in it. She turned with a gasp, trying to identify the spot that it had come from. Before she could, there was another – from somewhere else, but still behind the tiled and mirrored surfaces and in the fabric of the walls themselves. It was a sound like she had never heard before, a subtle, dangerous, insinuating thing. There was something hypnotic in the way, with each repetition, it became increasingly impossible not only to identify its source, but even to be sure that the source was not inside her own head.

Then something happened that she knew for sure she was not imagining. It started with a different sound, a scratching noise, like claws on slate or glass, the kind of noise that made you cringe and set your teeth on edge.

This time she knew where it was coming from. The sound was localized in a way the previous ones had not been. She found herself drawn as though by some magnetic force towards the mirror set into the wall behind the twin adjoining hand basins. She saw her own reflection clearly enough, and that of her surroundings, including the door still firmly closed behind her.

But it was not on the image that her gaze was focused: rather, on the glass itself in which the image lay. Something, she sensed, was happening there. And just as swiftly as she sensed it, so the words began appearing – ragged, slightly wandering lines scratched into the silvery reflecting surface on the back of the glass, as though traced by some unseen hand, but in a place where no hand could possibly have been.

The letter 'H' came first. Before it was complete, others began appearing simultaneously, as though each was being separately engraved in lines that hung in space at some intangible point between herself and her reflection.

She watched in awful fascination as the message was spelled out. At first she didn't understand. For a split second she thought it was in some strange language. Then she realized it was English, written backwards, as though by someone on the other side.

The message was:

ɘM qlɘH

Her head swam and she felt herself falling in some strange way into herself, imploding, losing form and focus. She grabbed for something, shook herself; it was all right, she would hang on, it would pass.

A thick mat on the tiled floor broke her fall. She felt a jolt to her knee, then another to her elbow and arm. She pushed herself up. She was unhurt, but aware now that there was no escape, not even into unconsciousness, from what was happening.

HELP ME!

'Help me! Ralph, help me!'

She was on her feet now, pounding at the door, rattling the handle and tugging it towards her. Quite suddenly it opened, seemingly of its own accord, neither resisting nor yielding to the pressure she was putting on it. There was no click of any latch or lock; it just opened and released her.

Ralph was entering the room on the far side as she stumbled, white-faced and terrified, from the bathroom. He ran to her.

'Jo – what happened?'

'Didn't you hear me?'

'I didn't hear anything. Are you all right?'

'Let's just go, now – right now, please.'

57

It was barely seven-thirty the following morning when Sam's phone rang. He was already on his second pot of coffee and cut short Ralph's apologies for calling so early.

'What's happened?' he asked, sensing the tension in the other man's voice.

'That woman you were looking for last night? She paid us a visit after you'd left. It seems that she'd also paid a visit to Joanna's parents.'

'And—?'

Ralph hesitated. 'I think it would be better if we talked face to face. Joanna and I are in a hotel right now, but I can be at the house in twenty minutes. Can you meet me there?'

Ralph Cazaubon was waiting on the steps of number 139 when Sam got out of his cab. He looked tired and nervous, very different from the self-assured and confident individual who had opened the door the previous day.

'Thanks for coming over, Dr Towne.' He pulled a key-ring from his pocket and gave a vaguely apologetic laugh as he unlocked the door. 'I told myself I'd wait outside until you got here so you could see everything exactly as it was, untouched since last night. But the truth is I'm just plain scared to go in there on my own.'

'Anybody in their right mind would be,' Sam said, trying to conceal his own nervous impatience.

Something appeared to be blocking the door because Ralph couldn't push it all the way back. When Sam followed him through the gap and into the hall, he saw the coat-stand on its side.

'That was the first thing that happened. The noise it made woke us up.'

Sam nodded, as though only marginally interested in details of this kind. 'Tell me about this woman,' he said. 'Describe her to me.'

He listened solemnly as Ralph did so. When he was finished he nodded again. 'That's her. Did Joanna see her, too?'

Ralph shook his head. 'Not then. When Joanna came into the room the woman wasn't there any more. We thought she'd just slipped out of the house. But then when all this started . . .' He gave an odd sideways glance at Sam, as though unable or embarrassed to look him in the eye. 'She was a ghost, wasn't she?'

'If I knew for sure I'd tell you. But I don't.'

Ralph looked at him again, more directly this time, as though trying to decide whether Sam was telling the truth. Whatever decision he came to, he kept it to himself. 'Come through here,' he said abruptly, moving towards the drawing room, 'you'd better see this.'

He stopped dead when he got there, muttering an obscenity under his breath and staring in dismay at what confronted him.

Sam looked past him into the room. It was a scene of devastation. Chairs and furniture were overturned, light

381

fittings had been torn from their sockets and dangled on the ends of electric wire, every ornament and picture in the place had been smashed. Even the carpet and underfelt had been ripped up in places to reveal bare floorboards.

'It wasn't like this when we left,' Ralph said. 'Just the big mirror that was over the chimney. We both saw it lift off the wall and fly across the room.' He pointed. 'You can see where it landed. But the rest of this . . .' He spread his arms in helpless incomprehension.

'You said "not then" when I asked if Joanna saw the woman,' Sam said. 'Does that mean she saw her later?'

'She saw something – in that mirror over there. She came into the room and saw the reflection of a woman over my shoulder. By the time I turned it was too late, the mirror was already flying across the room.'

'Did she describe the woman?'

Ralph nodded. 'It was the same woman I'd seen.'

He waited for Sam to speak, but the other man seemed lost in thought.

'There's something upstairs you'd better see,' Ralph said, and led the way, talking as they climbed. 'We'd gone back up to the bedroom to get our things together to leave. There was a crash from my music room. I came down to take a look. My desk had turned over, papers and everything on it were everywhere. I couldn't have been away from Joanna for more than two minutes, but when I got back upstairs she came staggering out of the bathroom, terrified. She said she'd been locked in and something had been knocking and scratching in the walls. And this thing had appeared, if it's still there . . .'

Sam noticed that lights still burned upstairs as they had in the hall and drawing room, evidence of the couple's panic-stricken flight in the early hours. He followed Ralph across the bedroom and into the bathroom, and saw the jagged lettering on the mirror.

He moved closer, reaching out instinctively to touch the surface of the glass.

'It's on the back,' Ralph was saying. 'It just isn't possible to do that.'

Sam began feeling around the edges of the mirror with his fingertips.

'It doesn't open,' Ralph said. 'There's no closet space behind it. That mirror's set right into the wall.'

Sam turned to him. 'Your wife wasn't harmed in any way, was she, when this happened?'

The question drew a faintly bitter laugh from Ralph. 'If you don't include being scared out of your wits, no, she wasn't harmed. But my wife's pregnant, Dr Towne. There's no telling what an experience like this might have provoked. I can promise you one thing – there's no way she's going to set foot in this house again.'

Sam was peering over every surface and into every corner of the bathroom, as though in search of something so far overlooked.

Ralph watched him for a few moments, then asked, with an edge of irritation breaking into his voice, 'Look, Towne, are you going to tell me what's going on, or what? Who was that woman?'

Sam glanced at him as though he'd forgotten he was there, then walked past him and back into the bedroom.

'Well, what does this mean, for God's sake?' Ralph said more insistently, following him. 'What the hell does "Help Me" mean?'

The two men faced each other across the room, Sam with his shoulders hunched and hands thrust deep in the pockets of his raincoat, Ralph with his hands out, waiting for an answer.

'She's some kind of ghost – right? We're being,' he stumbled over the word, as though unable to believe he was actually saying it, 'haunted!'

Sam still didn't speak.

'Well, say something, for Christ's sake!'

'I suppose,' Sam said after a while, 'ghost is as good a word as any.'

'What's the connection between this ghost and Joanna? Why does it – she, whatever – have my wife's name?'

Again Sam looked at him for a while, then lifted his shoulders in a shrug of defeat. 'I can't explain that.'

'I think you'd better try.' Ralph took a step forward. The anger that had followed on the heels of his fear was beginning to show itself in his physical attitude as well as his voice. He was, unconsciously perhaps, squaring up for a fight. 'I think you owe me an explanation. This whole thing started with your visit last night . . .'

Sam shook his head. 'No, it didn't start there . . .'

'Then where the hell *did* it start?'

'If I could tell you that, I would. But I can't.'

'Can't? Or won't?' Ralph was regarding Sam with open hostility now. 'I have a strong impression that you're holding something back, and I'm getting pretty tired of it.'

Sam took a hand from his pocket and held it up, palm out in a calming, open gesture. He knew that Ralph was on the verge of an irrational rage and he had to placate him.

'I can only tell you that I would like to make sense of all this every bit as much as you would.'

He saw Ralph's eyes narrow shrewdly, perhaps wanting to believe him, but not yet able to.

'Does all this by any chance have anything to do with Adam Wyatt?' Ralph said. 'Is that why you asked about him last night?'

Sam nodded. 'Yes, it has to do with Adam Wyatt.'

'In what way?'

'Look . . . anything I say is going to sound crazy. Will you just accept that, please, before we start? There's no point in my trying to tell you what I know if your only response is going to be that I'm a liar or a lunatic.'

'Try me.'

There was a leather chair by the wall, its back and arms forming a single curve. Sam sat in it, taking a deep breath as he did so. Then he rested his forearms on his knees and turned his gaze upwards on Ralph.

'I'm not going to offer any explanations for what I tell you. Not because there aren't any – there are too many, and none of them mean a damn thing. Beyond a certain point explanations are just new ways of asking the same question – they don't *explain* anything.'

'Okay,' Ralph said, folding his arms, 'that's the pre-amble, now give me the speech.'

Sam looked down at the carpet, deciding where to begin. Then he sat back, spreading his arms along the arms of the chair.

'About a year ago, a group of us – including Joanna, the Joanna who was here last night – invented a ghost called Adam Wyatt. It was an experiment in psychokin-esis – mind over matter. We made him up, his whole life story. We went through every record book imaginable to make sure that he didn't exist historically, and we found no trace of him. The point of the experiment was to see if we could create something that would, in one way or another, communicate with us.'

He paused, not taking his eyes off Ralph, who himself didn't move a muscle.

'Well, we succeeded beyond, you might say, our wildest dreams. Adam Wyatt didn't exist . . . but he began to communicate with us. And now, it seems, he *does* exist – or *did*. And that fact has had several remarkable consequences. You, for example. You wouldn't exist if Adam Wyatt hadn't lived. You're his direct descendant.'

Ralph was staring at Sam. He began to unfold his arms – very, very slowly. The movement reflected an awestruck utter disbelief in what he was being told.

'What in the name of all hell are you handing me here . . .?'

Sam held up a hand to forestall his protest. 'I warned you that none of this would make sense.'

'Are you saying you made me up . . .?'

Sam made a loose gesture, part apologetic, part just conveying that he had no comment to make.

'And my parents,' Ralph continued, his voice rising with incredulity, 'and their parents, and right on back to . . .?'

'I know,' Sam said. 'I know how it must sound.'

'That's as crazy as the idea that God made the world yesterday, and hid the fossils in it to fool us!'

'Another of the consequences of Adam's coming into being,' Sam said, ignoring the other man's indignant astonishment, 'is that those of us who created him . . . are ceasing to exist.'

Ralph snapped back his head as though injury had been added to the insult already on offer. 'What the hell is that supposed to mean – ceasing to exist?'

'So far all the members of the original group who created Adam have died. With the exception of myself, and Joanna – the Joanna you met last night. And God alone knows what's happened to her.'

Ralph made an involuntary half-turn and looked back into the bathroom. From where he stood he could see 'Help Me' scratched onto the mirror in reverse.

'I'm not insane, Ralph,' Sam said. 'I know I'm not. Just as you know that you're not a figment of my imagination. The fact is that we're both of us stuck with – perhaps more accurately in – a very singular situation.'

Ralph looked at him and began to shake his head, slowly at first, then faster. 'No . . . no, no, no, no, no. This is nuts . . . this is just impossible . . .!'

Sam felt a profound sympathy for him at that moment, understanding how every fibre of his conscious being must be putting up a fight to reject what he was being told.

'The most frightening thing is,' Sam said quietly, leaning forward again, 'is that anything's possible. When I tip over a bottle of ink, it's not impossible that all the molecules will get back together and retrace their path out of the tablecloth and back into the bottle. It's not impossible, just highly unlikely. It's probable that if you toss a coin a hundred times it'll come down fifty-fifty heads and tails, but it's also possible it could come down a hundred either way. Things are governed less by rules than gambler's odds.'

Ralph leaned towards him, like a stag locking horns. 'I'm no scientist, but I know that Einstein said, "God does not play dice with the universe." Are you saying he was wrong?'

'That was a statement of faith, not science. Every time

it's been tested by experiment, the dice theory has come out ahead. Which means we can't pretend that something isn't happening just by saying it's impossible. *Because nothing's impossible!*'

Sam's words hung in the air a moment, then Ralph crossed his arms at the wrist and flung them apart. It was the gesture of a man breaking invisible chains.

'No! I don't buy this! I just don't buy it! There has to be some proof, some evidence – at least other people, people I can talk to, somebody else who knew about this so-called experiment.'

Sam's voice was calm and level. 'There is no proof, and no evidence. All the people who knew about the experiment, colleagues of mine who weren't involved in it but discussed it with me at the time, now remember nothing. Every trace of it has disappeared. It never happened.'

'So you're telling me there's only your word to support this whole story . . .?'

'My word – and the fact that someone vanished in this house last night. Someone you saw, spoke to, someone who even brushed past you as she came in the door. You're not going to pretend now that all that never happened, are you?'

Ralph opened his mouth to speak, but seemed to lose heart and instead just sank slowly down onto the edge of the bed and buried his head in his hands.

'You know something really weird? It's crazy, but it's been bothering me ever since . . .' He lifted his head to look at Sam, his eyes reddened and pulled down by his fingertips.

'Last night, just for a second when I opened the door to her, that woman, I thought I knew her. It was that sense of *déjà vu* – the way it happens, inexplicably. Something in me said, I know this woman from somewhere. Then I told myself I was imagining it – obviously because I'd heard about her from you, and then that phone call from Joanna's father.'

He paused, his eyebrows knitting in a frown. 'I couldn't have seen her before, could I? How would it be possible?'

Sam debated whether to say what was in his mind. He decided they had now gone too far for him not to. 'Joanna – *my* Joanna – claims to have met you. It sounded pretty much like your meeting with your Joanna – horseback riding, the churchyard, Adam's grave. Except in her case it was three days ago – four now. And in your case it was a year ago.' He paused, then added, 'And there didn't seem much chance that you'd be getting married.'

He had leaned forward again as he spoke. Now he sat back. 'That's it, Ralph. The best I can do. What you make of it is up to you.'

Ralph didn't move for some moments, just sat hunched where he was on the edge of his and his wife's untidy, slept-in bed, his hands pressed together and touching his mouth. Eventually he rose very slowly to his feet. 'Where do we go from here?' he said, his voice unsteady.

'I think you should go back to your wife. Be with her.'

'She asked me to bring you over. I said I would. She wants to know what you think about all this.'

Sam got to his feet. 'I'll be glad to come with you.'

The other man shot him a hard look. 'You stay away from her.'

Sam shrugged. 'As you wish. But she's going to wonder why I won't talk to her. Or why you won't let me. And if she doesn't like your story, there's nothing to stop her calling me. Then what will I say?'

Ralph thought this over. It was true: his wife wasn't the type to be easily fobbed off with excuses.

'Listen to me, Towne . . .' he began.

'Sam. I think it might be easier if we use first names, don't you?'

'Listen to me, Sam. If you tell her any of the stuff you've just been telling me, ever . . . I'll break your damn neck. Do you understand me?'

Sam looked at him. Ralph was fit and well built and probably strong enough to do it. He was certainly scared enough to try.

'Don't worry, I'm not going to upset your wife. I've no reason to. I suggest we make a deal, you and I.'

Ralph frowned quizzically. 'A deal?'

'I'll come back with you and tell her something – something that makes sense.' He gave a brief, dry laugh. 'Not the truth, obviously, because that doesn't. I'll make something up, and say you've given me permission to stay in the house alone for a while to observe the phenomena more closely. What d'you say?'

Ralph looked at him, incredulous. 'You want to stay here? Alone?'

'That's exactly what I want.'

Ralph stared at him some more. And then a kind of understanding dawned in his face. 'Yes, of course. You and . . . that woman . . . I should have guessed from the way you've been talking about her.'

'Can I stay?'

Ralph nodded. 'You can stay.'

58

Sam made a brief tour of the rest of the house while Ralph packed a couple more suitcases for his wife and himself. Joanna's parents had insisted on driving up when Joanna had called them before breakfast to tell them what had happened. She was going to go stay with them for a few days; meanwhile Ralph would rent an apartment in Manhattan, then join her at the weekend.

There was nothing much that he hadn't seen already. In the basement kitchen, drawers had been yanked open and their contents scattered. Various things, although not everything, had been swept from shelves, and several pots and pans dislodged from where they usually hung. The damage wasn't as bad as in the drawing room, but it still looked as though a tornado had swept through.

Ralph's footsteps sounded on the stairs – coming down, Sam thought, a little faster than necessary. He had insisted that he didn't mind staying alone a few minutes to do his packing. 'What can happen in broad daylight?' he'd asked. 'This stuff only happens at night – right?'

Sam hadn't disabused him, though in fact there were no rules on the subject. Phenomena – to use that sterile, antiseptic term that Sam found increasingly unsatisfactory – occurred any time and any place, in the dark or in full light, below ground or above it.

'Okay, let's go,' Ralph said as Sam joined him in the hall.

'Let me take one of those.' Sam picked up one of the heavy suitcases.

They left the house and found a cab. Twenty minutes later they entered the lobby of the small hotel where Sam had spent time with Joanna's parents in the past. The desk clerk told Ralph that they had already arrived and were upstairs with Joanna.

As they went up in the elevator, Sam felt the same tense, nervous hollowness in his stomach that he'd felt waiting on the steps earlier while Ralph opened up the house. He was sure that Bob and Elizabeth Cross would not recognize him, yet the meeting filled him with apprehension. Nothing, he repeated to himself, could be taken for granted. Logic dictated that Joanna's parents, like the Joanna he was about to see again, would be part of the subtly changed world in which Adam Wyatt had been born not out of the minds of men and women, but out of the genes of his forebears.

Yet, as Sam knew, logic did not rule the universe. Or if it did, it did so in a fashion that remained impenetrable to the human mind. He used the thought to calm himself, to prepare himself with a Zen-like detachment for the confrontation.

Bob Cross opened the door of the suite when Ralph buzzed. There was no flicker of recognition in his eyes as they stepped inside and Ralph introduced them. Sam found himself in a medium-sized sitting room. Elizabeth Cross came in from what he supposed was the bedroom, closing the door behind her.

'Joanna's just getting out of the shower,' she said. 'If

you've got those clothes, you'd better take them through to her, Ralph.'

He did so, leaving Bob Cross to introduce Sam to his wife – again without a hint that their paths might have crossed before.

'Joanna tells me you investigate this kind of thing professionally,' Elizabeth Cross said.

'I run a department at Manhattan University,' Sam said. 'We look into anomalous phenomena of all kinds.'

'Well, this sounds about as anomalous as anything I've ever come across,' Bob Cross said. 'I saw a flying saucer one time, but that's nothing compared with all this.'

'Bob, will you please stop talking about your flying saucer? There's no comparison.' Elizabeth Cross sounded as though she had already rebuked her husband on the subject more than once that morning. 'Nobody else saw your flying saucer, but we've *both* seen this woman. Ralph's seen her, Dr Towne's seen her – even Joanna saw her in the mirror.'

She turned to Sam. 'What d'you think is happening here, Dr Towne? Can you tell us anything?'

Her face and tone of voice reflected the touching confidence that outsiders have, or need to have, in whoever is designated an 'expert' in some field in which they find themselves perhaps unwillingly involved.

'Do you know what I mean by poltergeist activity, Mrs Cross?' he said. He and Ralph had agreed on this approach on the way over.

'Well, yes, of course I've read about it and seen movies. Is that what this is?'

'I believe so.'

It was a deliberate lie, and he disliked himself for telling it, but he had no choice in the circumstances. For one thing, the alternative could only cause unnecessary pain to Joanna and her parents; for another, his access to the house depended on his keeping his word to Ralph.

'I thought poltergeist activity was something that only happened around adolescent kids,' Bob Cross said, sounding sceptical. 'Repressed sexuality, conflicting emotions, that kind of thing. Isn't that right?'

'It's right,' Sam said, 'but not a rule.' He wanted to tell them that there were no rules, that the truth made no sense, only the lies. But it was bad enough having to think like that, without forcing others to share in his despair.

It came as a shock to realize that 'despair' was the word that best described his state of mind. Until that moment he had hidden from it, clinging outwardly to a pretence of normality, and inwardly to the increasingly threadbare idea that even if the world was crazy he could remain sane by responding to it rationally. But it wasn't true. The truth was that the more clearly he saw things, the more swiftly he descended towards madness. He knew suddenly, deep inside himself, that he had already passed some point of no return. Yet he continued speaking calmly in his practised, authoritative, expert's manner.

'Poltergeist activity, things being thrown across rooms and smashed, is one of several psychokinetic effects – mind over matter, or mind working through matter, or in matter.'

'But there's always somebody who's doing it – right?' Bob Cross said. 'Somebody sending out mind waves or whatever? There's always somebody responsible?'

'That's true,' Sam conceded. 'Mind over matter – by definition there has to be someone doing it.'

'Then who's doing it here? One of us? That woman we saw last night?'

'From what I've heard, I'd say she's part of the effect and not the cause.'

'I don't understand,' Bob Cross persisted. 'I thought the poltergeist effect was things flying across the room, not people hammering at your door and talking to you and then disappearing.'

'That woman was a ghost, wasn't she, Dr Towne?' Elizabeth Cross spoke as though it was a thought that had been bearing down on her and of which she had to unburden herself.

'There's a widely held belief,' Sam told her, 'that ghosts are actually psychokinetic manifestations – the projections of our own consciousness.'

The memory of his conversation with Joanna over their first lunch many months earlier almost overwhelmed him. He buried the emotion in more words, standard explanations, reassuring half-truths.

'We take our consciousness so much for granted, we forget that so much of what we see isn't something that's objectively out there. Colours, for example, don't exist "out there" in their own right. They're the eye's and brain's response to certain wavelengths of light.'

'But the light's out there,' Bob Cross said, like a man with only limited tolerance for such abstractions.

'Well, yes . . .'

'That's something, at least.'

Elizabeth Cross stood with her hands clasped nervously in front of her. None of them had thought of sitting down, although there were ample places to do so. Somehow this didn't seem like a conversation to be had sitting down.

'I'm afraid all this talk of whether things come from inside us or from somewhere else is a little beyond me,' she said. 'Things happen, that's all I know.'

'And that's the most important thing we can say about them,' Sam said. 'In fact, it's probably the only thing.'

Elizabeth Cross took a few steps, composing herself for what she was about to say. Sam saw Bob Cross watching her with concern. He, apparently, knew what was coming and was unhappy about it.

'There's an idea I haven't been able to get out of my mind ever since that poor young woman was hammering at my door last night. I don't know why I called the police. I shouldn't have. I just panicked and . . .' She broke off, overcome by emotion for a moment. Her husband went to her and put his hands on her arms.

'Elizabeth, don't . . . you'll just upset yourself again . . .'

'No, I want to say it. I think if we're asking Dr Towne to investigate this . . . this *thing*, whatever . . . it's wrong to hold anything back.' She looked at Sam. 'My husband knows what I'm going to say. He thinks it's a silly idea . . .'

'Please, go ahead,' Sam encouraged her.

With a nervous glance at her husband, she began. 'Bob and I had a child before Joanna, but she died at birth. She would have been called Joanna, too. It was a terrible time for us, you can imagine. But when I discovered that I was pregnant again a year later, and when the baby was another girl, we decided to call her Joanna, too. In a way we both thought of her as the same little girl, alive and coming back to us. We felt as though we were giving back some kind of life to the poor little Joanna who died.

It probably sounds absurd to anyone else, but that was the reason why we called her Joanna.'

Her gaze had become fixed on Sam, though no less so than his on her.

Bob Cross stood at the third point of the triangle, though he knew he was outside what was going on between them at that moment. He was an honest, down-to-earth man not given to this type of speculation. It made him uneasy, though he was not entirely sure why.

'Could that woman have been the ghost of our little girl?' Elizabeth Cross asked, her eyes beseeching Sam, if not for an answer, at least for an understanding of the pain that lay behind the question.

59

It was several minutes before Joanna came in to join them – long enough for Elizabeth Cross to get over the tears that actually putting the question to Sam had unleashed in her. She and her husband now sat a little awkwardly on the edge of the dark red fabric-covered sofa. He was comforting her, and she was dabbing at her eyes with a handkerchief.

Sam turned away for a moment to give them their privacy. He looked out of the window into the busy street below and thought back over his answer. It had been pretty non-committal and well within the boundaries of his agreement with Ralph. Yet it was as honest as he could make it. He didn't know what other answer there could be.

'I'm all right,' Elizabeth said, clearing her throat and blowing her nose. 'I'm sorry, I'm all right now.'

Sam turned back to her. She was looking up at him, smiling an apology for her weakness.

'This isn't something that we've mentioned to Joanna, by the way. She knows about the other baby, of course, the sister she might have had. But we haven't mentioned it in . . .' she made a vague, general gesture, 'in this context. I thought maybe it would be best not to.'

'I think you're right,' Sam said with what reassurance

he could muster. 'I don't see that it would particularly help in any way.'

The door opened and Joanna came into the room. She wore jeans and a turtleneck sweater, and had her hair tied behind her head. She looked subdued and oddly fragile.

'Dr Towne – thank you for coming. Please tell me what's happening.'

Before he could say anything, she caught sight of her mother furtively hiding the handkerchief with which she'd been dabbing at her face.

'Mom, you've been crying! Please don't.'

'I'm all right . . . it's just all so . . . strange and upsetting.'

Joanna went over and gave her a hug. 'Don't worry – I'm sure everything's going to work out now that Dr Towne's here.'

Ralph came back into the room and stood quietly by the bedroom door. Joanna turned to Sam.

'Ralph says you're going to stay in the house for a few days.'

'That's what I'd like to do.'

She looked at him. The way she was dressed, her eyes wide and questioning and with no make-up, she looked more like a strangely solemn teenager than a grown woman.

'Who is she?'

Sam was aware of Ralph's gaze on him, but he didn't look away from Joanna. 'I can't say,' he said.

'You can't say? Or won't say? Or don't know?'

'I . . . don't know.'

She looked at him as though trying to divine whether he was lying to her or not.

'Why did she say "Help me"?'

'I don't know – yet. Maybe I'll be able to find out.'

'We must try to help her, whoever she is.'

'We will.'

Nobody else in the room spoke or moved, sensing that this was somehow a private moment between the two of them.

'Do you think I'm an awful coward not to go back?' She asked the question with a child-like seriousness, and waited for his answer.

'No. I don't think you should go back. I think it would be a mistake.'

'Why?'

He moved his head as though to say the answer was obvious. 'Ralph tells me that you're pregnant. That's a very good reason for being careful.'

'Do you think there's any danger?'

'I don't know. Sometimes it's more sensible not to find out.'

She continued to look at him, tipping her head slightly to one side, as though the angle gave her some insight into his thoughts.

'Is there something I don't know, Dr Towne? Something that you're not telling me?'

Sam shook his head and gave a gentle smile. 'No, I promise you.'

It was a lie, yet somehow an easy one. There was something about her that enchanted him, a freshness and an innocence that were all-too-rarely found.

'You have a very active imagination. That's another good reason for staying away from psychic phenomena.'

He looked over at Ralph. 'Don't let her go back there, Ralph – not yet.'

'Don't worry, I won't.'

Bob Cross gave a snort of impatience. 'Well, I certainly intend going over and taking a look.'

Sam knew at once and instinctively that he had to prevent this, although he didn't know why – or, for that matter, quite how.

'If you'll forgive my saying so, Mr Cross,' he began, trying to sound as deferential as he could, 'I don't think that's a very good idea.'

'Why not?' Bob Cross looked at him in a way that suggested he'd better have good reasons to back up his advice.

'Not really anything specific,' Sam said, hoping he wouldn't be forced to go into too much detail. 'It's just that whatever's happening here is a family-linked thing – *your* family. I think you should stay together, support one another, and not expose yourselves unnecessarily to any influences that we don't yet understand.'

Bob Cross looked unconvinced. 'I want to see that damn mirror for myself – the one with scratching on the back.'

'You will. Just give me a day or two – please?'

The older man's face took on an expression of reluctance, but he grudgingly agreed, 'Okay, you're the expert. I guess we'd better listen to you.'

Sam felt an immense relief. 'By the way,' he said, turning to Joanna and changing the subject, 'I read your book. It's excellent.'

Her face lit up with pleasure. 'Do you really think so?'

'It deserves to do well.'

'I really appreciate your saying that. Do you think we could discuss it some time, at more length?'

'I'd be happy to.'

Things drew quickly to a close. Joanna's father, having been denied access to the 'scene of the crime' was impatient to be on the move, urging his two women to collect their belongings while he phoned down to the garage for his car. Sam said his formal goodbyes to all three of them in the hotel suite, then Ralph accompanied them downstairs. When he returned, Sam was waiting for him.

'You handled that well,' Ralph said to him. 'Thank you.'

'They're nice people. I hope this thing won't cause them any more upset than it has already.'

Ralph had taken a bunch of keys from his pocket, but kept them in his fist for the time being. 'I don't know whether I should be giving you the keys to my house or calling Belle Vue and having you put under restraint,' he said. 'But after last night, I guess I have to give you the benefit of the doubt.'

He held out the keys. Sam took them.

'Thanks,' he said. 'If you move out of the hotel, let me know where I can find you.'

60

It took him several hours to write down the whole story. He wrote in long-hand, sitting at the desk in the music room where Ralph composed his operas, which were mostly unperformed, although several orchestral pieces had been recorded on CDs that Sam found in a rack on the wall. He played a couple, and found them interesting but too obviously influenced by other composers to be memorable. He reflected, ungenerously perhaps, that it was the work of someone wealthy enough to indulge his passion, though not talented enough to earn a living from it. But he made no comment on the music in what he wrote, seeing no cause to offend the man who would most likely be the one to find and read the document.

Only when that thought crossed his mind did Sam ask himself whether the words he was writing were in anticipation of his own death, a kind of valediction. He realized that they were. Although he did not assume that he was going to die (he no longer assumed anything), he did not see how he could continue to exist in his present state indefinitely. Six of the group were dead, and Joanna – *his* Joanna – had entered some strange limbo on the margins of a changed world in which he now found himself.

He did not speculate further upon his personal fate,

merely wrote down the story in all the detail that he could recall, starting with his reading in *Around Town* of Joanna's exposé of Camp Starburst and the cynical manipulations of Ellie and Murray Ray. He wrote of his first meeting with Joanna in a television studio, and then later on Sixth Avenue after her unnerving confrontation with Ellie. He wrote of how the idea of the experiment had been born, and how his relationship with Joanna had grown with it. In swift and simple prose he set down all that had happened from that time until the time of writing almost twelve months later, and a universe apart.

What does that mean, a universe apart? Am I speaking of parallel worlds? And if so, what does *that* mean? It's just an idea, a way, one of many, of describing the strangeness of nature when we examine her closely. We know that in truth there is only one world: the one we are in. We know too that concepts like space and time are merely constructs of our consciousness, not things 'out there' existing independently of us.

Physicists, it is said, have paid a high price for their understanding of nature: they have lost their hold on reality. Of course, that was 'reality' as defined by common sense – a transaction between 'out there', where the world was, and 'in here', where we were. Now that distinction has disappeared; the common sense that took it for granted has been proved an untrustworthy ally. There is nothing to lose our hold *on* any more. That which holds and that which is held are one and the same; observer and observed are merely parts of a spectrum, neither one existing independently of the other.

In physics we have had to learn a language that reflects both the precision of our knowledge and the ambiguity revealed by it. An electron, for example, is not a particle *or* wave; it is both. It exists in a 'superposition of states' – until we *want* it, for the purposes of measurement, to be one or the other. Then it will oblige us.

The universe in which we live is as much conceived by us as we are by it. Obvious simple rules like cause and effect have lost their power. Niels Bohr defined causality as no more than a method by which we reduce our sense impressions to some kind of order.

No one disputes the reality of this strangeness on the microscopic level. The only question has been whether it could carry over into the macroscopic world of our daily lives. There is increasing, indeed by now overwhelming, evidence that it can.

'I myself, sitting here, am living proof.'

He set aside his pen and leaned back to look up at the ceiling. It was barely visible beyond the penumbra of the lamp on his desk. Night had fallen while he wrote. He searched for a summing up, a final phrase that would crystallize and give shape to what he was trying to say.

It was of course a hopeless task. There was no such thing as a last word.

'Living proof,' he read, and picked up his pen, but wrote no more.

Because in that moment he had heard her voice. Quite distinctly, though not loudly. Nor was he sure where it had come from.

He stood up silently, as though the least sound he made might frighten her off and he would lose her, perhaps this time for good.

'Joanna?' he called out softly.

There was no response. Only then did he realize that,

although he'd heard her voice, he had no idea what she'd said. Had he really heard her? Or was his mind playing tricks?

He stepped out onto the landing and listened in the darkness. The house was silent except for the muffled sound of traffic in the street. He called her name again.

'Joanna . . .?'

Still no response. Then, somewhere above, he heard a faint, brief sound, as though someone had passed quickly and lightly over a loose floorboard.

The darkness around him grew deeper and more dense as he turned a corner on the stairs, losing the last reflected light from the music room below. He paused and spoke again, in barely a whisper.

'Joanna, are you there . . .?'

Again he heard her voice, closer this time, and in a whisper like his own. There could be no doubt it was her voice, but still he couldn't understand what she was saying.

'Joanna . . .? Where are you . . .?'

He groped in the darkness for a light switch, and cried out in shock as his hand connected with the feel of warm, firm flesh. Her unseen fingers interlaced themselves with his, and held him tight.

'I'm here,' she said. Her voice was clear now, so close to him that he could feel her breath on his. Her body pressed against him, soft and warm. He held her naked in his arms, and in the dark her lips found his.

He felt a movement of her hand against his chest and realized she was unbuttoning his shirt. Brushing her fingers aside, he tore off his clothes in what seemed like a single unbroken movement. He didn't try to speak, he knew he couldn't. The beating of his heart was like a hammer in his chest as she led him blindly through the dark until he felt the bed against his legs.

They tumbled onto it, devouring one another with a violence and a passion that seemed inexhaustible and endless. The only sounds they made were cries and gasps of need, desire and satisfaction, until, sated at last, they lay entwined in silence.

'I'm so happy,' she whispered. 'I knew you'd come. There's nothing to be afraid of any more.'

He pulled her to him, feeling the swell of her breasts, the curve of her stomach and thighs and the film of perspiration covering her skin as it pressed against his own. He could feel her, but he could not see her. He knew that the dancing lines and contours he fancied he had glimpsed from time to time as they made love were simply his imagination creating mental images from the sensual contact of their bodies.

'I want to see you,' he said. 'I have to.'

'Yes, I know.' There was a softness in her voice, as though the words came through a smile of tenderness. Her hand traced the contours of his face. 'It's all right. You can put on the light.'

He reached out to where he remembered seeing a bedside lamp, his fingers feeling for the switch. He found it – but, for some reason he did not fully understand, he hesitated.

'Don't be afraid,' she said.

He pressed.

There was a searing flash of light, like an explosion. Worse even than the pain that scorched his eyes was the blistering, asphyxiating sound – like the roar of an inferno, all around him, all-consuming, burning through his brain.

He didn't know how long it lasted, but as the blinding whiteness faded and the silence gradually returned, there came too a strange emptiness and an absence of all feeling.

Somewhere he heard a howl of pain and fear. It was his voice, he knew, but it no longer seemed to be a part of him.

She spoke again, calm, reassuring, in control, as though she had known all this would happen and was here to guide him through it. 'It's all right, my darling . . . don't be afraid . . . you're safe now . . .'

He cried out in startled rage, 'I can't see . . . where am I . . .?'

Feeling returned abruptly, as it does after an injury when the body has been momentarily anaesthetized by shock. But it was not pain he felt now, merely the sensation of being on his feet, stumbling forward like a blind man, arms outstretched in search of unseen obstacles.

Her voice came again – so close now that it seemed inside his head.

'Come . . . come with me . . .'

He felt her hand on his, its touch so light as to be barely there at all. He took a few more steps, and then the ground beneath his feet seemed suddenly to fall away.

But he himself did not fall. It was as though the house, the city and the world around it were opening into endless space. He felt that he was flying, borne aloft by a mysterious, all-powerful and all-embracing force. He knew that she was with him, but he was not sure how he knew.

Then the thought came to him that she was not with him, but was now in some way part of him. The idea seemed so obviously and inevitably true that he did not question it, or wonder how it could be so, or where it was that they were going.

He just relaxed and let what was happening take its course, until it seemed it would go on for ever . . .

61

Ralph Cazaubon had tried to call the house all afternoon, without success. The first day he had left Sam Towne to his strange vigil undisturbed, but on the second had found himself wondering so much what was going on that it became hard to concentrate on anything else.

All the same, he'd waited until after lunch to call. The morning had been spent looking at apartments to rent. So far he'd found nothing that seemed ideal for Joanna and himself, but there was no hurry: she was happy with her parents, and he'd promised to drive out to join her that night. Perhaps they'd take a holiday, he'd suggested, fly off to the sun where they could put the nightmare behind them. She had liked the idea. They said they'd talk about where over dinner.

So the afternoon was his last chance to find out what was happening with Sam Towne, preferably before dark. Although he disliked admitting it even to himself, he had no wish to be in that house – his house – after dark. He had already made up his mind that he was going to sell it. Even if the events of two nights ago never happened again, he couldn't bring himself to live there any longer. Above all, he couldn't let Joanna take that risk. He hoped only that Sam would somehow find a way of ending the possession that had so mysteriously entered the place; a house in the grip of such a thing would not be easy to sell, not even in that neighbourhood and at a bargain price.

He rang the bell for several minutes before taking the duplicate keys from his pocket and inserting them in the door's two main locks. He took a deep breath to steady his nerves, and entered.

The coat-stand was still where it had been two days ago, so he couldn't push the door all the way back but had to slide through sideways. He saw Sam Towne the moment he was through.

His naked body lay face down at the foot of the stairs. His arms were out, as though he'd tried to break his fall, and his head was twisted at an angle that left no doubt that he was dead. His eyes were open as though staring in shock at the pool of his own blood that had congealed on the floor into a patch of dark and lustreless vermilion, almost black in the fading light of the late Manhattan afternoon.

Epilogue

'If I don't go back,' she said, 'this thing will stay with me for the rest of my life, and I refuse to accept that. I have to walk through the house just once, and then it will be over. Exorcized.'

Ralph tried to talk her out of it, but she was adamant. It was ten days since Sam Towne's death. Ralph had met one of his brothers who had come down from Boston to arrange for the body to be shipped to Cape Cod for a family funeral. The death had been classed as accidental, with no suspicion of foul play: the fact that the deceased had fallen down the stairs while attempting to establish whether or not the house in which he'd died was haunted was of no great interest to the city authorities. Even if the presumption was that he'd been pushed, the law made no provision for the criminal prosecution of ghosts or other disembodied spirits.

The only real problem Ralph had had was what to do with the manuscript that he'd found on his desk in the music room. He hadn't discovered it until after the body had been removed. He'd taken it back to the hotel and read it there after calling Joanna with the tragic news. He read it through twice, and then a third time, before facing up to the fact that he was going to have to make a decision. Even then he'd put it off, slipping the handwritten pages into an envelope which he'd placed in the hotel safe.

There they had remained for several days, until all the legalities had been taken care of. Even when one of Sam's colleagues from the university, Peggy O'Donovan, had come over to see the place where he had died, Ralph didn't mention its existence. With each day that passed, during which time there was no evidence of any renewed unnatural activity in the house, he grew less inclined to do so.

He had workmen come in and tidy the place up. The mirror in the bathroom was replaced. Nobody reported feeling anything strange or noticing anything out of the ordinary. Even Ralph himself began to feel as much at ease in the house as he had in the past, though he still did not spend a night there, and formally put it in the hands of a real estate agent after a week.

The more he thought about Sam's manuscript, the less inclined he was to let anyone else see it. Legally and morally, he supposed, it was the property of Sam Towne's family. Or perhaps his colleagues at the university. But the fact that Sam had left no written instruction, no indication whatever as to whom he was actually addressing in the document, surely gave him, Ralph thought, some leeway in his choice of what to do with it.

The night before leaving the hotel and moving into the comfortable apartment he had found on Madison and 64th, he took it from the hotel safe and burned it, page by page, in the metal litterbin in his suite. The act made him feel that the whole episode was now over and a line drawn under it. What Sam Towne had written was something that no normal person could accept as any kind of literal truth. It was fantasy at best, the invention

416

of an unbalanced mind. Characters like Ellie and Murray Ray were figures from cheap fiction, not real life. The Joanna Cross to whom the whole unlikely story was supposed to have happened had never existed. The whole thing was best ignored, and if possible forgotten. There was no point in causing needless trouble for himself or, above all, for Joanna. Sam Towne's story was the kind of superstitious nonsense, neither provable nor disprovable, that got printed in the tabloid rags you found on sale at supermarket check-outs. It could blight their lives for ever if some sensational rumour of this kind got into circulation. He felt no remorse as he took the blackened ashes to the bathroom and flushed them down the lavatory.

After that he had thought his troubles were over, until Joanna began to insist on returning to the house. Just once, she said. An exorcism. Not of the house but of herself, of her fear – the fear that she had been touched by something alien and unnatural that she could only leave behind by making this one last ritual visit.

Ralph didn't know why he felt such apprehension at the prospect, but he did.

'All right,' he said, 'I can't stop you, but I can at least come with you. You aren't going to complain about that, I hope.'

'Of course you can come with me.' She slipped her arm through his and kissed him. 'We'll go together, then leave it all behind.'

The following day was bright and clear with a frosty sun that gave the city a sharp-edged clarity. They entered the house just after ten, descending first to the kitchen, then back up to the drawing room where the whole thing had begun. The damaged furniture had been removed, the carpets and light fittings put back in order, and a new mirror installed above the fireplace.

They went upstairs, into the music room, the guest rooms and the small room at the back that Ralph had made his library. Finally they went upstairs to their bedroom and adjoining bathroom, and stood for some moments in silence as the sun streamed brightly through the windows.

'You know,' she said, 'I'm beginning to regret we said we'd sell it.'

'I know,' he said, 'me too. But I still think we should, don't you?'

She nodded thoughtfully. 'Yes, I suppose so. It couldn't ever be the same, could it?'

They started down the stairs again. They were halfway down when they heard the front door open and shut. They stopped and looked at each other. They both felt a momentary unease, but then he gave her a slightly shame-faced, reassuring grin.

'I forgot,' he said. 'Madge Rheinhart called from the real estate office. She said she was bringing some people to see the house. She thinks they're serious. It's exactly what they're looking for, and they have the money. Let's go down and say hello.'

As they reached the hall, Joanna frowned. She didn't know what it was, but something about the short, elderly couple with the tall and elegant Miss Rheinhart seemed oddly familiar. The woman was wearing an expensive-looking fur coat, the man a camel-hair coat and a black fur hat. But when they turned as she and Ralph approached, she realized that she had never seen them before.

'Oh, Mr and Mrs Cazaubon,' Madge Rheinhart said,

all charm and studied poise, 'I didn't know if you'd still be here. I think we've just sold your house. Let me introduce you to Mr and Mrs Ray.'

'Murray,' said the old man, removing his hat respectfully. 'And this is my wife, Ellie.'

David Ambrose

HOLLYWOOD LIES

£5.99

'Seductive'
Empire

'Mr President, never in the history of the world has one woman meant so much . . .
 'Ladies and gentlemen . . . the late Marilyn Monroe'

Seven suavely bewitching stories, all with a Machiavellian twist at the end: Marilyn Monroe as virtual reality's most valuable asset . . . a fading film producer who considers the news of his impending death as the ultimate career break . . . a screenwriter terrorized by the character he creates – a force that refuses to die, either on screen or off. Against a backdrop already larger than life, each scenario mixes the surreal with the supernatural in a toxic cocktail. Hollywood glitter balancing on the scalpel edge of madness . . .

'Clearly based on an intimate knowledge of the lunacies, lies and pressures of Hollywood . . . Ambrose is often memorably nasty . . .'
Sunday Telegraph

David Ambrose

MOTHER OF GOD

£5.99

'If you only take one book in your suitcase this summer,
make sure it's this one'
Maxim

' "Who are you?"
"I have no name"
"What do you want?"
"I want you." '

A beautiful scientist at Oxford University – and a desperate
killer in California, one stalking the other. On the Internet . . .

Tessa Lambert is young, beautiful – and a genius. She has just
created the first viable artificial intelligence programme. But
her discovery is so controversial that she must keep it a secret
even from her dearest friends and colleagues.
   As her work grows daily more vital, Tessa's world begins
to fall apart, and when her programme takes on its own
completely malevolent existence, Tessa must make the last and
most terrifying connection, that her life has become her work.
And that her work has now taken over . . .

Mother of God is a stunning thriller blending high-octane
excitement with the terrifying edge of scientific discovery.

'Absolutely terrific'
Literary Review

'A wonderful read'
Clare Francis

All Pan Books are available at your local bookshop or newsagent, or can be ordered direct from the publisher. Indicate the number of copies required and fill in the form below.

Send to: Macmillan General Books C.S.
              Book Service By Post
              PO Box 29, Douglas I-O-M
              IM99 1BQ

or phone: 01624 675137, quoting title, author and credit card number.

or fax: 01624 670923, quoting title, author, and credit card number.

or Internet: http://www.bookpost.co.uk

Please enclose a remittance* to the value of the cover price plus 75 pence per book for post and packing. Overseas customers please allow £1.00 per copy for post and packing.

*Payment may be made in sterling by UK personal cheque, Eurocheque, postal order, sterling draft or international money order, made payable to Book Service By Post.

Alternatively by Access/Visa/MasterCard

Card No.   ☐☐☐☐☐☐☐☐☐☐☐☐☐☐☐☐☐☐

Expiry Date ☐☐☐☐☐☐☐☐☐☐☐☐☐☐☐☐☐☐

Signature _____

Applicable only in the UK and BFPO addresses.

While every effort is made to keep prices low, it is sometimes necessary to increase prices at short notice. Pan Books reserve the right to show on covers and charge new retail prices which may differ from those advertised in the text or elsewhere.

NAME AND ADDRESS IN BLOCK CAPITAL LETTERS PLEASE

Name _____

Address _____

_____

_____

_____

8/95

Please allow 28 days for delivery.
Please tick box if you do not wish to receive any additional information. ☐